Praise for Mary Kubica an… …ghts Go Out

"Mary Kubica knows how to do thrillers. [*When the Lights Go Out* is] a mystery that'll keep you turning pages." ***—theSkimm***

"Kubica brilliantly unravels the lives of two women in this tense and haunting tale of identity and deceit. [This novel] will keep you questioning everything—and everyone—until the riveting conclusion. A twisty, captivating, edge-of-your-seat read."

—Megan Miranda, *New York Times* bestselling author of *All the Missing Girls*

"Kubica is a helluva storyteller." ***—Kirkus Reviews***

"Will keep readers riveted… The ending brings a stunning ironic twist… This intensely moving novel about identity and deceit is strongly recommended." ***—Booklist***

"Creepy and oh so clever with a brilliant twist that I did not see coming! Best read with the lights on."

—Alice Feeney, internationally bestselling author of *Sometimes I Lie*

"As fact collided with fiction in Jessie's world, I was on the edge of my seat in real time trying to work out the truth…. And with an ending I never saw coming, I can truly say this book had my adrenaline going and energized me!" ***—First for Women***

Also by Mary Kubica

The Good Girl
Pretty Baby
Don't You Cry
Every Last Lie
The Other Mrs.
Local Woman Missing

MARY KUBICA

WHEN THE LIGHTS GO OUT

ISBN-13: 978-0-7783-0775-4

When the Lights Go Out

First published in 2018. This edition published in 2022.

Park Row Books
22 Adelaide St. West, 41st Floor
Toronto, Ontario M5H 4E3, Canada
ParkRowBooks.com
BookClubbish.com

Printed in U.S.A.

For
Dick & Eloise
Rudy & Myrtle

WHEN THE LIGHTS GO OUT

The mind is its own place,
and in itself can make
a heaven of hell,
a hell of heaven.

—John Milton, *Paradise Lost*

prologue

THE CITY SURROUNDS ME. A panorama. With arms outstretched, I can't help but spin, taking it all in. Enjoying the view, knowing fully well this may be the last thing my eyes ever see.

I stare at the four metal steps before me, aware of how frail and broken-down they look. They're orange with rust, paint flaking, some of the slats loose so that when I press my foot to the first step, it buckles beneath me and I fall.

Still, I have no choice but to climb.

I pull myself back up, set my hands on the rails and scale the steps. The sweat bleeds from my palms so that the metal beneath them is slippery, slick. I can't hold tight. I slip from the second step, try again. I call out, voice cracking, a voice that doesn't sound like mine.

As I reach the roof's ledge, my knees give. It takes everything I have not to topple over the edge of the building and onto the street below. Seventeen floors.

I'm so high I could touch the clouds, I think. The sense of

vertigo is overpowering. The ground whooshes up and at me, the skyscrapers, the trees starting to sway until I no longer know what's moving: them or me. Little yellow matchbooks soar up and down the city streets. Cabs.

If I was standing at street level, the ledge would feel plenty wide. But up here it's not. Up here it's a thread and on it, I'm trying to balance my two wobbly feet.

I'm scared. But I've come this far. I can't go back.

There's a moment of calm that comes and goes so quickly I almost don't notice it. For one split second the world is still. I'm at peace. The sun moves higher and higher into the sky, yellow-orange glaring at me through the buildings, making me peaceful and warm. My hands rise beside me as a bird goes soaring by. As if my hands are wings, I think in that moment what it would be like to fly.

And then it comes rushing back to me.

I'm hopelessly alone. Everything hurts. I can no longer think straight; I can no longer see straight; I can no longer speak. I don't know who I am anymore. If I am anyone.

And I know in that moment for certain: I am no one.

I think what it would feel like to fall. The weightlessness of the plunge, of gravity taking over, of relinquishing control. Giving up, surrendering to the universe.

There's a flicker of movement beneath me. A flash of brown, and I know that if I wait any longer, it will be too late. The decision will no longer be mine. I cry out one more time.

And then I go.

JESSIE

I DON'T HAVE TO see myself to know what I look like.

My eyes are fat and bloated, so bloodshot the sclera is bereft of white. The skin around them is red and raw from rubbing. They've been like this for days. Ever since Mom's body began shutting down, her hands and feet cold, blood no longer circulating there. Since she began to drift in and out of consciousness, refusing to eat. Since she became delirious, speaking of things that aren't real.

Over the last few days, her breathing has changed too, becoming noisier and unstable, developing what the doctor called Cheyne-Stokes respiration where, for many seconds at a time, she didn't breathe. Short, shallow breaths followed by no breaths at all. When she didn't breathe, I didn't breathe. Her nails are blue now, the skin of her arms and legs blotchy and gray. "It's a sign of imminent death," the doctor said only yesterday as he set a firm hand on my shoulder and asked if there was someone they could call, someone who could come sit with me until she passed.

"It won't be long now," he'd said.

I had shaken my head, refusing to cry. It wasn't like me to cry. I've sat in the same armchair for nearly a week now, in the same rumpled clothes, leaving only to collect coffee from the hospital cafeteria. "There's no one," I said to the doctor. "It's only Mom and me."

Only Mom and me as it's always been. If I have a father somewhere out there in the world, I don't know a thing about him. Mom didn't want me to know anything about him.

And now this evening, Mom's doctor stands before me again, taking in my bloated eyes, staring at me in concern. This time offering up a pill. He tells me to take it, to go lie down in the empty bed beside Mom's and sleep.

"When's the last time you've slept, Jessie?" he asks, standing there in his starch white smock, tacking on, "I mean, really *slept*," before I can lie. Before I can claim that I slept last night. Because I did, for a whole thirty minutes, at best.

He tells me the longest anyone has gone without sleep. He tells me that people can die without sleep. He says to me, "Sleep deprivation is a serious matter. You need to sleep," though he's not my doctor but Mom's. I don't know why he cares.

But for whatever reason, he goes on to list for me the consequences of not sleeping. Emotional instability. Crying and laughing for no sound reason at all. Behaving erratically. Losing concept of time. Seeing things. Hallucinating. Losing the ability to speak.

And then there are the physical effects of insomnia: heart attack, hypothermia, stroke.

"Sleeping pills don't work for me," I tell him, but he shakes his head, tells me that it's not a sleeping pill. Rather a tranquilizer of some sort, used for anxiety and seizures. "It has a sedative effect," he says. "Calming. It will help you sleep without all the ugly side effects of a sleeping pill."

But I don't need to sleep. What I need instead is to stay awake, to be with Mom until she makes the decision to leave.

I push myself from my chair, strut past the doctor standing in the doorway. "Jessie," he says, a hand falling gently to my arm to try and stop me before I can go. His smile is fake.

"I don't need a pill," I tell him briskly, plucking my arm away. My eyes catch sight of the nurse standing in the hallway beside the nurses' station, her eyes conveying only one thing: pity. "What I need is coffee," I say, not meeting her eye as I slog down the hallway, feet heavy with fatigue.

There's a guy I see in the cafeteria every now and then, a little bit like me. A weak frame lost inside crumpled-up clothes; tired, red eyes but doped up on caffeine. Like me, he's twitchy. On edge. He has a square face; dark, shaggy hair; and thick eyebrows that are sometimes hidden behind a pair of sunglasses so that the rest of us can't see he's been crying. He sits in the cafeteria with his feet perched on a plastic chair, a red sweatshirt hood pulled over his head, sipping his coffee.

I've never talked to him before. I'm not the kind of girl that cute guys talk to.

But tonight, for whatever reason, after I get my cup of coffee, I drop down into the chair beside him, knowing that under any other circumstance, I wouldn't have the nerve to do it. To talk to him. But tonight I do, mostly, I think, to delay going back to Mom's room, to give the doctor his chance to examine her and leave.

"Want to talk about it?" I ask, and at first his look is surprised. Incredulous, even. His gaze rises up from his own coffee cup and he stares at me, his eyes as blue as a blue morpho butterfly's wings.

"The coffee," he says after some time, pushing his cup away. "It tastes like shit," he tells me, as though that's the thing that's bothering him. The only thing. Though I see well enough inside the cup to know that he drank it down to the dregs, so it couldn't have been that bad.

"What's wrong with it?" I ask, sipping from my cup. It's hot and so I peel back the plastic lid and blow on it. Steam rises to greet me as I try again and take another sip. This time, I don't burn my mouth.

There's nothing wrong with the hospital's coffee. It's just the way I like it. Nothing fancy. Just plain old coffee. But still, I dump four packets of Equal in and swirl it around because I don't have a stir stick or spoon.

"It's weak and there are grounds in it," he tells me, giving his abandoned cup the stink eye. "I don't know," he says, shrugging. "Guess I just like my coffee stronger than this."

And yet, he reaches again for the cup before remembering there's nothing left in it.

There's an anger in his demeanor. A sadness. It doesn't have anything to do with the coffee. He just needs something to take his anger out on. I see it in his blue eyes, how he wishes he was somewhere else, anywhere else but here.

I too want to be anywhere else but here.

"My mother's dying," I tell him, looking away because I can't stand to stare into his eyes when I say the words aloud. Instead I gaze toward a window where outside the world has gone black. "She's going to die."

Silence follows. Not an awkward silence, but just silence. He doesn't say he's sorry because he knows, like me, that sorry doesn't mean a thing. Instead, after a minute or two, he says that his brother's been in a motorcycle accident. That a car cut him off and he went flying off the bike, headfirst, into a utility pole.

"There's no saying if he'll make it," he says, talking in euphemisms because it's easier that way than just saying there's a chance he'll die. Kick the bucket. Croak. "Odds are good we'll have to pull the plug sometime soon. The brain damage." He shakes his head, picks at the skin around his fingernails. "It's not looking good," he tells me, and I say, "That sucks," because it does.

I rub at my eyes and he changes topics. "You look tired," he tells me, and I admit that I can't sleep. That I haven't been sleeping. Not for more than thirty minutes at a time, and even that's being generous. "But it's fine," I say, because my lack of sleep is the least of my concerns.

He knows what I'm thinking.

"There's nothing more you can do for your mom," he says. "Now you've got to take care of you. You've got to be ready for what comes next. You ever try melatonin?" he asks, but I shake my head and tell him the same thing I told Mom's doctor.

"Sleeping pills don't work for me."

"It's not a sleeping pill," he says as he reaches into his jeans pocket and pulls out a handful of pills. He slips two tablets into the palm of my hand. "It'll help," he says to me, but any idiot can see that his own eyes are bloodshot and tired. It's obvious this melatonin didn't help him worth shit. But I don't want to be rude. I slip the tablets into the pocket of my own jeans and say thanks.

He stands from the table, chair skidding out from beneath him, and says he'll be right back. I think that it's an excuse and that he's going to take the opportunity to split. "Sure thing," I say, looking the other way as he leaves. Trying not to feel sorry for myself as I'm hit with that sudden sense of being alone. Trying not to think about my future, knowing that when Mom finally dies, I'll be alone forever.

He's gone now and I watch other people in the cafeteria. New grandparents. A group of people sitting at a round table, laughing. Talking about old times, sharing memories. Some sort of hospital technician in blue scrubs eating alone. I reach for my now-empty cup of coffee, thinking that I too should split. Knowing that the doctor is no doubt done with Mom by now, and so I should get back to her.

But then the guy comes back. In his hands are two fresh cups of coffee. He returns to his chair and states the obvious. "Caffeine is the last thing either of us needs," he tells me, saying that it's decaf, and it occurs to me then that this has nothing to do with the coffee, but rather the company.

He digs into his pocket and pulls out four rumpled packets of Equal, dropping them to the table beside my cup. I manage a thanks, flat and mumbled to hide my surprise. He was watching me. He was paying attention. No one ever pays attention to me, aside from Mom.

Beside me he hoists his feet back onto the empty seat across from him, crosses them at the ankles. Drapes the red hood over his head.

I wonder what he'd be doing right now if he wasn't here. If his brother hadn't been in that motorcycle accident. If he wasn't close to dying.

I think that if he had a girlfriend, she'd be here, holding his hand, keeping him company. Wouldn't she?

I tell him things. Things I've never told anyone else. I don't know why. Things about Mom. He doesn't look at me as I talk, but at some imaginary spot on the wall. But I know he's listening.

He tells me things too, about his brother, and for the first time in a while, I think how nice it is to have someone to talk to, or to just share a table with as the conversation in time drifts to quiet and we sit together, drinking our coffees in silence.

Later, after I return to Mom's room, I think about him. The guy from the cafeteria. After the hospital's hallway lights are dimmed and all is quiet—well, mostly quiet save for the ping of the EKG in Mom's room and the rattle of saliva in the back of her throat since she can no longer swallow—I think about him sitting beside his dying brother, also unable to sleep.

In the hospital, Mom sleeps beside me in a drug-induced daze, thanks to the steady drip, drip, drip of lorazepam and morphine into her veins, a solution that keeps her both pain-free and fast asleep at the same time.

Sometime after nine o'clock, the nurse stops by to turn Mom one last time before signing off for the night. She checks her skin for bedsores, running a hand up and down Mom's legs. I've got the TV in the room turned on, anything to drown out that mechanical, metallic sound of Mom's EKG, one that will haunt me for the rest of my life. It's one of those newsmagazine shows—*Dateline*, *60 Minutes*, I don't know which—the one thing that was on when I flipped on the TV. I didn't bother channel surfing; I don't care what I watch. It could be home shopping or cartoons, for all I care. It's just the noise I need to help me forget that Mom is dying. Though, of course, it isn't as easy as that. There isn't a thing in the world that can make me forget. But for a few minutes at least, the news anchors make me feel less alone.

"What are you watching?" the nurse asks, examining Mom's skin, and I say, "I don't even know."

But then we both listen together as the anchors tell the story of some guy who'd assumed the identity of a dead man. He lived for years posing as him, until he got caught.

Leave it to me to watch a show about dead people as a means of forgetting that Mom is dying.

My eyes veer away from the TV and to Mom. I mute the show. Maybe the repetitive ping of the EKG isn't so bad after all. What it says to me is that Mom is still alive. For now.

Ulcers have already formed on her heels and so she lies with feet floating on air, a pillow beneath her calves so they can't touch the bed. "Feeling tired?" the nurse asks, standing in the space between Mom and me. I am, of course, feeling tired. My head hurts, one of those dull headaches that creeps up the nape of the neck. There's a stinging pain behind my eyes too, the kind that makes everything blur. I dig my palms into my sockets to make it go away, but it doesn't quit. My muscles ache, my legs restless. There's the constant urge to move them, to not sit still. It gnaws at me until it's all I can think about: moving my legs. I uncross them, stretch them out before me, recross my legs. For a whole thirty seconds it works. The restlessness stops.

And then it begins again. That prickly urge to move my legs.

If I let it, it'll go on all night until, like last night, when I finally stood and paced the room. All night long. Because it was easier than sitting still.

I think then about what the guy in the cafeteria said. About taking care of myself, about getting ready for what comes next. I think about what comes next, about Mom's and my house, vacant but for me. I wonder if I'll ever sleep again.

"Doc left some clonazepam for you," the nurse says now, as if she knows what I'm thinking. "In case you changed your mind." She says that it could be our little secret, hers and mine. She tells me Mom is in good hands. That I need to take care of myself now, again just like the guy in the cafeteria said.

I relent. If only to make my legs relax. She steps from the room to retrieve the pills. When she returns, I climb onto the empty bed beside Mom and swallow a single clonazepam with a glass of water and sink beneath the covers of the hospital bed. The nurse stays in the room, watching me. She doesn't leave.

"I'm sure you have better things to do than keep me company," I tell her, but she says she doesn't.

"I lost my daughter a long time ago," she says, "and my husband's gone. There's no one at home waiting for me. None other than the cat. If it's all right with you, I'd rather just stay. We can keep each other company, if you don't mind," she says, and I tell her I don't mind.

There's an unearthly quality to her, ghostlike, as if maybe she's one of Mom's friends from her dying delusions, come to visit me. Mom had begun to talk to them the last time she was awake, people in the room who weren't in the room, but who were already dead. It was as if Mom's mind had already crossed over to the other side.

The nurse's smile is kind. Not a pity smile, but authentic. "The waiting is the hardest part," she tells me, and I don't know what she means by it—waiting for the pill to kick in or waiting for Mom to die.

I read something once about something called terminal lucidity. I didn't know if it's real or not, a fact—scientifically proven—or just some superstition a quack thought up. But I'm hoping it's real. Terminal lucidity: a final moment of lucidity before a person dies. A final surge of brainpower and awareness. Where they stir from a coma and speak one last time. Or when an Alzheimer's patient who's so far gone he doesn't know his own wife anymore wakes up suddenly and remembers. People who have been catatonic for decades get up and for a few moments, they're normal. All is good.

Except that it's not.

It doesn't last long, that period of lucidity. Five minutes, maybe more, maybe less. No one knows for sure. It doesn't happen for everyone.

But deep inside I'm hoping for five more lucid moments with Mom.

For her to sit up, for her to speak.

"I'm not tired yet," I confess to the nurse after a few minutes, sure this is a waste of time. I can't sleep. I won't sleep. The restlessness of my legs is persistent, until I have no choice but to dig the melatonin out of my pocket when the nurse turns her back and swallow those too.

The hospital bed is pitted, the blankets abrasive. I'm cold. Beside me, Mom's breathing is dry and uneven, her mouth gaping open like a robin hatchling. Scabs have formed around her lips. She jerks and twitches in her sleep. "What's happening?" I ask the nurse, and she tells me Mom is dreaming.

"Bad dreams?" I ask, worried that nightmares might torment her sleep.

"I can't say for sure," the nurse says. She repositions Mom on her right side, tucking a rolled-up blanket beneath her hip, checking the color of her hands and feet. "No one even knows for sure why we dream," the nurse tells me, adding an extra blanket to my bed in case I catch a draft in my sleep. "Did you know that?" she asks, but I shake my head and tell her no. "Some people think that dreams serve no purpose," she adds, winking. "But I think they do. They're the mind's way of coping, of thinking through a problem. Things we saw, felt, heard. What we're worried about. What we want to achieve. You want to know what I think?" she asks, and without waiting for me to answer, she says, "I think your mom is getting ready to go in that dream of hers. Packing her bags and saying goodbye. Finding her purse and her keys."

I can't remember the last time I'd dreamed.

"It can take up to an hour to kick in," the nurse says, and this time I know she means the medicine.

The nurse catches me staring at Mom. "You can talk to her, you know?" she asks. "She can hear you," she says, but it's awkward then. Talking to Mom while the nurse is in the room. And anyway, I'm not convinced that Mom can really hear me, so I say to the nurse, "I know," but to Mom, I say nothing. I'll say all the things I need to say if we're ever alone. The nurses play Mom's records some of the time because, as they've told me, hearing is the last thing to go. The last of the senses to leave. And because they think it might put her at ease, as if the soulful voice of Gladys Knight & the Pips can penetrate the state of unconsciousness where she's at, and become part of her dreams. The familiar sound of her music, those records I used to hate when I was a kid but now know I'll spend the rest of my life listening to on repeat.

"This must be hard on you," the nurse says, watching me as I stare mournfully at Mom, taking in the shape of her face, her eyes, for what might be the last time. Then she confesses, "I know what it's like to lose someone you love." I don't ask the nurse who, but she tells me anyway, admitting to the little girl she lost nearly two decades ago. Her daughter, only three years old when she died. "We were on vacation," she says. "My husband and me with our little girl." He's her ex-husband now because, as she tells me, their marriage died that day too, same day as their little girl. She tells me how there was nothing Madison loved more than playing in the sand, searching for seashells along the seashore. They'd taken her to the beach that summer. "My last good memories are of the three of us at the beach. I still see her sometimes when I close my eyes. Even after all these years. Bent at the waist in her purple swimsuit, digging fat fingers into the sand for seashells. Funny thing is that I have a hard time remembering her face, but clear as day I see the ruffles of that purple tulle skirt moving in the air."

I don't know what to say. I know I should say something, something empathetic. I should commiserate. But instead I ask, "How did she die?" because I can't help myself. I want to know, and there's a part of me convinced she wants me to ask.

"A hit-and-run," she admits while dropping into an empty armchair in the corner of the room. Same one that I've spent the last few days in. She tells me how the girl wandered into the street when she and her husband weren't paying attention. It was a four-lane road with a speed limit of just twenty-five as it twisted through the small seaside town. The driver rounded a bend at nearly twice that speed, not seeing the little girl before he hit her, before he fled.

"He," she says then. "He." And this time, she laughs, a jaded laugh. "I'll never know one way or the other if the driver was male or female, but to me it's always been *he* because for the life of me I can't see a woman running her car into a child and then fleeing. It goes against our every instinct, to nurture, to protect," she says.

"It's so easy to blame someone else. My husband, the driver of the car. Even Madison herself. But the truth is that it was my fault. I was the one not paying attention. I was the one who let my little girl waddle off into the middle of the street."

And then she shakes her head with the weariness of someone who's replayed the same scene in her life for many years, trying to pinpoint the moment when it all went wrong. When Madison's hand slipped from hers, when she fell from view.

I don't mean for them to, but still, my eyes fill with tears as I picture her little girl in her purple swimsuit, lying in the middle of the road. One minute gathering seashells in the palm of a hand, and the next minute dead. It seems so tragic, so catastrophic, that my own tragedy somehow pales in comparison to hers. Suddenly cancer doesn't seem so bad.

"I'm sorry," I say. "I'm so sorry," but she shoos me off and says no, that she's the one who should be sorry. "I didn't mean to make you sad," she says, seeing my watery eyes. "Just wanted you to know that I can empathize. That I can relate. It's never easy losing someone you love," she says again, and then stands quickly from the armchair, gets back to tending to Mom. She tries to change the subject. "Feeling tired yet?" she asks again, and this time I tell her I don't know. My body feels heavy. That's as much as I knew. But heavy and tired are two different things.

She suggests then, "Why don't I tell you a story while we wait? I tell stories to all my patients to help them sleep."

Mom used to tell me stories. We'd lie together under the covers of my twin-size bed and she'd tell me about her childhood. Her upbringing. Her own mom and dad. But she told it like a fairy tale, like a *once upon a time* kind of story, and it wasn't Mom's story at all, but rather the story of a girl who grew up to marry a prince and become queen.

But then the prince left her. Except she always left that part out. I never knew if he did or if he didn't, or if he was never there to begin with.

"I'm not your patient," I remind the nurse but she says,

"Close enough," while dimming the overhead lights so that I can sleep. She sits down on the edge of my bed, pulling the blanket clear up to my neck with warm, competent hands so that for one second I envy Mom her care.

The nurse's voice is low, her tone flat so she doesn't wake Mom from her deathbed. Her story begins somewhere just outside of Moab, though it doesn't go far.

Almost at once, my eyelids grow heavy; my body becomes numb. My mind fills with fog. I become weightless, sinking into the pitted hospital bed so that I become one with it, the bed and me. The nurse's voice floats away, her words themselves defying gravity and levitating in the air, out of reach but somehow still there, filling my unconscious mind. I close my eyes.

It's there, under the heavy weight of two thermal blankets and at the sound of the woman's hypnotic voice, that I fall asleep. The last thing I remember is hearing about the snarling paths and the sandstone walls of someplace known as the Great Wall.

When I wake up in the morning, Mom is dead.

I slept right through it.

EDEN

May 16, 1996
Egg Harbor

AARON SHOWED ME THE house today. I'm in love with it already—a cornflower blue cottage perched on a forty-five-foot cliff that overlooks the bay. Pine floors and white-washed walls. A screened-in porch. A long wooden staircase that leads down to the dock at the water's edge where the Realtor promised majestic sunsets and fleets of sailboats floating by. *Quaint*, *charming* and *serene*. Those are the words the Realtor used. Aaron, as always, didn't say much of anything, just stood on the balding lawn with his hands in the pockets of his jeans, staring out at the bay, thinking. He's recently taken a job as a line cook at one of the restaurants in town, a chophouse in Ephraim. The cottage will more than cut his commute time in half. It's also a steal compared to our current mortgage, and set on two acres of waterfront land that spans the heavily wooded backcountry to the rocky shores of Green Bay.

And there's a garden. A ten-by-twenty-or thirty-foot space overrun with brambles and weeds. It's in need of work, but already Aaron has promised raised beds. There is a greenhouse, a sorry sight if I've ever seen one, set in a sunnier patch of the yard where the grass still grows. Small, shedlike, with aged glass windows and some sort of clear, corrugated roof meant to attract the sun. The door hangs cockeyed, one of its hinges broken. Aaron took a look and said that he can fix it, which comes as no surprise to me. There isn't a thing in this world that Aaron can't fix. Cobwebs cling to the corners of the room like lace. Already I'm imagining rows and rows of peat pots of soil and seed soaking up the sun, waiting to be transported into the garden.

Nearby, a swing hangs from the mighty branch of a burr oak tree. It was the tree that cinched it for me. Or maybe not the tree itself, but the promise of the tree, the notion of children one day causing ruckus and mayhem on the tree's swing, three feet of lumber fastened to the branch with a sturdy rope. I envision them climbing deep into the divots of the tree's trunk and laughing. I can hear them already, Aaron's and my unborn children. Laughing and screaming in delight.

Aaron asked if I loved it as much as him, and I didn't know if he meant whether I loved the cottage as much as I love *him*, or if I loved the cottage as much as he loves the cottage, but either way I told him I did.

Aaron left the Realtor with our bid. It's a buyer's market, he said, trying to finagle the asking price down a good 10 percent. Me, I would have paid asking price, too afraid to lose the cottage otherwise. Tomorrow we'll know if it's ours.

Tonight I won't sleep. How is it possible to love something so much, to want something so badly, when only hours ago I didn't know it existed?

with a short story, letting her imagination run wild. never showed anyone her writing. She'd learned g ago that she didn't have any talent. But she still oyed writing. She either threw the pieces out or hid em away in boxes in her closet. She didn't know why e wrote. It was just something she'd always done.

When Harper was little, she used to show people er stories. They were just silly ones about whatever ught her fancy. But she'd been proud of them. Then ne day, when she was eight, her mother had called her nto her office.

"Harper James-Muir!" Her mother's voice rang out in their New York City condominium. "Come into my office, please."

Harper had been sitting at the kitchen table, idly kicking her legs and eating cinnamon toast while staring at the ice-crystal design on the window. Hearing her mother's voice, she froze and darted a fearful gaze at her nanny. Her mother used her full name only when she was in trouble, and to be called into her office meant this was serious.

Luisa, her nanny, shook her head to indicate she didn't know what this was about.

Harper set down her toast while Luisa rushed to her side to wipe crumbs from her mouth and school uniform. She smoothed Harper's hair, then, taking hold of her shoulders, guided her to her mother's office.

Georgiana was sitting in her book-lined office

And who was that girl? Dora wondered, stunned at Harper's outburst. The mouse had roared! And Dora had to admit, she admired this side of Harper she'd never seen before. She had gumption, and that was something Dora could respect.

Dora's anger was quickly replaced by remorse. She slumped onto the chair and stared at her reflection in the mirror. Her cheeks were pink from the sun but her hair was mousy and her Bermuda shorts and bra looked like something her mother would wear. How could she be upset with Harper when Harper was right? Dora hated the way she dressed.

Was Harper also right about those other things? Did Dora push people away? She thought of Cal. How many nights had she pushed him away, claiming fatigue and headaches? She knew plenty of women used any number of those excuses on the nights they weren't in the mood, but it got old with Cal, and he got angry. "You're never in the mood," he'd complained. She couldn't explain to him that not feeling pretty, sexy, desirable, or even feminine was often the real source of the problem. Pushing people away was easier than letting them get close.

Harper was right. Again. She had pushed her away. She'd been jealous. She'd always thought both Harper and Carson lived exciting lives. They'd traveled the world while Dora had never left the South. They were younger, slimmer, richer—or at least Harper was. Dora's claim to fame was her marriage, her child, her stability. She'd held up the facade of her being the perfect Southern woman. Until the facade crumbled, leaving her with nothing to feel good about.

Facades were easier to maintain over distance.

But it was about time that *all* their facades were cracking and crumbling. Since they'd all returned to Sea Breeze, the truths were slowly being unearthed. Carson had been brutally honest, sharing the sordid details of her childhood. Harper revealed the loneliness behind the wealth of the James family. Why had Dora been ashamed to tell her sisters about the divorce?

The voice in her head that told her divorce was an embarrassing scandal, something to avoid at all costs, was the same harsh critic that whispered she was fat, not pretty. Were her insecurities what made her act so inflexible and stuck in her ways? Was she too judgmental, always finding fault and pushing people—and any hope for happiness—away?

She brought her hands to her face. In the past week she'd caught a glimpse of how her life could change. She liked the way she was beginning to feel about herself. In her reflection she was catching a glimpse of the young girl she once was. The girl who had confidence and dreams. The girl who believed anything was possible.

How could she break the old patterns that had grown like kudzu vines around her heart? How could she quiet the negative voices and listen to the positive ones?

Dora dropped her hands and slowly raised her eyes to the dresses hanging on the wall hooks. Harper had

told her she had looked pretty in the had told her she was beautiful. When wa start believing?

"Oh, give me that damn dress," Dora s as she rose to her feet and grabbed the firs reach.

Harper sat at a small table in City Lights ca napkins covered in her handwriting on the ta her. Whenever she was hurt or angry, Harpe therapeutic to write out in dialogue all the t wished she'd had the courage to say. She'd scr a heated fury a vitriolic scene of Dora and herse changing room, hurling insults, throwing clothe catfight. Finished, she sat back in her chair, relea pen, and grabbed her latte.

She finished her drink, set down the empty and looked around the coffee shop. Big stainless espresso machines lined the wall, pastries were arra on the counter. Women and men of all ages sat at small tables, talking, reading, typing on laptops. found the heady scents of freshly brewed coffee a sweet pastries comforting, and she needed that now.

In New York, she often went to coffee shops wi her laptop and people-watched. She enjoyed descri ing what she saw—the people, the setting, what th ordered. She jotted down comments she found amu ing or poignant. Sometimes she'd be so inspired by conversation she'd overheard that she finished the sn behind a sleek ebony desk. She was dressed in her work clothes, a stylish black houndstooth wool suit. Harper crinkled her nose at the stench of the cigarette smoke that always made her stomach upset.

"Come in," Georgiana said. "And shut the door behind you. That will be all, Luisa."

Harper heard the officious tone and, nervous, did as she was requested. She stood with her hands held before her.

"Sit down."

Harper walked across the plush carpeting to sit in one of the hot-pink velvet chairs with her shoulders back and ankles crossed, as she'd learned to do. Her gaze swept her mother's desk for clues as to why her mother had called her in. She spotted her handmade book, *Willy the Wishful Whale*. Harper had been especially proud of this story of the adventures of a young whale searching for his family. She'd painted the illustrations herself, bound the book using a three-hole puncher and ribbon. She'd even written a song to go with it. She released a sigh of relief, thinking that her mother, an editor of books, would be proud of her effort. After all, she'd created her first book!

Georgiana lifted the paper book. "Did you write this?"

"Yes."

"Do you write many stories?"

Harper smiled, encouraged. "Yes. Well, sometimes. I mean, I just do it when I get an idea."

"Where did you get the idea for this one?"

Harper shrugged. "I don't know. It just popped into my head."

"It just popped into your head," Georgiana repeated slowly. "I see."

Harper knew that when her mother became frosty, she was on the verge of losing her temper. Harper waited, holding her breath.

"Are you lying to me?"

Harper paled and her stomach suddenly felt sick. "No!"

"You got this idea from one of the books you read, didn't you?"

"I . . . I . . ." Harper didn't know what to say. Her mother was frightening her. "I don't know."

"I thought so," she said, taking a drag on her cigarette, then setting it down on the ashtray. She folded her hands on the desk. Harper stared at her perfect pink nails. "Harper, listen to me very carefully. You must never, ever copy the work of others. In the publishing world, that is called plagiarism. And it's a crime. Not to mention a scandal. I won't have it, not even for play. Do you understand me?"

Harper nodded, rendered speechless at the cruel accusation that she was lying and cheating when she wrote her book. The idea came to her as they all did—while she was dreaming, while reading, while listening to people talk. Sometimes they came to her while she was at the park or zoo with Nanny, just watching the animals. Was that copying? Was she being bad?

"Why are you writing books, anyway?" her mother

asked, clearly upset. Then she skewered her with a pointed gaze. "Are you trying to be like your father?"

Harper shook her head no. She knew they'd suddenly moved onto treacherous ground.

Her mother's eyes glittered with anger, as they did each time she brought up the topic of Parker Muir. "Well, don't. You didn't know him. I did, and trust me, you don't want to be like him. He was a lush and ladies' man. A ne'er-do-well." She pointed one of her perfectly polished fingers at her. "You're a James and you're better than him. Better than the lot of them." Her face hardened with the tone of her voice. "Your father wasn't a writer," she said with derision. "His work was derivative. He didn't have the talent. And," she said, lifting Harper's handmade book and dropping it onto the desk as if it were trash, "neither do you."

Harper felt her enthusiasm and pride for her book wither in her heart to be replaced by shame.

Georgiana took a final puff from her cigarette and blew out a stream of smoke as she eyed her daughter sitting slump-shouldered on the chair before the desk. Then she reached over to the ashtray and snuffed it out.

"I'm glad we had this little talk," her mother told her. "You're my daughter. I love you and have great expectations for you. I know you won't disappoint me." She smiled then, the same smile she gave to guests when they left the house, the megawatt one that made them feel like they'd been given a gift. "You can go now. I'll see you at dinner, all right?"

Harper shivered at the memory and reached for her mug of coffee, frowning when she saw that it was empty and cold. She was bored with waiting and ready to leave. Where was Dora? she wondered irritably. She cupped her chin and let her gaze wander the café, then out the front window. She spied Dora through the window, approaching the store. She sat up, expectantly. The bell over the door chimed and Dora walked in.

Harper felt all the frustration and anger pent up in her chest release in her short laugh of delight. Dora was beaming, wearing one of the dresses that Harper had selected for her. It was a navy print with vertical lines that complemented her figure. Harper didn't know what had brought about this change of heart in Dora, but it meant the world to her. Smiling, she shot her hand in the air and waved it in an enthusiastic arc. Dora spotted her and her eyes lit up at seeing her.

"You look gorgeous!" Harper exclaimed, standing to greet her. "I love you in that dress."

Dora swept her in a bear hug and whispered by her ear, "And I just plain love you."

They held tight for a moment, then a moment longer, not needing words this time to express their apologies and the enduring, unbreakable bond between them.

Dora released her and stepped back, a bit flustered. Harper could see the redness in Dora's eyes that revealed she'd been crying.

"Want some coffee?" Harper asked.

"I'll get it. My treat. I kept you waiting long enough."

Harper watched Dora get in line to place the order with the barista. As she waited, a rush of ideas flooded her head, fun things they could do together—just two women, two friends, two sisters, with a free afternoon on King Street. Smiling, she hurriedly gathered the napkins filled with her angry scribbling and, crumpling them in her hands, walked across the room and tossed them into the trash.

The afternoon sun was lowering by the time the girls returned to Sea Breeze. Mamaw had been waiting by the front windows, watching for them.

"Lucille!" she called out, her heart beating a mile a minute. "They're here!"

Lucille came rushing out from the kitchen in her stiff-legged gait, drying her hands on her starched white apron.

"At last," she huffed. "I hope they didn't eat nothin'. I've been cooking this rabbit food for an hour, trying to give it some taste."

"I hope they'll like what I've done," Mamaw said nervously. She turned to Lucille. "Do you think they will?"

"'Course they'll like it. Who wouldn't?"

"I don't want them to think I'm being, well . . ."

"Scheming?"

Mamaw frowned. "Such a harsh word. I like to think *generous* does the job."

Lucille guffawed. "Well, look at them, laughing together. I 'spect your *generosity* been workin' with those two."

Mamaw felt her worry ease. "Yes. I swanny, they've been like oil and water."

"Baking soda and vinegar, more like it. Hush now, here they come. Lord help us, looks like they done cleaned out the stores."

The front door opened and Mamaw heard the laughter before she saw Harper and Dora saunter in, laden with brightly colored shopping bags in their arms.

"We're back!" Dora called out gaily. "We had the best time! Harper is the sweetest girl in the whole world. Come see what we've bought! Or Harper bought. That woman is wild with that credit card!"

Mamaw turned her head to share a surprised glance with Lucille. This was certainly a change of heart between the girls, and Mamaw's elation bubbled over in her greeting.

"Dora, you look stunning! Why, you're positively transformed!" she exclaimed, walking toward her with her arms open.

Dora's blond hair had been highlighted to punch up her color and trimmed in a sleek new style. The chic summer dress made her look as if she'd lost an additional ten pounds, and Mamaw wasn't sure whether it was her happiness or the new makeup, but her face was positively glowing.

Dora was beaming as she stepped into Mamaw's arms. "It's all Harper. She did a complete makeover."

Mamaw turned to find Harper already busily spreading out the shopping bags on the Chippendale sofa and opening boxes. It didn't appear that Harper had bought anything for herself, which spoke volumes to Mamaw.

"You're quite good at this," she told Harper. "You should open a business!"

"I can't afford it," Harper said with a light laugh.

Dora gushed, "You think *I'm* bossy? I'm a piker compared to this girl. She made me get my hair done, and my makeup, and look! A mani-pedi. Lucille, what do you think of the color?" She held out her hands to reveal a bold hot-pink color. "Doesn't it just scream *summer*?"

Lucille bent over her hands. "It screams somethin', that's for true."

Dora giggled and hurried to the sofa to dig in one of the large bags. She fished out two small ones. "We picked out these for you together. Oh, Harper, you should give them. I'm forgetting my manners."

Harper just laughed and waved her hand, enjoying Dora's excitement. "Go ahead."

Mamaw accepted the bag with surprise. "For me? Gracious, girls, I don't deserve anything. It's not my birthday."

"It's nothing, really," Harper replied, watching. "A *petit cadeau*."

Mamaw pulled a scented candle out of the bag. "Thank you, precious. It's lovely," she said.

Lucille had received a candle as well.

"They're different scents," Harper said. "Hope you like them."

"You should," Dora added. "They cost the world."

Harper laughed and shook her head, embarrassed.

Lucille had pulled on her reading glasses and was studying her candle. "Says here it's called Summer Nights. I don't know what that means, but this smells like jasmine to me. I love me my night-blooming jasmine." She looked up, grinning.

Dora returned to the bags on the sofa. "Wait till you see what else I got."

"Girls," Mamaw said, clasping her hands close to her breast. She glanced at Lucille, who nodded in agreement. "There's something I'd like to show you first. It's my own little makeover."

Dora released the shopping bag and glanced at Harper. "Is this connected to all that knocking and pounding of the past few days?"

"You'll just have to look and see," Mamaw replied cagily.

"I love surprises," Harper said.

"Good. I hope you like this one. Come with me."

Mamaw led them from the living room down the hall toward her bedroom. She opened the doors that led into the anteroom of the suite, where a framed photograph of Mamaw and Granddaddy Edward greeted them over a small foyer table. Immediately to the left was a small computer room that had been built into a large closet. They proceeded into the large bedroom, adorned with a collection of paintings of the lowcountry landscape that Mamaw adored, all done by local artists. Every spare inch of her walls was covered in paintings. She'd often told the girls that lying in bed, especially now that Edward was gone, she felt surrounded by friends.

Mamaw went to stand before a pair of sliding wood doors separating her bedroom from her sitting room that were not there several days before.

Harper looked to Dora and they shared a look of confusion.

Mamaw's gaze swept over their expectant faces. "I've done a bit of work, as you've heard," she began. She let her gaze rest on Harper.

"Harper, dear, you've been a true gem putting up with being evicted from your bedroom this summer without a peep of complaint. We've all appreciated it."

"Of course, Mamaw," Harper said. "It's nothing. And I've enjoyed bunking with Dora." She glanced at Dora with a smile.

"Precisely the spirit I'm referring to. Nonetheless," Mamaw continued, "Carson and Nate are due back in a few days and I've done a bit of rearranging that I hope will suit you. This is your room now."

Mamaw turned to grasp the large brass door handles and with a push slid open the doors. Sunlight poured into the bedroom from the bay windows, revealing a sitting room transformed into a bedroom. Instead of the settee and armchair, a feminine antique bed with scrolls and curves was set at an angle from the windows, a soft blue patterned Persian rug at its feet.

Harper sucked in her breath and walked slowly into the sunny room, her head turning from left to right to take in the changes. The small desk from Dora's room had been painted a cream color and moved under the bay windows, and atop it, fresh flowers were arranged in the Chinese Rose Medallion vase she'd once told Mamaw she liked. Only Mamaw could be so attentive to the smallest details.

"You created a room . . . for me?" Harper asked in a small voice.

"It wasn't much. I had that bed and armoire in storage. You don't have a closet, I'm afraid. But you can have Edward's computer room for yourself. It just sits there unused. Other than that, Lucille and I just moved things around a bit. Oh"—she indicated the pale blue coverlet on the bed—"we thought you'd like to pick out a new coverlet yourself."

"Oh, Mamaw, I would have been content with an air mattress on the floor."

Mamaw laughed in the manner that implied what Harper said was absurd. "That is precisely why it brought me so much pleasure to do this." She kissed Harper's forehead. "I had the doors added so you could simply shut me out. They lock, see?" she said, pointing out the brass bolt. "I also had a door added so you can have a private entrance from the porch. I know how you like your privacy."

"Thank you, Mamaw. I'm . . . I'm overwhelmed." Harper had been raised to hold her emotions in check and blinked rapidly, trying to stop the tears.

Dora stood in the background, her eyes taking in the new room with wonder. "I have to admit, I'm going to miss sharing a room with you."

Mamaw looked to Dora to seek out any signs of jealousy that Harper had received such a boon. It was with relief that she saw nothing but genuine pleasure in Dora's face. It made her feel all the more eager about her next surprise.

Mamaw said to Dora, "You don't think I've left you out, do you? We've begun work on your room, too. Come take a look."

They followed Mamaw, giggling, through the living room again to the west side of the house. As they passed the library, the smell of fresh paint permeated the air. Looking over her shoulder to make certain that Dora was behind her, she smiled at seeing all three women with expressions on their faces like children on Christmas morning. Without delay, she pushed open the door.

The small bedroom was in the chaos of transition. Most of the furniture had been moved out, a painter's tarp covered the floor, and all the trim was freshly painted glossy white. One wall was covered with a pale pink-and-white-striped paper, feminine and chic.

"There's a lot left to be done," Mamaw said. "I had to call in every chit and I've been on the phone nagging seamstresses all over town." She proudly walked them around the room, pointing out changes. "The wallpaper will be hung tomorrow and we can get the curtains in as soon as all is dry. I only have a small window of time, and I'm determined to have everything in place before

Carson returns from Florida. You'll have to sleep in her room until then. If that's all right with you. Lucille's changed the bedding. All is in the ready."

"Of course," Dora sputtered. "I don't know what to say. I didn't expect anything like this. I would've been happy with a bigger bed. But . . ." Worry had now entered her voice. "Mamaw, all this effort and expense. I . . . we'll only be here for a short while . . ."

"I know, but I'm having so much fun and the Realtor told me I needed to freshen things up a bit. So it had to be done anyway." She shrugged with a roll of the eyes and said, "*Que sera sera*. Now, Dora, there's one object in particular I want you to see. It's what sparked all this effort in the first place," she said, guiding Dora out of the room. "I put it in Carson's room for now. Come see."

"A new bed, I hope?" Dora said. She hated sleeping in that twin.

"That, too," Mamaw assured her. "I'm having a full bed brought over from storage."

"Thanks be to . . ." Dora muttered before her voice stuck in her throat.

Mamaw opened the door to Carson's room and in the corner, dominating the space, she saw Mamaw's imposing French vanity. Dora stood staring at the beloved priceless antique, speechless.

"The vanity is yours, Dora."

Dora walked slowly to the vanity, her hand reaching out to delicately trace the elaborate curves of the brass mirror.

"Oh, Mamaw," Dora said breathlessly. "How did you know how much I loved this?"

Mamaw smiled indulgently. "I'm your grandmother. I *should* know such things."

Dora turned to face her. "But what will you use?"

"Oh, child, at my age, the less I look in the mirror, the better." She glanced at Lucille, who stood by the door beaming with pleasure. "Especially not if that old bird won't give me her skin cream recipe."

Lucille's grin widened. "Too late now, anyway!"

Mamaw sniffed and shook her head with resignation. Turning to Dora, she took her hands. "My dear girl, you've worked so hard to rediscover how very beautiful you are, inside as well as out. I hope you'll look in this mirror every day and see that beauty reflected." She squeezed Dora's hands. "You hear?"

Tears spilled over Dora's eyes as she nodded, her laugh broken with a choked cry.

"You're ruining her makeup!" Harper cried, laughing.

Mamaw held Dora in her arms, relishing the softness of her, the sweet scent of tuberose in her perfume, and the depth of feeling Dora was allowing herself to unleash, at last.

Chapter Twelve

The glimmering candlelight on thick white cotton tablecloths, the original lowcountry art on the walls, the orchids in bud vases, the hum of conversation punctuated with occasional laughs, the clinking of silverware—all combined to create the ambience of a perfect dinner date.

Dora shifted nervously in her seat and swirled the cabernet in the large crystal bowl of her wineglass. She took note of her perfectly polished pink nails. Tonight she wore her new shimmering blue silk dress that Harper had found for her during their shopping spree. Mamaw's large, creamy pearls graced her neck, and she knew she looked her best in the elegant Charleston restaurant.

Across the table, Devlin studied the oversized menu. He, too, was transformed tonight, handsome in his beautifully cut tan suit, a blush-pink shirt, and a

Ferragamo tie. She studied his hands on the menu—they were not long-fingered, like Cal's. Rather, they were wide and ruddy from being out on the water. A man's hand. On his ring finger he wore a thick gold signet ring. She sipped her wine, her imagination taking a turn in this romantic restaurant. What, she wondered, would those hands feel like on her body?

Devlin looked up from the menu and, catching her perusal, smiled.

"You look beautiful tonight. That reminds me . . ." He set the menu down and, with a gleam in his eyes, reached into his breast pocket to pull out a small jeweler's box. He set it on the table before Dora.

"What's this?" she asked, feeling a sudden panic.

"Nothing big, just something I saw that I thought you might like. Go ahead, open it."

Dora cast him a glance of mock suspicion and reached for the gray velvet box. Opening it, she found a pair of large blue-stoned earrings within a border of tiny diamonds.

"They're beautiful!" she exclaimed, shocked at their size. They had to have been costly.

"I always said your eyes are the color of aquamarines. Topaz are too clear. Yours are a deeper blue, like the deep ocean."

"I can't accept these. They're too expensive."

"Please, don't play that game. We're way past that. I saw them, I want you to have them, and they match your dress. Aren't those enough reasons to put them on right this minute and let me enjoy seeing you in them?"

Dora grinned and plucked the earrings from the box. It took a moment to slip the pearls from her ears and replace them with the aquamarines. When she was finished, she searched her purse for a mirror and pulled it out to study her reflection. The large aquamarines were dazzling and they were, indeed, the same color as her eyes, making them pop against her soft tan.

"I was right," Devlin said, leaning back in his chair with a smug grin.

"Thank you," Dora said, lowering the mirror to give Devlin her full attention. "Thank you times ten. I've never had such beautiful earrings. I'll treasure them."

"Don't be putting them in a box, afraid to wear them. You should wear them every day. If you lose them, I'll get you another pair."

Dora listened to the words with wonder. Cal had always been so frugal. He never splurged on a gift of jewelry for her. He was the type to buy her an appliance or a scarf. Tonight Devlin was offering her dinner at a five-star restaurant, fine wine, and now a gift—this was a full-court press.

The waiter stepped up to the table. He was dressed in black pants, a white shirt, and a black bow tie. After a few words of chitchat he launched into a description of the evening's specials with a flourish. Dora's mouth was watering after weeks of low-fat, lean meals.

Devlin picked up the menu and began ordering.

"Let's start with some lobster cakes. Then we'd like the she-crab soup." He glanced at Dora. "It's the specialty of the house. You've got to have some." Looking again at the waiter, he said, "That honey-roasted duck sounds good, too. And I can tell you right now we're both going to want some of your famous coconut cake."

"Devlin, wait . . ." Dora interrupted.

Devlin turned his head, expectant.

Dora turned to the waiter. "We're going to need a few more minutes."

The waiter nodded and discreetly stepped away.

"Dev, I can't eat all that. I'm on a . . ." She didn't want to use the word *diet*. "The doctor said I can't eat all that fatty food. Lord, the she-crab soup alone could kill me."

Devlin's smile dropped as his eyes widened. "I'm sorry. I forgot. What an idiot I am."

"No," she said in a hurry, not wanting him to feel bad. "You were being a gentleman. But I think it's best for me to order my own dinner."

"Of course," Devlin said, but she could tell he was flustered at his mistake. He raised his hand briefly and the waiter quickly reappeared.

"The lady will order her own dinner," Devlin said.

"Certainly." The waiter turned his attention to Dora.

She cleared her throat and studied the enormous menu. "I'll have the chef's summer salad, no dressing . . . the grilled shrimp, and hold the hushpuppies. And could I substitute the creamed corn for collard greens?" She closed the menu and, handing it to the waiter, added, "No dessert."

"Well played," Devlin said. He closed his menu and returned it to the waiter. "I'll have the same. Except, I still want some of that coconut cake." He glanced at Dora again. "I might convince the lady to try it."

"Dev . . ."

"One bite!" he exclaimed, then laughed.

Their laughter was interrupted by the ringing of her cell phone. Dora immediately drew her evening bag closer and pulled it out. She kept her phone turned on in case the call was about Nate.

"Hello?" she said.

"Hi, Dora. It's me, Cal. I thought I'd better give you a call and check in."

"Uh, Cal, I can't talk now. Can I call you back?"

"Where are you?"

"I'm out to dinner."

"Oh. Okay." There was a pause. "With who?"

"I have to go. I'll call you back. Bye."

She slipped the phone back into her bag and, a little sheepishly, looked up at Devlin. He was watching her with a skeptical expression.

"Sorry about that. I thought it was about Nate."

"That was your husband?"

The word *husband* coming from his lips while they were on a date sliced the air of intimacy they'd been enjoying.

Dora cringed, thinking, What were the odds that Cal, who rarely called, would pick tonight? "Cal, yes."

"Does he call you often?"

"Actually, no."

"You *are* separated . . . getting a divorce?"

"Yes, of course," Dora replied, bristling. "You don't

think I'd be having dinner with you, accepting gifts, if I weren't?"

He spread out his palms. "Just asking."

Dora couldn't respond. An awkward moment passed while she sipped her wine. It was with great relief that the first course arrived.

The remainder of the evening continued in an uncomfortable vein. It was as though Cal had pulled up a chair and joined them at the table. Their conversation was stilted; a bad first date. All the natural ebb and flow that they usually enjoyed had run dry. By the time the famous coconut cake was presented, neither Dora nor Devlin wanted any and were eager to go.

The short drive home to Sea Breeze seemed long, even in his luxury BMW sedan. It was a dark night. Heavy cloud cover obscured the moon and stars. Dora was tired and, closing her eyes, listened to moody ballads sung by Michael Bublé. When they pulled into the driveway, Devlin put the car into park but kept the engine running.

"You don't have to walk me up," Dora said in the darkness. Then, turning toward him, she added in a soft voice, "Thank you for a lovely evening. I had a wonderful time."

There was a pause, then Devlin switched off the engine. He turned and slid his arm around her waist. She stiffened, but he didn't release her.

"You don't have to be polite. You didn't have a wonderful time," he said in a low voice.

"I . . . It was a delicious meal."

He nodded in agreement. "It was. But I'm sorry I got all messed up by Cal's phone call. Plus, that whole scene is not my style. I just wanted to impress you."

"Impress me? Why? I've known you since we were kids."

"That's exactly why. You knew me when I was flat broke. I couldn't ever have afforded to take you out to a restaurant like that or buy you pretty earrings. I wanted to, but I never had the money."

"Dev, you and I . . . we never needed any props between us. It's always been just you and me, having a good time because we were together."

He reached out to take her hands. Looking at them, he played with her fingers, then tapped the wedding ring she still wore on her hand. "But you married him."

"Yes."

"Tell you what," Devlin said, looking at her face. "Give me another chance to take you out again. We'll go out on the boat, like we used to. Take a spin through the creeks. Do it proper." He drew her closer. "What do you say?"

Dora let her arms slide under his suit jacket and around his waist, and she leaned against him. She felt his warmth and smelled the faint remnants of his after-shave. It was a spicy scent and, smiling, she thought she wouldn't be at all surprised if he was still wearing Old Spice. She turned her head up toward his.

"I'd love to."

His smile came slow and easy as he wrapped his arms around her and lowered his mouth to hers. His arms tightened as his kiss deepened, and all thoughts of Cal evaporated into the night like an exorcised ghost.

The following morning, Dora stood at the wooden kitchen table overflowing with produce that had been delivered from a local farm. She was packing a bag of snacks for her boat trip with Devlin. She'd washed and cut up carrots and celery, added a bag of cherries and almonds, and put them into a large canvas bag beside bottles of water. A month ago she would have packed cookies, a candy bar, and soda. Though she still craved sugar, with every day that passed the desire loosened its hold on her as her refined taste buds began to appreciate the natural sweetness of fruit. After talking with Carson about Nate and his colorful schedule, Dora had affixed her own routine and diet calendar to the fridge. Every *X* on the calendar gave her strength to stay on her diet another day.

Across the room Lucille was at the stove, stirring a pot of vegetable soup. Lucille and Mamaw stuck by their word unwaveringly, clearing all the processed foods and sweets from the cabinets. There were nights when she'd prowled the kitchen for something *good* to eat—meaning cookies, candy, anything sweet—cursing them for not leaving a single morsel of chocolate. Dora had gained a whole new understanding of Carson's addiction to alcohol.

"That soup smells wonderful!" Dora exclaimed.

Lucille grunted. "It'd be a whole lot better if I could

put a ham bone in it. Nothin' a good soup needs more than a ham bone. That's what gives it the flavor."

"So put one in."

She grunted. "Can't. Miss Harper can sniff out a bit of pork like a coon dog does a possum. Nothing gets past her. It'll be good," she said, stirring. "Just not *as* good, that's all I'm sayin'."

"We're sure putting you through your paces this summer with all our demands, aren't we? No alcohol, no fat, no salt, no butter."

"No taste," Lucille grumbled.

"It's healthy," Dora offered.

"I do what I gots to do," Lucille said with the sigh of the long suffering. "But I won't give up my corn bread. I don't care how much Miss Harper complains about my bacon grease, I will not give up my mama's corn bread!"

"God forbid!" Dora agreed. "Bless her heart, she's from New York and doesn't appreciate the virtues of pork. But she's making an effort. And you're a genius in the kitchen. Everything still tastes wonderful. I, for one, know I wouldn't be able to stick to this diet without your support. I swear, Lucille, your cooking is holding this family together."

Lucille appeared mollified and half smiled. "Ain't nothin' I wouldn't do for this family."

Dora paused and stared at the woman bent over the stove. Lucille had the heart of a lion but she was normally shy of expressing her affection in words. She showed her love through action—breakfast in bed on birthdays, an ironed dress for a special occasion, fresh flowers on the bureau. To hear these words now took Dora by surprise. She went to Lucille's side and kissed her cheek.

Startled, Lucille drew back, her dark eyes wide. "What's that for?"

"Does it have to be for something? *You're* family, you know."

Lucille, clearly flustered by Dora's show of emotion, awkwardly tried to smile as she turned back to the stove. "Just caught me by surprise, is all. You're not one to give kisses."

Dora wondered about that comment as she returned to the table. For so long she'd held herself back from excessive shows of affection. Cal was not physically affectionate. No pats on the behind or arms around her shoulder during a movie. She was especially restrained with Nate, knowing that he'd get upset if she spontaneously hugged or kissed him. Did that restraint come naturally to her? Was she, as Cal had insinuated, frigid?

Dora stuffed a few paper napkins into the canvas bag. "I'm sure Cal would agree with you. Maybe I should change that, eh?"

"This surely is a summer for changes."

Dora laughed, hearing the truth in that.

"Where are you off to this time?"

"We're going boating."

"We?"

"Me and Devlin."

Lucille paused her stirring, her lips twisted in

thought. "I know that name. How do I know that name?"

"Devlin Cassell," Dora replied. "You remember him. I went steady with him back in high school. Blond hair, blue eyes, tan. Surfer. He was here all the time. Practically lived in the kitchen. Used to steal your cookies."

Lucille swung around, eyes wide. "*That* Devlin? Lord help us. Was that the man you got all trussed up for the other night?"

Dora laughed. "Sure was."

Lucille clucked her tongue. "Back when, your mamaw was on her knees praying most nights that boy wouldn't get into your skivvies, worried 'bout what else he'd steal beside cookies. And now it's startin' up all over again." She turned back to the stove and said in a lusty wail, "My, my, my . . ."

"Mamaw doesn't have to worry about my cookies any longer," Dora said drily. "Let's just say things aren't as hot and heavy now as they were back when we were teenagers."

"You talk like you're an old woman."

"I'm thirty-six. Almost thirty-seven. With a child."

"You got the same parts, don't you?"

"Last time I looked."

"And they still work?"

Dora smirked. "I wouldn't know. It's been so long."

"Seems to me it's high time you find out."

Now it was Dora's turn to be flustered. "Well, it wouldn't be right," she stammered. "I'm not divorced yet."

"You ain't been living as man and wife for a long time."

"It would be wrong for me to, you know, be with another man."

"Who says?"

"My lawyer, probably. My mother, most certainly."

Lucille grunted in a manner that gave no doubt she didn't care for Winnie. "Who's gonna tell them? That's one woman who'd be a lot happier if someone took the long pole out of her backside."

"Lucille!" Dora burst out with a laugh.

"You know it's true. And don't you tell me you're not thinkin' the same thing."

Dora giggled at Lucille's unexpected burst of temper. Her mother had never given Dora that little talk mothers were supposed to give their daughters at puberty. Dora didn't think Winnie could bring herself to say the words. When Dora was thirteen, she had found a pamphlet on her bed written by some priest or bishop. It was all about the mystical body of Christ, and Dora couldn't figure out what they were talking about.

"She was always pretty rigid about rules, I'll give you that. And sex. I don't think she finds sex very ladylike."

"It was a miracle you were born, child," Lucille said. "When Winnie talks about Adam and Eve, I'll wager all she can think about is how they committed some sin. What's that special name they call it?"

"Original sin."

"That'll be it. Ain't we learned nothin' since then? Still calling sex a sin. Sex is as natural as the birds and the bees." Lucille grew agitated, putting one hand on her hip as she spoke. "God put a man and a woman together, buck naked in paradise. 'Course He knew what was gonna happen. Way I see it, that was the plan all along. Else how would Cain and Abel be born? Or any of us?"

She covered the pot of soup and turned off the stove. "Don't listen to your mother. You ain't sixteen no more. You're a woman, fully growed. Make up your own mind. Just remember, we're all Eve's daughters." She caught Dora's gaze and held it. "This is your one and only life, girl. Your time in the garden."

Lucille pointed the wooden spoon at Dora. "What you waitin' for?"

Dora stood on the dock, staring into the current of the Cove. Even with Nate on holiday, Dora still acutely felt the weight of her responsibilities. She felt more and more sure of her decision to proceed with the divorce. This opened a Pandora's box of decisions. Where would she move? She'd have to find a school for Nate, a job for herself. This was a watershed moment in her life.

A large fish jumped and landed in the water with a noisy splash, creating ripples that fanned out farther and larger across the water as Dora watched. She sighed—the ripples of her decisions would have long-lasting consequences as well.

The growl of outboard motors broke her dark thoughts. Lifting her head, she saw the tip of a blue-and-white boat heading toward the dock. Squinting, she spotted Devlin waving at the wheel and immediately broke into a grin and waved back.

As the big boat drew near, Dora couldn't help but notice it was a very nice one. A Boston Whaler, at least twenty feet in length with a pretty, bright blue canopy. Devlin always liked his toys, she thought as she stood on the edge of the dock with her arms outstretched, ready to catch the rope.

Dora loved boating—she was good at it. When the girls came to Sea Breeze for the summers, it was Dora who drove the boat while Carson and Harper rode the inner tubes or water-skied. Dora wasn't much for getting wet. She preferred the feel of the wheel in her grasp and the throttle of engines at her control.

The boat's engine bubbled in the water as Devlin slowly brought the boat alongside the dock. Dora deftly caught the rope and secured it. Her legs stretched precariously between the dock and boat as she tied the line. She almost lost her balance for a moment, not having the control she did when she was younger. She blushed and looked up at Devlin.

He was busy tying up the line in fast, sure movements. He was stocky but moved across the boat like a dancer. Knowing boats, she appreciated his speed and confidence. That, she knew, came only with years of experience.

Devlin looked up from the boat, grinning behind

his dark sunglasses at seeing her. A worn Ducks Unlimited cap tamped down his blond, windblown hair and his skin was tanned. Devlin was an outdoorsman, as comfortable on the water as on land, and Dora found that very attractive. She smiled back and tossed him the canvas bag, then reached out to accept Devlin's hand. At his touch she felt an electric-like charge, calling to mind the conversation about natural urges she'd had earlier with Lucille. He must have felt it, too, because he squeezed her hand again before releasing it.

Devlin went to the cooler and retrieved two beers. He put them in koozies and handed one to Dora.

"Make yourself comfortable, pretty lady," he told her as he rushed back and forth across the boat untethering the ropes. When he was done, he went to the wheel.

Dora opened her can, then moved to stand close to him under the awning. He reached out to slip an arm around her and tugged her closer.

"Glad you're here," he said, giving her bottom a modest pat.

Dora laughed for the pure joy of going out on the boat with Devlin on such a perfect day. "Me, too."

It was still early. The sun was rising overhead in a cloudless sky. Devlin slipped his arm away to lean back, half standing, half sitting against the captain's chair. He reached for the throttle with one hand, while the other was on the wheel as he slowly revved the motors. They growled and gurgled as he guided the Whaler through the narrow marsh creeks.

Dora held on to the rocking boat as she moved to sit in the second seat beside him. She held her beer, but her fingers itched to drive the boat. She knew a captain didn't like to give up his wheel and she didn't want to press—at least not on their first outing.

As the boat took off, she thought back to when they were young and she and Devlin had been out on his boat. He used to let her drive. When her hands were on the wheel, he'd come up behind her and put his hands on her waist. He'd told her he was steadying her, but as they bounced along the waterway he'd leaned closer, wrapped his arms tighter around her, and buried his lips in her neck. Her toes curled as she remembered the rush of feelings.

She remembered how great a kisser Devlin was. Day after summer day they went out on the boat alone to explore the winding creeks and deserted hammocks, stopping at frequent intervals to explore each other's bodies with equal excitement and adventuresome spirit.

Dora opened her eyes and studied the man at the wheel from behind her sunglasses. Was it really twenty years ago? Where did the time go? He'd aged some, as she had. She could see the weather-beaten texture of his skin, the first gray hairs at the temple. Their bodies were fuller, softer. Her gaze traveled to his mouth and she smiled furtively. He still had those beautiful lips.

They had traveled years apart, too, she realized. Yet today, back on a Boston Whaler in these familiar creeks, with Devlin, she thought, *I feel sixteen again.*

Devlin guided the Whaler out of creeks into the wide and heady Intracoastal Waterway. Once there he slowed the boat to a stop, stepped aside from the wheel, and waved his hand, indicating Dora should come closer.

"Come on, honey, let's give you a chance at the wheel. I seem to recall you were pretty good at handling one of these things."

Dora burst into a grin. He'd remembered! Clearly she wasn't the only one taking a trip down memory lane. She set her beer into a holder and began walking across the boat when another boat roared past them, sending huge wakes their way. Dora lost her balance in the rocking boat and tottered with her arms stretched out wide.

Devlin grabbed her waist. "Hold steady, girl."

Dora clung to his arm a moment, like it was her anchor. When she got her balance, he released her and she clumsily walked the few feet to the wheel and grabbed hold.

Looking up, she spotted the speeding boat weave past another boat in the queue ahead. It was filled with four teenagers, all insolent, bronzed, and beautiful.

"Damn hooligans. Someone ought to arrest those boys, speeding like that," she blustered.

Devlin laughed beside her. "Aw, hell, Dora. We were just like that. What goes around, comes around. Come on, sugar. Let's show 'em how it's done."

She glanced over at him. She couldn't see his eyes behind his shades but knew there was a boyish sparkle of mischief in them.

"You're a bad influence on me," she said.

"Always have been"—his lips spread to a grin—"Mrs. Dora Tupper."

He'd used her married name for the first time. She hadn't been aware that he knew it.

"What you waitin' for, girl? Let's get this ol' tub going!"

Dora reached down to grab the throttle and pushed it forward. The Whaler's engine growled again and they took off along the waterway. Dora lifted her chin, feeling the vibrating, powerful engines under her control, the push of wind against her cheeks.

"Put a little muscle on it, Dora. You drive like a girl."

Dora burst out in a laugh and accepted the dare. She gripped the throttle with her hand and pushed forward hard. The engines screamed as they churned water and the boat tore off down the Intracoastal Waterway. The boat bounced on the small waves like a bronco, cool droplets splashing her face, and the wind coursing through her hair, streaming it back like a flag. She let out a whoop while beside her, Devlin let loose a rebel yell. She hadn't felt this alive in years.

Devlin stepped behind her and placed his hands on her waist.

"Just like old times," he said, lowering his lips to her ear.

Dora leaned back against him, enjoying the feel of his hard body against hers. She slowed the boat, wanting to enjoy the moments as they cruised the waterway. She rolled her palms along the wheel, one eye on the shallows, the other on signals, passing slower boats with finesse.

"Stay left at the split," Devlin called, pointing out the direction.

"Aye aye, Captain." She veered left, maneuvering the boat to a narrow creek bordered on both sides with cordgrass growing so high that she could barely see over it. It felt more like they were traveling through a long tunnel.

"Where are we going?" she asked. "It's getting narrow in here. If the tide goes out, we can get stuck."

"We're good here," he told her with confidence. "This is deep water." He leaned forward, his lips close to her cheek. "Don't you remember where we are?" he asked, his voice suddenly husky.

She caught the scent of beer on his breath and enjoyed the feel of his chin grazing her skin. She studied the long stretch of cordgrass and for the life of her couldn't remember. She shook her head. "No."

"Keep going," he told her encouragingly.

She drove the boat at a slower pace through the narrow creek before it opened up again to a wide area of water spotted with several small hammocks. The breeze picked up in the open area and brushed away the cobwebs in her memory.

"I know where we are!" she exclaimed, turning

around to face Devlin, laughing. "This is our old hangout."

He slipped his arms tighter around her waist and said teasingly, "More than a hangout, if memory serves."

She blushed and faced forward again, her eyes lingering on the rounded hammock in the distance, a jungle of tall palm trees, live oaks, Chinese tallow trees, and shrubs. This had been their spot. The isolated place they'd anchor and make out and talk for hours. This secluded haven was where she'd lost her virginity. She smiled, realizing Devlin remembered.

"You ol' horn dog," she said with a playful push.

"Can't teach an old dog new tricks."

He nuzzled her neck and she felt again she was racing along the Intracoastal.

"We can pull anchor right up yonder," he said, pointing to a shallow spot near what had been their favorite hammock. "Seems as good a place as any to have some lunch."

"Lunch? I didn't pack lunch, just some things for us to munch on."

"You weren't supposed to. You don't think I invited a lady out for a trip without seeing to the details, do you?"

"I don't remember you ever bringing food to this hammock before."

"Yeah, well . . ." Devlin rubbed his jaw in embarrassment. "I've grown up a bit since then. Learned some manners at my daddy's knee."

"Your daddy? I'll wager you learned through trial

and error with all the pretty girls you've brought to this hammock since me."

"None of them were as pretty as you."

Dora felt embarrassed by the compliment. Of course she wasn't the prettiest.

"Stop it, Devlin. You don't have to say that."

"Say what? It's the truth. You're beautiful."

"I said stop it," Dora snapped. "We both know I'm not." She turned her gaze away. "At least, not anymore."

Devlin took the wheel as the mood shifted. Dora went to stand at the opposite side of the boat. Devlin brought the mighty engines to a stop and set anchor. The boat rocked lightly in the current, immersed in a sudden great silence.

Dora stared at a pair of white ibis standing in the shallow water along the shore, their elegant orange down-curved bills digging in the mud. They appeared so beautiful, so serene.

Devlin walked to her side and, taking her waist, turned her to face him. He took off his sunglasses. Then he reached out and took off Dora's. This close, Dora could see the network of fine lines around his stunningly pale blue eyes. She couldn't look away.

"Dora Muir Tupper," Devlin said. "You're still the prettiest girl I ever saw."

When Dora looked into his eyes, she saw a pulsing kindness and sincerity that couldn't be faked. She felt her own eyes fill with tears and thought to herself, *Lord help me, I still have a crush on this man.*

Their gazes locked. Everything that needed to be

said was said in that long look, words that the intervening years had made too complicated for translation into syllables. Dora raised her arms around his neck, not worrying this time if her body wasn't slim and perfect, if he felt more skin than was there before. He'd called her beautiful and she'd seen the truth in his eyes. She would, she decided, believe him.

When Devlin lowered his head, Dora knew that this time, she wasn't a fumbling sixteen-year-old. No, not at all. She felt every inch a luxurious woman. As she pressed her curves against him, she thought, *We are all Eve's daughters*.

It was late by the time Devlin drove Dora back to Sea Breeze. He kissed her good-bye once, then again, then once more. They giggled softly, each acknowledging that they didn't want to stop. When, at last, she extricated herself from his arms, she adjusted her shirt and smoothed her hair, glad for the darkness.

"See you tomorrow?" he asked.

"Call me."

"Soon as I wake up."

She looked at him askance. "Lord, what time is that?"

"Whenever I open my eyes."

Dora chuckled. This was one dog that would not be tied to the post.

She opened the car door and closed it as softly as she could, not wanting to wake up the household.

Mamaw had kept the light burning for her. She was likely asleep, and Harper was likely still tapping away at her keyboard, lost in whatever it was she was madly working on. Feeling safe from discovery, she waved and watched Devlin drive off into the night.

No sooner did she start walking toward the front door than Lucille's porch lights went on.

"Shit," Dora muttered under her breath.

The cottage's front door opened and Lucille came out in her long white nightgown and blue floral-patterned robe. Dora didn't know if she'd ever seen Lucille in her nightclothes before and she couldn't quite grasp it in her mind.

"Sorry if I woke you up," Dora said in a loud whisper, walking closer to the cottage porch.

"You didn't. I couldn't sleep."

Dora reached the foot of the porch. "Are you okay?"

Lucille waved her hand in dismissal. "Oh, just an old woman's aches and pains. I ain't had a good night's sleep since I turned sixty. Gettin' old is not for sissies. I reckon I'll just sit out on the porch awhile, let this fine night cast its spell."

"Want some company?"

"Why, sure. Love it. Want something to drink?"

"Not a thing," Dora answered, stepping up the stairs onto the porch. She took the rocking chair beside Lucille, dropping the canvas bag on the floor.

Lucille's dark eyes studied her. "You look like you got some sun."

"Lots of it. Hope I don't peel."

"Put aloe on your skin tonight and drink lots of water."

"I will."

They rocked awhile before Lucille said, "That sure was a long boat ride."

Dora closed her eyes as images of Devlin flashed across her thoughts. That first kiss on the Boston Whaler had lit a fire in her that she hadn't felt in a very long time. It felt both as though she and Devlin had picked up right where they left off when they were teenagers, and like they were exploring something fresh and new. They were older, more world-wise, certainly more experienced. Being with Devlin was like scratching an eighteen-year-old itch. She felt again the ripple of pleasure she'd experienced when he'd found the itch and scratched it, but good. Again and again.

Dora stopped rocking and looked at Lucille. "I discovered something today."

"Oh, yeah?"

"I'm sure as hell Eve's daughter."

A knowing smile spread across Lucille's face. "Well, good for you! I'm glad to hear it." She chuckled and commenced rocking. "That boy's been waiting long enough. I reckon it was worth it?"

"Oh, yes," Dora said with a slight laugh. "Definitely."

"You gonna see him again?"

"Definitely," she repeated. After rocking awhile Dora said, "He wants to see me again tomorrow. And the day after that. I think I should cool it a little, don't you? I mean, I feel this nervousness, like I'm in high school all over again. That's not normal, is it? Is it always like this when you have a crush on someone? At my age?"

"Don't ask me. I ain't never felt that."

Dora looked at Lucille and it suddenly dawned on her how little she knew about Lucille's personal life. Lucille was always the much-loved woman who lived at Sea Breeze and took care of all of them. That was a child's vision of the person, she realized with a burn of shame.

"Lucille, why didn't you ever get married?"

"I didn't want to."

"You never fell in love?"

"Didn't say that. Said I didn't never want to get married."

"Why not?"

"Why you want to know?"

Dora rocked awhile. "No reason. I just realized I don't know much about you. About your family. And I've known you all my life."

Lucille stopped rocking. "What you want to know?"

"Do you have a family?" Dora asked.

"No, not no more. My family used to live here on Sullivan's Island. You know that."

Dora nodded.

"A lot of black families used to live on Sullivan's. But times got hard, and we left to move to the city when I was not much older than Nate. My mama found work, but my daddy . . . One night he went off and we never saw him again. Never found out what happened to him. My mama died a few years later. I was just thirteen."

"Lucille, I'm sorry. That's so sad. Did you go to live with relatives?"

"My two younger sisters went to live with my aunt upstate. It was hard on them taking on two more mouths to feed. They had their own chilluns to worry about. I was the eldest and they couldn't take on the extra burden, so I went out on my own."

"At thirteen?" Dora asked, aghast. "What about an orphanage?"

"There weren't no orphanages back then, not for colored folk." She shook her head and commenced rocking.

Dora studied the woman's tight lips and didn't press with more questions.

"I made my own way," Lucille continued at length. "My mama, she took in ironing and taught me. When she passed, I had her iron, so I had some work. There were some nice women who looked out for me." She turned away, frowning. "Some not so nice."

Dora couldn't begin to imagine what life must have been like for a young, orphaned black girl in the 1950s, making a living for herself. It would have been Dickensian.

"The Lord looked out for me, though. I went into service with your mamaw when I was eighteen and I been with this family ever since." She turned her head. "You're my family, hear?"

Dora nodded, comprehending the depth of the comment.

"So you think you're in love with Devlin? That what you saying?" Lucille asked in an upbeat tone.

Dora understood Lucille wanted to change the subject. "It's way too early to say that. I like him. A lot. But with all that's going on, I don't think I should encourage him."

"A little late for that."

"A fling is one thing. A relationship is another. I mean, do I really want to take on another relationship so soon? All I want is to have a little fun. I've got enough to deal with without sparking gossip."

"Honey, no one's looking that close. If any tongues wag, they're just jealous. Look at your sister. Carson goes through men like nobody's business. You think she cares what people think?"

"I'm not like Carson."

"No, you ain't. You ain't like Harper, neither. Each of you girls have changed some since you were little and you're gonna change more in the years to come. But you're the same at the core. Carson, now she's what you might call fearless. She takes the world head-on. But she gets knocked down on her bottom plenty, too. Harper, she likes to watch. She might seem to be on the sidelines, but she's taking everything in. That girl don't miss a trick. Something's bubbling in that brain of hers, and I don't know what it is. She might not either. Yet." Lucille half turned to look at Dora and let her gaze sweep slowly over her.

"And me?"

"And you, Dora, you're the rock. You always have both feet planted firmly on the ground. The one we can depend on."

"I don't feel like a rock."

"You're going through an earthquake now. Your world is shifting. That's okay. Happens to all of us. Some folks crumble, but not you. You'll settle again, and when you do, you'll feel solid and strong again. Maybe even more than you did before. I know it."

Dora reached out to take Lucille's hand. "Oh, Lucille, thank you. I needed to hear that tonight."

"It's all gonna be all right," Lucille said in a soothing voice, patting Dora's hand over hers.

"Can I come back again, to chat like this? Just you and me?"

Lucille smiled and her eyes grew misty. "Why, I'd like that. For true."

Chapter Thirteen

The day was starting out to be a scorcher on Sullivan's Island. No cloud broke the sun's relentless heat, no breeze blew from the ocean. Sweat poured down the overheated faces of both Dora and Harper as they fought backbreaking struggles with deep-rooted monster weeds in the garden. They'd been at it for over an hour and had managed to clear nearly half of the garden. They'd been ambitious with their original design, but once they comprehended the great battle, they edited the garden to a more manageable size.

Today, even that felt like too much.

"Why are we even doing this?" Dora whined, pausing her digging to swipe the sweat from her brow. "My back aches and my mouth feels like it's stuffed with cotton balls."

"Because it's fun?" Harper replied in jest, whacking at the parched earth with her hoe.

"Yeah, it's a riot," Dora said with heavy sarcasm.

Harper leaned on her hoe and caught her breath.

"Really, what's the point?" Dora asked. "Mamaw's just going to sell the place. We won't see it come to glory."

"Maybe not," Harper said. Wiping her brow, she left a mud streak in the sweat. "But we'll know it's here, won't we? Like it used to be."

Dora wasn't convinced. "So what . . ."

"*So what,* indeed," Harper muttered as she let her gaze sweep Sea Breeze.

The view from the Cove was its best side, she decided. Her Muir ancestors knew what they were doing when they'd chosen this spot on the quiet end of Sullivan's Island. The old house was well situated on higher ground, with a broad rear porch facing the Cove. The porch provided a magnificent vantage point from which to view the Intracoastal Waterway. Mamaw had added the long black-and-white awning that provided shade for the oversized black wicker chairs, with their plump black-and-white cushions. A few steps down from the porch was another level of decking that surrounded the swimming pool and stretched the entire length of the porch. From this level, more steps led to the small patch of grass that continued on a downward slope to where the wild grasses bordered the marsh.

This was where the long wooden dock extended over the marsh to the winding water of the Cove. The old, elegant Southern house, the broad veranda with chairs, the dock with a boat tied up were, for Harper, the very definition of a lowcountry setting. She was surprised by the love she felt for this place and how heartsick she was to see it leave family hands. *So what*, she wondered, feeling a bubbling resistance to the idea that she'd never be able to come back here, to Sea Breeze, to the only place she'd ever truly felt safe. *So what* . . . She didn't want that to happen, that was so what.

She heard Dora laughing and turned her head to see her sister looking at her with amusement.

"What's so funny?"

"You. Even digging in the garden, you make a fashion statement."

Harper looked down at her long-sleeved white cotton shirt and designer jeans. "It's all I had," she said, a tad defensively.

"I don't want to think how much those jeans cost," Dora said.

"After today, they'll be worthless. And this shirt will officially be my gardening shirt because it won't be fit to wear in public. Sort of like yours," she teased, indicating Cal's old Gamecock T-shirt, now relegated to garden duty. Dora's jeans might've been Cal's, too. They were too big and unhemmed. Under her large floppy straw hat, Dora's face was as bright as a cherry.

"Maybe we should both take a break," Harper said. "You shouldn't push too hard, with your heart and all. I don't want you digging your grave here."

"Don't worry about me," Dora said with a dismissive wave. "The doctor wants me to have a good cardio workout every day and I'm thinkin' this applies."

"I have to admit, this is a lot harder than I thought." Harper wiped at her brow. "How big did you say your garden was in Summerville?"

"A quarter acre."

Harper shook her head, incredulous. "Amazing. And ambitious."

"It was already framed out when I moved in. And I was younger." Dora laughed. "It was in the same sorry shape as this when I took it over. Lord, I slaved over that plot of earth. But it was worth every minute. I grew all our vegetables for Nate. Everything was natural, no pesticides. And the butterflies!" She smiled wistfully.

Harper brushed clumps of dirt from her shirt. "After all that work, why'd you let it go to seed?"

Dora had asked herself that question many times over the years. There wasn't an easy answer. "With Nate, it just came down to choices. I could go out to the garden or spend time with Nate. Nate won out every time. And later I homeschooled, which took a lot of time. Then there were his enrichment therapies, speech therapy . . . so many different therapies over the years." She added pointedly, "I don't regret how I spent my time."

"Of course not," Harper readily agreed. "I don't know if I'll ever have kids, but if I do, I hope I'm half as dedicated a mother as you are."

The compliment caught Dora by surprise. Harper couldn't know what it meant to her.

"That was so nice to say. Thank you."

Mamaw called from the porch, "Come take a break, girls. I've brought iced sweet tea!"

"You go get me one, would you?" Harper said. "There's something stuck in here and I've almost got it out." She gritted her teeth with determination. "Hand me that shovel."

Dora relinquished the shovel with relief. She plucked off her garden gloves as she strolled across the scrubby patch of grass, slapping them against her thighs to shake out the dirt. Looking over her shoulder, she laughed at the sight of Harper digging in the hole like a terrier with a bone. That tenaciousness was a side of her sister that she was coming to recognize and appreciate.

"Bless you, Mamaw," Dora said, accepting the glass. The tea was icy sweet, and as she gulped it down, her throat felt like parched ground welcoming a rushing river.

"You're making progress," Mamaw said, lifting her sunglasses as she looked out at the garden. "It does my heart good to see the garden return to its former beauty."

"It won't be as fancy as your last one."

"It'll be glorious, because you girls created it. Now drink up. You know what I always say."

"*You have to stay hydrated,*" Dora replied, then dutifully took a sip.

"And wear sunscreen. I've given you good genes, but you have to do your part." She lowered her voice and took a step closer. "And get Lucille's recipe for face cream. I swanny, she'll go to the grave with it."

Dora chuckled at Mamaw's lifelong quest to get Lucille's face cream recipe. "Where is Lucille?" she asked. "I haven't seen her around this morning."

"No, she's feeling poorly, bless her heart."

"That doesn't sound like her. I can't remember the last time she got sick."

"I know. She's usually fit as a fiddle, but we have to accept that she is getting older. Even if she won't admit it."

The porch door opened and Lucille stepped out, blinking in the light. She was dressed in her usual summer uniform of a pale blue cotton shirtwaist dress. Mamaw had told her many times over the years that she no longer was required to wear a uniform, but Lucille preferred to and stubbornly continued to do so. When Lucille had her mind made up, she couldn't be swayed.

"I won't admit what?" Lucille asked, walking toward them.

Dora didn't like the stiffness to Lucille's gait or the grayish cast to her skin. She looked frail, too, like she'd suddenly aged.

"Are you sure you should be out of bed? You don't look so good."

"That's because I don't feel so good. But I just go stir-crazy lying in my bed all day. I can sit just as well out here on the porch." She turned to Mamaw. "I won't admit what?"

"That you're getting older," Mamaw replied archly, walking over to the large black wicker chairs in the shade.

"I'm still younger than you!" Lucille snapped back, then mumbled something unintelligible.

Dora trotted over to help Mamaw drag a chair deeper into the shade, then carried the ottoman over as well.

"Come sit down, Lucille," Mamaw said. "You should rest."

Lucille obliged, sinking with a soft grunt into the thick black-and-white-striped cushions. She put her feet up on the ottoman and rested her head back, already fatigued from the mild exertion. Dora caught Mamaw's eye and saw her own worry reflected there.

"You don't have a fever, do you?" Mamaw asked, hovering over Lucille. "Is it the flu?"

"No, I ain't got no flu. I'm just tired. Like you said, I'm old."

"Not that old," Mamaw said.

Lucille looked at Mamaw and shared a laugh.

"How about a nice glass of sweet tea?" Dora asked.

"That'd be real nice." Lucille glanced at Mamaw. "Want to play a little gin rummy?"

Mamaw's eyes lit up. "I'll get the cards."

A call from Harper in the garden interrupted her departure.

"Hey! I found something!"

Mamaw's hand flew to her heart. "Heavens, she found buried treasure!" she exclaimed dramatically. "We've been looking for the Gentleman Pirate's treasure for generations. Legend has it that pirates buried their treasures for safekeeping in the deserted dunes and woods of these islands," she told Dora. "And, with our history, well, it should be here somewhere. Although," she said with a sigh, "no one has found anything so far."

"I'd better get out there before she claims finders keepers," Dora exclaimed. "Just what a James needs, more treasure," she added with sarcasm. "It'd be just my luck, too." She took a final swig of iced tea. "I'm coming!" she yelled, and trotted to the garden carrying a frosty glass for Harper.

Harper was on her knees before a deep hole at the fringe of the garden, bent over a mud-encrusted object in her lap.

"It looks like some kind of chain," she said as she busily knocked off clumps of dirt. Then she paused to gratefully accept the drink from Dora.

"Maybe it's a gold chain," Dora said, excitement building.

"Or just a chain. It's metal. And it's heavy." Harper gulped down half the glass of tea, set the glass down, and returned to knocking dirt from the object. Gradually the object became a recognizable shape. Harper took off her sunglasses and lifted the item higher in her hands. She cocked her head, studying it.

"I'm not sure," Harper said a bit breathlessly, "but I think it might be handcuffs of some kind."

Dora scooted lower, then looked over to Harper with amazement and awe. "*Slave shackles?*" Though she would have preferred to have unearthed a thick gold chain from pirates, there was a historical significance to the shackles that rendered her speechless.

Harper rose to her feet with the chain. "Let's go rinse it off with the hose and show it to Mamaw and Lucille. They'll know."

Mamaw and Lucille were sitting up in their chairs on the porch, necks craned as they followed Dora's and Harper's progress from the garden to the hose.

"What you got there?" Mamaw called out.

"Not sure," Dora called back. "Be right there."

Dora held out the chain as Harper hosed the gushing water over the unknown hunk of metal. Water sluiced off the final layer of mud and muck, revealing what looked like thick, rusting, heavy metal handcuffs joined together with a chain. Neither woman spoke but stood in almost a reverential silence. Harper turned off the hose, then followed Dora across the porch to the two waiting elderly women. Their eyes were wide with curiosity.

"What is it?" Mamaw asked.

Lucille sat up and lowered her legs from the ottoman.

Dora lay the dripping object on the ottoman. It settled with a clanking sound.

Lucille sucked in her breath and stared at the object. Then with seeming trepidation, she reached out to place her dark, wrinkled hand on one of the handcuffs.

"Lord above, girl, you done found slave manacles," she said in a soft voice that shook with emotion.

"I thought that might be what they were," Dora said.

Mamaw drew closer to study the heavy metal cuffs. "They say if you dig anywhere on this island you'll uncover history. When we renovated the house, we found Revolutionary War bullets, Civil War coins, buttons, broken pottery, all manner of memorabilia. But never any pirate's treasure. Or anything as profound as this," she said, indicating the shackles. "This is a part of our history I'm not proud of."

Lucille's hands shook under the weight as she lifted the manacles and put them in her lap. "They so heavy I can hardly lift them."

"Can you imagine how they managed to walk with those?" Dora said.

Harper asked, "What are slave shackles doing on Sullivan's Island? I thought the slaves all went to the market in Charleston."

Mamaw's face grew reflective. "The slaves weren't sold at the market. They were usually sold at the Charleston ports, right off the boat. After quarantine. The local residents were terrified of infectious diseases like cholera, measles, and smallpox coming in on the ships. This was a major port for the country, don't forget. So they built pest houses here on Sullivan's Island for quarantine. It was a convenient location, a barrier island right along the port entry. Throughout the eighteenth century, slaves flowed through our port in large numbers. And all of them were sent for quarantine before they were sold."

"If they survived the journey," Lucille added somberly.

Mamaw rested her hand over her friend's. "Sadly true."

"How many slaves came through Charleston Harbor, do you know?" asked Harper.

"No one knows for sure," Mamaw answered. "So many died here in the pest houses—men, women, and children."

Lucille said sadly, "I heard somewheres between two hundred and four hundred thousand slaves came through."

Harper gasped. "That many?"

Lucille glanced at her. "You think that's a lot? It ain't so many when you know ten to twelve million were shipped out of Africa." Lucille sighed as she stared down at the shackles. "Africa done bled her children."

"Charleston was the major port of entry for slaves in America," explained Mamaw. "Near half of African Americans in this country can trace their roots through Charleston. And most of them were quarantined right here on this island." She looked at the shackles and added, "I've always felt that we needed to do more here on Sullivan's Island to honor all those slaves who died here. A monument of some kind. After all, this was an Ellis Island for the hundreds of thousands of slaves who passed through."

"Hardly Ellis Island," Harper corrected Mamaw. "Immigrants who passed through that island came willingly and sought a better life, political or religious freedom. Ironic contrast, wouldn't you say?"

Dora felt a flurry of irritation. Harper always had to argue a point. And it rankled because she was usually correct.

"My ancestors came here on a slave ship," Lucille said in a low voice.

She was bent over the shackles, her hand resting on the metal protectively. It appeared to Dora that the old woman was folding into herself.

"Only the strong in spirit survived the journey," Lucille continued. "Black families lived on Sullivan's for as long as I know. Used to be small farms here." She stretched out her hand toward the garden. "Big gardens. There were chickens, too. Maybe a pig. But they's all gone now. Poor folk moved to Daniel Island when this one got built up. Now they gone from Daniel Island, too." She paused as her mind seemed to drift back to the past.

"Do you miss your family?" Harper asked gently.

Lucille blinked and seemed to return to the present. "No, there's only me." She looked at the other women. "And y'all. And that's all right. We all have our time, there's no use fightin' it. I like to think we'll meet up again someday on the other side."

"You have your ancestors' strength," Dora said emphatically.

Lucille appeared moved by the comment. "I hope so. I'll need it when times get hard." She looked at Harper. "What you plan to do with these?"

"I don't have any plans," Harper replied. "Donate them to a museum maybe?"

"If you don't mind, I'd like to hold on to them, just for a while."

"Of course," Harper said. "Take them. They're yours."

Lucille looked down at the shackles in her lap. "Thank you. I'd just like to study them awhile. Maybe I will go back to my cottage now," Lucille said. "I'm tired." She attempted to rise, but with the heavy chain weighing her down it took more strength than she had. Alarmed, Dora and Harper each took a side while Mamaw grabbed hold of the chain. They helped Lucille to her feet.

"You better go back to bed," Mamaw told her.

"I might do that," Lucille said in a pant. "I am weary." She reached out for the shackles.

"I'll carry those for you," Harper said.

Lucille turned her shoulder and took the shackles from Mamaw. "No, no, child. I got them. I want to carry them. I want to know what it feels like to be worn-out and still have to walk, carrying this burden."

Chapter Fourteen

Dora received a text message from Devlin asking her to come by a house he was working on. He wanted her to see it and then join him for dinner.

It was easy to text back an enthusiastic yes. Dora loved houses, especially on Sullivan's Island, where so many—large and small, historic and new—had unique settings, or views, or history. She hopped into the golf cart with a bottle of water and bumped along the road to the southern side of the island, checking the address. She turned down a side street that led toward the marsh. Many old live oaks created heavy shade cover, welcome on a steamy summer day. She checked the address again and came to a stop before a small cottage barely visible behind a jungle of overgrown shrubs and palm trees. The driveway had long since been converted to dirt. Revving the engine, she drove the golf cart up beside Devlin's big truck. When she reached for her purse, she heard her phone ringing.

"Hello?" she said, expecting it to be Devlin. She was shocked when she recognized Cal's voice.

"Dora? It's me."

"Yeah. What's up?"

"Well, you never called me back."

Dora cringed. She'd completely forgotten about him. "Oh, I'm sorry. I, uh, I've been really busy."

"Oh yeah? Doing what?"

"Oh, uh . . ." She swallowed, thinking of an excuse. "Harper and I have started a garden. It's been a lot of work."

"A garden? In July? Are you sure you should be doing that kind of intensive labor? With your heart?"

"My heart is fine," she replied, irritated that he still thought she was sick. "And we're being careful. Anyway, I'm sorry I never called back. Is there something in particular you wanted to discuss?"

There was a pause. "Yes," he said in that tone that implied she should have known there was a topic. "We were going to discuss whether you were going to move into the condo. With me."

"I thought I was clear about that. I'm going to stay at Sea Breeze for the summer."

"I thought you might change your mind. You see, there are problems at the house."

Dora's stomach dropped. Of course, that was why he was calling. "What kind of problems?"

"The painters say that there was water damage on

some of the upstairs bedrooms. That they can't paint, so they're stalled. They're guessing it's from the roof. So now we have to have someone come in to assess water damage in the attic. It's never-ending," he said with a hiss of frustration.

"What do you want me to do about it? I'm out here on Sullivan's. You're in Summerville."

"Dora," he said, reining in frustration. "That's why it makes sense for you to be here. The house is a bigger project than we'd anticipated. It needs someone's full-time attention to keep the crews in line."

"It's not bigger than we anticipated," she argued. "We always knew it was a big job, and that's why we didn't start, or at least that's what you always told me. I'm going to say again what I told you at the lawyer's office. Sell the house as is if you don't want to take charge of the renovations."

"We can't do that. We'd lose our shirt."

"We've already lost our shirt."

"Dora, please. I'm up to my ears in work right now. Can't you help me?"

Dora groaned inwardly. "Oh, all right. I'll come to Summerville and take a look at the house. Make a few phone calls. But that's it. I'm not moving into your condo, Cal. I'm not ready to go that far."

"Okay, that's fine. But you'll call someone about the leak, right?"

She rolled her eyes and laughed shortly at his transparency. "I'll call. Bye." She ended the call and tossed the phone into her purse.

Dora stretched her arms over her head, trying to release the frustration from Cal's phone call before she saw Devlin. She didn't want Cal in the room between them, again. She heard the high hum of a power tool from inside the house and, curious, followed the noise to the front door. It had been left ajar.

"Hello?" she called out, poking her head in. It was hard to be heard over the roar of the power tool. She stepped inside and saw Devlin in goggles, standing behind a woodcutter and slicing what looked like a piece of wood paneling. She had to pause to take in the sight of Devlin doing construction. It was another side of him she didn't know about.

"Hello!" she called again when he'd stopped.

Devlin jerked his head up and broke into a wide grin. He lifted his goggles from his head, shaking sawdust into the air, and stepped forward to offer a quick kiss.

"You're here!"

"Just got here," she said, brushing away sawdust from his hair. "What's going on?" she asked, looking around the house with curiosity. The cottage had been gutted and was now in the process of a major renovation. A lot of work had already been done—new walls, cabinets, counters, appliances. Dora had dreamed of renovating her house in Summerville for so long that she always got a thrill at the sight of a renovation.

"This is a house I bought last year when the market dropped. Got it on a foreclosure. I'm renovating it in my spare time. When I'm done, I'll put it back on the market."

"*You're* renovating it? I didn't know you were a handyman."

"A carpenter, thank you very much," he said in the manner of someone who'd been doing it for a very long time. "That's what got me in the real-estate business in the first place. I used to work construction—thought you knew that. I bought a fixer-upper back when I could afford anything on Sullivan's, did all the work myself, then sold it for a big profit. I just kept on going, flipping houses, making profits. Found out I had a good eye for real estate." He shrugged. "I was lucky and got in for the boom. The rest is history."

She looked at Devlin, seeing him in a new light.

"Why are you looking at me like that?"

"Like what?"

"Like you're about to have me for dinner."

She laughed, coloring. "I guess because I find the fact that you can do your own renovations very sexy."

He laughed, raised his brows, and set the piece of paneling down. "Well, hell, lady," he said, reaching out and grabbing her around the waist, tugging her closer. "If I'd a known that, I'd a shown you my power tools right off."

He kissed her then, long and slow and deliberate, and she felt the humming in her veins. When the kiss ended, she leaned back in his arms and smiled coyly. "I wish I'd known you had this talent a few months ago. I could have used your help."

"Yeah? Why?"

She disentangled from his arms and began walking around the room, not wanting to bring Cal and the house in Summerville into the conversation. Devlin was installing cypress wood paneling into the back room, creating a lovely lowcountry feel. The back wall had been replaced with a long wall of windows overlooking the marsh. Dora crossed her arms and stood looking out over the wide swath of waving grass and the Intracoastal glistening in the sunlight.

"This view never gets old."

Devlin followed her to the windows and stood beside her. "That's because it's always changing. Folks from off who come to buy always want the ocean views. I can find that, too. But it's the wetlands that shows the change of scenery. The migrating birds, the changing grass—bright green in the summer, gold in the fall, brown in the winter, then the soft greening again in the spring."

He turned his head and looked at her, his gaze serious. "Why could you have used my help a few months back?"

Dora sighed, resigned, and looked up at him. "I have to put my house in Summerville on the market. We bought it as a fixer-upper, only we never did the fixing-up. There was never the money. Now that we're getting a divorce, we're putting the house on the market. Suddenly everything that I've been waiting years to get done has to get done in a hurry."

"So, you're trying to flip the house."

"Not even. We're just trying to get it in decent

enough shape to sell it. Cal wants to spend money we don't have, and I want to sell it as is. He won, of course."

"Why of course?"

"Because whenever it's an issue of money, Cal makes the decision."

"Even when the outcome affects your financial situation?"

Dora moved to the other side of the room, where a new fireplace mantel was being installed.

"Cal is not as concerned about my financial situation."

Devlin gave a little laugh. "He's an ass."

"Yes, well . . ." Dora looked closely at the wood trim of the mantel. She heard Devlin draw closer.

"How can I help?"

Dora turned and found he was standing very close. "Cal just called. There's a problem of a leak. It's probably the roof. He wants me to find someone who can take a look and tell us what needs to be done."

"He wants you to find the person?"

She nodded.

Devlin pinched his mouth, keeping what she was sure was a string of unsavory comments from flowing out.

"I'll take a look. And I should send him a whopping bill, just to teach him a lesson. Only you'd get stuck paying the bill. We can drive up together and I'll take a good look around and give you my opinion, for what it's worth."

"That would be so great. Apparently the workers are slacking off, too."

"I've got good crews who can do the work for a good price. If your guys are jerks, we'll send them packing."

"What can I do to thank you?"

Devlin gave her a wicked look that promised mischief, then pointed to the box of paneling. "Grab some gloves, woman, and lend me a hand. I've got work to finish before I cook you dinner!"

They spent the rest of the afternoon paneling the back room together while Devlin's old CD boom box played rock and roll. With the hum of the power tool and hammering, they couldn't talk much. Instead they sang out the lyrics to songs they remembered from their youth, and during the occasional slow song, Devlin strolled over to her side, swinging his hips to wrap her in his arms and dance with her. He held her close, hummed in her ear, and smelled of sweat and wood, and it was pure heaven.

When at last the room was paneled, Dora and Devlin stood back to admire their work. She'd actually helped panel a room, she thought with stunned surprise. And it had been fun! This is what she'd always imagined it would be like for her and Cal in the house they'd bought. Working together, side by side, taking pride in their accomplishments, sharing in the glory. It was never going to happen, not if they'd lived in that house for another ten years. She knew that now. It wasn't the time or the money. Cal didn't have Devlin's skill or the desire to do the transformation himself. He wasn't interested in anything but seeing it done. Cal was, simply, not Devlin.

"Nice job," Devlin told her, obviously pleased with the turnout.

"I can see how you got hooked," she said.

"You had a good time, did you?" he asked, curious.

"I did," she replied honestly. "I never knew how physically exhausting it was, but I had a great time. Can I help with something else?"

Devlin laughed then and wrapped her in his arms. "I knew you were a good 'un." He kissed her nose, then patted her bottom in a signal they were done. "Let's take a swim before dinner."

"I didn't bring a suit."

"Yeah? So?"

Dora made a face. "I'm not going skinny-dipping."

Devlin wagged his brows, then grabbed her hand. "Come on, I won't look. Much."

Dora laughed but pulled away. "No way."

"Chicken. All right. Come on, then, and help me pull up dinner."

"Where are we going?"

"Down the dock, of course."

He took her hand again and she followed him outdoors. They walked single-file in the path he'd made through the tall grass that led to the wood dock. It was very long and very narrow, double the length of Mamaw's dock at Sea Breeze, because it had to stretch much farther out over the grass to reach water.

"It's kinda rocky in spots, so be careful," Devlin warned.

Dora followed Devlin down the rickety walkway over pluff mud and grass. A few slats had rotted through, and Devlin was careful to point each one out along the way. At last they reached the end, where a rickety dock met the waterway.

"I'll have to replace the dock, too," Devlin said. "Whew, it sure is hot today." He took off his T-shirt and wiped his brow with it. "That water sure looks refreshing." He glanced at Dora.

Dora stuck out her hands. "Don't. Just don't!"

"Kick off your sandals, darlin'."

"Devlin!" She kicked off her flip-flops.

In a flash he grabbed her hand, pulled her close to the edge of the dock, and they both let loose a howl as they jumped together into the water.

She hit the water, and it was cool and refreshing. She burst out laughing as she came up for air, her hair flowing back and the sun shining on her face. Devlin swam to her side and kissed her again, holding her close, beginning again the slow dance in the water.

Later, they climbed back to the dock, refreshed. Devlin went to the edge and pulled up on a thick rope attached to the piling. His wet shirt clung to his body, revealing taut muscles straining as he pulled on the rope, hand over hand, until a large, black iron cage emerged, dripping water. Dora drew closer, curious, then stepped back when she saw at least a dozen crabs skittering noisily inside the trap.

Devlin lifted the trap high and laughed. "You're as skittish as one of these crabs. Haven't you ever gone crabbing before?"

"Never!" she exclaimed, warily watching the claws snapping in the air.

"Stand back," he said, easing the trap onto the dock. "We've got dinner!"

Dora helped Devlin again, this time cooking the crabs in a big stainless-steel pot on a gas burner out on the back porch. Dora wore a towel like a sarong and slicked back her hair from her face. There was an old picnic table on the patio that was still standing . . . barely. Devlin spread newspaper over it, set candles in empty beer bottles, and laid out two wooden mallets and a roll of paper towels, while she shucked corn and melted butter. The boom box played golden oldies by Otis Redding.

The sun was setting and Dora was on her third beer by the time the feast was ready. In the distance the glassy waters shimmered in hues of lavender and rose, setting a romantic mood. Devlin lit the candles and guided her to a seat on the bench.

"I know this isn't quite the setting of the restaurant the other night," he said by way of apology.

"No, it's not," Dora replied, swinging her leg around the bend and sitting. "It's better."

Devlin lowered his face to kiss her neck, and she shivered in anticipation of what was to come. Once again, Devlin helped Dora wield a hammer, this time on the crabs to crack the shells and dig out the sweet meat. Putting the crab to her lips, she tasted the pungent Old Bay seasoning and the salt from the sea on her fingers, thinking she'd never in her life tasted anything so delicious.

Tonight, no specter of Cal came between them. They talked seamlessly about whatever came to mind—Nate's progress, Devlin's plans for the house. Later they journeyed back to shared memories of the years they'd dated, laughing at crazy antics, calling out the names of old friends, favorite songs, rumors they'd heard, truths revealed.

When they were done feasting, Devlin took her in his arms and once again they began to dance. He held her close as they moved left to right to the beat of the music, no longer remembering old times they'd shared, but dreaming of new ones to come.

Chapter Fifteen

Florida

Today was special. Nate was becoming increasingly relaxed in his interactions with the dolphins from the floating dock. He'd learned hand signals and played games with the dolphins using balls and rings. He'd even had a T-shirt painted by a dolphin. Today, however, Nate was going to swim with the dolphins.

"How do you feel about getting in the water with the dolphins today?" Carson asked Nate over breakfast. She put a spoonful of cold cereal in her mouth and began chewing, giving him time to answer. Earlier in the summer, Nate had swum daily with Delphine in the Cove behind Sea Breeze. Carson worried that he'd be nervous about going back in the water with a dolphin after Delphine's accident.

Nate scooped his cereal into his mouth and continued reading the back of the cereal box. When he finished, he set down his spoon and nodded seriously.

"Good," he said.

"What's good? The cereal or swimming with the dolphins?"

Nate scowled, as though frustrated with his ninny of an aunt.

"Good to swim with the dolphins."

That was all Carson needed to know. That, and the excited look in his eyes gleaming against his tanned skin, spoke volumes.

Once there, Nate ran ahead to the lagoon as usual. Carson moved slowly, feeling lethargic in the relentless Florida heat. Watching the boy trot along the path, she reflected on the transformation from a shy, timid boy into this happier, more relaxed version. He wasn't outgoing; that was not his nature. Yet she could see he felt comfortable here after days of routine. Welcomed. The staff called out his name as he ran along the path, and though he didn't verbally respond, he raised his hand in a wave of acknowledgment. Most telling of all was the joy she captured on film when he swam with the dolphins.

Joan and Rebecca were waiting and guided them to a different section of the park. This was on the opposite side from where the female dolphins lived. It was a break in his routine from the front lagoon and Carson held her breath as she watched Nate tap his fingers against his mouth, a sign she recognized now as nervousness. But Joan led the way with confidence, marching Team Nate past the wood railings that bordered the lagoon and the houses where the sea lions lived. Two sleek females were basking like mermaids on rocks.

Turning a corner, Carson paused to take in the wide expanse of gorgeous Florida Bay.

"So these are the bachelor pods," she said.

A long coral causeway was covered with the same thatched island-style roof found at the front lagoon. It created a shaded space for guests while they watched the dolphins. Each side was lined with spacious enclosures, partitioned to house different pairs or small groups of dolphins.

When they reached the partitioned dock that Nate would use today, Carson grabbed a spot on the bench in the shade.

"Are you sure you don't want to join us in the swim today?" Joan called to her. "You're welcome to, and it'll be fun."

"No, thanks. I want to take pictures," she called back. She lifted the camera hanging around her neck to prove the point.

"We have a photographer," Joan reasoned. "He'll make sure to get plenty of great shots of Nate."

Carson paused.

A part of her wanted to go into the water with Nate, to feel the rubbery skin of the dorsal fin under her hand again and glide across the lagoon. That feeling was unlike any other. But she couldn't face swimming with another dolphin. Not yet. She'd had such a rare and unique bond with Delphine. She missed seeing Delphine's bright, inquisitive eyes, hearing her high-pitched whistle or her nasal staccato laughs. Swimming with another dolphin would be too painful.

She shook her head. "My stomach's feeling a bit off," she called back. "Better not. But thanks."

Carson bent over her huge canvas bag where she kept all their supplies and pulled out the lenses she wanted to use today. A dog's bark from the far end of the lagoon caught her attention, and turning her head, she was surprised to see a large black dog on the lower dock at the end of the pavilion. A dog near the dolphins wasn't the norm. Curious, she rose and joined the cluster of tourists craning to watch the interaction between the big black dog and a dolphin. They were laughing and pointing.

Carson lifted her camera. Through her lens she saw the big dog lower its pointy nose as it inched with agonizing slowness toward the edge of the dock. The dolphin appeared equally curious about the dog and was rising higher in the water, angling closer.

Carson held her breath, her finger on the button.

The big dog reached the edge, then stopped. The dolphin moved forward to touch its rostrum against the dog's nose.

Carson clicked the camera. "Got it!" she said, grinning. She felt as if she were the big black dog as its tail began wagging a mile a minute. Carson kept clicking away as the dolphin returned for more kisses. It was clear the two animals were having a good time.

When a man came to take hold of the dog's collar and, with a gentle pat, lead it away from the dock's edge, she lowered her camera and joined the chorus of groans from the audience who were enjoying the tender scene. He tied the dog to the dock post in the shade and gave the dog's big head several more pats. When he returned to the lower dock and looked out, Carson realized that the man was Taylor.

She knew she should go right back to Nate's dock, but she couldn't resist watching Taylor give signals to the two dolphins at his dock with the ease and authority of any of the other trainers. He was working with two male dolphins, one huge and the other small. She poised her camera and photographed Taylor giving a command that sent the dolphins swimming off underwater. Clicking rapidly, she caught shots of them leaping skyward in a beautifully synchronized leap. The big dolphin reached a remarkable height, while beside him the smaller one climbed not nearly as high.

Carson's heart lurched when she saw a chunk was missing from the smaller dolphin's tail fluke, like Delphine's. She followed the small dolphin with her camera, focusing in on the details. When the small dolphin emerged again at the dock to receive a fish, she saw that part of its dorsal fin was missing as well. The crowd applauded and Carson caught a great shot of Taylor's face breaking out into a reluctant grin.

"I could watch him all day," a young woman to her left remarked to her friend. "And I'm not talking about the dolphin."

"Mm-hmm," her friend agreed, before they bent their heads together, giggling.

Perusing the group, Carson couldn't help but notice how many of the women had their gazes not on the dolphins but on the handsome trainer. With her camera she captured his muscles exposed beneath his sleeveless T-shirt, the long swim trunks falling from his hips. Besides his good looks, his movements were graceful like a dancer's. What made him all the more attractive was his being oblivious to the attention he was receiving. His focus was solely on the dolphins.

Carson lowered her camera, feeling an undeniable racing in her blood, a spine-tingling attraction to the Marine. She was only human, after all. But then Blake's smiling face popped into her head, and she felt guilty that the first time she'd left Blake, her gaze was wandering.

Carson covered her lens and hurried back to the other side of the pavilion to Nate's dock. She quickly took several photos of Nate chest-deep in the water, grinning ear to ear while confidently giving signals to a big dolphin. Then she went back to the bench and, pulling out her phone, placed a call to Blake. She wanted to hear his voice. Blake had been out doing fieldwork for the past several days, out of phone range. Once again, her call was sent to voice mail.

Sighing and putting her phone in her bag, she looked up to see Nate engaged in a splash battle with the dolphin. Clearly the dolphin was winning and Nate was loving it. As she watched, her mind drifted back to Blake. She'd never been in love before, but she thought what she felt for Blake might be love. So her attraction to Taylor was a red flag.

"Still stalking me, I see."

Carson whipped her head up to see Taylor standing by the bench, a crooked grin on his face. He held on to a thick, black "Service Dog" harness attached to the black dog she'd seen on the dock. The dog was so big that, sitting on the bench, she was eye to eye with it.

"Taylor!" she exclaimed a little too loudly, rattled that he'd snuck up on her just as she was thinking about him. "I didn't know if I'd see you again. And certainly not training dolphins."

Taylor's grin widened as he took a seat on the bench beside her. He seemed more relaxed today, and she wondered if it was because of his session with the dolphins or because he was with his dog.

"Didn't I tell you I was having sessions here?"

"You did, but I thought you were doing what Nate's doing, not training. You looked good out there, by the way," she said, then blushed slightly at the double entendre. "I took some pictures. Here, take a look."

He leaned closer to look into her camera's LCD panel, their shoulders touching. Once again she felt a jolt of attraction. She flicked through the photos, enjoying the sound of his deep laughter and his occasional "That's a good one."

"I've got to get copies of Thor with the dolphin," he told her.

"Sure. I'll send them to you. What's your e-mail?"

"I don't have a pen or paper," he said.

"No problem." Carson turned to dig again into her bag, pulling out her card. "Here's my card. Just e-mail me and I'll send them to you."

"Great. Thanks." He tucked the card into his shorts.

"You were great out there," Carson said.

"I've been training here for almost a year now." He smiled a bit sheepishly. "They've offered me a job."

I'll bet, she thought to herself. There'd be a line of women at the gate clamoring for tickets. "Congratulations." She grinned and, turning her head, stared into a pair of dark brown eyes. "And your dog, too?"

He laughed and reached out to pat the dog's head. "Where are my manners? Carson, this is Thor. Thor," he said to the dog, "say hello to the pretty lady."

Thor shifted his adoring gaze from his master to Carson and lifted his giant paw.

"Whoa," she said as the paw hit her lap. "That's a pretty big paw you got there, pal." Carson loved dogs, especially big, gentle ones. Thor reminded her of Blake's dog, Hobbs, with his large block head, wide chest, and floppy ears. He also had large, soulful eyes she could lose herself in. They reminded her of Blake's eyes.

"He's a great dog," she told Taylor, who was watching Thor with affection.

"Yep, he is," Taylor agreed, patting his head again. "He was rescued from the pound and trained as a service dog. He's a mutt, but I'm guessing he's part Great Dane and part Lab and part something else that gave him that patch of white on his chest that looks like a lightning bolt. Reckon that's how he got his name."

Carson began to absentmindedly scratch Thor behind his ears, and his tail started thumping in response. Taylor was a Marine with a service dog, she thought to herself. Interesting.

"You said you were in a program with Joan?"

Taylor looked across the walkway to where Joan sat on the dock watching Nate.

"I was here for the Wounded Warrior Project."

Carson wasn't surprised to hear that. She'd read that the Dolphin Research Center had a program for wounded warriors. Yet, when she thought of a wounded warrior, she thought of someone with physical injuries.

After an awkward silence Taylor said in a softer tone, "I know what you're thinking. Where's the wound, right? You don't see the injury."

Carson couldn't reply. Blunt though it was, he was right.

"You can't see all wounds," Taylor said. "Especially not in this war. Sure, some of us in the Wounded Warrior program have missing limbs, or are in a wheelchair. Some have serious burns. But *all* of us have PTSD."

Carson knew quite a bit about post–traumatic stress disorder because she'd studied the symptoms after Delphine's accident on the dock. It was a debilitating condition that followed a terrifying event. She'd had bad nightmares after the fire that killed her mother, and she'd tucked away that traumatic memory in her mind for years, only to begin to deal with it now. After Delphine's accident she had been stricken with guilt and regret, but she'd been able to move on. She'd read how PTSD left one feeling emotionally numb, especially toward people they were once close to. Learning that had helped her to understand Nate's angry behavior toward her.

"I think my nephew, Nate, had PTSD from the accident."

"What kind of accident?"

"Actually, it involved a dolphin. Delphine. She used to come by our dock on Sullivan's Island. One morning she got caught in the fishing line and was badly hurt. Luckily we got her to a rehab facility in Florida, but Nate was pretty traumatized by it. You see, he was the one who'd put out the fishing lines."

Taylor turned a sympathetic glance toward Nate. "Poor little guy. He must have taken it all pretty hard."

"So did I," Carson added, her voice catching unexpectedly. She cleared her throat. "Joan's doing a wonderful job bringing him out of it."

"She's good at that."

"What made you want to start training dolphins?" she asked Taylor.

"A lot of it has to do with that little dolphin out there." He jutted his chin to indicate the lagoon.

"Which one?"

Taylor scanned the water, then reached out to point to a smaller dolphin. "That dolphin swimming near the dock closest to us. That's Jax."

"The little guy. I noticed that he's missing part of his tail fluke."

"Yeah, Jax is a real survivor. He was just a calf when he was found near dead in the water near Jacksonville. That's how he got the name. They captured him and brought him to Gulf World in Panama City. The tip of his dorsal fin, half his left fluke, and part of his pectoral fin were bitten off before he got away. You can still see the scars left by the shark's teeth on his flank. From the measurement, they figured he was attacked by a bull shark."

Carson shuddered, remembering her own near miss with a bull shark earlier that summer.

"It's a good guess Jax's mother was killed trying to defend her calf. They saved his life at Gulf World, then he was placed here for a permanent home."

"He wasn't released?"

"He never would've made it out in the wild. Not only because of his injuries, but because without a mother to teach him the ropes, he'd starve or be shark bait. He was only about a year or so when he came here. Now Jax is part of the gang. He has his injuries, of course. And he's younger than the others and still has some growing to do, so he doesn't jump as high as the other males." He grinned. "But Jax doesn't care. There's nothing he can't do. He jumps, leaps, does all the routines right with the pack. Here's the thing. The other dolphins don't see Jax as injured. And Jax doesn't see himself as injured." He swallowed hard. "That says it all."

Carson heard the emotion in his voice and understood why Taylor felt such a strong connection to the brave young dolphin.

"The program directors gave us this," Taylor said, reaching up to pull out a silver chain from under his shirt. He turned so she could see a small silver dolphin tail fin attached to the chain; the left tail fluke was missing. "That's Jax's fluke."

Carson reached out and took the small silver fin between her two fingers, tracing the intricate lines. She looked up at Taylor.

"Aunt Carson!"

Carson had been so caught up in Taylor's story, she hadn't noticed that Nate had finished his session. She was surprised at how fast the time had flown and embarrassed that she hadn't given Nate her full attention. Nate ran up to her, eyes aglow from his session, but stopped short at seeing Taylor and Thor at her side. Instantly he grew wary.

"Nate, you did great! I'm so proud of you," Carson exclaimed. "Come closer, I want you to meet my new friend Taylor. And guess what? He trains the dolphins."

Nate looked at his feet without a word.

Taylor didn't seem the least bothered by Nate's silence. "Hey, Nate. Do you want to meet Thor?"

Nate looked at the dog. "Is Thor the dog's name?" Nate asked.

"Yes."

Nate studied the dog a moment, then asked, "Can I pet him?"

"Sure."

Nate approached the dog slowly. Thor looked patiently at the boy and remained calm while enduring the petting.

"How much does he weigh?"

"One hundred and twelve pounds of pure muscle," Taylor answered with a hint of pride. "He loves to swim in the ocean."

"With the dolphins?"

"No, they don't come close enough in the wild. But he would if he could."

Nate petted the dog again, then, his curiosity sated, turned to Carson. "I'm hungry."

"I'll bet you are after all that swimming. Let's head back home and think about going someplace special for dinner. It's our last night."

"Why not let me take you to dinner?" Taylor offered. "Since it's your last night and all."

Carson was taken aback by the invitation. It was completely unexpected. Taylor waited for his answer.

"What do you think, Nate?"

Nate looked away and shrugged.

Inside her gut, warning bells were going off, telling her to beg off with some excuse. Ignoring them, she said, "All right, that's real nice of you. I should warn you, though, we'll need to go someplace that serves food Nate will eat. He's pretty picky."

"I'm hungry *now*," Nate said.

"I am, too, pal," Taylor told Nate. "Why don't we get cleaned up and I'll come by your place, and we'll go right out to eat. The Shipwreck is close by and they have a pretty standard menu. It'll be an early dinner or a late lunch. Whatever you want to call it."

You can call it anything but a date, Carson thought to herself as she smiled back at Taylor.

"Okay, Nate, it's time to turn off the game," Carson called out. "Bedtime."

"No, not yet. Just a little longer," Nate whined.

"We're almost done with this level," Taylor added, not taking his eyes from the screen.

"You're not helping," Carson told Taylor, raising an eyebrow in hopes of transmitting some sort of silent adult signal.

Taylor turned his head briefly from the screen and shot her a teasing glance, then went back to the video game.

Carson stood sipping coffee in the small galley kitchen, watching the big man and the slight boy sitting together on the futon in front of the game screen. Life was full of surprises, Carson thought, but Taylor took the cake. It was surprising enough to discover that he trained dolphins. Then he asked her and Nate to dinner, and they'd had a lovely time. But the last thing she'd expected was for Taylor and Nate to become such pals. Who knew they'd bond over video games? Nate was enthralled by his new hero—Taylor knew all the cheat codes.

She was also surprised by her attraction for him. Taylor had shown up in pressed pants and a long-sleeved shirt. She always was a pushover for a man in crisp attire. His shirt was unbuttoned at the collar and the bright white contrasted with his deep tan. Dinner had been pleasant, if a bit awkward with Nate. It wasn't a date—Carson kept reminding herself—but it felt like it could have been if they'd been alone. The possibility made her nervous. They were just friends, she told herself again. Nothing to feel guilty about. But why, then, did she feel just that?

She reached for her phone and checked her messages. Still no word from Blake. Damn, how long was he going to be out in the field? She needed to talk to him, to hear his voice. To feel a connection with him. She also felt the need to send Taylor packing.

"Sorry, guys, time to break it up. We've got an early start tomorrow. No complaints," she said in automatic response to Nate's immediate outcry. "We're going to see Delphine, remember?"

The mention of Delphine was enough to assuage Nate's outburst. He sighed, more for show, then promptly saved the game and relinquished his remote.

"I think you've got it down pat, buddy," Taylor assured him.

"You get in your pajamas and brush your teeth while I get your futon ready, okay?" Carson said.

Nate rose slump-shouldered and began walking away.

"What do you say to Taylor?" Carson asked, stopping him.

"Thank you," he said dutifully.

Taylor smiled. "It was nice meeting you."

Nate didn't respond. He hurried into the bedroom, closing the door behind him.

Carson looked after Nate's retreating figure with

affection. "He really did appreciate it, Taylor. It's rare for him to get along so well with a stranger. He thinks you walk on water. How did you learn to play so well?"

"I'm not that good," Taylor said modestly. "I played a lot of virtual reality games for PTSD therapy."

"You played video games for therapy?" The idea seemed out there.

"Well, the idea is that by reenacting a traumatic experience or confronting an irrational fear in a safe place, we'll become used to that experience. Or fear. The trauma doesn't disappear, but it becomes manageable. It worked for me."

"And the cheat codes?" she asked.

"Ah, well." He rubbed his jaw. "Those I figured out on my own."

She offered a smile. "I've got to get Nate to bed. Do you need to go?"

"I can stick around."

"Oh," she said, surprised. "Uh, okay. I'll just be a few minutes. Do you mind waiting outside on the patio? There are chairs out there." She pointed to the futon and said in way of explanation, "This is Nate's bed."

"Sure," Taylor said good-naturedly. "I'll grab a smoke."

Lord, she thought to herself as she followed Nate into the bedroom. What was going on here? She really didn't need to help Nate much. He was nine and had his routine down. She'd thought it was an obvious hint for Taylor to leave. Going out to the restaurant with him had gone well—and innocently—enough. Sitting on the bench chatting with him in public was okay, too. But being alone with him tonight in the cottage was another thing altogether. Especially with the undercurrent zinging between them.

Once Nate was ready for bed, he and Carson returned to the main room. Nate hopped onto the futon, and she tucked him in. Looking at his tanned face and watching him yawn, Carson thought how much he'd returned to the boy who'd leaped into the Cove and swam like a fish earlier in the summer. The boy who saved his smiles for her. Coming here had been the right thing to do. *Thank you, Harper,* she thought to herself, *for coming up with the idea of bringing Nate here. And thank you, Dora, for allowing it.* She hoped they could keep up the good vibes when they got back to Sea Breeze. A lot, she knew in her heart, depended on what happened with Delphine tomorrow.

"Good night, Nate. I'll just be outside."

"Aunt Carson?"

"Yes?"

"Do you think Delphine will remember me?"

She paused. She'd wondered where his thoughts lay concerning the dolphin. Now she knew he was worried. Perhaps even guilt-ridden. She sat down on the futon beside him.

"I can't say for sure, but I think she will. She's very smart. She remembered me."

"But she loves you."

Carson felt her heart twinge. "Yes, Delphine loves me. But she loves you, too."

Nate yawned the words: "I love her too. I always will. Even if I never see her again after tomorrow."

Out of the mouths of babes. Carson felt love bloom in her heart for the boy. He must have discussed this with Joan. This boy understood the difference between a wild dolphin and a dolphin in a facility better than most adults.

"I couldn't have expressed my own feelings any better," she told him. "Good night, sleep tight. Don't let the bedbugs bite."

"There aren't any bedbugs," he told her matter-of-factly. "I checked."

Carson laughed lightly at the literal workings of his brilliant mind. "Good night," she said again, and then she went to the door, turning off the light as she exited.

Outdoors she could hear the gentle lapping of the waves against the shore. She saw his broad-shouldered silhouette standing on their patio, staring out at the Gulf. A trail of smoke rose from his cigarette.

"Here you are," she said in way of announcement.

Taylor tossed the cigarette to the ground and stomped on it.

"I should be going."

"Okay," she said, not sure if it was relief or disappointment she felt. He walked closer to her, and in the shadows she could make out the contours of his face—his strong, Roman nose, his full lips. God, he had a beautiful face, she thought.

"I had a nice time," he said.

"Me, too. And so did Nate," she hastened to add. "It was nice of you to take us out on our last night."

An awkward silence. The night's sultry summer breeze felt like a caress against her skin. It was heavy with the scents of the sea and a sweetness that had musky notes. She felt his closeness, the slim margin of space between them narrowing as they imperceptibly drew closer and desire welled up, unbidden.

Like the dolphin and the dog earlier on the dock, they inched toward each other, each tentative, almost shy. She closed her eyes, surrendering to the tug. In a single move their lips touched. The fullness of his lips cushioned hers. His arms encircled her, so strong, as they pressed harder together.

This kiss felt so good.

Yet it felt so wrong.

Carson opened her eyes, stiffening her back. She put her hands against Taylor's chest and drew away, the light dimming in her eyes. She looked out at the moonlight to allow her breath to slow and gather her wits. What was going on in her head, she wondered. Her body enjoyed the kiss. It wasn't like her to not simply let go with her feelings. The old Carson would have kissed this man good and hard. She wanted him. Yet tonight, even a small kiss had felt like a betrayal.

"Carson?" Taylor's voice was tentative but he held on to her forearms.

"I'm sorry," she said, unsure of how to explain her feelings. "I . . . I can't do this. I'm dating someone."

"Oh," he said, and, letting go of her arms, took a step back.

Carson blew out a plume of air and lifted her long shank of hair from her back. "This is so weird. I don't know what to say."

"Are you engaged?"

"No," she replied, shaking her head. "No," she said again.

"I'm glad."

Carson didn't want to encourage him. "But we have this understanding. It's kind of exclusive."

"I respect that," Taylor said.

A bird called out in the night, a melancholy sound.

"I better go."

"Look, Taylor," she said, stopping him. "I'm really glad I got to know you. You're a great guy." She leaned forward and kissed his cheek. "And I meant it when I said if you're near Sullivan's Island, look me up. We can be friends, can't we?"

He offered her his crooked grin. "Good luck tomorrow with Delphine."

Carson watched him walk away with a pang of regret. Taylor had never answered her question.

Chapter Sixteen

Sullivan's Island

The moon was a slim crescent in the velvety sky. Venus shone bright to the north. Harper sat at the edge of the dock, her feet dangling in the cool water, and looked up at the night sky, thinking how much she loved being here, sitting under a sky that mirrored the South Carolina flag. When did this love affair with the lowcountry begin? she wondered.

She kicked her legs back and forth, feeling the power of the current. She'd always enjoyed her visits here, but when she was a child she thought of Sea Breeze as a kind of camp. A place to run wild and have fun with the other girls. Someplace that one returned home from. Like Dora had said, being at Sea Breeze wasn't real life.

Or was it? This summer Harper had returned as a woman—despite Mamaw's insistence on continuing to call them her "summer girls." In the past months

Harper had come to appreciate that the slower-paced life here in the lowcountry was indeed real. It was just very different from what she knew in New York, or in the Hamptons, or England. Or, she thought, was this summer only a respite from the pressing demands and expectations that she would have to face at summer's end?

She heard a footfall on the dock, felt its vibration, and turning her head, she saw a dark silhouette coming toward her.

"Dora?" she called out.

"Found you!" Dora exclaimed, stepping down to the lower floating dock. "What are you doing out here all alone?"

"Nothing."

"Want some company?"

"Love some." Harper patted the dock beside her.

Harper caught the scent of Dora's floral perfume as she settled beside her and slipped her legs into the black water.

"Seems strange to be out here without Carson," Dora said.

"Yeah. I half expect to see Delphine pop her head out of the water. Poor Delphine . . ." In her mind's eye she saw the sweet smile of the dolphin and felt a prick of conscience for what the consequences of their actions had cost it.

"When is Carson due back?" she asked Dora.

"Not sure. Tomorrow or the day after."

"I saw on the weather report there's a tropical

storm brewing off the coast of Africa and the computer models say it will head our way."

"Please . . ." Dora said with a wave of her hand. "Whenever there's any disturbance from that direction, the weathermen go wild, stirring us up into a frenzy. I swear they're disappointed if the storm veers off. I don't pay any of the warnings any mind until it's hugging our coast."

Harper was the type to study the computer models, and at the moment, the majority of them had this storm hitting Charleston.

"You've lived here longer than I have," Harper conceded. "If Carson comes back tomorrow, she'll just beat the storm. I'm hoping she and Nate don't get stuck driving in a downpour."

Dora's face clouded at the slightest possibility of Nate being in a storm. "Maybe I will check those storm warnings."

Harper saw the worry on Dora's face and regretted bringing up the topic of the storm. "They'll be fine," she said in consolation.

"Oh, sure . . ." Dora's voice was troubled.

"You must miss Nate a lot."

"Terribly. It's been wonderful to have some time to myself, but it's been long enough. I want my baby home."

"I miss him, too."

Dora turned to face Harper. "It's also been really nice spending time with you this past week."

Harper smiled into the water.

"I've gotten to know you better," Dora continued. "I feel closer to you. I'm trying to break old patterns, and you've really helped me." She paused. "Thank you."

Harper looked up and in the moonlight saw the sincerity in Dora's eyes. "We're sisters," Harper said. "You don't have to thank me." She broke into a broad grin.

Dora released a wide smile and nodded, looking out at the moonlight dancing on the Cove. "I like that."

"You know, I don't know who was the tougher sell on getting Nate to go—you or Nate."

Dora laughed. "I think it's a miracle he agreed to get in the car with Carson in the first place! But I have to hand it to her. She's done a real good job. She's been sending me pictures every day of Nate's progress. He looks so good, so tan. For a boy who rarely smiles, Nate was smiling all the time! It was a side to my little boy I rarely see. I've sent the pictures to Cal. He needs to see that side of his son." She paused. "Carson doesn't seem to have a problem having a good time with Nate, does she?"

"Carson? She doesn't have a hard time having a good time with anyone. It's her gift."

"And yours. You play with Nate, too. On the video games."

"Well, yeah . . ." she replied hesitatingly, remembering the terse words when Dora discovered Harper playing video games with Nate.

"I shouldn't have snapped at you like that. I'm so sorry. It . . . it wasn't the video games I was upset about. I was jealous," she admitted.

"Jealous?" Harper asked, shocked at the confession. "Of what?"

"Jealous that you found a way to have fun with Nate. Like Carson did. This isn't easy to say, but I don't know how to do that." She mulishly kicked the water.

"He's your son," Harper said, not understanding how a mother wouldn't know how to play with her own child.

"Moms are the rule makers. It's not always a fun job. There has to be balance, and I see now that I've been so obsessed with helping Nate because of his Asperger's, I forgot to have fun with him. I don't want to just be his keeper, the one who tells him what to do, tidies up after him, feeds him." Dora glanced at her sister. "In the dressing room you said something to me that made me think."

"Oh-oh . . ." Harper recalled she'd said some harsh things in that tight space.

"No, really, it was good. I know Nate loves me." Dora took a breath. "But I'm not sure he really likes me."

"Aw, Dora, of course he likes you."

Dora shrugged and said in a small voice, "He doesn't like to play with me."

"It's easy. Find something *he* likes to do."

"I'm trying . . . but it's not easy with Nate. He doesn't like imaginary games and he prefers to play by himself most of the time. I can't count the number of games I've initiated with him or the outings we've gone on that are instructive or will help him learn some skill. He shuts me out."

"That's the problem. Stop being his teacher and just have fun."

"But I *am* his teacher. I love Nate, more than life itself. I'm trying to make life easier for him, to somehow make him *better*. He needs help if he's going to learn to deal in the normal world."

"But not all the time. Nate's a pretty remarkable boy just the way he is. Instead of trying to change him, once in a while try hanging out with him without an agenda. See what he's interested in. He'll let you know."

Dora put her face in her palms. "God help me, I know you're right."

"I'm speaking from personal experience here," Harper said. "There's a difference between compelling your children to do what *you* want them to do, and just letting them discover for themselves what *they* want to do."

"Is that what your mother did?"

"In spades," Harper answered. "That's why I've always enjoyed coming here, to Sea Breeze. Mamaw let us run wild and play our own games." She released a short laugh of pleasure. "You know, whenever I think of the best times in my childhood, they're always here at Sea Breeze."

"Me, too."

"We sure had great summers, didn't we?"

When Dora didn't answer immediately, Harper turned her head. She watched Dora stare out at the Cove as though she were going through personal memories. The moonlight made her hair appear an almost unworldly shade of gold.

"We surely did," she said in a faraway voice.

"So, there's your answer. Be like Mamaw and do the same thing with Nate. Let him go wild. Go exploring. Have fun just for the sake of doing it together." She wagged her finger. "No lesson plans. Okay?"

Dora laughed. "Okay."

Harper took a breath and asked Dora the question that had been niggling at her brain the past few days. "Dora, are you going to introduce Nate to Devlin?"

Dora leaned back on her arms. "I don't know. I don't think so. Not right away."

"Why not?"

"There's no hurry. Besides, Nate doesn't do well with change. He's already upset that his father isn't around. He might feel threatened if Devlin came into the picture right away. And, selfishly, when he gets back, I want some time alone with him."

"Are you sure you're not pushing Devlin away?"

Dora shook her head. "I thought about that, but no. Not at all."

"I think he's good for you."

"You do?" Dora asked, delighted to hear this opinion from Harper, whose opinion she was learning to respect. "Why?"

"He's the yin to your yang. More relaxed, a little wilder, earthy. Not afraid to mess things up. I think this fellow might give you that balance you're looking for."

Dora felt as though Harper's words lit a light inside of her. She felt herself glowing with pleasure.

"We dated all through high school and into college."

She glanced at her sister and said, "He was my first, you know."

Harper looked up, surprised. She didn't know. She smiled encouragingly for Dora to go on, reveling in the rare moment of true sisterly bonding.

"Not that there were a lot of others," Dora continued after a huff of embarrassed laughter. "Dev was the only other man I've slept with besides Cal."

"Really?" she asked, her tone incredulous.

"Why? How many men have you slept with?" she asked, sounding a little defensive.

Harper burst out in a laugh. "I don't know," she said, evading the truth. She didn't want to shock her sister with what she'd think a scandal, not when they were finally getting along. "A few more than two, I guess. Let's just say they weren't that memorable."

Dora smirked, indicating she knew Harper was being evasive. "Uh-huh, sure."

"I'm serious."

"Has a man told you he loved you?"

"Sure. Plenty of times," Harper said flippantly. "The problem is, I never believed them."

Dora glanced at her with uncertainty.

"I'm what you might call"—Harper lifted her fingers to make quotation marks—"'a good catch.' I'm decent enough looking, well educated, have—or rather, had—a good job. But that's not the real lure. No, sirree," she said in a self-mocking manner. "I'm an heiress. Rich. With a pedigree. I'm the whole package. Mothers are throwing their sons at me." She laughed bitterly.

"Whenever a man tells me he loves me, I'm never quite certain if it's me he desires, or my fortune."

"But even so, didn't you ever fall in love? With any of them?"

Harper considered the question seriously, letting her mind roam over a litany of faces she'd known throughout her teens and into her twenties.

"There were some I liked quite a bit. One or two I dated for several months. There was one chap in England my grandmother almost called the banns for." Harper lifted one shoulder insolently. "Unfortunately, she liked him better than I did. Honestly? I can't say I ever did fall in love. It's rather sad, isn't it?"

"You're only twenty-eight!" Dora said with a light laugh. "You've got lots of time left. Lord, you make it sound like you're over the hill."

Harper didn't laugh. She didn't want to make light of this. "Think of our father and his track record. He never fell in love. He was incapable of making a commitment. And I'm always told Jameses don't marry for love." She changed her voice, taking on a British upper-class accent. "Jameses marry for alliances." She smirked. "My ancestors have married for money for generations."

"How royal of you," Dora said as a tease.

Harper laughed at the truth in that statement. "God knows my mother never loved anyone but herself. I honestly don't think she's capable of that emotion. Not even for her own daughter. She despised our father."

Dora burst out in a laugh. "You mean Mamaw was

right after all? Your mama just wanted him for his sperm?"

"I'm afraid so," Harper replied, coloring faintly. "But don't ever tell her I said so. I'll never live down the fact that I am the product of such an ill-advised union."

"My lips are sealed. But I'm glad she did. I have you as my sister."

Maybe it was the oddly intimate spell the night seemed to be casting over them as their feet dangled in the cool water, but Harper finally felt like she could share her deeper feelings. "Do you think there's something inherently wrong with me?"

"What?" Dora blurted. "Lord, no."

"I've been thinking about this," Harper persisted. "Maybe it's in my genetic line to be incapable of love. I worry about that. There might be something missing in my DNA."

Dora reached over to lay her hand on Harper's. "You're crazy if you think that. Love is out there. You just have to find it."

Harper smiled weakly. "I want to believe in love," she confessed. "But I'm not willing to settle. I refuse to be shackled by my fortune. I will *not* be like my mother," she said with heat. "I'm holding out for true love."

Dora studied her sister. "You are wise beyond your years, Harper," she said slowly.

Slightly embarrassed at the compliment, Harper elbowed Dora in the ribs. "That romanticism must come from the Muir side, eh? What with the great love affair of the Gentleman Pirate and Claire, right?"

Dora laughed, then looked out over the water, lost in thought.

"What about you?" Harper asked. "You said you kinda-maybe-might love Devlin. Does that mean you've decided to leave Cal for good?"

A bemused expression slipped over Dora's face. "I've been wondering about that myself," she replied. She shook her head and said in a low voice, "It's so hard to know what to do. I just don't know."

"What don't you know? You know Devlin loves you. Does Cal?"

Dora looked trapped. "I know he needs me."

"Oh, great," Harper exclaimed, throwing up her hands. "That's so romantic." She turned to face Dora. "You just told me how you want to have some fun with Nate. Why should it be any different with your *husband*? Dora, you're a caretaker. It's what you do. Granted, taking care of Cal is one part of a marriage, and an important part, at that. But do you have fun with him?"

Dora gave a tiny shiver. "No."

"I didn't think so. I've been watching you these past weeks, and clearly you're having fun with Devlin."

"But is that enough for a relationship?"

"It's a good start. If you don't mind my saying so, you're a stickler for what you think a marriage *should* look like. How's that working out for you so far?"

Dora stared at the water.

"Let me ask you this. Is it Cal you want to stay with? Or the marriage?"

Dora didn't reply. She sat twisting her wedding ring on her finger.

Harper asked gently, "Are you *in love* with him?"

Dora raised up her left hand. The luster of the gold shone in the moonlight.

"When you talked about feeling shackled by your fortune, all I could think was how I feel shackled to my marriage. Right now"—Dora lifted her left hand—"this ring feels like a manacle, every bit as heavy and binding to an institution I don't want to be part of anymore."

Dora lowered her hand to her lap. "I loved Cal when I married him." Her gaze met Harper's. "But, no. I'm not in love with him. I can't go back." Looking at the ring, she cried, "I want to be free."

Dora began tugging the ring from her finger, but it was snug and unyielding.

"What are you doing?" asked Harper.

"This ring has been on my finger for fourteen years," Dora said with an edge of panic to her voice. "It won't come off."

"Well, stop pulling at it," Harper told her. "You're just making your finger swell more. Try dipping your hand in the cool water."

Dora leaned far over the edge of the dock and stuck her hand into the water.

"Why are you doing this now?" Harper asked, surprised by her usually cautious sister's impetuousness.

"It's your fault," Dora told her, letting her hand wade back and forth in the water. "When you said that about the shackle, I couldn't get that image out of my mind. I've got to get it off." Dora pulled her hand from the water and moved to sit on the dock. She grabbed the ring once more.

"Wait, wait," Harper said, putting an arresting hand on Dora's arm. "Granny James once had a ring stuck on her finger. The jeweler came to cut it off." She laughed. "The ring, not the finger. But first he had her soak it in cool water and then he eased it off her finger, real slow, so the skin didn't bunch up at the knuckle. He used hand lotion. Or we could use some soap. I'll go inside . . ."

"Let me try first." Dora puffed out some air, then very slowly eased and twisted the ring. "I think it's coming." She kept at it, rolling the ring over her knuckle while her face grimaced in pain. Slowly, it slid down her finger.

"It's off!" she exclaimed, holding the gold band in the air between two fingers.

Harper hooted aloud, bringing Dora's hand closer for perusal. Dora's hand was pink and pickled from the cold water, and there was a bruised spot below the knuckle of her fourth finger.

"I'm free!" Dora shouted, pumping the air with her fist.

"Not legally," Harper said, giving Dora her hand back. "At least not yet," she amended.

"Maybe not. But from now on, Cal can take care of himself!"

"Dora," Harper said. "I think we were meant to find those manacles this summer." She leaned forward, eyes gleaming. "Let's make a pact. You and I will no longer be bound by the expectations of others. No more shackles."

Dora grasped Harper's hand. She'd always been a bit jealous that Harper and Carson had their own rallying call: Death to the ladies! Now she and Harper had their own call, as well. In a burst of joy, Dora reared back and threw the ring into the Cove.

Together they shouted, "No more shackles!" Their whoops of glee echoed over the quiet waters.

Chapter Seventeen

Florida

Nate's fingers tapped his lips as he and Carson followed Lynne Byrd through the long halls of the Mote Marine cetacean hospital. Lynne was kind enough to take Nate on a tour of the lab and the sea turtle hospital, describing all the patients. His head turned from left to right, seemingly taking in the colorful murals of sea life that adorned the walls. Carson knew, however, that the little guy was searching anxiously for Delphine.

At last Lynne pushed open the doors to the outdoor arena. The sunlight was so bright that Carson had to squint until her eyes adjusted. The enormous pool in the center of the arena now had netting arcing over it.

"Good news," Lynne said to Carson. "Delphine has been doing so well, we've moved her into the large pool, where there's room for her to exercise. She's still on antibiotics, but she's a remarkable healer with a strong will to live."

Lynne led them toward the pool. "She was weighed this morning and is continuing to gain, which is a very good sign. It's been touch and go with the condition of her mouth. At the beginning we only fed her live mullet and snapper, but now she's accepting the dead fish—a mix of herring and capelin, too. She's also interacting more with her environmental enrichment devices." She turned to smile at Nate. "Toys."

"Where's Delphine?" he asked pointedly.

"You'll see her, don't worry," Carson assured him. Like Nate, she wanted to break free and run to the pool to see Delphine.

At last they reached the edge of the pool. Nate wanted to go closer but was cut off by Lynne's outstretched arms.

"Here's how we're going to do this," Lynne said in a tone that brooked no argument. "Carson, you know the drill. You can help me give Delphine her antibiotics. While I get the meds, you can go in the water and let Delphine know you're here." She turned to Nate. "Sorry, Nate, but you can't go in the water."

Nate looked stricken. "But I went in the water with the other dolphins."

"I know. But this is a hospital. It's not allowed. But . . ." Lynne smiled at Nate, who reluctantly met her eyes. "How about I let you play with Delphine using some of her favorite toys? Her very best favorite is that pink ball in the bin over there." She gestured toward a basket by the wall. "See it?"

Nate scanned the room and, spotting it, nodded.

"Okay, go stand by the wall and wait until I say you can throw it to her, okay? Carson and I have to give Delphine her medicine first. Stay by the wall," she said.

"That's the rule," Carson added for clarity, knowing he'd take it very seriously when put in that context.

"Carson, if Delphine will let you, you can give her a rubdown. She loves those."

Carson was surprised she'd still be allowed to touch Delphine, now that the dolphin was so much improved. She knew Lynne didn't want human interaction with the wild dolphins if possible, especially not touch. It made her wonder if decisions had been made as to where Delphine would be transferred once she was deemed healthy.

"Is Delphine already slated to go to the Dolphin Research Center?"

Lynne shook her head. "No. We haven't given up on trying to release her into the wild."

"But the rubdown . . ."

"It's helping her heal, which is our top priority. This particular dolphin gets depressed in isolation. We had to make a call based on her needs. As for her release—when and where—the jury's still out on that."

The pool was enormous and deep and the vast screening over it provided lovely dappled light that made patterns on the water. Carson stood at the edge and squinted into the shifting shadows, searching for the dolphin. Not seeing her, she lowered herself to sit on the edge and slipped her legs into the water. It was cool but not cold, refreshing against the searing temperature of the air. She searched the water for some sign of Delphine. Carson kicked her legs in the water, hoping the vibration would alert the dolphin and bring her close, if only out of curiosity.

Nothing.

Carson added a whistle. Sharp and clear, it pierced the quiet. It was the same whistle she'd always used at the Cove when she called Delphine. She glanced over her shoulder at Nate. He stood keen eyed and alert, watching.

Suddenly she saw a gray shadow streaking through the water toward her. Her heart skipped a beat as the shadow swam close, then veered, doing a glide-by. She knew Delphine was checking out the stranger in the pool. Carson gasped with a laugh when a glistening head suddenly emerged from the water right before her. Two shiny bright eyes studied her for a moment. Then Delphine shot high in a vertical jump and released a whistle that sounded to Carson's ears like a yelp of joy.

"Delphine!" she cried, her heart near bursting. From behind her, she heard Nate shout out Delphine's name and run toward the pool.

"It's her! It's her!" he exclaimed, arching on his toes excitedly and pointing.

Swimming past them again, Delphine tilted to her side, looking up. Passing Nate, she stopped and rose up, whistling.

"She sees me!" Nate exclaimed, rushing to the pool's edge.

Carson watched as Nate looked into the dolphin's

eyes, overwhelmed with gratitude that Delphine had recognized Nate. There was an attentiveness between them—a connection—that went beyond words.

Two female volunteers came closer from the other tanks, intrigued by what was happening in the pool.

When Nate crouched at the pool's edge, Carson put her hand out to stop him from getting too close. "Honey, I'm sorry, but you have to go back against the wall until Lynne tells you it's okay to come close."

"No!"

"Remember what Lynne said." Nate was jumping up and down, getting overexcited. She feared a meltdown and spoke calmly but firmly. "Go stand by the wall. That's the rule. If you do what Lynne says, you can play with Delphine. You'll have your turn."

Reluctantly Nate went to stand by the wall, but he rose up on his toes and kept his eyes glued to Delphine.

Delphine kept rising up in the water to peek out over the edge of the pool, obviously looking for Nate.

"She knows you're here," Lynne called out to Nate. "She's happy to see you. I told you she would be!"

"What are all those marks on her body?" Nate asked, looking stricken.

Carson looked at Lynne, who nodded at Carson, giving her the silent go-ahead to explain.

"Those are her scars. But don't worry, they will get better. Look how healthy she is. That's what's important."

Delphine began chattering excitedly, then took a rapid run around the pool before returning to where

Carson stood. She tilted her head to study Carson with her shiny black eyes.

Carson lowered her head closer to the dolphin's. "Yes, it's me. I'm back." She braced herself with her arms and slipped into the pool. Delphine swam very close, her eyes big and eager looking. The dolphin stopped in front of her and waited, as though inviting Carson's touch. Carson tentatively reached out a hand in the water and held it inches from the dolphin, giving her time. Delphine moved to gently nudge the tip of her rostrum against Carson's hand, then nudged her head against Carson's fingertips. Carson felt the old connection and relaxed, letting her hands slide gently over the rubbery skin.

"Hey, Delphine," she murmured.

Over and over Delphine swam past Carson, each time allowing Carson's hands to rub her sides in a circular massage. After several minutes, Delphine faced Carson again, this time remaining under the water. Carson heard a quick staccato sound and felt a tingling on her abdomen, like tickling. Laughing, she tried to shoo Delphine away but Delphine was persistent, returning over and over to send the sonar to her belly.

Lynne walked up carrying medical equipment in her arms. "What's she doing?"

"She's echolocating. She won't stop. She keeps coming back and doing it over and over. Look at her—here she comes again." Delphine was gently poking her rostrum near Carson's abdomen. Still laughing, Carson turned around, showing Delphine her back. "Is this a new game for her?"

"Not that I'm aware of," Lynne replied, slipping into the pool beside Carson. She handed Carson a long plastic feeding tube. "Sometimes she echolocates on the metal pole when we sweep the pool. I can feel the tingling on my palms. It's kind of a weird feeling."

"Exactly."

Lynne gave Carson a curious look. "You're not pregnant, are you?"

Carson barked out a laugh. "God, no. Why do you ask?"

"A few years back I was in here with a dolphin and the same thing happened to me. The dolphin kept coming by and echolocating my belly. Over and over." She laughed. "A week later I found out I was pregnant."

Carson felt her body go cold in the water. "You mean, the dolphin . . ." She couldn't say the words.

". . . saw my fetus before I even did," Lynne finished for her. "Amazing, huh? It could see something was different inside me and was curious. That little fetus is three years old now. Makes for a good story, doesn't it?"

Carson couldn't reply. Of course she wasn't pregnant, her mind screamed. Blake always used protection. Still, just the possibility freaked her out. She turned her head to look at Delphine, who was floating nearby, her mouth open and relaxed, watching her with an angelic smile.

What do you know? Carson thought irritably.

Carson had to focus as she assisted Lynne with

administering the medication to a compliant Delphine. Then, at last, it was Nate's turn to play. Carson climbed from the water to sit alongside the pool with her feet dangling in the water and watched Nate toss the ball over and over to Delphine. The dolphin was like a dog, never tiring of going after the ball and tossing it back. The two of them were in heaven. Nate didn't need to get into the water. He was seeing for himself that Delphine was okay, that she didn't blame him.

Delphine isn't the only one on the mend, she thought with a bittersweet smile. She remembered Taylor's words: *Not all wounds are visible.*

An hour after Carson and Nate had said their emotional good-byes to Delphine, with a promise from Lynne to keep Carson apprised of the dolphin's progress, Carson stood with her hands on her hips, staring uncompromisingly at the little white stick lying on the bathroom counter. It was an exercise in frustration, like waiting for a pot of water to boil. She lowered her head and closed her eyes. She'd never realized how long three minutes could be. Nor that a heart could pound so fast or her hands feel so cold. Lifting her head, she checked the wall clock. Three minutes . . .

She licked her lips, took a breath. Her hands were shaking as she held up the tip of the little stick to the color chart on the box.

Carson stared at the stick and felt the blood draining from her face. She slipped slowly to the floor, feeling faint. Over and over her dazed mind kept screaming, *There must be some mistake.* She lurched for the box and read the directions again. Then she looked at the stick again. The two little lines were a bright, unyielding, mocking pink.

Carson leaned back against the wall and stared at one long, narrow crack in the bathtub's porcelain. It forked in the middle of the tub and became two cracks. She kept tracing the crack back and forth, her brain unable to think beyond the glaring truth of those two lines.

She was pregnant.

Chapter Eighteen

Charleston, South Carolina

Mamaw pulled the Camry into a space in front of the Medical University and craned her neck, searching for Lucille. Usually Lucille drove while Mamaw preferred to be the passenger. The Camry belonged to Lucille, and Mamaw didn't feel comfortable with the strange car, but since she'd given the Blue Bomber to Carson she no longer had "wheels," as Carson said. Today she'd driven Lucille to another of several recent doctor appointments. Mamaw did not like how weak Lucille was looking and insisted on driving her to the city. In turn, Lucille had insisted that Mamaw not wait in the hospital for her. Instead, Mamaw could do a little shopping in town, a rarity these days. She had tried to get into her old groove on King Street, but found that most of her favorite boutiques had closed, replaced by hip little cafés and trendy shops.

There was a time she could walk into a boutique

and expect the clerk to have a card on file with her sizes. Today no one knew her name. She'd spent her entire life in this city, was a sixth-generation Charlestonian. Generations of her family were buried in this city—her husband, her son—as someday she would be.

And yet, sitting between these massive hospital buildings, watching the traffic go by and throngs of people crowding the sidewalks, she didn't feel that it was home any longer.

What was keeping her? she wondered. Not more than a minute later she spotted a slightly stooped woman in a navy-and-white shirtdress pushing through the hospital revolving door. She stopped on the sidewalk and stood clutching her bag, looking from left to right, the wind picking up the hem of her dress.

"Lucille!" Mamaw called out the window.

Lucille lifted her hand to acknowledge she'd seen her.

When did Lucille get so old? Mamaw wondered as she eased the car into drive. *And so frail?* It seemed to have happened overnight. Worry creased her brow. A body didn't get so frail so quickly with the flu. A shiver of fear swept over her as she pulled up to the curb.

Lucille climbed into the passenger seat with a soft grunt. She fumbled with the seat belt buckle. Once Mamaw heard the click, she flicked on her blinkers and carefully steered the car back into traffic.

"I'm sorry if I kept you waiting," Lucille said. Her voice sounded tired and she leaned her head back against the seat and closed her eyes.

Mamaw glanced at the woman beside her. Lucille looked drawn, her usually plump cheeks sunken. In her hand she carried a large paper bag from the hospital. Medicine, Mamaw guessed. She drove carefully through the tight traffic on narrow city streets, turned onto East Bay, then headed for the bridge.

She breathed easier once she was on the expansive Ravenel Bridge that towered over the Cooper River. She glanced again at Lucille. Her head was turned as she sat quietly looking out at the expansive view of the Cooper River.

"You have indeed kept me waiting," Mamaw said.

Lucille turned her head to look at her. "What's that?"

"I'm wondering," Mamaw said, her eyes on the road ahead, "just how much longer you're going to keep me waiting."

"What do you mean?"

"When are you going to tell me the truth?" She quickly glanced at Lucille. "What's going on?"

Lucille turned her head and looked straight ahead through the windshield.

"I thought we were friends," Mamaw said.

Lucille said nothing.

Mamaw glanced again from the road. Lucille clutched the bag tighter but her face gave nothing away.

"That we didn't keep secrets from each other," Mamaw continued.

"You told me you didn't want no more bad news," Lucille said.

"What? When did I say that?"

"A while back. In this very car."

Mamaw was flustered. "I don't remember saying that, and even if I did, I certainly didn't mean to be taken literally. Lucille, for pity's sake, I know you don't have the flu. Please tell me what's going on."

Lucille turned to look at her. Then she said in a flat voice, "I got the cancer."

Mamaw felt her heart skip a beat, even as her stomach dropped. "Oh, no." She swallowed hard, then asked, "What kind? What do the doctors say?"

"Slow down," Lucille said, tapping the dashboard. "You're gonna kill us both."

Mamaw hadn't realized she'd been accelerating her speed. She applied the brake and slowed to the speed limit. She took the Sullivan's Island exit from the bridge and drove up Coleman Boulevard to the first parking lot she spied. She pulled in and stopped the car. Turning, she faced Lucille.

"Tell me everything."

Lucille looked at her with compassion in her eyes. "I know what you're thinking. You're already making a list of what doctors to call, what treatments to try. Now, Miz Marietta, you're just gonna have to listen to what I'm going to tell you without interrupting me. Okay?"

Mamaw nodded and said uncertainly, "All right."

Lucille shifted her weight in the seat. "A while back I got these pains. I tried to manage them, but when they wouldn't go away I went to see my doctor. He sent me to another doctor here at the hospital and they gave me a mess of tests."

Mamaw feared the worst. "What kind of—"

Lucille put up her hand to stop Mamaw's question and Mamaw snapped her mouth shut.

"They told me I had cancer. Pancreatic cancer."

Mamaw sucked in her breath, then exhaled. "Oh, Lord."

"Today they told me it spread to my other organs. That's why my stomach pains are so bad."

Mamaw had to ask. "What stage is the cancer?"

"They call it stage four."

Mamaw clenched her hands together. Pancreatic cancer was always bad, but stage four was a death sentence and they both knew it.

Lucille looked down at her lap. "There's nothing to do now but wait," Lucille said. She smiled ruefully. "Today the doctor told me I'm not gonna have to wait too long."

"No!" Mamaw blurted out. She'd agreed to keep silent, but now the story was told and she couldn't hold back any longer. Lucille appeared so defeated, so willing to accept the diagnosis. Mamaw couldn't—she wouldn't—lose Lucille without putting up a fight.

"I won't accept that. There are several procedures you can try. My friend had pancreatic cancer and she had some surgery, something to do with a Whipple. I'll find out her doctor's name. We have to try something. I'm sure there's some procedure."

Lucille put her hand up in a gesture to silence Mamaw. "First off, I ain't got insurance."

"I don't care. I'll pay for it."

"Now, Miz Marietta, we both know you can't afford to take that on right now. And I wouldn't let you. Besides, it's too late. There ain't no cure for what I got."

"Maybe not a cure, but we can buy more time. There's chemotherapy and radiation."

"No." Lucille shook her head, her voice resolute. "I'm not doing no chemo or radiation. I'm not puttin' that poison in my body."

"You don't expect me to just sit here and let you die!"

Lucille smiled sadly. "That's exactly what I expect you to do."

Mamaw choked back a cry as her hand covered her mouth. "That's absurd! I can't do that."

Lucille's face softened. "You must. Miz Marietta, the plain truth is, it's too late for any of that. The cancer's too far gone. I talked to the doctors and I've made up my mind."

Mamaw brought a hand to her face and turned her head away as she wept, shaking her head in denial.

Lucille dug into her purse and pulled out a tissue. Handing it to Mamaw, she said, "Here, now. Take this. Your eyes always puff up like a sea urchin when you cry."

Mamaw let out a laugh and grabbed the tissue.

Only Lucille could get away with saying such things to her at a time like this.

"This is such a shock. I didn't see it coming. I'm older than you are. I'm supposed to go before you."

"Seems God has different plans."

Mamaw blew her nose and composed herself. "I can't accept this."

"Now, Miz Marietta, listen to me." Lucille waited for Mamaw to face her again, then spoke in a slow, stern voice. "I've seen you be strong when Parker passed, then Mr. Edward. I'm asking you to be strong for me."

A rush of memories flooded Mamaw's mind—the nursing, the companionship, the steady encouragement, the exhausting hours, and, finally, the unutterable grief. She knew what was coming. She comprehended fully what Lucille was asking of her.

Mamaw nodded almost imperceptibly. "I will. You know I will."

"And be strong for the girls."

"The girls," Mamaw said, suddenly remembering them. "When are you going to tell them? They'll be devastated. They love you so much."

"I was hoping I wouldn't have to tell them. I didn't want to ruin their summer with this sorry business. I figured they'll all be leaving at summer's end, flying off like the shorebirds to wherever their lives take them. I hoped I'd just be like one of them. Flying off. No fuss."

"Flying off and leaving me alone!"

"I know that. But it don't change things, does it? You've got your plans, and now I've got mine."

Mamaw brought her trembling hand to her eyes. "Lucille . . ."

"I'm not afraid to go," Lucille said in a peaceful tone. "Seeing those manacles made it right clear in my mind. We're all shackled to this life for the duration. We carry our load. Looking back, I've lived a good life. I've no regrets. Way I see it, it's my time to cross the water. I like to think I'll face the crossing with the same courage of my ancestors." She looked up and smiled. "I'm gonna be set free."

Mamaw tightened her lips.

"I'm only afraid of one thing," Lucille said in a soft voice, looking at the bag of medicine in her lap.

"What's that?"

Lucille lifted the bag. "The pain. They give me all these pills. But they're not working so good no more. The cancer's taken a turn. The time for all this hospital rigmarole is done." She shook her head resolutely. "I don't want no treatments. I know that. But . . . I don't want to face this alone."

Mamaw looked into Lucille's dark, watery eyes. They bulged slightly, unblinking against a chalky face. Mamaw saw a ghostly image of what was coming. She grasped Lucille's hand and held it tight. "I'll be right here, sitting by your side all the way. You won't be alone."

Lucille's lips quivered and she held tight to Mamaw's hand. "That's all I needed to know."

Chapter Nineteen

Carson crossed the Ben Sawyer Bridge over the Intracoastal Waterway as dusk settled over the lowcountry. The water shimmered in dusky twilight pinks, and bordering the banks, thick rows of palms formed dark shadows.

She turned off the air-conditioning, rolled down the windows, and let the sultry air flow into the stale car. She breathed deep the scents of mud and salt, raking her hand through her hair, loosening the elastic, and letting her hair catch the wind. She was nearing home.

When she'd arrived at Sea Breeze the previous May without a job or a place to live, she'd thought that she'd hit rock bottom. She'd been penniless and adrift. In retrospect, compared to how she felt now, that seemed like a cakewalk.

During the long trip home from the Keys, Nate had mostly slept, exhausted from his busy week, and she had plenty of time to think about the new life growing inside of her. She vacillated between benign curiosity, idly tapping her belly like a cat playing with a bug, and abject terror of an alien life growing inside of her. She had to first decide whether to tell Blake. Part of her wanted to make her decisions without involving him. It wasn't his body, after all.

Despite her independence, however, it felt selfish, even wrong, not to tell him. Blake wasn't a one-night stand. He was someone she had a relationship with, someone she cared deeply for. Someone she might even love. The father of this unborn child. Didn't he have the right to know?

She'd always been self-reliant. She'd spent most of her youth taking care of her father; she'd been more a maid than a daughter. When she turned eighteen she'd left to live alone, existing hand to mouth most of the time. She was not accustomed even to accepting help, let alone asking for it.

Carson ran her hand through her hair, weary and bleary-eyed. She'd been going over and over this issue in her head for twelve hours and was no closer to a decision. All she knew for certain was that she was exhausted and thirsty, and needed to pee. And that this fetus inside of her felt like an uninvited guest.

She glanced in the rearview mirror at the young boy sleeping in the backseat, strapped in by his seat belt. His head hung loosely to the side and his mouth was open; he was snoring gently. Her heart pinged with affection as tears filled her eyes. She loved that little boy and knew he loved her, in his own way. In retrospect, she had truly enjoyed being with Nate, taking care of him, watching him mature. Would she have these feelings for her own child? Could she be a good mother?

Glancing at the road, Carson saw she was nearing the turnoff for Sea Breeze. Her hands clenched the wheel and her heart rate shot up as her base instincts reared. All she wanted to do was to drop off Nate, then put the pedal to the metal and roar out of the driveway. To keep on driving. To run far, far away.

The following evening, Carson was sitting at the wood table in Blake's apartment staring at a plate of shrimp and grits. It was a hot and humid night heralding the oncoming storm, but he'd slaved over the stove to prepare the meal for her homecoming. Thunder rumbled and the ceiling fan over the table was causing the tapered candles to drip wax onto the tablecloth.

Across the table from her, Blake was looking anxiously at her face. Shrimp and grits was her favorite dish but she couldn't eat. She'd managed a few bites of the grits but the rich, buttery sauce was too much for her. Just the smell of seafood made her feel sick. More than the smells, however, the news she had to share had her stomach tied in knots.

Hobbs lay patiently under the table, watching for the piece of shrimp she slid under the table into his waiting mouth.

"More water?" Blake asked, already lifting the pitcher.

"Yes, thank you." Her mouth felt filled with unspoken words.

Carson quietly watched him pour, heard the ice clink as it fell into her glass. She knew she was being sullen and withdrawn. To make up for it, he was being exceedingly solicitous, tiptoeing around her.

He set down the pitcher and looked at her full plate. "Aren't you hungry? You've hardly taken a bite."

"No," she said, slowly shaking her head. She felt bad for all his effort for naught. "I'm not feeling well."

"Oh, baby, I'm sorry. You should've told me. You do look a little off."

She snorted a short laugh. "Do I?"

"You still look great," he hurried to add. "Beautiful. As always."

Carson's face was glistening with sweat, and she knew she was being testy. It wasn't Blake's fault she was pregnant . . . at least not entirely. She set her napkin on the table and pushed back a bit in her chair. Hobbs moved back with a dissatisfied grunt.

"Blake, I have something to tell you."

Blake looked at her warily. "Okay."

"I'm pregnant."

Blake sat motionless, his eyes wide. After a moment he blinked, and she could see he was gathering his wits. "Are you sure?"

She wanted to scream, *No, I'm making it up!* "Yes, of course I'm sure. I was late and took a pregnancy test in Florida. It's positive. I took the test three times to be sure."

He leaned back against his chair and averted his gaze. Then, meeting her eyes, he smiled with a kind of wonderment. "You're pregnant," he said. "That's, well, wow . . . that's great."

Carson blinked, not sure she'd heard right. "Great? What do you mean, that's great? It's *not* great."

"It's better than what I thought you might say. Look," he said, laying his palms on the table. "I know we didn't plan it, but it happened." He leaned back on the hind legs of his chair and scratched his head. "How *did* it happen?"

Carson snorted again and looked at him askance.

He brought the chair back aright and grinned wickedly. "I know *how* . . ." His smile fell and he grew serious. "But how did you get pregnant? We were careful."

"That's what I want to know," she replied, narrowing her eyes with accusation.

Anger flashed in Blake's eyes. "What? No way. What do you take me for? If I wanted to knock you up, I'd be up-front and honest about it."

"Well, you *did* knock me up!" she shouted.

"Well, I'm sorry!" he shouted back.

Hobbs jumped up and ran to the door, barking.

"Hobbs, hush," Blake fired off.

The dog immediately stopped barking and returned to sit on the floor by Blake's feet with a grunt.

Blake and Carson stared each other down for a moment, the silence thick around them.

Finally Blake wiped his brow, his face pinched in concentration. "Look," Blake said in a calmer voice. "Obviously something just failed. It's rare but here we are. And you weren't on the pill . . ."

"You knew that," she said defensively, and looked away, embarrassed for her lapse in good judgment. She'd gone off the pill before she'd left Los Angeles. She wanted to give her body a break from the hormones and she wasn't planning on starting up any relationships. She had meant to go back on the pill when she returned from Florida. She'd thought they were being careful. Stupid, stupid, stupid.

"I'm just saying . . ." Blake said in a conciliatory tone. "We're in this together, okay?" He reached out to tap her hand lying flat on the table. When she looked up he held her gaze. "*Okay?*"

Carson reluctantly nodded.

"When did you find out?"

"Day before yesterday. It was so bizarre. I was in the water with Delphine and she started echolocating on my abdomen. Turns out she knew I was pregnant before I did."

"No kidding?" he said, incredulous.

"It freaked me out, let me tell you. As soon as we left the Mote I went to the pharmacy to buy one of those home pregnancy tests. I took all three in the box and all three of them said I was pregnant." She wiped a wayward lock of hair from her face. "When I found out, it turned on some goddamned switch in my body. Suddenly I'm as sick as a dog. I'd think it was psychosomatic except I couldn't fake being this sick."

"Okay," he said, pushing away his unfinished plate. "It's going to be okay. I have money in savings and I've got good insurance."

"Wha— Wait!" Carson blurted, sitting straight with alarm. "I'm not sure I'm even having it!"

Blake's face tightened. "Not sure you're having it?"

"It's a big decision. I need to take a step back and think about it."

"I love you. You love me. What do you need to think about?"

Carson tossed her napkin on the table and stood. She felt the walls of the room closing in on her. "I need to go."

Blake pushed back his chair and went to her side to take hold of her arm.

"I know you're freaked out. You're afraid. But don't be. I'm here."

He was saying all the right things and she wished they made her feel better, but they didn't.

"Carson, you know I love you, right?"

She sniffed, unable to look him in the eye. "Yes."

"There's a simple answer. We can get married."

"No . . ." she said, shaking her head. "Not like this."

"Honey, I want to marry you. I've wanted to marry you from the first moment I saw you at Dunleavy's."

"You wouldn't be asking me if I wasn't pregnant."

"Maybe not tonight. But whether it's now or next year, it doesn't matter as long as we're together." He lowered his lips to kiss the top of her head, then slipped his arms around her, holding her close to his chest.

"We can get married right away, it doesn't have to be fancy. Then you can move in here. We'll make my office the nursery. At least until we find a bigger place."

Blake had it all planned out, apparently. Except Carson didn't come here tonight for him to have all the answers or to plan her life. She just wanted him to listen to her, to be there for her and let her spill out all her fears and worries, to be her sounding board so she could gain some perspective on what decision to make. Instead, he was pushing her to do what he wanted her to do. Planning her life so she would just say yes. Getting married, having a baby . . . these things were on his agenda, not hers.

Carson felt her breath come quick in a panic. His arms around her felt like a trap. She tensed and broke free of his arms.

"Blake," she said in a shaky voice, putting her fingers to her temples. "Right now my head feels like it's going to burst into flames. I can't talk about getting married and moving in. I'm not sure I want to have a baby at all, much less get married! This is all going way too fast. We've only known each other a few months!"

He stared back at her, arms hanging at his sides.

"I didn't ask you to marry me. I don't want you to tell me what to do. That's not why I'm here tonight." She began pacing the room, eyeing the door. "I'm just trying to do the right thing, to tell you that I'm pregnant. That's all. That in itself is a stretch for me. I'm not ready to be a mother. I don't even have a job! How am I going to take care of a baby?"

"I'll support you and the baby."

"I don't want you to! I don't want to depend on you. Don't you get that yet?"

He went still, his expression bruised. "I'm beginning to."

She hadn't meant to hurt him. That's not why she came here. Now everything was worse. "I'm sorry," she said. "It's just that I'm afraid of this . . ." She trailed off, indicating her belly with a swipe of her hand. "This thing."

"Why?"

"Everything will change."

"Nothing will change. Not between us."

"Of course it will. Because I'll change."

"How will you change?"

"I don't know!" she cried, knowing she was sounding irrational, but that she was right. "I just will."

"Carson . . ."

"No! I'm not ready to talk about this. About us. I thought I was strong enough to handle it, but I can't do it."

Blake's eyes dimmed and he lowered his head.

"I have to go."

Blake's arm shot out to grab her hand, stopping her. "Carson. Don't have an abortion."

"Blake . . ."

"I mean it." His dark eyes deepened.

Carson felt an instinctive rush of rage, rearing back

and swiping away his firm grip. "It's my body. I'll decide what I'm going to do."

"I love you, Carson. But if you do that, it's a deal-breaker for me."

Her breath caught in her throat. This was precisely why she hadn't wanted to tell him. She came here hoping he'd be sensitive and understanding, the man who listened to her, helped her make decisions without judgment. But why did she think that? Blake was one of the most opinionated men she'd ever met.

Carson grabbed her purse from the chair as she made her way to the door. She opened it, but before leaving she turned and said, "Please, don't call me for a while, okay?"

"Are you breaking up with me?"

"No. Yes . . ." She gave a huge sigh. "I don't know," she said, and fled, closing the door behind her.

That evening, Dora lay on Devlin's big sleigh bed, her head on his shoulder, drowsy in a post-sex daze. It had been the first time they'd made love on his king-size bed—on land, for that matter. The space seemed luxurious compared to the cramped boat.

It would feel luxurious under any circumstances, Dora thought as her gaze swept the room. His was a large house on the Breach Inlet side of Sullivan's Island, new construction in the Southern style, with lots of porches with rockers facing the ocean. The bedroom porch doors were open wide, allowing the ocean breezes to flow in. Those who grew up on the island preferred the sultry air to air-conditioning. It was indeed an impressive house, she thought again, but she wasn't sure she didn't prefer the quaint cottage on the marsh.

They'd kicked off the sheets and lay exposed to the cooling breeze. Her hand caressed his bare chest, her fingers mingling with the soft curls. Devlin's hand stroked her shoulder in a lazy swirling pattern, as he hummed to the song that was playing on his CD.

"I like this song," Devlin said in a low voice. "Makes me think of us." He began to join in the chorus, singing in an off-key baritone.

"I saw you last night and got that old feeling."

"You know the words," Dora said teasingly. "I'm impressed."

"I live to impress you."

Dora burrowed her head comfortably into his shoulder. Cal was not a cuddler, and of course, neither was her son. With Devlin she found she craved this gentle intimacy, almost more than the sex. The sex was wonderful, but this . . . Dora sighed. She needed to be held, to feel treasured.

Devlin began to sing again in his wobbly voice, *"The spark of love is still burning."*

"Nice . . ." she murmured absently.

"Woman, didn't you listen to the lyrics? I'm trying to say something here."

Dora went very still, suddenly appreciating that Devlin wasn't joking around.

"That's how I feel about you, Dora. About us. That old feeling is back. It's like we're getting a second chance."

"Honey, we've only just started dating. Let's not get ahead of ourselves."

"How long don't matter. It's like the song says. I saw you and got that old feeling."

"Dev, wait," Dora stammered, sitting up and pulling the sheet around herself.

"What's the matter, honey?" Devlin asked, his smile falling. He moved to sit up, exposing his nakedness. Dora had to look away, still embarrassed at the sight. She'd never felt comfortable naked, not even as a young woman and never before Cal, who was, she could see in retrospect, a prude.

Devlin took the hand that clutched the sheet tight and pulled it away. As it slipped off she lurched to clutch it back, but he reached out to hold both of her hands in his. She blushed, flustered.

"You're not wearing your wedding ring," he said, looking down at the pale skin on her ring finger.

"No."

He didn't say anything; he just nodded and let his finger rub the empty space on her ring finger for a moment.

"I thought you'd be glad to know how I feel about you. How I've always felt about you."

She dragged her gaze to his and was caught by the sincerity in the brilliant blue.

"You were the one for me back when we were teenagers, and you're still the one for me now. All these years we've been apart, I think I've been lost. I know now that I never got over you. I never should have let you go."

Dora felt the impact of those words deep in her heart. She couldn't respond. Couldn't move.

"Did you hear what I said?" he asked.

"Yes."

"I know you feel it, too," he said. "I know it."

"I do," she replied. "When I saw you after all these years, you made me feel like I was sixteen again."

"That's how you always will be to me."

"But I'm not sixteen. I'm thirty-six. With a child."

"Hell, I know all that. What matters is that we feel the same about each other. Right here, right now."

"Right now," she said, "I don't feel sixteen. Nor do I think of you as that teenager anymore." She laughed at his puzzled expression. "Thank God! I've lived those years, gone through so many experiences, learned so much . . . I don't want to be that young, foolish girl any longer. Malleable, obedient, gullible even. I like being the woman I am today. Devlin, you've made me feel beautiful again. Womanly. Sexy. Right now."

She looked at Devlin and leaned forward to stroke his face. "And I like who *you* are today. The man you've become. I don't want to go back to being those kids again."

Devlin reached out to take hold of her shoulders. "I feel the same. That's what I've been trying to say in my own clumsy way. "Dora . . ." he said, his voice tight with emotion. "I . . . I love you. I always have and I always will."

Dora drew back, and her heart began to flutter. "Dev . . . this is all moving so fast."

Devlin's smile slipped and he released her shoulders.

"Because you don't have feelings for me? You don't love me."

Dora let out a guttural groan. "Of course I have feelings for you. Deep and very real. But love? I'm not going to rush into using that word again. I'm not ready. I'm not even divorced yet!"

"Well, I am," he shot back. "And I'll tell you what. A piece of paper don't make a damn bit of difference. It's what's in here that counts." He made a fist and pounded his heart. He went very still. His tone turned indignant. "Eudora Tupper, do you still love your husband?"

"Devlin, how can you ask me that?"

"I can because you broke my heart once over that man. I don't aim to have it broken again."

"When did I break your heart?"

He looked stunned that she could ask. "When you broke up with me!"

"Oh, for . . . Dev, I was eighteen years old!"

"Nineteen. We dated all freshman year you were at Converse and I was at USC. All that summer and part of the next year."

Dora stared back at him, stunned that he knew this, and by the raw hurt and pain so evident in his voice.

"Then you met your high-and-mighty Calhoun Tupper and you traded me in for a fancier model."

"I did not!" she said, annoyed that he would say such a thing. "That's not why we broke up."

"Then why?" he asked, eyes glaring. "You never told me. Not really."

Dora shifted. "I . . . I don't know. We grew up. We changed. I fell in love with Cal," she stammered.

"Or your mama did." His tone was bitter.

"Don't be ridiculous."

"Am I? You know your mama never liked me. She never thought I'd amount to much."

Dora crossed her arms. "What does she have to do with this?"

"Everything! You were a mama's girl. She said jump, you said how high. It was always like that with her. She never liked me, but I can just imagine her putting Cal's picture in front of you whenever I called. I'm damn sure she never gave you half of my messages once you hooked up with Tupper."

Dora averted her gaze.

"You married him because your mama told you to."

"Stop, Dev," Dora said, looking into his eyes. "That's not fair. I married Cal because I loved him."

"Shit," he said in a long drawl, shaking his head. Pointing his finger at her, he declared, "I don't believe you."

Dora straightened, mouth agape.

Devlin angrily flipped back the covers and rose from the bed. He crossed the room in long strides, slamming the bathroom door behind him.

Dora wrapped her arms around herself and sat alone in the king-size bed. The moon rose higher in the sky, like a resplendent queen. A few minutes ago, she'd felt as golden and full of light as that moon. Now she felt eclipsed and cold. She dragged the thick coverlet from the bottom of the bed over her shoulders. Staring out at the night, she ran her fingers along the cable pattern of the wool.

Patterns, she thought—there was that word again. Dora was beginning to comprehend the power that patterns had to influence behavior. What Devlin had said was true. Winnie had made no secret of her disapproval of Devlin. Was she being a good girl and following the pattern set by her mother, and her mother before her, when she'd married Cal? She thought back to how Winnie had pointed out to Dora that Cal wasn't the heavy drinker her father was, or Devlin was. Winnie had always railed against the evils of alcohol, using her father as the prime example of how a life could be corrupted by it. She'd also reminded Dora how Cal was from a family with deep Charleston roots and strong connections. He would provide for her the comfortable lifestyle she was accustomed to.

Dora had loved Cal in her girlish fashion. She had felt from the first that with Cal she was on a trajectory toward marriage. When he dropped to one knee and proposed, she could only answer yes.

They'd married at St. Philip's Episcopal Church in a traditional ceremony on a sunny day in June. She'd worn white lace; the bridesmaids blush-pink taffeta. Dora had chosen an Aynsley China pattern like her mother's and her grandmother's silver pattern.

Was it fair to say that she had judged Devlin by her mother's stringent measures? Dora swallowed hard. She had to admit it was. Lord help her, she thought, feeling the sting of shame.

Dora tossed the throw off her shoulders. The thick, unyielding wool was irritating her tender skin. As she sat scratching her neck and arms, she wondered how long she would continue to blanket herself in the old patterns that had only brought her unhappiness.

The bathroom door opened and Devlin walked out, tying the belt of an expensive-looking waffle-weave robe. His blond hair was disheveled and his feet bare. He had the heavy-footed walk of confidence mixed with anger.

How times had changed, she thought. She couldn't help but wonder what her mama would think of Devlin now. This was no longer the clever but poor island boy she'd grown up with. Dev was a self-made millionaire. He'd brought himself up from almost nothing. He'd become a man, had a successful business, married, divorced, was a father. Yet despite the changes and years, he still loved her.

He stopped at a tray table laden with bottles of liquor and poured himself a drink. He turned to glance her way.

"Want a cognac?"

She could tell from his tone he was upset, but still resigned to being a gentleman. "No, thanks. I'd love a water."

He paused, then turned back to the tray and put

the stopper back on the crystal bottle. He then opened two bottles of water and carried them to the bed.

He handed her a bottle, then slid beside her on the mattress. She moved to make room for him against the headboard. He stretched his legs out beside hers and leaned back, taking a long swallow.

Dora leaned against his shoulder, relieved that he'd returned to the bed and not stayed away in a show of pique. Only a man with confidence would do that, she thought. She reached out to take hold of his hand on his lap. Immediately, he squeezed it.

"Dev, we haven't talked yet about *your* marriage," she said, glad that they were both sitting against the headboard, looking out at the ocean, not at each other. It made the honesty somehow easier. "Did you love your wife?"

"I thought I did. I won't deny it."

"I'm glad," Dora said. She wouldn't have liked to think he hadn't been in love with his wife.

"Ashley and I got married a long time after you and I broke up," he clarified.

"Why did you divorce?"

A long sigh rumbled in Devlin's chest. "I screwed up. Screwed around. I was too young to get married and too stupid to appreciate what I had. We hung on for longer than we should've. I don't think either of us wanted to admit we'd made a mistake. Especially after Leigh Anne came along. But when Ashley finally made the call, I didn't fight her. I couldn't. I'm not gonna lie. The divorce was hard to go through. We both still bear the scars. But I can look back and see it was for the best."

"How is she?"

"Ashley's doing okay. Getting married again."

She looked over at him. "Are you okay with that?"

"Sure," he replied quickly. Then, more sincerely, "I'm happy for her. He's a good guy. He'll be a good father for Leigh Anne. But she'll always be *my* little girl. I'd do anything for her. Getting a divorce doesn't change how a father feels about his child."

Dora thought about Cal and believed Devlin was right, unfortunately for Nate.

"Where do they live?"

"Over in Mt. Pleasant. They have a real nice house on the creek. Not far."

"Do you see your daughter often?"

"Every other weekend, and we work out holidays. I haven't missed a school function or a dance recital," he said with a measure of pride.

She smiled, glad to hear that.

He shifted against the headboard to look into her eyes. "Honey, I know we talk about the past a lot and what we remember from back when we were sixteen. I like that you make me feel like that again. And that I make you remember." He paused, playing with her fingers.

"But I know we aren't kids any longer. I got the aches and pains to remind me." His laugh rumbled low. "I'm not that reckless surfer that you used to know.

I'm a man now. But just because I've grown up doesn't mean I have to be old, now does it?"

She shook her head and moved a hand to place it over his. "No, not at all. I love that you're still spontaneous and fun. You make me happy."

He cocked his head. "I hear a 'but' coming . . ."

She smiled ruefully. "But . . . like you said, I enjoy a quiet life, my home and my garden. My son. I like staying home at night. While you . . ." She looked into his eyes. "You go out all the time. You walk into the bar and Bill knows your drink. You called Dunleavy's your office."

"It's the nature of my business. I go out with clients when they can go, which is often on weekends and in the evenings. I take them to restaurants to talk about deals and to add some local color."

"It's all business?"

"No, of course not." He paused. "What are you asking? Do you think I can't settle down?"

"I only know what I see."

He looked at her hands again. "Did it occur to you that I might be lonely?"

She abruptly looked up at his face. The blue of his eyes burned like torches against the ruddy tan and burned a hole right through her arguments. She couldn't quite grasp the concept: Devlin Cassell, lonely?

Dora had not considered that possibility. She shook her head, then lowered it onto his broad, strong, capable shoulder. He wrapped his arm tighter around her.

"Dev," she said, pushing herself to be honest. "It means so much to me that you love me. Be patient with me. I can't say the words. Not yet. It might just be paper, but I need to get my divorce signed, sealed, and delivered before I can move forward. I'm not ready for anything more."

He sighed, but his hand gently patted her shoulder. "Okay, honey. I won't rush you."

"Thank you."

"As long as you're not pushing me away again."

"I'm not. I promise." Dora patted his chest with her hand. "I'm right here."

He bent and kissed the top of her head. "That's where I want you to stay."

Dora awoke the following morning filled with light. As soon as she reached the beach she began to run. She didn't stretch. She simply took off, with her fists pumping at her sides. Her feet pounded the hard-packed sand, one foot after the other. To her right, the ocean was a roiling mass of choppy, white-tipped waves.

You're strong. You can do it. You can make your goal.

She said the words over and over, like a metronome keeping the pace. She had to believe the words, too.

Sweat poured down her brow, but she pushed on, past the lighthouse on her way to Breach Inlet. She remembered the first time she'd reached this point, the first day of her walking program. She was tired, thirsty, barely able to put one foot in front of the other. That was the morning Devlin had found her. She'd looked her absolute worst and he'd thought she was beautiful. Dora laughed out loud, hearing the joyful sound like a clarion call in the early morning wind.

She reached the inlet and turned back, keeping up the pace. Her heart felt ready to burst, but Dora kept on running the final lap. Her muscles were screaming, but she'd come too far to quit before she reached her goal. No more excuses. Today she was going to make it.

She ran, her strong heart pounding, until she reached as far north as she could run on the tip of Sullivan's Island. At last Dora came to a stop, panting hard, her hands on her hips, sweat pouring down her face. She was exhausted but triumphant. A grin stretched wide across her face. She'd made it!

She stood on the sand, letting the brisk wind cool her body, as her gaze swept across the stretch of beach of this small island she loved. Beyond, the vast Atlantic Ocean was stirring like a great beast, growling and spitting, awakened by the storm.

She laughed out loud, her voice mingling with the roar of the waves. She had come a long way to reach this morning. Her namesake, Eudora Welty, had been right, she thought. A love of place could heal the soul.

Dora turned her head to look toward the back of the island, to where the Cove raced with the tides, where the cordgrass rustled in the wind, where the egrets feasted. Above the treeline she could barely make out the widow's walk of Sea Breeze. She smiled as Mamaw's words sang out in her mind.

Find yourself, and you will find your way home.

Chapter Twenty

Dora showered and dressed in a light summer shift, then carried her coffee and bowl of whole grain cereal out to the back porch. The sun was a ghostly eye in the sky, obscured by an armada of gray clouds. She sidestepped several vegetable and herb flats as she crossed the porch to join Mamaw and Lucille playing cards in their usual spot under the awning. The awning was rattling in the gusts of wind.

She took a seat at the table beside Carson, who was reading the *Island Eye*.

"Good morning," she called out as she approached. "Storm's coming."

The women looked up and greeted her warmly.

"You were up and out early," Mamaw said.

"I hope I didn't wake you."

"Lord, no," Mamaw said. "At my age one never sleeps well. Harper woke up just minutes after you left." Mamaw looked out to the garden. "Dear girl made coffee, fueled up, and went straight to work on planting those flower beds." She sipped her tea, watching, then as she lowered her cup said, "I swanny, look at that girl lift those bags of soil. They must weigh as much as she does."

Looking out to the backyard, Dora saw Harper lifting enormous bags of compost and dumping the contents into two new raised garden beds.

Lucille chuckled. "She's little but she's feisty."

"Dora, why aren't you out in the garden with her?" Mamaw asked. "Isn't it your project, too?"

"Hell, no," Dora said, chewing her cereal. "Harper took over that garden. I just get in her way."

Carson lowered her newspaper and laughed. "That's a switch."

"Not really," Dora said with a bemused expression. "She's not the meek little mouse I used to think she was. I'm kind of afraid of her."

Mamaw laughed as she picked up a playing card and held it in the air, deciding whether to keep or discard it. "She must've ordered every garden book ever written. Her room is littered with them. I'll wager she'll read each one, too."

"What are all of those?" Carson asked, pointing to the flats.

"Vegetable starter plants," Dora replied.

"Just what we need," Lucille muttered, picking up a card. "More vegetables. Wish she took a hankering to raising me a nice pig. Or a couple of chickens."

"Don't mention it to her!" Mamaw exclaimed. "Or we'll have chickens arriving tomorrow." She threw down a card.

"Don't worry. Sullivan's isn't zoned for livestock," Dora said.

"That won't stop Miss Harper if she puts her mind to it," Lucille said, picking up Mamaw's card.

"Bless her heart," Mamaw muttered. "Hush now, here she comes."

The women stopped talking as they watched Harper walking across the yard, slapping dirt from her clothes. It was a futile gesture. She was streaked from head to toe with soil that was fast becoming mud in her sweat.

"She doesn't even look winded," Dora said with awe.

"Hi, y'all," Harper said as she approached.

The three women stared at her wide-eyed with shock that their New Yorker greeted them in the Southern style.

"If that don't beat all," Lucille said under her breath.

"I'm just playing with you," Harper said with a light laugh. "Though I must say that expression is catchy." She turned to Dora as she poured herself a glass of water from a thermos. "Dora, glad you're back. I could use your help. I've got to get all these plants in before the rain comes."

"Sorry, Mrs. Green Jeans," Dora said, but she didn't look the least bit sorry.

Harper harrumphed and turned an imploring gaze on Carson.

"Carson . . ."

"Don't look at me," Carson said. "I hate gardening."

"Aw, come on," Harper moaned. "I need to get all those plants in before the rain." Her eyes sparkled with enthusiasm as she launched into a monologue of her progress. "I've come too far to mess it all up now. There's three different kinds of lettuce, patio tomatoes, and oh, the herbs! They smell heavenly. Parsley, thyme, rosemary, sage, oregano, dill, and lots of basil. Aren't they sweet? So tiny and all. I call them my babies." She turned to Lucille. "Lucille, this will be your very own kitchen garden," she said proudly. "In a few weeks, you can just saunter out and pick whatever you like."

Lucille smiled sweetly. "That's nice. Thank you, baby." She glanced at Mamaw.

"I really would help you, Harper," Dora said. "But I'm going out to play with Nate. We have a kayaking lesson this morning. Although . . ." She looked up at the gathering clouds. "I hope it isn't canceled because of this storm."

They all looked up at the clouds heralding the tropical storm that was barreling in from the south.

"It's really moving in," Mamaw said. "You shouldn't go out on the water today no matter what."

"Those clouds now have an official name," Carson informed them. She looked to Lucille. "Guess what it is." When Lucille shrugged, Carson said, "They named it Tropical Storm Lucy! Isn't that a hoot? I think it's only fitting they named a storm after you, you ol' windbag."

The girls laughed at the joke as Carson moved to kiss Lucille's cheek.

Lucille grunted. "I ain't never been called Lucy in my life and never will. I've always been Lucille."

Mamaw didn't laugh. "These midsummer storms can be surprisingly strong. They can pack a punch. I've lived through too many of them not to take each one seriously. Last summer Tropical Storm Debby wiped out our dunes. Cut them clean away." She clapped her hands together, rousing the group to action. "Girls, plans or no plans, today we have to prepare for this storm. We must take all the cushions inside, put anything light or loose that can be picked up by the wind into the garage. Harper, all your garden tools have to be put away. We don't want anything to become a missile in the wind and break a window. We can't be too careful."

"Mamaw, you always panic with every storm," Dora said. "This house has weathered storms for over a century."

"That's because I prepare! And I'll have you know; young lady, that this house might still be standing, but I've done many repairs over those years. Hugo almost took the whole house away. Once you live through that, you never turn your back on the ocean."

"Amen," Lucille muttered.

"Lucy's gonna be a real storm," Carson said, looking up at the sky. "I can always feel it in my bones. It's the shift in the barometric pressure."

Dora looked at the sky again, feeling the foreboding every person in the lowcountry experiences at the approach of a named summer storm. "At least it's not a hurricane."

"But the forecast calls for high winds," Harper said, looking warily at the sky. "I'm worried about my plants." She took a deep breath. "I'm off. Got to get them in before the storm hits." Harper marched off to retrieve a flat of herbs and hoisted them in her thin arms with the ease of a common laborer.

"Who is that girl?" Carson asked, resting her chin in her palm. "And where does she get all that energy?"

"It's the enthusiasm of a convert, my dear," Mamaw replied. "It's irrepressible."

"Speaking of energy," Dora said to Carson, "I noticed you slept in again this morning. You haven't been out surfing or kiting since you got back. With those waves building in the storm, I thought for sure you'd be with those other crazy risk takers out there."

"I'm still just tired from the trip. Not feeling that good, that's all." She looked to Lucille. "I think I've got what you've got."

Lucille snorted. "Honey, you ain't got what I got."

Carson leaned against Lucille's shoulder and declared with humor, "Well, you sure ain't got what I got."

The way Carson said it had Mamaw looking up quickly to catch Dora's eye, then Lucille's. In that moment the three women shared a knowing look. In a synchronized movement, all heads turned toward Carson with narrowed eyes.

Dora bent closer to her sister. "Carson, are you pregnant?"

"The air's so wet I could drink it," Mamaw said. Pearls of sweat formed on her brow, and her hair was frizzing.

Tropical Storm Lucy was gathering strength as it moved north along the coast. The sea was roaring in anticipation, echoing throughout the island. A heavy humidity hovered over the lowcountry like a pall. They'd all pitched in to prepare for the storm's predicted arrival that evening.

Mamaw took a final look-see around the property to make certain all the flowerpots, garden supplies, cushions, and knickknacks were safely stored indoors.

"We're done here. And we're hot and sweaty," Carson said, her arms above her head to redo her ponytail. "We're going to the beach."

Mamaw was glad to see a little more color in her face this morning. She was wearing a bikini top and yoga pants that hung low off her hips. Looking at her flat belly, Mamaw found it hard to believe a new life was growing in there. Carson refused to discuss her pregnancy, not even with her. After she'd admitted to the truth, she'd stormed off to her room and shut the door. Mamaw had thought she might hear a rap on her bedroom door and that Carson would slip in, like she usually did for a chat. Carson was resolutely silent.

Harper approached in a black Speedo suit and

sarong, and on her head she wore a large floppy hat. She carried beach towels under her arm.

"Want to come?" she asked Mamaw.

"Oh, I don't think so, dear. Not today."

Behind her, Dora carried a large canvas bag. Nate's face bore streaks of white suntan lotion.

"Why don't you come, Mamaw?" Dora asked. "You haven't been to the beach much this summer. It'll be like old times."

"I don't want to leave Lucille alone," Mamaw replied. "Besides, I have a few things I want to get done before the storm. You children go on and have a good time. But Carson"—she pinned her granddaughter with a no-nonsense look—"no going in that ocean, hear? Listen to it roar. That undercurrent is deadly."

Carson only smirked and did not reply. Mamaw knew that good waves in Charleston waters were powerful bait for local surfers. She also knew that as with everything else, Carson would do what Carson wanted to do.

"You, too, Nate," she said, turning to Dora. "Don't you let him in the water."

"Don't worry, Mamaw. We won't."

Mamaw watched the group saunter off, her fingers tapping her thigh. As soon as they disappeared around the hedge, Mamaw checked her watch and hurried back up the stairs into the house. She went directly to the kitchen phone and dialed a number she'd written on a Post-it note. After two rings, a man answered the phone.

"Devlin Cassell."

"Devlin, it's Marietta Muir."

"Mamaw!" The reply rang with warmth.

Mamaw couldn't respond for a moment, taken aback at the shock of Devlin calling her Mamaw.

"Forgive me for being so familiar, Mrs. Muir. Old habits die hard."

"That's quite all right. But perhaps *Mrs. Muir* is better, given the nature of our business."

"Yes, ma'am, Mrs. Muir."

"The girls have gone to the beach. Do you have time now?"

"For you? Of course I do. I'll be right over." He chuckled low in that easy manner she remembered from long ago. "I know the way."

Mamaw opened the door to a broad-shouldered, well-dressed man wearing dark sunglasses. He removed the sunglasses and smiled, and she recognized the astonishing blue eyes.

"Devlin Cassell. I hardly recognized you!"

He was taller and broader than she remembered. His blond hair was trimmed neatly around his head, but still uncontrolled. It gave him a youthful look, even in his sophisticated creased khaki pants and bright blue, expensive polo shirt.

"Mrs. Muir, you haven't changed a bit," he said with a wide grin.

"Please come in." She ushered him inside. "You'll

have to excuse the look of the place at the moment. The girls and I have spent the day turning the house upside down, readying it for the storm!"

Devlin's head moved from left to right as he entered, allowing his gaze to sweep the rooms. She wished the sun were shining. Sea Breeze showed so well with sunlight pouring in through the windows, but with the storm coming, the rooms appeared gloomy. Mamaw had turned the lights on in each room. As they walked through the house, the golden light gave the pine floors an added luster. Devlin paid close attention to the historic details they both knew added value to the house. From time to time he'd stop to jot something in his notebook or make a comment. *You don't see moldings like that every day.* When they stepped out onto the back porch, Devlin paused, put his hands on his hips, and stared out at the vast expanse of the Cove. It was high tide and a silvery mist from the incoming storm hung low over the wetlands, making the scene appear otherworldly.

"This is what they'll come for. The million-dollar view," he said after a while. "Or in this case, multimillion." He released a soft whistle. "I'd forgotten how well situated the house is."

"Yes, well, I believe you had your eyes on Dora at the time."

He caught her eye and chuckled. "I surely did. Still do." He paused, then asked, "Do you mind?"

She was touched that he cared enough about her opinion to ask. "It depends on your sincerity." She tilted her head and clasped her hands, choosing her words carefully. "She's a traditional woman with traditional values. This divorce is hard on her."

"I know that."

Mamaw wrapped her arms around herself, surprised by the drop in temperature.

"I've always found that if a person truly wants to be a part of your life, he will make an effort to do so." She turned toward Devlin, her gaze direct. "We haven't seen hide nor hair of Calhoun Tupper since Dora returned from the hospital. But I believe she's seen quite a bit of you in the past few weeks."

He nodded.

"Have you met Nate?"

"Not yet. I'd like to. But Dora wants to wait."

"She's very protective of that boy. Too protective, perhaps, but she has good reason."

Devlin turned back to face her, his gaze sincere. "I'm trying not to rush her. She told me not to. But," he said in earnest, "I want you to know that my feelings for Dora are true. And they run deep. I won't hurt her. Or Nate. In fact, the one who's likely to get hurt in this deal is me."

Mamaw's smile lit up her face. What a nice, genuine man Devlin had grown up to be.

"Then I think neither of us has anything to be worried about. Let's go inside, shall we? It must've dropped ten degrees just since you arrived and the rain can't be far behind."

They returned to the front of the house. Devlin's

gaze fell on the cottage and he stopped in front of it, studying the quaint house. "May we go in and take a look?"

"Not today. Lucille isn't well and she's resting. I don't want to disturb her. And with the change in the weather, I fear the girls will return momentarily. It's as tidy and tight as a ship."

"And the garage?"

"Dusty and filled with cobwebs and junk, but solid."

"Good. Well, then. I'll go to the office and work up some comps so we can begin talking about the price." His eyes gleamed. "But I can tell you right now, there's nothing else like it on the market right now. With both the historic factor and the killer views . . ."

"So you think it might sell quickly?"

He smiled. "I've got folks on my Rolodex I can call right now who are just waiting for a house like yours to come on the market. Yes, Mrs. Muir. I think it could sell very quickly."

Mamaw was filled with relief and sudden gratitude toward him. She looked over to the cottage, imagined Lucille lying in there. Mamaw planned to call a few doctors and see whether there were some procedures that could be done. With money in hand, she could fight the cancer.

"I'm so pleased."

"When would you like to put it on the market?"

"As soon as possible."

Devlin's brows shot up. "Really? I thought Dora said you were going to wait until the fall."

"That was my original thinking. But some recent developments have changed my mind. Though I do not want to leave Sea Breeze until the summer's end."

"Yes, ma'am. I reckon I have my marching orders. I'll get back to you as soon as possible." He turned and walked to his car. It was a large German automobile, black, polished, and expensive-looking. He bent to open his car door, then stopped and looked toward the street.

Mamaw heard the voices as well and felt her stomach drop. She'd hoped they'd finish their business before the girls returned home. Thunder rumbled and a gust of wind sent dry sand swirling in the air. Dora and Nate appeared, walking between the tall hedges that bordered the property. Dora was talking to Nate but stopped short when she saw Devlin. Harper soon followed, then Carson, who smiled and waved when she saw Devlin.

"Well, hey, Dev!" Carson called out, coming to Devlin's side. "I was wondering when you'd show up. How are you?"

"Good. Real good," he replied genially, and glanced worriedly at Dora.

Dora said nothing. She stood silently beside Nate.

"My, don't you look handsome, all dressed up," Carson teased. "Are you here to whisk our girl out to dinner?" She looked over her shoulder at Dora and gave her a questioning look.

"I, uh . . ." Devlin hesitated and glanced at Mamaw for guidance.

Mamaw stepped forward. "I asked Devlin to come. He's here to give me an estimate on the house's value."

Carson looked stricken. "You're putting the house on the market *now*?"

"I'm just getting some information, so let's not fuss. Let the poor man get home before the storm hits."

"Devlin, wait," Dora said, coming closer to him. "Since you're here, I'd like you to meet my son." She waved Nate closer. "Nate, come meet my good friend Mr. Cassell."

Devlin's eyes widened along with his smile. "Hey there, Nate. I'm glad to meet you at last. Your mama told me all about you. In fact, she can't stop talking about you." He held out his hand.

Dora cringed inwardly, knowing Nate would not shake it.

"Hi," said Nate, looking away at the house.

To Devlin's credit, he let his hand move to his hips without offense. "I hope you'll come out on my boat sometime. I know spots where there are lots of dolphins and where they do that strand feeding. Do you know what that is?"

Nate shook his head.

"Then I'll show you. Your mama tells me you like dolphins."

Nate glanced at the man, nodded abruptly, then turned to Dora. "Can I go inside now? I'm cold."

"I'll take him in," Harper said. "Hi, Devlin," she added in passing.

"See you, Dev," said Carson with a short wave, following Harper. "You'd better hurry. The sky looks ready to rip."

Mamaw offered her hand. "I'll be looking forward to your report," she said, and without further word turned and hurried up the stairs.

Dora waited until the others went indoors. Lightning flashed across the sky and by the time the front door was closed, a ripping crack of thunder rent the air. Dora stepped closer to Devlin and he wrapped his arms around her, tugging her against him. Looking up with a coy smile, she surprised him with a long, slow kiss.

"What did I do to deserve that?" he asked lazily, not ready to stop.

"You were kind to my son. And I missed you."

"I'm *here*," Devlin said. Then, locking her gaze in his, he said, "Every day and every night. And I'm not going anywhere."

Chapter Twenty-One

That evening, as predicted by the forecasters, Tropical Storm Lucy whistled and rattled the windows. Rain pounded the roof. But inside Sea Breeze, the lamps were glowing cheerfully. The women decided to mock the storm by having an indoor picnic. They moved the living room furniture, laid out blankets on the floor, and pulled out food from the refrigerator.

Mamaw sat back in her chair and listened to her granddaughters chatting like magpies as they stretched out on the blankets. When they got together, it was almost as if she were invisible. It was a revelation to hear their stories of their worst dates, fad diets they'd tried, fashions they adored, and favorite memories of their days as children at Sea Breeze. As the evening drew on, the stories became more serious. Occasionally she'd spy Harper jotting down notes on her ever-present computer.

While they talked they feasted on cold chicken and shrimp, savory crackers and assorted cheeses, pickles and olives, ripe avocados, and as much ice cream as they could eat. Mamaw feared the electricity would go out and it would all melt.

At nine o'clock the storm ratcheted up a notch. The wind started screaming like a banshee and rain hit the windows horizontally. Suddenly the lights flickered, then everything went black. Mamaw clutched Lucille's hand beside her, heard the girls suck in a collective breath and Nate's shriek.

Carson reached for the flashlight she had at her side. With a flick, the long beam of light immediately restored calm to the room. "No need to worry," she called out. "There are candles and matches on the table."

Soon the room was alive with dancing light on the walls and ceiling.

"It's like camping." Dora turned to Nate. He was sitting rigid, knees close to his cheeks and eyes wide. She smiled encouragingly. "Isn't it?"

He didn't reply but scooted closer to her.

"The storm's getting pretty strong," Harper said. She looked at the windows with a worried frown. "Are you sure it's not a hurricane?"

"No, child, that ain't no hurricane," Lucille said with a light, cackling laugh. "If it were, you'd know it. This whole house would be rattling, not just the windows. And we wouldn't be sitting here. We'd be off this island waitin' it out somewhere north. After Hugo,

I won't stay on the island for no hurricane. Uh-uh," she said with a shake of her head. "So don't you worry none. This be just a good summer storm."

Suddenly the lights were back on.

There was a gasp of surprised delight.

"See?" Lucille said with a smug smile. "What'd I tell you? Just the summer wind."

Mamaw had an idea that she hoped might distract everyone from the worsening weather. She went to the stereo and searched her CD collection. Her fingers ran along the cases until she found Frank Sinatra. Pulling the CD out, she put it in the stereo and pushed play. There was a click and whirr, then the velvet voice of Frank Sinatra sang out.

The summer wind came blowin' in from across the sea.

"Edward and I used to dance to this during storms," Mamaw said, remembering with wistfulness to her tone.

"I remember," Carson said, rising to her feet. "At the big house on East Bay. Once, I hid on the stairs and watched you." She held out her arms. "Mamaw, dance with me."

Mamaw took Carson's outstretched hand. "I'd love to," she said, then laughed lightly as Carson led her in the dance. They were both tall and glided gracefully across the floor.

Dora stood and held out her hands to Nate. "Come on, Nate. You're the man of the house. You have to dance with the ladies."

To everyone's surprise, Nate stood up. They all cheered him on as he took his mother's hands and began to dance a clumsy two-step.

"I don't think she'll ever forget this dance," Carson whispered to Mamaw.

"Nor shall I."

"I love you, Mamaw."

"I know you do. I love you, too. My love is unconditional. You know that, don't you?"

Tears sprang to Carson's eyes and she nodded, tightening her lips.

Harper sprang to her feet. "Come on, Lucille. We can't be left out!"

Harper helped Lucille to her feet and as she took her hands, they began to dance, slow and easy.

Mamaw felt aglow as she looked around the candlelit room to see everyone dancing. No one was running out the door, catching a plane, or sulking in her room. Here they all were, her summer girls, together as she'd always hoped they would be. She said a prayer of thanks for this midsummer storm that had brought them all together for this special night.

They played the song again and switched partners, dancing once more to the heavy beat. Nate wouldn't dance with anyone except Dora, so this time Carson danced with Harper. Mamaw took Lucille's hand and led her in a gentle weaving back and forth, humming the tune.

Suddenly Lucille gasped and bent over in pain.

Everyone froze.

Mamaw clutched Lucille's arms and held on tight as she fired off orders. "Carson! Help me get her to the sofa. Dora, her pills are in my bathroom. Run and get them. Harper, fetch a glass of water."

The girls sprang to action. Within minutes, Lucille was resting on the sofa with Mamaw's arm still around her shoulder. Carson, Dora, and Harper clustered around them, unsure and anxious. Nate sat quietly on the blanket.

"This isn't the flu." Carson looked to Mamaw for confirmation.

Mamaw shook her head. "It's not for me to say." She looked to Lucille.

There was a silence in the room, save for the howling wind outside the windows. Lucille slowly brought her eyes up to look at Carson. Then she turned to look at Harper and Dora. The pain had subsided some, and though she still gripped her abdomen, her face appeared serene.

"Now don't look so worried," Lucille said, her voice weak. "What's happening is as natural as the wind blowing outside those windows. I'm sick, is all."

"What kind of sick?" Dora asked.

Lucille sighed with resignation. "Cancer."

There was a shocked silence, then Carson went to her knees and laid her head on Lucille's lap. "Oh, Lucille."

"What kind of cancer?" Harper wanted to know.

The girls all jumped in after that, with an outpouring of follow-up questions, suggestions, and recommendations of the top medical centers Lucille could go to for treatment.

"Stop all this jabbering," Lucille said, putting her hands up. "I've gone through all this with your grandmother and I don't have the energy to go through it again. I made up my mind, hear?" she said firmly, silencing them all. "I lived my life with dignity. I intend to die with dignity."

"I know how hard it is to accept," Mamaw told the girls. "But Lucille's made her decision. It's up to us now to make sure she's as comfortable as possible."

"Now I hate to break up the party," Lucille said, "but I'm tired and need to go to bed. Gimme your hand, girl," she said to Carson. "Help an old woman up."

Mamaw and Carson each took an arm and helped Lucille slowly to her feet. She grunted softly and grimaced, the pain obvious. Dora and Harper grasped each other's hand for support.

"Take her to my room," Mamaw said.

"What? No, no. I want to lie in my own bed," Lucille said.

"Later, when the storm subsides. For now, just rest awhile in my bed."

Despite Lucille's complaints, she settled in Mamaw's big four-poster bed. Dora and Harper fluffed up pillows behind her.

"Go on back to your party." Lucille waved her hand dismissively. "This ain't no death watch. I'm just tired. Go on with you." She added, "My precious girls."

Carson, Harper, and Dora took turns kissing Lucille

good night, reluctantly leaving the room. Mamaw ushered them out the door. "She'll be all right. She needs her rest. I'm going to bed, too. We'll see you in the morning. Mind you blow out the candles before you retire."

She closed the bedroom door with a sigh of relief. What a night it had been. She felt exhausted by the whole of it. She quickly changed into her nightgown and brushed her teeth, listening to the storm still pounding the rooftop like a drum. Turning off the light, she entered her bedroom, lit only by the eerie blue light of her night-light.

"I can go to my own bed now," Lucille said, flipping off the blanket.

"Oh, no, you don't," Mamaw said, hurrying to Lucille's side and smoothing the blanket back over her chest. "It's gale winds out there, as bad as we've had in a long spell. I don't want you alone out there in that cottage. You just settle in, my friend, because you're sleeping in this house till it's over."

"But there's no extra bed!"

"That's why you're going to sleep here."

"Where will you sleep?"

"Right next to you."

"I can't . . ."

"Don't fuss at me. I'm too tired to argue. I doubt either of us will get much sleep anyway, with that wind howling like that and the rain beating against the roof."

Lucille looked to the window. "It's raining like the Lord's flood."

"I hope Harper's poor little plants survive. She

worked so hard . . ." Mamaw sighed as she climbed into the bed beside Lucille. She tried to move slowly so as not to jiggle the mattress. Lucille had told her the pain was worsening and it weighed heavily on Mamaw's mind. Mamaw knew it was only a short while before she'd have to call hospice.

Mamaw lay on her back and brought the blanket up to her chin. Glancing over, she saw Lucille beside her, propped up by pillows, lying absolutely still as though afraid to move.

"This is a first," Mamaw said with a giggle.

Lucille chuckled softly. "One for the books."

Mamaw giggled. She certainly couldn't imagine lying in the same bed with her maid fifty years ago. "We've lived a lot of years, my friend. Gone through many changes."

"Maybe not as many as just this summer."

Mamaw laughed a tired laugh.

Lucille smacked her lips.

"Want a glass of water?" Mamaw asked.

"No. This medicine makes my mouth dry, is all."

"Some ice, then? You could chew it."

"I'm fine."

They lay in silence, listening to the storm.

"I'm glad you told them. They needed to know. To prepare."

"I expect so."

"They love you very much."

"I know that." Lucille turned her head toward her. "It's a comfort."

"I'm going to miss you," Mamaw said in a broken voice.

"I know that, too," Lucille said. "But I'll be watching over you, same as always."

"It won't be the same. Who will give me what-for after you're gone? You're the only one who keeps me in line."

Lucille laughed lightly in the dark. "Oh, I 'spect them girls will carry on."

Mamaw sighed. "I expect you're right."

Mamaw and Lucille could hear the sounds of the three women talking in the living room.

"I worry about them," Mamaw said softly.

"Mmm-hmm."

"Harper seems so alone. She carries such a burden of expectations from her family. Her mother . . . How will she ever find what *she* wants to do? Or find a husband who can measure up to the James standards?"

"You worry about *Harper*?" Lucille huffed. "Why, she's the one I'm *least* worried about."

"Why do you say that?"

"First off, she's the youngest. Only twenty-eight. What cause have you to worry if she finds herself a fella or not? She's got plenty of time."

"In my time, most young women were married by twenty- eight," Mamaw said primly.

"Well, that time is long, long gone. Second, she's rich as Croesus. Or her mama is. That child don't need to find no husband or no job to live. And live proud." She jerked her chin, emphasizing that point. "I never got married on account I never wanted no man to tell me what to do. I like living on my own. Who's to say Harper don't feel the same way?" A grin eased across Lucille's face. "If I had money like Harper. Lord . . ." She rolled her eyes and grinned.

"What would you do?" Mamaw said, curious.

"What wouldn't I do?"

The women laughed together in the manner of old friends, comfortable in the bond of their decades-long friendship.

"You don't need to worry about our Dora, neither," Lucille added.

"Don't I? She still has so many decisions to make. The divorce isn't final . . . if there's even going to be a divorce."

"Oh, there'll be a divorce."

"What do you know?" Mamaw asked.

"Can't say. Just that it ain't Calhoun Tupper she's dreaming of no more."

Mamaw half smiled, having come to the same conclusion.

"It's that other one I lose sleep over." Lucille wagged her head.

"Carson . . ."

"What we gonna do with that girl?"

"I don't know," Mamaw confessed. She was very afraid for Carson.

"I thought we got her on the road to mend. Now this baby. What's become of her young man? I ain't seen him come by in a while."

"Blake? I heard she's broken it off."

"Lord have mercy. She runnin' from another one?"

Mamaw sighed. "She needs us now more than ever."

"She needs you," Lucille amended. "I'm not going to be here."

"Don't say that! Of course you will."

Lucille didn't reply.

"Thank heavens she stopped drinking," Mamaw mused. "To think if she'd been drinking when she conceived that baby. It's a small miracle. Poor girl has her father's curse and I'm proud of how hard she's trying. But she can't drink a drop while she's carrying."

"Is she even gonna have the baby?" Lucille asked.

"Of course she'll have it."

"Best to just wait and see what happens." She gave Mamaw a long look. "No meddlin'."

"I have a right to worry."

"Worry, yes. Meddle, no."

"Stop giving me the eye, you old banty hen."

Lucille just cackled a laugh in response.

"We raise our girls to grow up to be strong and independent women," Mamaw said in a more serious tone. "And they are. But Lord, I'm embarrassed to admit I still think of them as my little girls. I want to see them all settled. Married. Am I too old-fashioned? The girls think I am . . ."

"You and me, we're from another era. Things are different now. These girls want more, expect more, even demand more. Who's to say being married is the answer? Look at Dora! She done everything right.

Got married at a tender age to a respectable man in that fancy wedding you and Mr. Edward paid for. She moved into a big house, had a child. Marched to the tune y'all been singing since she was born. And now what?"

Mamaw was silent.

"I'll tell you what," Lucille said. "Our girl Dora's pickin' herself off the floor, straightenin' her shoulders, and startin' anew. She's settin' a good example for her younger sisters. I'm so proud of her my buttons are poppin' off my chest."

Mamaw reached out and grasped Lucille's hand. "Thank you, Lucille. I needed to hear that. See? That's what I mean," she said with a sniff. "You're my best friend. What am I going to do without you?"

"You gonna get older and wiser. That's the way of things." She paused. "We had fun tonight, didn't we?"

"We did," Mamaw said with a whisper of a smile.

"That summer wind was blowin' but we danced. You needs to remember tonight, Marietta. When the hard times come, just dance."

Chapter Twenty-Two

Dora sat cross-legged beside Harper on the four-poster brass bed. The storm and the late hour had brought a chill and dampness, and they were wrapped in blankets. She let her gaze wander over the changes in her bedroom—the petal-pink-and-white wallpaper, the brass-and-mirrored vanity, the Aubusson rug. The physical changes of the room reflected Dora's taste and were an outward sign of the changes that had taken place within herself this summer.

And for her sisters, as well. Harper's room was more serene and classic. Carson's was lowcountry, more shabby chic. In giving them rooms of their own, Mamaw had offered each granddaughter a safe haven at Sea Breeze from the storms they each faced.

Dora looked up to see Carson standing at the window, her arms crossed like a shield in front of her, looking out at the fronds of the palm trees shaking in the wind. The relentless roar of the surf echoed, and Dora wondered at the changes she'd see on the beach in the morning.

"Carson, come join us," Dora called.

Carson came to join her sisters on the bed. Harper scooted closer and tugged at the blanket around her shoulders to place part of it over Carson.

"This is nice, all of us huddled together, talking," Dora said.

"Like old times," Harper agreed.

"But it won't always be like this, will it?" Carson asked, her tone depressed. "The thought of losing Sea Breeze is hard enough. But now Lucille?" She shook her head. "Unbearable."

"But that doesn't mean we can't still be together," Dora said. "Somewhere."

"Doesn't it?" Carson asked.

"That depends on us," Harper answered. "All those years Sea Breeze sat here and none of us came. We have to decide to make the effort."

"Yeah, well, let's remember it was Mamaw who brought us back," Carson said. "What happens when she is gone? When Sea Breeze is gone?"

"Don't be morbid," Dora said.

"I'm not. I'm just facing reality. I can't help but worry now about what's going to happen to her. She's eighty. What's she going to do without Lucille?" Carson asked. "Especially when we all leave?"

Carson looked at the streaks against the window and thought it looked as though even the house was crying.

"That's *why* Mamaw brought us back," Dora said. "She knew this day was coming and she wanted us to be close again, as sisters should."

"Even if her methods were a little Machiavellian." Harper smiled wryly.

"I feel," Carson said, her voice low and trembling, "like everything I love is slipping through my fingers."

"This place has always been the touchstone for all of us," Dora said, aware of her role as the older sister. "We're all feeling shaken. I admit, even though Mamaw talked about selling Sea Breeze, it just never felt real. Until today when I saw Devlin come by for an appraisal. I don't know about y'all, but that brought it home for me. Mamaw's not fooling around. She's going to sell this house and we won't have Sea Breeze to come back to any longer." She looked at Harper and Carson. "So what are we going to do after Sea Breeze is sold? Are we going to stay in touch?"

"Yes," Harper readily agreed. "Though, I don't know where I'll be or what I'll be doing. I've got a month to figure out where I'll be going from here."

"Aren't you going back to New York?" asked Dora.

"Maybe. But definitely not to live with my mother." She shook her head, then tucked a copper-colored shank of hair away from her face. "I couldn't go back to that. I've thought about going to England," Harper added. "Even if for a visit. Just to sniff around a bit, see how I feel. I'd like to visit Granny James for a while. I thought I'd be nervous and scrambling around, handing in my resume to a zillion companies. But I'm not.

I'm not in a hurry." Harper tucked the blanket closer. "I know this sounds a bit out there, but I feel like something's going to happen to make everything clear."

"Like what?" Dora asked, intrigued.

"I don't know," Harper said with a small smile. "I'm not just sitting around," she hastened to add. "I'm looking at my options. Lining up a few things. But, I'm also kind of . . . waiting."

"Waiting?" Dora asked dubiously. "That sounds so not like you."

Harper shrugged and looked a bit embarrassed. "I'll know when it happens. But wherever I end up, I promise I'll stay in touch."

"That's the big question for all of us, isn't it? It's like we're on some ship waiting to dock. I'm not sure where I'll end up either," Dora said. She made a face. "By the end of summer I'll be in the midst of a divorce. *And* selling my house." She put her hands together in supplication. "Please, God, let someone buy it." She lowered her hands and began counting off her fingers. "*And* I have to find a new place to live. A job. A new school for Nate." Dora blew out a plume of air with a soft whistle. "I've got more on my plate than I can eat, that's for sure."

"You've got Devlin in the wings," Harper reminded her.

"Dev . . . He's a good ol' boy with one eye always on the tides. It's what I like most about him. He's laid-back where I'm uptight. But he's also smart, successful. He keeps me grounded. And Lord, he knows how to push my buttons in a good way." She smiled with a little embarrassment. Dora looked at the empty space on her ring finger. The bruising was gone but the skin remained pale where the ring once lay.

"I've made a decision. A big one." She looked up to see Carson and Harper staring at her. "I'm going forward with my divorce. I can't go back to Cal. I feel sad," she admitted. "It's hard to break up a family. Except, we weren't much of a family, and I know I can't live like that anymore. I know we'll both be happier apart than we were together."

"I'm glad you made the decision." Harper reached out to place a hand on her shoulder. "I know it wasn't easy."

Carson looked sideways at Dora. "Is it because of Devlin?"

Dora's cheeks colored. "For sure, my feelings for Dev helped me make the decision. But he wasn't the deciding factor. Cal had already left the marriage, don't forget. We were on the way to a nasty divorce when I had that attack. Sister mine, if I learned one thing this summer, it's that I'm not going back to a loveless marriage. It's not enough for me."

Carson tilted her head and studied Dora as a smile eased across her face. "Good for you."

"But I'm not looking to hitch my star on any man right now, either," Dora continued. "I think I want to be an unmarried woman for a while." She glanced up. "This summer is *my* time. I used to think that was selfish, just focusing on my needs and what I wanted. I've spent my entire life thinking about other people's needs—trying to make them happy, seeking approval. I'm heading on forty. It's high time I start thinking about how I want to spend the next forty years of my life." She sat straighter and the blanket slid from her shoulder. "You know, I've never lived on my own before."

Harper shook her head in disbelief. "Never?"

"Nope," Dora replied, yanking the blanket back over her shoulder. "I went straight from my mother's house to Cal's house." She waved her hand. "Not counting college, of course. But I lived on campus with a slew of roommates. That doesn't count." She sighed. "I've always lived where I was told to. I never rented my own apartment. I'm kind of looking forward to it."

"Where?" asked Carson.

Dora considered this. "I won't go as far as New York or England, that's for sure," she added with a quick smile toward Harper.

Devlin's face flashed in her mind, their times out on the boat together, cooking crabs, drinking beer, watching sunsets. She thought of the exhilaration she felt running on the beach, watching the changing tides, collecting shells with Nate.

"I'll stay in South Carolina, definitely. I want a small house, with a tiny bit of land I can garden that needs little to no maintenance. I see now how I isolated myself. And ate to compensate for the void I was feeling. This time, I'm going to reconnect with old friends, make some new ones, rejoin my community. I think I'll stay right here in the lowcountry. I love it here," she admitted with heart. "Nate does, too." Her son's smiling face came to mind. "He's better when he's near the sea." She took a breath and looked at Carson and Harper.

"Wherever I end up, I'll keep in touch. I promise. I'm going to need my sisters to get through this."

Dora and Harper turned to look at Carson.

"What about you, Carson?" Harper prodded.

Carson only looked down and offered a noncommittal shrug.

"Are you okay?" asked Dora.

"No. I'm not okay," she fired back, almost as a challenge. "I'm pretty far from okay." She looked at her sisters, her eyes flashing. "You both have support systems in place, imperfect as they might be. You have families who've got your back. For me, it's only Lucille and Mamaw. This house. And now that's all being blown away like the sand out there in the wind. Predicting what I'll be doing in the fall feels damn impossible. Forgive me if I can't get past next week."

Dora reached over to put her hand on Carson's shoulder. "You have us, too. Me and Harper are right here. Oh, honey, we know this is a tough time for you. But we'll be here for you all the way. Hey, you can come live with me," she said with a nudge of encouragement. "It won't be fancy, but I'll help you take care of that baby."

Carson recoiled from Dora's hand. "Baby? I'm not having a baby."

Dora looked confused. "But I thought . . ."

Carson went rigid and her voice turned cold. "You thought wrong."

Understanding flooded Dora's features. "You're considering an abortion?"

"Of course I am," Carson said, clenching her fists under the blanket. "I'm unmarried, without a job, without a place to live . . ."

"Carson," Dora said, leaning forward and slipping off her blanket. "What about Blake?"

Carson's voice trembled with raw emotion. "Don't go there."

"Carson, I—"

"Dora," Harper said in a warning tone. "Can't you see she's struggling? This isn't your decision. Let it go."

Dora stared at Harper, letting her words penetrate. *Let it go*. Letting things go without a fight was what she'd been trying to do all summer. But this was so important. She had things she should say to stop Carson from making a decision she might live to regret. Like how hard it was for her to conceive Nate. How she'd suffered one miscarriage after another, staying in bed for months at a time and gaining fifty pounds in the process. How Carson should keep the baby.

Dora looked at Carson, sitting straight, bowed up for a fight, tears flashing in those blue Muir eyes. Then it hit her. She thought of her mother and how she always had a *should* at the ready at moments like this to keep her daughter in line. Dora didn't want to tell Carson what she *should* do. That hadn't worked out well between them in the past.

Dora wanted a relationship with her sister, one based on love and trust. She thought again of all the phone calls they'd shared while Carson was in Florida and how they'd talked about everything and nothing. Dora wanted her sister to pick up the phone and call her after they left Sea Breeze.

Dora pressed her fingers to her eyelids. Harper was right. Her opinions were not what her sister needed to hear now. Dora's life might be a shit storm at the moment, but she was beginning to see the light breaking through the clouds. That's what Carson needed now. Just a sliver of luminosity to give her hope.

Dora looked at Carson and spoke in a calm voice without contention. "A few months ago, I might have told you what I thought you should do." She laughed in a self-deprecating manner. "I wouldn't have been shy to tell you my opinions, either."

"I think I can guess what you'd say," Carson said flatly.

"Probably. Those are *my* opinions," Dora said honestly. "We're so different. We share the same father, but we haven't had the same upbringing, the same religious beliefs, culture, lifestyle. The list goes on and on."

"Even if we grew up in the same house," said Harper, "we'd all be different."

"Well, yeah," Dora conceded. "Honey, I'm stuck in my own mud pile right now. I don't need to be flinging any of it around. I'm the last person who should give you advice."

She stopped when she saw the stunned expressions

on Carson's and Harper's faces. It was slightly irritating, but gratifying at the same time—their shock confirmed for Dora that she had done the right thing.

"What I'm trying to say," Dora pressed on, needing to get the words out, "is I don't really know what you're going through. When I got pregnant I didn't have to make a choice. I was married. I wanted a baby. And yet I still had problems."

Carson's face lost its belligerence, and Dora saw that she was listening.

"I had miscarriage after miscarriage. Each one broke my heart. I wanted a baby so badly and I just couldn't carry one. I felt I'd failed. And then I had Nate. My sweet, darling boy."

Tears came to her eyes, and Dora wiped them away. She didn't want to be emotional now, just honest.

"Being a mother is hard." She took a long breath and exhaled. "Okay, I'm just going to say this. I've never said it before, at least not aloud." She clenched the blanket tighter around her shoulders. "I was brokenhearted when I got Nate's diagnosis of autism. At the beginning I didn't know how bad it was going to be, if he'd learn to speak, to communicate at all, even go to the bathroom. I was told I was being selfish, that I had to think about my child and not myself. I tried. I really did." Dora swallowed hard, feeling the old emotions well up.

"But deep inside I grieved over the loss of the child I'd planned on having. The perfect child . . ." She shook her head. "I know that sounds awful. That's why I could never talk to anyone about those feelings. Not even Cal." She snorted. "Especially not Cal."

Dora looked up to gauge her sisters' reactions, sensitive to criticism or judgment in their eyes. Not finding any, she continued. "I've been on a long journey since then. I know now there is no such thing as a perfect child. I love Nate for who he is, just the way he is. I may have to teach him about emotional cues, but he's had to teach me, too. Sure, I know it will always hurt when I visit my son at school and find him eating alone, or when he's not invited to a birthday party. Or when I can't take away his anguish when he's trapped in the throes of a tantrum. But any mother feels this when she can't make life perfect for her child." She smiled tremulously and shrugged. "It's not easy being a mother. But this is the part I want you to know. I'll be thankful every day because I thought I'd never be able to have a child and now I have this amazing gift."

Dora searched Carson's face and saw the vulnerability in her eyes. She knew there was so much more she could say. She felt the words aching in her chest. But Carson was too fragile. Dora needed to tread softly.

"It's not going to be easy, no matter what you decide. In either case, your life will never be the same." She reached out and put her hand on Carson's shoulder. "You're my sister and I love you. Whatever you decide, I'll be here for you."

Carson leaned forward and slipped her arms around Dora.

"Thank you," Carson said, with a tremulous whisper.

"I'm here, too," Harper said, wrapping her slender arms around both her sisters.

Carson lay on her side, her hands tucked under her head and her eyes wide open. She'd been lying in bed, listening to the storm slowly dissipate as it moved off island. Outside the house, as well as inside, a temporary peace had been restored. She saw the first faint gray light of dawn through the slats of the shutters. She heard the dawn song of the birds in the surrounding trees, vigorously heralding the new day.

The dawn had always called to Carson. She rose from her bed and slipped a silk kimono over her underwear. Tying it at the waist, she walked out into the hallway, careful not to awaken her two sisters sleeping side by side on Dora's bed. She'd heard them talking into the wee hours of the morning.

She opened the front door, cringing when it creaked loudly in the silence. Stepping outdoors, she was met immediately with the moist sweetness in the air that always followed summer storms. Raindrops lay heavy on the leaves of the oak tree, along the bark, and in puddles on the ground. A pearly mist hung over the island, and as she walked down the stairs she felt as though she were entering another world.

A noise caught her attention and she followed the sound, turning her head toward the cottage. She saw Lucille in her robe and slippers slowly climbing the stairs up to her front porch. Carson hurried across the cold gravel to Lucille's side.

"Let me help you up the stairs," she said, taking hold of Lucille's arm. The old woman's bones felt as light and hollow as a bird's. They reached the porch and paused while Lucille caught her breath. Carson couldn't remember ever seeing Lucille so winded and it scared her.

"I want to lie in my own bed," Lucille told her.

"Of course. I'll open the door for you and turn on a light. We don't want you falling in the dark."

"I could walk through my house with my eyes closed," Lucille muttered, but she waited while Carson turned on the lights, then held open the door for her.

Carson followed Lucille into the cottage. All was as neat as a pin. The walls were painted stark white but the artwork covering the walls was alive with the vivid colors of popular African-American artists of Charleston. Everywhere she looked she saw signs of Lucille's personality and handiwork—the sweetgrass baskets, the embroidered pillows, the knitted throw. It was easy to see that Lucille loved her cottage and was happy here.

Stepping into Lucille's bedroom, however, Carson caught the stale scent of illness and medicine. She helped Lucille out of her robe and into the black iron bed. Lucille had shrunk in size, and her robustness had disappeared along with the pounds. She looked like a child with her dark eyes wide in her face, her gray hair frizzled around her head like a halo, engulfed in the brightly colored crazy quilt. Carson let her gaze flutter around the room, capturing Lucille's robe lying across the small lady's parlor chair, the large bouquet of summer flowers, and the bedside table filled with medicine bottles.

"There, that's better," Lucille muttered. "I like lying in my own bed. Under my own roof." She blinked heavily several times, seemingly exhausted. Then her gaze sought out Carson, and finding her, Lucille smiled weakly and patted the mattress. "Come closer, child."

Carson came to sit on the edge of the mattress, careful not to jostle Lucille. It was heart-wrenching to see Lucille so weak and frail. For her, Lucille had always been the strong, opinionated, unwavering pillar of support. This woman had raised her. She'd been a mother to her every bit as much as her grandmother had. Carson held her breath, trying in vain to stop the tears.

"Why you crying?" Lucille asked.

Carson sniffed and shook her head. "I don't know," she blurted.

"Must be something, 'cause you hardly never cry. Tell me."

Carson didn't want to tell her she was crying because she couldn't bear to see her so weak, so sick. How she couldn't imagine life without her. So instead she told her of the other source of her tears, knowing Lucille was probably the one person who would listen and not judge her.

"I feel so lost. And scared."

"About that life you got growing inside of you?"

Carson took a deep breath and nodded. "I don't know what to do."

"You don't have to do anything."

Carson couldn't look at her. "I think I do."

"I see." Lucille went quiet.

"You don't think I'm a terrible person?"

Lucille snorted and shook her head. "You're in trouble. And you're scared. I can see that."

"I'm thinking of going away."

"'Course you are."

Carson frowned and looked up. "Why do you say that?"

"'Cause whenever trouble comes, you run away."

"No, I don't!"

Lucille patted her hand, her thick knuckles and stubby nails beautiful to Carson. "Yes, child, you do. Always have. I've known you since you were born. When someone gets too close, you cut loose. Carson, you can't ever outrun the kind of fear you got bottled up inside. You think if you don't let anything or anyone get too close you won't get hurt again, like you were when your mama died, or when your daddy took you away from us to go to California. I never thought your mamaw should've let that happen. You cried then like you're crying now." She sighed heavily. "And now, you're upset I'm gonna leave you, too. Now, don't deny it," she said, waving her hand against Carson's open mouth. "The plain truth is, I *am* going to die and there's nothing you can do and it scares you. I see it in your eyes. And you're afraid your mamaw's gonna die, too. Well, child, one day she is!"

"No," Carson cried, her shoulders shaking as the tears gushed. She lowered her head to Lucille's shoulder as she did when she was a little girl. "Don't leave me. I don't want you to go."

Lucille patted her hand as Carson released the pent-up tears that she'd held at bay for too long. Tears of sorrow for Lucille's illness, for the pregnancy, for her breakup with Blake, for her guilt over Delphine, for all the sorrows she knew were as yet coming.

When she finished Carson pulled herself back up and reached for a tissue.

"Feel better?"

Carson shrugged. "I feel drained."

"A good cry is like letting loose the steam from a pipe. Gotta do it before it bursts."

Carson blew her nose. "I'm crying a lot lately."

"Hormones."

"Oh, God . . ." Carson said with a long sigh.

"You and I, we're both participating in the cycle of life. The beginning and the end. I find that kind of reassuring, don't you?"

Carson looked out the window.

"We all enter and leave this world alone." Lucille tapped Carson's hand, drawing back her attention. "But it's sharing our lives with others what makes life worth living. And makes the leaving easier. When your time comes, you know you're leaving a part of yourself behind, with them."

Lucille moved to sit higher up against the pillows. Her face scrunched up in pain with the effort while Carson fluffed up the pillows. Once she settled back, Lucille looked again at Carson, her dark eyes piercing. "What's really ailing you, child?"

Carson lowered her head. Her confusion and despair were like a black hole, sucking the light from her life. She squeezed her wildly swinging emotions into three tiny words: "I am afraid." She hastily wiped her eyes. "You're right. I don't like being afraid. I feel frozen, like I did back when I was floating in the ocean staring into the deadly eyes of the shark. I couldn't move. That's how I feel now. My mind can't make a decision."

Lucille made a face and scoffed at the notion. "But you got away! You made it to shore. See? That's what I'm talkin' about. Girl, you got good instincts. I used to watch when you went out in that ocean riding them waves and wonder what that must feel like."

"I didn't know you watched me surf."

"Well, I did. Your mamaw and I both did. You know how to move your feet and your legs, when to move a bit to the left or right, how to ride that wave back to shore." She released a gentle laugh. "You might look like a natural out there, but I know how you got up early and went out there day after day, no matter what the weather. After all them years, your body just knows what to do. And *now* you're doubting yourself? Girl, get out of your head! We might all be cheering you on from the beach, but it's like I was saying. You're alone out there on the water. You got to trust your instincts to take you where you're supposed to go."

"This isn't the ocean. This is life. It's different."

"No it ain't." Lucille gave her a no-nonsense look, her beautiful, intelligent eyes radiating faith and encouragement. "Carson, honey, life is like that ocean out there. It's deep and bountiful, and the waves just keep on comin'. Sometimes the waves get choppy, sometimes they smooth. You just got to ride them, Carson, same as you always done."

Lucille's smile fell as her voice weakened. "Whatever you decide, don't be afraid. I don't never want to hear you say those words again. You hear?"

Carson nodded.

"You've got good instincts. Listen to them. You'll know what to do." Her eyelids lowered and she patted Carson's hand a final time. "Now I'm tired. Didn't sleep a wink in your mamaw's bed. Go on and let me rest, eh? Just a little while."

Carson bent to kiss Lucille's cheek. She smelled of vanilla.

"Sweet dreams, Lucille," she whispered.

Carson stepped outside the cottage and closed the door quietly behind her. She stood on the edge of the porch and raised her face to the warmth of the morning sun. The fog had lifted, though a soft rain still fell. The shrubs, flowers, and grasses were no longer bent over by the pounding rain and struggled to stand taller, shaking off the drops. Bits of leaves and debris lay scattered across the gravel, remnants of the storm. Looking up, she saw the ball of sun pushing rays of golden color through the dispersing clouds. Behind them, soft hues of rose and blue already were stretching across the morning sky.

Overhead, the calls of the birds grew increasingly strident, and beyond, she heard the roar of the ocean. As always, she followed its call. Carson walked across the gravel toward the beach, eyes on the sky.

Chapter Twenty-Three

Mamaw awoke slowly. She pried open an eye, yawned, then gathered her wits after the long, trembling night. Suddenly remembering, Mamaw turned to look at the pillow beside her.

Lucille was gone.

Of course she was, she thought with a weary sigh. Lucille no doubt sneaked out at the first sign of the storm's abatement. She did love her own bed.

The sliding door to her former sitting room, Harper's room now, was open. Supporting herself on one elbow, Mamaw craned her neck and peeked in. She saw that the bed had not been slept in. She'd heard the girls chatting like magpies in the other room until she'd fallen asleep. She wondered how late they'd stayed up. She hoped it had been one of those all-night bonding experiences that would stay with them long after the summer had passed, keeping them close despite the distance between them.

The house was silent. Mamaw slipped into her pink silk robe and slippers, then went into her bathroom and took her time with her toiletries, washing her face and brushing her teeth, adding moisturizer and running a comb through her hair. She opened the window and felt the breeze, carrying with it the scent of pluff mud and an earthy sweetness from the storm.

She slipped into underwear, a pair of soft pants, and a tunic, then went out into the living room, relishing the sight of sunlight pouring in through the windows. Peering out, she surveyed the storm's damage. She was especially anxious about the ancient live oak tree that dominated the front yard. Those giant limbs hanging over the house were always a worry. She smiled with relief, seeing that once again the old tree had weathered the strong winds. *Good ol' tree*, she thought with affection.

It would be a good day, she thought with a light step as she made her way into the kitchen. The clock chimed eight times. So late? Strange that the house was still so quiet. She busied herself measuring coffee grinds into the machine and water into the teakettle. Then she put two pieces of whole grain bread into the toaster. Humming a nameless tune, Mamaw pulled out the floral tray that was Lucille's favorite and set out a Limoges floral china bowl, matching teacup and saucer, and silver. She put the kettle on the stove and hurried out the front door to collect the newspaper. The pavers were soaked through and the scattered leaves of trees and shrubs littered the ground like dead soldiers after a war. There was cleanup to be done later in the day, she thought. As she glanced at the cottage, all was quiet. She was glad Lucille was still asleep.

The kettle was whistling when she returned to the kitchen and the rich aroma of fresh coffee filled the air. She poured herself a cup, then set about preparing Lucille's breakfast. She ate so little these days, Mamaw had to tempt her with her favorite foods and a nice presentation. If she served her several small meals a day, Lucille ate more. Mamaw didn't want her to lose any more weight. She plucked the hot toast from the toaster and, skipping the butter that bothered Lucille's stomach, slathered a thick coating of her favorite blackberry jam over the bread. Next she filled a bowl with blueberries, poured the tea, then arranged it all prettily on the tray. Lucille, for all her no-nonsense brashness, liked pretty things.

Humming again, she lifted the tray, steadying herself, feeling its weight. She might feel like a girl, but she had the strength of an old woman, she chided herself. Nonetheless, she moved on through the house, navigating doors, steps, pavers, and gravel to cross the driveway to Lucille's cottage. She set the tray on the porch table, knocked as a courtesy, then opened the door.

"Lucille! It's me!"

Picking up the tray, she walked into the cottage, humming the cheery tune. "Breakfast," she called out as she made her way down the hall to Lucille's bedroom.

The drapes were drawn and the room held a strange crepuscular light.

She pushed open the bedroom door with her shoulder. "The storm is over and the sun . . ."

Mamaw stopped talking when she saw that Lucille was still asleep in her bed. Poor thing, she thought. She must be tuckered out after all the excitement of the night. Mamaw set the tray down on the bureau, relieved of the weight, and turned to approach the bed.

She stopped short. Suddenly, all her joy drained from her, replaced by a sudden sense of dread. In the shadowy light, Lucille lay on her back, her arms at her sides, her head tilted toward the windows. Mamaw felt her blood go cold. Lucille was not asleep. She appeared to be looking out at the morning sun. Only Mamaw knew her eyes no longer saw.

Mamaw's heart beat like a trapped bird's as she stepped closer to the bed. She hesitatingly stretched out her arm and laid a hand on Lucille's chest. There was no heartbeat. She lay still, her gaze vacant and empty. Mamaw moved to grasp Lucille's hand. Her body was not yet cold. Despair immediately filled Mamaw.

Have I just missed her passing? If only I hadn't dallied. If I'd hurried, if I'd woken just a little earlier . . . She was alone when she passed. With a choked cry, Mamaw brought Lucille's hand to her mouth and kissed it, then held it close to her breast. *I didn't get to say good-bye.*

After she had sat by Lucille's bedside for some time, alternating between crying heaving tears and staring blankly at the shell that had housed her dearest friend, Mamaw went out of the cottage. She paused at the threshold of the porch, leaning against the white pillar. She stared out at a world that, though in many ways was the same world she'd stared out at earlier that same morning, was now somehow all changed.

Lucille gone. She couldn't grasp it. She knew Lucille was dying, realized the end would come—but not so soon. Not today. They'd spent the night talking. It still didn't seem possible that they'd never talk again.

She brought her hand to her throat as her practical nature took stock. There were things to do, phone calls to make. She was, sadly, experienced in matters of death. She should go to the house and begin, she thought. But she couldn't so much as move a muscle. All the energy she'd felt only a short while ago when she was rustling through the kitchen had fled, leaving her feeling so very old. Numb.

The weight of her deadened heart made her weary. She walked slowly to the rocking chair. Water had pooled in the seat. She was beyond caring. She eased into the seat, feeling the cold dampness through her pants.

Mamaw was no stranger to grief. There could be no grief worse than the death of one's only child. Yet she'd survived. When Edward had passed a year after Parker, she thought she'd go mad. She didn't believe she could continue. Or want to. It was Lucille who had nursed her back, who would not allow her to wallow. And again, she'd persevered.

But now? Lucille wasn't here. Her loved ones were gone. What was the point of continuing the fight?

A gust of wind sprayed droplets of rain from the tree's leaves across her face. Mamaw sucked in her breath at the chill of it. Turning her head from the rain, she saw Lucille's chair beside her rocking back and forth. Mamaw's breath caught in her throat. She sensed Lucille's presence, very real and very close. So close that she called her name.

"Lucille?"

There was no reply. Only the calls of birds and the rustle of leaves. "You old fool," she muttered to herself. It was just the summer wind. Yet, closing her eyes, she still felt Lucille's presence.

Thunder rumbled softly in the distance. Mamaw opened her eyes and saw that the sun had emerged from behind the clouds. She gripped the arms of her rocker and rose to her feet to stand again at the edge of the porch. Stepping into the mist, she felt the cool moisture against her skin. Looking at the dewy, fresh surroundings, Mamaw remembered Lucille's words. *When the hard times come, just dance.*

She stretched out her arms and lifted her face to welcome the sun and the rain. Going up on tiptoe, she swirled around. She was alive! The night had been filled with terror, but the morning sun rose on another day. Lucille would want her to be grateful, even joyful, in this moment, despite the grief and the pain.

Mamaw lowered her arms and walked back toward Sea Breeze, taking the time to let her gaze sweep over her house and the landscape she loved. The old house with its mullioned windows, graceful, sweeping stairs, and gables had survived the storm, too. She didn't want to go inside quite yet. Inside the house, the girls were still sleeping. Mamaw wanted a few more moments alone with her memories.

She took the pebbled path around the side of the house. She passed the outdoor shower and near the porch spotted Harper's raised garden beds. The small stalks of starter plants were bent over from the storm's driving rain and wind. Some of the tiny leaves were plastered with the mud. But a few hearty ones had already straightened, and in time, most of them would perk up in the sunshine.

She stepped out of the dappled shade into the light. The sun felt warm on her damp skin. The wet grass soaked her slippers but she ignored it, walking on toward the Cove. The air was heavy with the pungent scents of pluff mud and that powerful post-rain sweetness she called the perfume of the lowcountry. She breathed deep, feeling cleansed, looking at the refreshed green of the sea grass. She walked with arms swinging across the rain-drenched ground to Harper's garden.

Who knew her Harper had a green thumb? Sweet city girl was growing roots in the lowcountry, she thought as she took in the newly planted flowers. Drops of dew hung fat and heavy on the roses that she knew had been planted especially for her. Bending, she plucked the best one and cradled it in her palms. It was a bright pink, just opening its petals to the sun. She brought it to her nose. The bud didn't have much scent, but she gloried in the fact that it was the first rose she'd gathered from this garden in years.

She heard the piercing cries of an osprey from the Cove. She looked up, searching for the great fish hawk. She'd always loved that plucky bird. Putting her hand like a visor over her eyes, she spotted it, circling gracefully over the water, on the hunt. This time of year there would be babies on the nest, squawking for breakfast.

"There she is!" came a call from the porch.

Turning her head toward the house, she saw her granddaughters walking toward her in the light. Her summer girls. Dora in a flowing floral robe, Harper in a sleek silk sheath, Carson already in her swimsuit and shorts. So different, yet united by blood. Together . . . Mamaw felt her chest swell, knowing that she and Lucille had done the right thing in bringing the three women back home to Sea Breeze for this final summer. This was their shared triumph. These young women were their legacy.

Mamaw felt her heart warm in her breast and pump with love. Despite all the as-yet-unsettled questions, regardless of the many decisions yet to be made, on this troubled morning, looking at her granddaughters, she rediscovered her purpose for living.

Yes, they needed her, perhaps now more than ever. Yet not, she knew, as much as she needed them.

She raised her arm over her head in a wide-arc wave.

They were coming toward her.

Mamaw opened her arms.

"I'm here!"

Acknowledgments

I owe a great debt of thanks to Dr. Pat Fair at NOAA for her mentorship and friendship; to Stephen McCulloch at Florida Atlantic University; and to Lynne Byrd at the Mote Marine cetacean hospital. A heartfelt thanks to the dedicated team at the Dolphin Research Center, especially Joan Mehew, Mandy Rodriguez, Linda Erb, Rita Irwin, Mary Stella, Becky Rhodes, and Sheri Peiloch. A shout of congratulations to Joan Mehew for winning the Wounded Warrior Project's 2013 Carry Forward Award! Some readers may recognize the Dolphin Research Center and the Mote Marine cetacean hospital described in the book, but the depicted sessions, characterizations, and dialogue are strictly from my imagination and presented with their approval.

As always, I send my sincere thanks and love to Marguerite Martino, Angela May, Kathie Bennett,

Buzzy Porter, Ruth Cryns, and Lisa Minnick for all their invaluable support.

Heartfelt thanks to the fabulous team at Gallery Books: Lauren McKenna, Louise Burke, Jennifer Bergstrom, Elana Cohen, Jean Anne Rose, Ellen Chan, Natalie Ebel, Liz Psaltis, and everyone there who has continually supported my books. Love and thanks to my agents at Trident Media Group: Robert Gottlieb and Kimberly Whalen, Sylvie Rosokoff, Adrienne Lombardo, and Tara Carberry. Many thanks also to Joseph Veltre at Gersh.

I especially want to acknowledge the children's picture book *Shackles*, written by Marjory Wentworth (Legacy Publications). Her beautiful story of the discovery of slave manacles in her backyard on Sullivan's Island inspired me.

Finally, my love and thanks to my husband, Markus, for all the cups of coffee, glasses of wine, handfuls of almonds, and words of encouragement during all hours of the day and night.

The Summer Wind

Mary Alice Monroe

Introduction

The second book in Mary Alice Monroe's Lowcountry Summer trilogy, *The Summer Wind* continues the story of three half-sisters and their grandmother experiencing the highs and lows of a poignant summer on Sullivan's Island.

For Dora, the winds of change force her to cope with the aftermath of a messy divorce. Dora must let go of her facade of the perfect wife and mother and discover a renewed purpose before she can move on with her future. For Carson, the summer brings a road trip with her nephew that will change and heal them both. For Harper, a summer of self-reflection leads her to reveal the weight of the expectations placed on her as the heir to her family's fortune.

As a rough island storm brews and a health crisis threatens a beloved member of the family, the summer girls' bond strengthens—just as Mamaw had planned.

Discussion Questions

1. Mamaw sometimes reflects on her sneaky methods—"blackmail," Harper calls it—for keeping the girls together at Sea Breeze for the summer. Do you think she was right to use manipulation to get the girls to stay? In other words, do you think that a mother's or grandmother's good intentions can justify her actions?

2. How do the girls' relationships with one another change over the course of the novel? Take time to consider each of their one-on-one relationships, as well as the dynamic of the three of them together.

3. As Dora stands in her and Cal's old house, she compares it both to herself—"She felt rather like this old house. . . . Beneath her ever-present smile, she was crumbling"—and to her and Cal's marriage—"Everywhere she looked, Dora saw . . . that no amount of effort on her part could save it." In what ways does Dora feel trapped in the house, and how is she able to free herself of it? On a separate but similar note, if the old house represents Dora's marriage and unhappiness, what does Sea Breeze represent?

4. Which moment do you think was the bigger turning point for Dora—her "broken heart syndrome" stress cardiomyopathy attack, or her realization in the store dressing room after Harper's out-

burst? What other major turning points does Dora encounter, and how do they affect her life and her relationships?

5. Dora's role as Nate's mother is not easy, but her sisters suspect she puts more pressure and strain on herself than she needs to. What does Dora discover about her relationship with Nate through allowing him to travel to Florida with Carson?

6. Though he is continually withdrawn due to his Asperger's, Nate's transformation from the sad, outburst-prone boy at the start of the novel to the more accepting, slightly more outgoing boy at the end is clear. What factors and events most contributed to this transformation? Do you think the change is temporary or permanent, and why?

7. What do you consider to be the main priorities of each summer girl—Carson, Dora, Harper? How, if at all, do you think their priorities change over the course of the novel?

8. Monroe's theme of humans and animals sharing a connection is evident in *The Summer Wind.* Consider Carson and Nate's connection with Delphine, Cara's connection with the sea-turtle hatchlings, and Taylor's connections with Jax and Thor. How do these bonds affect their lives and the lives of those they love? Discuss ways in which you can develop your connection with animals and with nature.

9. Harper talks of the expectations placed on her as the heir to the Jameses' fortune. How do you think those expectations have shaped the woman she has become?

10. What are the major differences between Dora's relationship with Cal and her relationship with Devlin Cassell? What positives and negatives do you see for her in each relationship, and which would you encourage her to pursue? Why?

11. Consider the role that guilt plays in the novel. Which characters suffer from it, and why? Are all of the characters able to overcome their guilt? Or are there any characters left with guilty feelings at the end of this book?

12. The unearthing of the slave manacles is a poignant moment for the girls—and especially for Lucille. What do you think the manacles represent to her? What emotions do you imagine are stirred in her when she sees and holds them?

13. "We should never underestimate how important our loved ones are to us. Or how powerful one's grief can be." Mamaw's words foreshadow the loss that is to come in the novel's final pages. Lucille's passing signifies the end of a long era at Sea Breeze; truly she had become a member of the family. Discuss Mamaw and Lucille's long friendship, and the impact each woman had on the other's life.

14. At the end of the novel, Carson is faced with a life-changing decision. Do you think she will decide to have her baby? Do you think she'll repair her relationship with Blake? What are your predictions for her in the final novel of the Lowcountry Summer trilogy?

15. The theme of healing is dominant in this book, as Dora heals from "broken heart syndrome" and the dolphin Delphine heals from her injuries. Discuss the parallels of their healing: What do both Delphine and Dora have to let go of from their past? What must they find? What are the possibilities for their future? Are other characters undergoing healing in this book?

Reading Group Enhancers

1. On the very first page of the novel, we learn that "being out on Sullivan's Island, sitting in the shade of a live oak tree, sipping iced tea, and waiting for the occasional offshore breeze" is Mamaw's "very definition of summer." What's yours? Ask each member of your reading group to write down how they define summer on an index card, then take turns sharing the definitions out loud.

2. Carson's best friends when she was a child were her books—"*A Wrinkle in Time, The Lion, the Witch, and the Wardrobe*, and anything by Judy Blume." Have the members of your group bring their favorite childhood books along to share, and discuss the role reading played in your lives when you were younger.

3. The three summer girls were named after their father's favorite Southern authors—Harper after Harper Lee, Carson after Carson McCullers, and Dora after Eudora Welty. Split your reading group into three teams, and give each of the teams one of these authors to research, asking them to consider what each author may have in common with her namesake.

4. In gardening, Dora and Harper find an activity that brings them closer together. Bring a bit of nature into your reading group: Purchase packets of seeds,

small pots, and a bag of soil ahead of your reading group date, then let each member of your group plant their own mini-garden to take home with them.

5. If playing cards is more your speed, skip the gardening and go straight for discussing the novel over a game of gin rummy—in Mamaw's honor and Lucille's memory. Don't know the rules, or need a quick refresher course? Check out http://www.bicyclecards.com/card-games/rule/gin-rummy.

6. Taylor, the Marine Carson meets while in Florida, is a participant in the Wounded Warrior Project—a program for which the real-life Joan Mehew won the Carry Forward Award in 2013. To learn more about the vision and purpose of the Wounded Warrior Project, visit http://sandbox.woundedwarriorproject.org.

7. To discover more about Mary Alice Monroe and her books, read her blog, view a list of her upcoming author appearances, and more, visit http://www.maryalicemonroe.com.

Turn the page for an exclusive sneak peek of

The Summer's End

Book Three in Mary Alice Monroe's
Lowcountry Summer Trilogy

Available May 2015 from Gallery Books

Chapter One

The dawn of another summer day. Mamaw tightened the soft cashmere throw around her thin shoulders. Slivers of light pierced the velvety blackness over the Cove and pewter-colored shadows danced on the spiky marsh grass like ethereal ghosts.

Mamaw sat huddled on an oversized black wicker chair on her back porch, her legs tucked beneath her. The fog was moist on her face and the predawn chill went straight to her bones. She couldn't seem to get warm with Lucille gone. As had happened nearly every night since she'd lost her dearest friend, she'd awoken from a fitful sleep and had come outdoors hoping the fresh air would settle her nerves. She found scant comfort or peace. In the distance the Atlantic Ocean, her mercurial friend, roared like a hungry beast. The waves were devouring the dunes in a relentless rhythm. Echoes reverberated over Sullivan's Island.

One wave after another, she thought, *like the flow of days that ceaselessly followed one after the other.*

Over a week had passed since Lucille's death. Yet she

still felt her old friend's presence around her, hovering in death as she did in life. Dear Lucille. Death came to us all. She knew that. Mamaw was no stranger to death. At eighty years of age, she could hardly have been spared the loss of loved ones. She'd buried her parents, her husband, and, too early, her son. Yet tonight she felt the past more alive than the present. Memories of her loved ones played vividly in her mind.

Mamaw took a long, raggedy breath. From faraway, she heard the mournful bellowing of a ship's foghorn. In contrast, a bird in the nearby tree began calling out his strident dawn whistles . . . *a cardinal,* she thought. Mamaw listened, stirred from her lethargy by the dawn song. She watched as the morning light, in degrees, brightened the skyline, revealing the Ravenel Bridge appearing as two great sailing vessels in the distance. Slowly, as the sun illuminated the darkness, her despair dissipated like the mist. Mamaw felt the tension in her chest relax and she took a deep breath. The worst of the night was over.

Foolish old woman, she chided herself. *Sitting in the dark, mourning your friend. Wouldn't Lucille give you a what for if she spied you moping like this outdoors in the damp chill, still in your nightclothes?* Who had time to lollygag? Their plan for the summer was not finished! She'd invited her three nearly estranged granddaughters—Dora, Carson, and Harper—to Sea Breeze in May, and they'd come. The first time they'd been together in over a decade. True, it had been a tumultuous summer of change and growth, ups and downs, joys and heartaches. But it was her triumph that they'd weathered the vicissitudes *together.* Her granddaughters had rediscovered the love they'd shared as children when they played together during the summers here on Sullivan's Island. She should be crowing like a rooster.

Yet there was still much to be done, and she was running out of time. It was already August. The sea turtles were finishing another season, the children were heading back to school, the ospreys would soon head south with the other migrating birds and butterflies. Summer's end was fast approaching. Soon, too, her Summer Girls would be leaving.

Mamaw felt a twinge of loss at just the thought. She would miss them—their sweet faces, their chatter, tears, laughter. The footfall in the house, the drama, the hugs and kisses liberally offered. What a summer it had been! When her granddaughters left in the fall she would, she realized, be utterly alone.

Mamaw lowered her cheek to rest in her palm. But where would they go? Each of the women was unsure of what her next step would be when they left the safe embrace of Sea Breeze. They were adrift. Dora's divorce was pending, Carson was pregnant, and Harper was completely at a loss.

"All right, Lucille," she said aloud to the presence she felt hovering in the pearly light. Renewed determination shot through her veins, stirring her to sit upright. "Enough of my bellyaching and self-pity. At my age, I'm lucky to be here to greet the new dawn! Life is to be savored, not squandered. Time is precious, and I still have some left," she said, tapping her fingers. "Not much," she added ruefully. "But I pray at least until summer's end."

"Ah Lucille, you were the one who always rallied me in my dark moments. But now I must depend on myself. We brought them here. And now I have much yet to do to finish our plan."

Mamaw's eyes rose to the sky where great shafts of pink and blue were just starting to break through the horizon. A smile eased across her face. *The moon may be gone,* she thought. *But the sun was rising on another day.*

In another room of Sea Breeze, Harper lay on her bed in the steely light, her hands tucked beneath her head, listening to the mighty roar of the ocean. *How loud the sound of the waves is,* she thought. The echoes reverberated in the still morning. She thrilled to the sound, so different from what she was accustomed to in New York City.

In New York, Harper awoke to the blare of police sirens, honking horns, and loud garbage trucks. So much was different here. *She* was different here. Since she'd arrived on Sullivan's Island her body had slowly acclimated from the fast pace and sense of urgency she had in the city to the slower, quieter rhythm of the lowcountry. She no longer went out to parties or bars till late at night, nor did she charge out of bed in the morning at the sound of an alarm. At Sea Breeze her days were ruled by the sun. Early to bed, early to rise.

Harper smiled, wondering if she ever foresaw how much she'd enjoy this lifestyle. No, she didn't think she had. She stretched languidly while the light brightened, giving the room a pearly glow. She turned to her side to look out the window when her hand brushed against sheets of paper. Surprised, she sat up to investigate. Sheets of paper lay strewn across her bed and scattered on the floor.

She rubbed her eyes as understanding took hold. Her book . ...

She must've fallen asleep while reading her manuscript, she realized, yawning. She rose from her bed and gathered the two hundred some sheets into a pile, taking her time to put the pages in order. As she did, her eyes reread a sentence here and there. *Not bad,* she thought to herself. The emotions in the words felt true. Then again, she was a biased judge. Her mother had made it brutally clear when she was a girl that she didn't have talent like her father. Her mother was a renowned editor so Harper had taken her words as fact. Those fateful words still stung, even after a decade. Since then, Harper hadn't shown her work to anyone. She'd pursued a career as an editor, discovering she had a talent in assisting others with their work's story structure. It was still playing with words.

Yet she'd found editing others' work didn't bring her the same satisfaction as writing her own words. So she'd continued writing—in her room, in coffee shops, on trains—in secret. Like a sinful pleasure she could indulge in when she wanted to dish out her anger or amusement and, too, her joy at life's vicissitudes. It wasn't until this summer, this block of time she'd given herself without interruption, that Harper had decided to write a book. A whole body of work with a beginning, a middle, and an end. She wouldn't know she could actually write a book until she'd finished one. And, she thought with pleasure, picking up the papers and holding them in her hands, she was nearly done.

Harper placed the manuscript on her desk, resting her hands on the pile of papers a moment longer with a sense of ownership.

Her book.

Her sisters thought she'd been taking the summer off, being idle and relaxing while they scrambled to find jobs and apartments. True, she'd been enjoying her break at Sea Breeze, gardening, swimming, talking with her sisters and roaming the far ends of the island. But she'd been privately working, too. She didn't dare tell anyone about it because, if she did, she knew they'd want to read it. Or at the very least for her to tell them the story.

No, she thought, tapping the manuscript firmly with the palm of her hand. She would keep her manuscript all to herself. She wasn't as outgoing as her sister Carson, who was quick with a witty repartee, funny, a shining star. Nor was she as bold as her eldest sister, Dora, who had strong opinions on every subject and could be intimidating when she offered them—even when not asked for. Harper expressed herself best on paper.

And, she thought with a rueful smile, her sisters wouldn't be pleased to learn that she was writing about them.

Harper slipped the manuscript into the desk drawer and locked it.

Outside her window she heard the strident dawn whistles of a bird singing in a nearby tree. She paused to listen, wondering what kind of bird it was that awakened her most mornings. She vowed to find out. She wanted to learn the names of the birds and the trees and the plants of this island that she'd come to love. She'd spent all her twenty-eight years in beautiful places—her mother's fashionable apartment overlooking Central Park in New York City, the house in the Hamptons, and her grandparents manor house in England. Not to mention the exclusive boarding schools and Ivy Colleges. But nowhere did she feel so at home or content or as much herself as she did here in the lowcountry, by the ocean, at Sea Breeze.

She'd be leaving soon.

The thought came unbidden and struck a chord of sadness in the morning's sweet music. Harper went to the window and opened the wooden slats of the plantation shutter to peer out. Dawn had not yet broken in full. Pale gray light illuminated the shadows. She'd thought she was a night person, someone more productive in the wee hours. Here at Sea Breeze, however, she'd discovered she enjoyed rising with the sun. Perhaps it was because Carson waxed poetic about how glorious it was to be out on the water when the dawn exploded over the ocean.

How it was her favorite time of the day. Carson could be so passionate about anything connected to water.

And yet . . . Harper had listened to her words, could see that sunrise in her mind's eye, and suddenly felt a stirring to witness that for herself. Why not now? she asked herself. Before it was too late. What was she waiting for?

Harper felt lighthearted as she slipped into denim shorts and a swimsuit top. She laced up her running shoes. As quietly as the mouse she was nicknamed after, she slipped open the sliding door that separated her bedroom from her grandmother's. It rattled on the track and, grimacing, she paused to listen. She didn't hear Mamaw stir in her dark bedroom. Harper tiptoed quickly across the carpet, closing the door behind her.

The house was quiet, everyone was asleep. Making good her escape, Harper flew out the front door, aware that the sun waited for no man or woman. She was met with a surprisingly cool and sweet-tasting breeze. The wind that had roiled the ocean had chased away the humidity and heat, leaving the morning air unusually refreshing for August. The morning was still, amplifying sounds. Above her, the leaves of the great oak tree rustled in the soft breezes and the palm fronds scraped like castanets. Beneath her feet the gravel crunched loudly as she hurried across the driveway to the garage.

The rusty, trusty old bicycle was leaning against the garage wall. She pulled it out, swung her leg over the seat and took off.

Despite her twenty-eight years, Harper felt no older than thirteen as she pedaled furiously along the streets. The neighboring houses appeared blanketed in the shadows, their occupants still asleep in the hush over the island. Only a few feral cats darted soundlessly across the roads. She hadn't seen as many feral cats clustering on the island this summer as she remembered from her girlhood. People said it was the coyotes. She kept her eyes peeled as she pushed on along the muted street that cut through Sullivan's Island. Past Stella Maris Catholic Church with its hallowed steeple. Past the ominous, giant, mole-like burrows of Fort Moultrie. Past the tight cluster of restaurants, shuttered now and deserted. Only a few joggers and an occasional automobile shared the road with her.

At last she reached the northern tip of the island where Carson had told her the surfers gathered. She turned off Middle Street toward the sea. Several cars, all with roof racks for surfboards, crowded the narrow side streets, but she wasn't surprised because Carson had told her this was a popular place for kite surfers. At the beach path Harper had to push the bike through the tall barrier of shrubs. She could hear the echoes of the waves pounding the shore. The surf was unusually loud this morning. Her excitement built as she pushed the wheels of her bike through the soft sand of the path. When at last the path opened up to the beach she stopped to catch her breath. The panorama of sand and sky spread out before her into infinity. A gust of onshore wind caught her hair and sent it fluttering about her shoulders. Lifting her face, she smelled the sea and tasted salt on her lips.

Harper's chest expanded as she took in the vista. A dusky blue sky and gray sea came together to form one infinite horizon line. The sun did not rush to her glory. She rose at her own pace, imperious, radiant, bursting in her display of achingly beautiful pastels. The colors reflected, shimmering, on the water. Harper felt so small in the presence of something so profoundly beautiful. Something never-ending. Yet, at the same time, she felt connected to it, empowered to be part of this godlike perpetuity. She stood motionless as she stared out, holding firm to the handlebars. In that dazzling moment she felt the glistening light enter her soul to fill her with hope.

Harper understood at last why Carson rose early to catch this moment, day after day. It truly was spiritual.

Harper clutched the handlebars of her beach cruiser tightly in the clarity of the dawn's light. The new day was spread out before her like a blank page, ready for her to fill with her words, thoughts, feelings. She'd given herself this one summer to discover—at long last—what *she* wanted to do with her life. No longer would she continue meekly following what *her mother* had planned.

She didn't know what her future would bring. Yet standing in the glow of the rising sun, Harper was filled with a tingling sensation that her future was only just beginning.

The sea was calling her. Carson lay in the dim light of her bedroom listening to the incessant roar of her old friend, the ocean. It was rare for the waves to come in hard, like they were now. When they did, Carson had always joined her friends to grab their surfboards and get to the water. It was her nature to do so. Salt water ran in her veins.

Carson didn't jump from her bed this morning, however. She continued to lie on the bed, her palms resting on her abdomen. She no longer was free to follow her whims. No longer the fearless surfer or world traveler, able to pick up and leave when she wished.

She was pregnant.

She let her fingers gently stroke her belly, still flat despite the life growing beneath the taut skin. She herself hadn't guessed. It took the echolocation of a dolphin to tell her.

"Oh baby," she crooned. "What am I going to do with you? I'm not married, I don't have a job, I don't even have my own place to live. How am I going to take care of you?"

She brought to mind her last conversation with Lucille. The night she'd died. Carson had been struggling with what to do about the pregnancy and went to Lucille to sit at her knee, as she had so many times growing up, and once more ask for advice. Lucille didn't tell her what to do. That wasn't her style. Instead, the old woman guided Carson's thoughts to find her own answer. Carson would never forget her words.

You've got good instincts. Listen to them. Trust them. You'll know what to do.

Carson knew Lucille was right. When she was surfing, Carson had to trust her instincts on the wave to know when to step left or right. It was all a matter of balance.

She had to listen to her instincts. It didn't make sense for her to have a baby now. All her rational arguments were against it. But over the rational thoughts her instincts spoke loud and clear. That and her raging hormones, she thought with a snort. Lying on the bed, listening to the echoing sound of the waves rolling to the shore, Carson knew she had to ride this wave home.

"Well, baby," she said, patting her tummy. "It's me and you now. I'm not running away."

Dora's arm shot out to silence the alarm clock. She groggily opened one eyelid: 7 a.m. "Rise and shine," she mumbled.

She moved in a stupor, accustomed to the routine. She dressed quickly in running clothes, splashed cool water on her face, applied SPF moisturizer, then did a few stretches. This past summer she'd learned that she had to get her exercise done first thing in the morning, because if she waited, she'd slip into a thousand lame excuses why she didn't have time. She'd learned to make time for the things that mattered to her.

And nothing mattered more to her than her son.

Dora swiftly walked down the hall to Nate's room. She very gingerly pushed the door open. The room had that stuffy, closed-in smell but Nate, unlike the rest of the inhabitants of Sea Breeze, did not like to sleep with his windows opened. He was adamant about his likes and dislikes, quick to let you know if something was right or, more often, wrong. She went to the side of his bed and stood for a moment staring into her nine-year-old son's face.

Her heart bloomed with love for him. Did a child ever look more angelic than when asleep? she wondered. Nate's long pale lashes fluttered against his cheeks. His lips were slightly parted as he breathed heavily. One small hand rested on the pillow above his head, like he was fencing. He was small for his age but his thin frame had filled out this summer at Sea Breeze, and his skin glowed with a tan. This summer at Sea Breeze had been good to Nate on many levels. He loved the water. She called him her little fish. As her eyes hungrily roamed his face she noted that his shaggy blond hair needed a trim, and she made a mental note to take him to the barber. It would be a fight, she thought with a sigh. Nate hated to have his hair cut.

Poor little guy, she thought as she reached out to gently stroke his hair away from his forehead. She felt the moisture of perspiration on his brow. Cutting his hair was the least of the changes he'd be facing soon. Her obstinate, fretful son, who hated any change. In a short period of time she'd have to help her son transition from homeschooling to a classroom setting. It was a big decision, long and hard in coming. She'd found a private school that specialized in bright children with special needs, like his Asperger's. The school offered highly individualized instruction and positive behavior support. This summer she'd faced the reality that Nate was older and needed more than she could offer. He needed to communicate and socialize with his peers.

Dora sighed. They both did. Isolation had not been good for either of them.

On the heels of this decision was her intention to move to Mt. Pleasant, closer to the school. A new school . . . a new home . . . Dora said a quick prayer that she'd find the strength.

She bent to lightly kiss Nate's cheek, breathing in the scent of him. When he was awake, he didn't like to be kissed.

"We'll be fine," she whispered close to his ear. "Mama's here. I won't let you down."

While Harper pedaled back to Sea Breeze her mind was filled with words that could capture that glorious sunrise. *Iridescent, shimmering, glittering, ethereal, inspiring* . . . Harper parked the bike in the garage and hurried toward the house, eager to slip quietly back into her bedroom and begin writing. She wanted to describe what she'd seen and the feelings that had swirled in brilliant colors around her. As she made her way across the back porch a cough drew her attention. Harper turned her head to the back corner of the porch and was surprised to see her grandmother sitting tall and straight-backed in one of the large black wicker chairs. In the dim light, wearing her long white cotton nightgown, Mamaw appeared almost ghostly.

"Mamaw!" Harper exclaimed. "What are you doing out here?"

Mamaw smiled as Harper approached, but it was a tired smile. Her pale blue eyes were sunken and her arms were wrapped around her slender body as though she were chilled.

"I couldn't sleep," Mamaw replied. "I woke very early and my mind kept wandering." She shook her head. "It's so exhausting when that happens. A curse of old age. I just gave up and came out here to sit a spell. I thought the fresh air might help."

On the glass-topped table Harper saw a line of playing cards. Her heart pinged, realizing Mamaw was playing solitaire. The image of Mamaw and Lucille playing endless games of gin rummy together on the porch at all hours of the day and night flashed in Harper's mind.

Harper hurried to put her arms around her grandmother's shoulders. "How long have you been out here?" she asked, alarmed. "You're chilled to the bone." She rubbed Mamaw's arms briskly with her hands, trying to warm her.

"Mmm . . . that's nice," Mamaw said. "Thank you, dear."

Harper pulled up a chair and dropped into it. She leaned forward, elbows resting on her knees.

"What's got your mind wandering?"

"Oh . . . I was thinking of Lucille," Mamaw said wistfully.

Of course, Harper thought.

"It was a nice funeral, wasn't it?" Mamaw asked.

"It was. I'd never been to a Gullah funeral before. So much song, tears, and rejoicing."

"And 'Amens'," Mamaw added wryly.

Harper smiled in agreement. She'd been moved by the unrestrained calling out at the service, the passion, the strong sense of community.

Mamaw looked back out over the water. "I was sitting here, looking across the Cove, and it brought to mind what the preacher talked about at Lucille's service. How their ancestral spirits who came to the lowcountry—those by force and those who came after—lived, thrived, and died here. They worked hard, cooked rice, cast nets for shrimp, raised children, and now they've all moved on to the bounty of the afterlife. That's what Lucille believed, you know. She was tired at the end, I daresay looking forward to crossing the water." Mamaw sighed, remembering. "I confess, lately I feel as though I might be ready, too."

Harper leaned forward to grasp Mamaw's hand.

"Don't go yet," she said. "We still need you."

Mamaw's lips slipped into a wobbly smile, briefly, then fell again. "I'm having a hard time believing she's really gone."

"It all happened so fast." Harper also felt deep sorrow at Lucille's swift battle with cancer.

Mamaw looked at Harper and asked pointedly, "Do you believe in an afterlife?"

Harper released Mamaw's hand and, leaning back, scratched her head, thinking this was a heavy conversation to have before a first cup of coffee. She'd never warmed to the idea of a God that rewarded the good with heaven and the others an eternity of brimstone and fire. It seemed so unforgiving. Still, after much soul searching she'd come to believe there was a higher being. She'd felt a connection to that infinite power this morning while staring out at the sunrise.

"I guess so," she said with hesitancy. "I don't think much about it."

Mamaw smiled ruefully. "You're young. You think you're immortal. When you get to my age, you'll think about it . . . a lot."

"I don't like to see you out here alone, playing solitaire and thinking of death. It's a tad morbid."

"I'm not feeling the least bit morbid. Quite the opposite." Mamaw patted Harper's hand with a weary smile. "Death is becoming an old friend."

Harper rose and tugged gently on Mamaw's arm.

"Come inside and I'll make you a nice breakfast. Something warm."

"I'm not hungry." Mamaw resisted, leaning back in her chair. "I've just got the dwindles."

"How about I bring you a nice hot cup of coffee?"

Mamaw perked up at the suggestion. "Well, I wouldn't say no to that."

"Coming right up." She paused. Mamaw was always an elegant woman who took great care with her appearance. She had been a leading Charleston socialite known for her extravagant parties as much as her polished beauty. To see Mamaw sitting on the porch still in her nightclothes, her white hair flowing, unbrushed to her shoulders, and wrapped up in a coverlet like a bag lady shook Harper to the core. This was an outward sign of the state of her mind.

Harper made a bold suggestion. "Mamaw, while I make coffee, why don't you get dressed?"

Mamaw turned her head to deliver a stern face with a brow raised. "I beg your pardon?"

Harper rushed on. "Don't you remember, you used to tell us that while in France Thomas Jefferson wrote his eleven-year-old daughter letters on deportment. He admonished her to always rise and dress promptly. Neat and clean and tidy." Harper paused, pleased to see her grandmother was listening. "You told us your mother read you his letters and you read them to us. Why, if you caught us lying about in our jammies, you sent us straight to our rooms to get dressed."

Mamaw raised one brow. "I'm delighted to learn you paid attention." She offered her hand in a regal manner. Harper took it and helped Mamaw to her feet. "Very well," Mamaw said. "The sun is up and so I should rise with it. It is, to paraphrase Scarlett O'Hara, another day."

July 1, 1996
Egg Harbor

The boxes are plentiful. There is no end to the number of cardboard boxes the movers carry through the front door, delivering them to their marked rooms—living room, bedroom, master bath—stomping across our home in dusty work boots. Sixteen hundred square feet of space needing to be filled as Aaron and I divvied up our gender-appropriate tasks, he directing the movers with couches and beds while I unpacked and washed the dishes by hand and placed them in the cabinets. I watched the many laps they took, each man's head beginning to glimmer with sweat. Aaron's too, though he hardly carried a thing, and yet the authority in his voice, the obvious clout as grown men trailed him through our home, heeding his every word, was enough to catch my eye. I watched him round the home time and again, wondering how I was so lucky to have him all to my own.

It wasn't like me to be lucky in love. Not until I met Aaron. The men who came before him were deadbeats and drifters, bottom-feeders. But not Aaron. We dated for a year before he proposed. Tomorrow we celebrate two years. Soon there will be kids, a whole gaggle of little ones spinning circles at our feet. As soon as we're settled, Aaron always said, and now, as my eyes assess the new home, the sprawling landscape, the sixteen hundred square feet of space, three bedrooms—two vacant and left to fill—I realize the time has come and like clockwork, something inside me starts to tick.

When the movers' backs were turned, Aaron kissed me in the kitchen, pinning me against the cabinets, hands gripping my hips. It was unasked for and yet very much wanted as he kissed with his eyes closed, whispering that all of our dreams were finally coming true. Aaron isn't one to be sentimental or romantic, and yet it was true: the cottage, his job, leaving the city. We'd both wanted to get away from Green Bay since the day we were married, his hometown and my hometown, so that two sets of parents couldn't show up at our door on any given day, unsolicited, waging a secret battle as to which in-law could occupy the most of our time. We hadn't gone far, sixty-seven miles to be precise, but enough that visits would be preempted with a simple phone call.

Tonight we made love on the living room floor to the glow of candlelight. The electricity had yet to be turned on and so, other than the dance of candlelight on the whitewashed walls, the house was dark.

Aaron was the first to suggest it, discontinuing my birth control pill, as if he knew what I was thinking, as if he could read my mind. It was as we lay together on the wide wooden floorboards staring out the open windows at the stars, Aaron's prowling hand moving across my thigh, contemplating a second go. That's when he said it. I told him *yes!* that I am ready for a family. That *we* are ready. Aaron is twenty-nine. I am twenty-eight. His paycheck isn't extravagant, and yet it's enough. We aren't spendthrifts; we've been saving for years.

And even though I knew it wasn't possible yet, the pill in my system nipped any possibility of pregnancy in the bud, I still imagined a creature no bigger than a speck starting to take form as Aaron again let himself inside me.

July 9, 1996
Egg Harbor

Our days begin with coffee on the dock, bare feet dangling over the edge, downward toward the bay. The water is cold, and our feet don't reach anyway. But as promised, there are sailboats. Aaron and I spend hours watching them pass by, as well as sandpipers and other shorebirds that come to call, their long legs wading through the shallow water for a meal. We stare at the birds and the sailboats, watching the sun rise higher into the sky, warming our skin, burning off the early-morning fog. Heaven on earth, Aaron says.

As we sit on the dock, Aaron tells me about his nights at the chophouse that steals him from me for ten hours at a time. About the heat of the kitchen, and the persistent noise. The rumble of voices calling out orders in sync. The sputter of boneless rib eye on the grill, the dicing and hashing of vegetables.

His voice is placid. He doesn't complain because Aaron, ever easygoing Aaron, isn't one to complain. Rather he tells me about it, describing it for me so that I can see in my mind's eye what he's doing when he's away from me for half the day. He wears a white chef jacket and black chef pants and a cap, something along the lines of a beanie that is also white. Aaron's been assigned the role of *saucier*, or sauce chef, one that's new to him, but no doubt comes with ease. Because this is the way it is with Aaron. No matter what he tries his hand at, things always come with ease.

Our property is fringed by trees so that as we sit on the deck's edge, Aaron and me, it feels as if we're all alone, partitioned from society by the lake and the trees. If we have neighbors, we've never seen them. Never laid eyes on them. Never spied another home through the canopy of trees. Never are we disturbed by the sound of voices, but only the colloquy of birds as they perch in the trees and yammer back and forth about whatever it is birds talk about. On occasion the helmsmen will wave a hearty hello from behind the steering wheel of their sailboats, but more often than not they're too far away to see Aaron and me at the dock's edge, feet dangling southward, holding hands, sitting in silence, listening to the breeze through the trees.

We're marooned on an island, stranded and shipwrecked, but we don't mind. It's just the way it should be.

Aaron's work shift begins at two in the afternoon and ends when the last customer leaves and the kitchen is clean, most nights stumbling into bed around midnight or after, smelling of sweat and grease.

But the days are ours to do with as we please.

Last week, Aaron repaired the greenhouse door and we stripped it of cobwebs and bugs. We spent days cultivating the garden and Aaron made good on his promise of raised beds, three feet by five feet by ten inches deep, made of white cedar that will one day house cucumbers and zucchini. But not this year. It's far too late in the season to grow produce this year and so for now, we buy it from any number of tatty roadside farm stands. We live two miles from town and even though the population around here expands sevenfold in the summer months thanks to a healthy tourist population, outside town it's still mainly rural, long stretches of open country roads that intersect with nothing but sky.

Instead of planting produce this year, Aaron and I sowed perennial seeds to enjoy next year: baby's breath and lavender and hollyhocks because all the fences and cottages around here, it seems, are flanked with hollyhocks. We placed them in peat pots of gardening soil in the greenhouse and set them in the sunniest spot we could find. In a month or so, we'll transplant them to the garden. They won't bloom for some time, not until next spring. But still, I stand hopeful in the greenhouse, staring at the peat pots, imagining what might be happening beneath the soil's surface, whether the seeds' roots are taking hold, pushing down into the soil to anchor the seedling to this world, or if the seed has merely shriveled up and died in there, a dead embryo in its mother's womb.

As I clear out the last of my birth control pills and run a hand across what I imagine to be my uterus, I wonder what is happening inside there too.

JESSIE

I HAD MOM CREMATED at her request. I carry her around now in a rhubarb-glazed clay urn with a cork in the top, one she bought for herself when the cancer spread. It's cylindrical and inconspicuous, the cork stuck on with an ample amount of Gorilla Glue so I don't lose Mom by chance.

Mom had two wishes when she died, ones she let slip in the last brief moments of consciousness before she drifted off to sleep, a sleep from which she would never wake up. One, that she be cremated and lobbed from the back end of the Washington Island Ferry and into Death's Door. And two, that I find myself and figure out who I am. The second hinged on the esoteric and didn't make obvious sense. I blamed the drugs for it, that and the imminence of death.

I'm nowhere near accomplishing either, though I filled out a college application online. But I have no plans of parting with Mom's remains anytime soon. She's the only thing of value I have left.

I haven't slept in four days, not since some doctor took pity on me and offered me a pill. Three if you count the one where I nearly nodded off at the laundromat waiting for clothes to dry, anesthetized by the sound of sweaters tumbling around a dryer. The effects are obnoxious. I'm tired. I'm grumpy. I can focus on nothing and my reaction time is slow. I've lost the ability to think.

Yesterday, a package arrived from UPS and the driver asked me to sign for it. He stood before me, shoving a pen and a slip of paper up under my nose and I could only stare, unable to put two and two together. He said it again. *Can you sign for it?* He forced the pen into my hand. He pointed at the signature line. For a third time, he asked me to sign.

And even then I scribbled with the cap still on the pen. The man had to snatch it from my hand and uncap it.

I'm pretty sure I've begun to see things too. Things that might not be real, that might not be there. A millipede dashing across the tabletop, an ant on the kitchen floor. Sudden movements, immediate and quick, but the minute I turn, they're gone.

I keep track of the sleepless nights in the notched lines beneath my eyes, like the annual rings of a tree. One wrinkle for each night that I don't sleep. I stare at myself in the mirror each day, counting them all. This morning there were four. The surface effects of insomnia are even worse than what's going on on the inside. My eyes are red and swollen. My eyelids droop. Overnight, wrinkles appear by the masses, while I lie in bed counting sheep. I could go to the clinic and request something else to help me sleep. Some more of the clonazepam. But with the pills in my system, I slept right on through Mom's death. I don't want to think about what else I'd miss.

At McDonald's, I'm asked if I want ketchup with my fries, but I can only stare at the worker dumbly because what I heard was *It's messed up when boats capsize*, and I nod lamely because it is disastrous and sad, and yet so out of left field I can't respond with words.

It's only when he drops a stack of ketchup packets on my tray that my brain makes the translation, too late it seems because I hate ketchup. I dump them on the table when I go, the mother lode for someone who likes it. On the way out the door I trip, because coordination is also affected by a lack of sleep.

Two hours ago I dragged my heavy body from bed after another sleepless night, and now I stand in the center of Mom's and my house, deciding which of our belongings to take and which to leave. I can't stand to stay here much longer, a decision I've come to quickly over the last four days. I've spoken to a Realtor already, figured out next steps. First I'm to pack up what I want to keep, and then everything else will be sold in an estate sale before some junk removal service tosses the rest of our stuff in the trash.

Then some other family will move in to the only home I've ever known.

I'm eyeing the sofa, wondering if I should take it or leave it, when the phone rings. "Hello?" I ask.

A voice on the other end informs me that she's calling from the financial aid office at the college. "There's a problem with your application," she says to me.

"What problem?" I ask the woman on the phone, afraid I'm about to be cited for tax evasion. It's a likely possibility; I'd left blank every question on the FAFSA form that asked about adjusted gross income and tax returns. I might have lied on the application too. There was a question that asked if both of my parents were deceased. I said yes to that, though I don't know if it's true.

Is my father dead?

On the other end of the line, the woman asks me to verify my social security number for her and I do. "That's what I have," she says, and I ask, "Then what's the problem? Has my application been denied?" My heart sinks. How can that be? It's only a community college. It's not like I registered for Yale or Harvard.

"I'm sure it's just a weird mix-up with vital statistics," she says.

"What mix-up?" I ask, feeling relieved for a mix-up as opposed to a denied application. A mix-up can be fixed.

"It's the strangest thing," she says. "There was a death certificate on file for a Jessica Sloane, from seventeen years ago. With your birth date and your social security number. By the looks of this, Ms. Sloane," she says, and I amend *Jessie*, because Ms. Sloane is Mom. "By the looks of this, Jessie," she says, and the words that follow punch me so hard in the gut they make it almost impossible to breathe. "By the looks of this, you're already dead."

And then she laughs as if somehow or other this is funny.

Today I'm looking for a new place to live. Staying in our old home is no longer a viable option because of the residual ghosts of Mom that remain in every corner of the home. The smell of her Crabtree & Evelyn hand cream that fills the bathroom. The feel of the velvet-lined compartments in the mahogany dresser. The chemo caps. The cartons of Ensure on the refrigerator shelf.

I perch in the back seat of a Kia Soul, trying hard not to think too much about the call from the financial aid office. This is easier said than done. Just thinking about it makes my stomach hurt. A mix-up, the woman claimed, but still, it's hard to grapple with the words *you* and *dead* in the same sentence. Though I try to, I can't push them from my mind. The way she and I left things, I'm to provide a copy of my social security card to the college before they'll take another look at my application for a loan, which is a problem because I don't have the first clue where the card is. But it's more than that too. Because the woman also told me about some death index my name was found on. A *death index*. My name on a database maintained by the Social Security Administration of millions of people who have died, nullifying their social security numbers so that no one else can use them, so that I can't use my own social security number. Because, according to the Social Security Administration, I'm dead.

You might want to look into that, she'd suggested before ending our call, and I couldn't help but feel shaken up by it even now, hours later. My name on a death database. Though it's a mistake, of course.

But still I pray this isn't some sort of foresight. A prophecy of what's to come.

I gaze out the window as some woman sits behind the wheel of the Kia, steering us through the streets of Chicago. Her name is Lily and she calls herself an *apartment finder.* The first I'd heard of Lily was days ago, when I'd come home from a cleaning job—hating the feeling of coming home to Mom's and my empty house alone, wishing she was there but knowing she would never be again, making a flip decision to sell the home and leave. I came home, leaving my bike on the sidewalk, and there, hanging on the handle of our front door, was an ad for Lily's efficient and cost-free services. An apartment finder. I'd never heard of such a thing, and yet she was just the thing I needed. The door hanger was in-your-face marketing, the kind I couldn't recycle with the rest of the junk mail. And so I called Lily and we made an appointment to meet.

Lily's parallel parking skills are second to none, though it seems easy enough for someone like me who's never driven a car before. Growing up in an old brick bungalow in Albany Park, there was never a need to drive a car. We didn't have one. The Brown Line or the bus took us everywhere we needed to go. Either that or our own two feet. I also have my Schwinn, Old Faithful, which is surprisingly resilient in even the worst weather, except for, of course, three feet of snow.

I was fifteen when Mom was diagnosed with cancer, which meant that for the time being, my life was on hold, anything that wasn't essential set aside. I went to school. I worked. I helped with the mortgage and saved as much as I could. And I held Mom's hair for her when she puked.

She found the lump herself, slim fingers palpating her own breast because she knew sooner or later this would happen. She didn't tell me about the lump until after she'd been diagnosed with cancer, one mammogram and a biopsy later. She didn't want to worry me. They removed the breast first, followed by months of chemotherapy. But it wasn't long before the cancer returned, in the chest and in the bones this time. The lungs. Back for vengeance.

Jessie, I'm dying. I'm going to die, she had said to me then. We were sitting on the front porch, hand in hand, the day she learned the cancer was back. At that point, her five-year survival rate took a nosedive. She only lived for two more, and none of them great.

The cancer, it's hereditary. Some aberrant gene that runs through our family line, red pegs lined up in my battleship already. Like Mom and her mom before her, it's only a matter of time before I too will sink.

I claimed the back seat of the Kia after Lily dropped her purse into the passenger's chair. She drives with one hand on the horn at all times, so she can scare pedestrians out of the way, those she hollers at from behind safety glass to *shake a leg* and *scoot your boot*. I have no credit history and no bank account, which I've confessed to Lily, and instead carry a pocketful of cash. Her eyes grew wide when I showed her my money, thirty hundred-dollar bills folded in half and stuck inside a wristlet.

"This might be a problem," Lily said, shrugging her shoulders not at the cash but rather the shortage of credit, the absence of a bank account, "but we'll see."

She suggested I offer a landlord more up front to offset the fact that I'm one of those people who keeps all my money in a fireproof safe box beneath my bed. The checks I earn cleaning houses get cashed at Walmart for a three-dollar service fee, and then deposited into my trusty box. I considered signing on with a temp agency once, but thought better of it. There are perks to my job I won't find anywhere else. Because I'm cleaning houses, I don't have to pay taxes to Uncle Sam. I'm an independent contractor. At least that's the way I've always rationalized it in my head, though, for all I know, IRS agents are hot on my heels, planning to nab me for tax evasion.

And still, I load my cleaning supplies into a basket on the back end of Old Faithful each day and pedal off to work, earning as much as two hundred dollars some days by cleaning someone else's home. I do it in peace with my headphones on. I don't have to make small talk. No one supervises me. It's the best job in the world.

"Either that," said Lily as she easily navigated the streets of Chicago, pulling in to an alley behind a high-rise on Sheridan and putting the car in Park, "or you'll need to find someone to cosign on the loan," which isn't an option for me. I have no one to cosign on the loan.

The apartment search is nearly an abject failure.

Lily shows me apartment after apartment. A third-floor unit in a high-rise in Edgewater. A mid-rise on Ashland, newly rehabbed, in my price range though at the high end of it. Unit after unit of boxlike rooms enclosed by four thin gypsum walls, foggy windows that inhibit the light from coming in. The window screens are torn, one stuffed full with an air-conditioning unit, which is supposed to make me happy because, as Lily points out, renters usually have to buy them themselves, those repulsive window units that bar any natural light from entering the room.

The kitchens are tight. The stoves are old and electric. Freckles of mold grow in the showers' grout. The closets smell like urine. Lightbulbs have burned out.

But it isn't the mold or the windows that bother me. It's the noise and the neighbors—strange people just on the other side of drywall, their domestic life partitioned from mine by a paltry combination of plaster and paper. The sense of claustrophobia that settles under my skin as I pretend to listen to Lily as she goes on and on about the two hundred and eighty square feet in the unit. The laundry facilities. The high-speed internet. But all I hear is the noise of someone's hair dryer. Women laughing. Men upstairs screaming at a ball game on TV. A phone conversation streaming through the walls. The ding of a microwave, the smell of someone's lunch.

Four days without sleep. My body is tired, my mind like soup. I lean against the wall, feeling the force of gravity as it threatens to tug my heavy body to the ground.

"What do you think?" Lily asks over the noise of the hair dryer, and I can't help myself.

"I hate it," I say, for the eighth or ninth time in a row, one for as many apartments as we've seen. Insomnia does that too. It keeps us honest because we don't have the energy to manufacture a lie.

"How come?" she asks, and I tell her about the hair dryer next door. How it's loud.

Lily keeps composed, though inside her patience with me must be wearing thin. "Then we keep looking," she says as I follow her out the door. I'd love to believe that she wants me to be happy, that she wants me to find the perfect place to live. But ultimately it comes down to one thing: my signature on a dotted line. What a lease agreement means for Lily is that an afternoon with me isn't a complete waste of time.

"I have one more to show you," she says, promising something different from the last umpteen apartments we've seen. We return to the Kia and I buckle up in the back seat, behind the purse that's already riding shotgun. We drive. Minutes later the car pulls to a sluggish stop before a greystone on Cornelia, gliding easily into a parking spot. The street is residential, lacking completely in communal living structures. No apartments. No condominiums. No high-rises with elevators that overlook crappy convenient marts. No strangers milling around on street corners.

The house is easily a hundred years old, beautiful and yet overwhelming for its grandeur. It's three stories tall and steep, with wide steps that lead to a front porch. A bank of windows lines each floor. There's a flat-as-a-pancake roof. Beneath the first floor there's a garden apartment, peeking up from beneath concrete.

"This is a three flat?" I ask as we step from the car, envisioning stacks of independent units filling the home, all united by a common front door. I expect Lily to say yes.

But instead she laughs at me, saying, "No, this is a private residential home. It's not for sale, not that you could afford it if it was. Easily a million and a half," she says. "Dollars, that is," and I pause beneath a tree to ask what we're doing here. The day is warm, one of those September days that holds autumn at bay. What we want is to climb into sweaters and jeans, sip cocoa, wrap ourselves in blankets and watch the falling leaves. But instead we drip with sweat. The nights grow cold, but the days are hot, thirty-degree variants from morning to night. It won't last long. According to the weatherman, a change is coming, and it's coming soon. But for now, I stand in shorts and a T-shirt, a sweatshirt wrapped around my waist. When the sun goes down, the temperature will too.

"This way," Lily says with a slight nod of the head. I hurry along after her, but before we round the side of the greystone, something catches my eye. A woman walking down the sidewalk in our direction. She's a good thirty feet away, but moving closer to us. I don't see her face at first because of the force of the wind pushing her dark hair forward and into her eyes. But it doesn't matter. It's the posture that does it for me. That and the tiny feet as they shuffle along. It's the unassuming way she holds herself upright, curved at the shoulders just so. It's her shape, the height and width of it. The shade and texture of a periwinkle coat, a parka, midthigh length with a drawstring waist and a hood, though it's much too warm for a coat with a hood.

The coat is the same one as Mom had.

I feel my heart start to beat. My mouth opens and a single word forms there on my lips. *Mom*. Because that's exactly who it is. It's her; it's Mom. She's here, alive, in the flesh, coming to see me. My arm lifts involuntarily and I start to wave, but with the hair in her eyes, she can't see me standing there on the sidewalk six feet away, waving.

Mom doesn't look at me as she passes by. She doesn't see me. She thinks I'm someone else. I call to her, my voice catching as the word comes out, so that it doesn't come out. Instead it gets trapped somewhere in my throat. Tears pool in my eyes and I think that I'm going to lose her, that she's going to keep walking by. And so my hand reaches out and latches on to her arm. A knee-jerk reaction. To stop her from walking past. To prevent her from leaving.

My hand grabs a hold of her forearm, clamping down. But just as it does, the woman frees her face of the hair and casts a glance at me. And I see then what I failed to see before, that this woman is barely thirty years old, much too young to be my mother. And that her face is covered in an enormity of makeup, unlike Mom, who wore her face bare.

Her coat is not periwinkle at all but darker, more like eggplant or wine. And it has no hood. As she nears, I see more clearly. It isn't a coat after all, but a dress.

She looks nothing like Mom.

For a second I feel like I can't breathe, the wind knocked out of me. The woman tugs her arm free. She gives me a dirty look, scooting past me as I slip from the sidewalk, my feet falling on grass.

"I'm sorry," I whisper as she skirts eye contact, avoids my stare. She moves to the far edge of the sidewalk where she'll be two feet away, where I can't reach her. "I thought you were someone else," I breathe as my eyes turn to find Lily with her arms folded, trying to pretend that this didn't just happen.

Of course it's not Mom, I tell myself as I watch the woman in the eggplant dress move on—faster now, no longer shuffling along but now walking at a clipped pace to get away from me.

Of course it's not Mom, because Mom is dead.

"You coming?" Lily asks, and I say yes.

I follow Lily as we sneak along a brick paver patio and into the backyard. My heart still beats hard. My nerves are rattled. The backyard opens up to reveal a patio and a yard, and behind that, a red brick garage with a jade green door. "This is why we're here," says Lily, gesturing to the garage, and I stop where I am and ask, "You want me to live in a garage?"

"It's a carriage house," she says, explaining how there's living space up above, as is apparently evidenced by a window or two on the second and third floors. "These are quite the find. Some people love them. The minute they come on the market, they're usually gone. This listing just came in this morning," she says, telling me how carriage houses used to be just that in the olden days, a place to park a horse and buggy and for the carriage driver to live. Servants' quarters. They're tucked away on an alley, camouflaged behind a far less humble house, living in the shadows of something bigger and better than them.

Which seems to me to be just the thing I need. To be camouflaged, to live hermit-like in seclusion, in the shadows of something grand.

"Can we see?" I ask, meaning the inside, and Lily lets us in through a tall, tapered front door and immediately up a flight of rickety stairs.

It's larger than anything we've yet seen, nearly five hundred square feet of living space that is dilapidated and old, everything painted a hideous brown. The wooden floors have taken a beating. The boards are squeaky and uneven, with square-cut nails that lift right up out of the floorboards to a toe-stubbing height. The kitchen lines a living room wall, if it can even be called a kitchen. An old stove, an old refrigerator and a small bank of cabinets lined in a row beside where a TV should go. The lighting fixtures are archaic, giving off a scant amount of light. The place is minimally furnished; just a couple pieces of furniture that look to be about as decrepit as the home.

The bathroom appears to have had minor renovations. The fixtures, the paint are new, but the floor tile looks to be older than me. "You won't hear a neighbor's hair dryer from here," Lily says. The so-called bedroom is up a second flight of precarious stairs, a loftlike space with an arched ceiling that follows the low roofline.

On the top floor I can't stand upright. I have to hunch.

"This is hardly suitable living space," says Lily, bent at the neck so she doesn't hit her head. Her wedge sandals struggle down the wooden steps, her hand clinging to the banister lest she fall. She doesn't think I will like it, but I do.

Carriage homes like these, Lily says, don't follow the same rules as prescribed in the city's landlord-tenant ordinance. I wouldn't be protected in the same way. They're overlooked when it comes to regular safety inspections. There's only one door, which generally goes against fire codes that require two. Because garbage bins are relegated to the alley that abuts this home, it can be loud. The smell, especially in the summer months, can be sickening, she says.

"Rats are bent on eating from garbage bins, which means…" she begins, but I hold up a hand and stop her there. She doesn't need to tell me. I know exactly what she means.

"What do you think?" Lily asks.

I listen for the sound of women's laughter. For rowdy men screaming at a TV. There are none.

"How do I apply?" I ask.

Lily takes care of the paperwork. The landlord is a woman

by the name of Ms. Geissler, a widow who lives alone in the greystone. We never meet, though Lily provides her with my completed application, a list of references—ladies whose homes I clean—and a letter of recommendation from a former high school guidance counselor. I kiss three grand goodbye, enough to cover first and last months' rent, plus two more for good measure. As they say, money speaks.

At Lily's suggestion, I wait in the car while she goes inside to meet with the landlord. I hold my breath, knowing it's liable the landlord will soon discover the same slipup as the college's financial aid office. That my social security number belongs to a dead girl. And she'll deny my application.

But, to my great relief, she doesn't. It takes less than fifteen minutes for Lily to emerge through the front door of the greystone, a key ring in hand. The keys to the carriage home. I breathe a sigh of relief. As it turns out, Lily let on about my mom and for that reason, Ms. Geissler approved the application without vetting me first. Out of sympathy and pity. Because she felt sorry for me, which is fine by me, so long as I have a place to live. A place that doesn't remind me of Mom.

As we pull away, I stare out the window and toward the imposing home. It's masked in shadows now, the sun slipping down on the opposite side of the street, burying the greystone in shade. The house is dignified but solemn. Sad. The house itself is sad.

From the third story, I watch the window shade slowly peel back, though what's on the other side I can't see because it's shadowy and dim. But I imagine a woman, a widow, standing on the other side, watching until our car disappears from view.

EDEN

July 26, 1996
Egg Harbor

IT JUST SO HAPPENS that we do have neighbors.

They came this afternoon after Aaron had gone off to work, a pregnant Miranda and her two boys, five-year-old Jack and two-year-old Paul. They came trudging down our gravel drive, Miranda pulling both boys in a red Radio Flyer wagon so that by the time they arrived she was sweaty and spent. She'd come to deliver a welcoming gift.

It was the sound of wheels on gravel that caught my attention as I stood on a ladder, painting the living room walls a pale gray, the windows and doors open to expel chemical scents from the air. This is how I now spend my days when Aaron is away. Unpacking boxes of belongings. Cleaning the insides of closets and cabinets. Painting the home.

I saw them through the window first, heard the tired woman growl at the boys to *stop crying* and to *behave*, her cheeks flushed red from the heat and the pregnancy and, I guessed, the desire to impress. Her blond hair blew around her face and into her eyes as she walked. Her body was cemented with a short maternity dress, fastened to her with sweat. On her feet were Birkenstocks. In her eyes, exhaustion and discontent. From the moment I first spied her out the open window I knew one thing: motherhood did not suit her well.

I set down my painting supplies and met them on the porch. Dropping the wagon's handle, Miranda introduced herself first and then the kids, neither of whom said hello, for they were far too busy clawing their way out of the wagon, elbowing one another for room on the porch step. I didn't mind. They had blond hair like their mother, and if it weren't for the apparent age difference could have easily been twins. They fought one another, vying for the right to their mother's free hand. The bigger of the two won out in the end and as he slipped his hand inside Miranda's, the little guy fell to the ground in a puddle of tears. "Get up," Miranda commanded, her sharp voice jabbing through the placid air, apologizing to me for their manners as she tried hard to raise Paul from the ground. But Paul was a deadweight and wouldn't stand, and as she tugged on his underarms he cried out in pain that she'd hurt him. Tears came pouring from his eyes.

"Damn it, Paul," she said, pulling again roughly on those underarms. "Get up."

What she saw were naughty children making a fuss, embarrassing her, making her feel humiliated and ashamed. But not me. I saw something else entirely. I dropped down beside little Paul and held out a hand to him. "There's a tree swing in the backyard. Let's go have a ride on it, and let Mommy rest awhile?" I said. His pale green eyes rose to mine, snot gathering along his nostrils, running downward toward his lips. He wiped at his nose with the back of a dirty hand and nodded his sweet little head.

Miranda had walked far to bring us a blueberry loaf, more

than a block in the heat. The pits of her dress were damp with sweat, the cotton pulled taut across the baby bump. When she spoke, her voice was breathless, exhausted, burned-out from the energy it took to raise two boys on her own, and she confessed to me that this time—while running a hand over that baby—she was hoping for a girl.

She sat on a patio chair, kicking off her Birkenstocks and resting her swollen ankles on another seat as I poured us each a glass of lemonade, conscious of the dried paint on the backs of my hands.

Miranda's husband, she told me, is employed by the Department of Public Works. She stays at home with Jack and Paul, though what she always wanted to be—what she used to be in her life before kids—was a medical malpractice attorney. She asked how long Aaron and I have been married and when I told her, her eyebrows rose up in curiosity and she asked about kids.

Do we have them?

Do we plan to have them?

It seemed an intimate conversation to have with someone I hardly knew, and yet there was a great thrill at saying the words aloud, as if cementing them to reality. I felt my cheeks redden as I thought of that morning before dawn when Aaron rose, dreamlike, above me, lifting my nightgown up over my head. Outside it was dark, just after four o'clock in the morning, and our eyes were still drowsy, heavy with sleep, our minds not yet preoccupied by the thoughts that arrive with daylight. We moved together there on the bed, sinking into the aging mattress. And then later, while grinning at each other over mugs of coffee on the dock, watching as the fleets of sailboats went floating by on the bay, I had to wonder if it happened at all, or if it was only a dream.

When Miranda asked, I told her that we're trying. Trying to have a child, trying to start a family. An odd choice of words for creating a baby, if you ask me. *Trying* is how one learns to ride a bike. To knit, to sew. To write poetry.

And yet it was exactly what we were doing as Aaron and I made love with reckless abandon, and then followed it up a week or two later with a home pregnancy test. The tests were all negative thus far, that lone pink line on the display screen notifying me again and again that I wasn't yet pregnant. I tried not to let it get the best of me, and yet it was hard to do. It wasn't as though Aaron and I minded the time spent *trying*; in fact, we enjoyed it quite a bit, but with every passing month I yearned exponentially more for a baby. For a baby to have, a baby to hold.

I never mentioned to Aaron that I was taking the pregnancy tests.

I took them while he was at work, watching out the cottage window as his car slipped from view and then, when he was out of sight, rushing to the bathroom, where I closed and locked the door in case he mistakenly left something behind and had to return for it.

And then, when the single pink line appeared on the display screen as it always did, I wrapped the negative pregnancy test sticks up in tissue and discarded them discreetly in the garbage bins.

Miranda beamed when I told her that we're trying. "How exciting!" she told me, her smile mirroring the one on my own face.

And then, helping herself to a slice of her own blueberry loaf and running a hand over her bump for a second time, she said that her baby and my baby could one day go to school together.

That they could one day be friends.

And it was a thought that filled me with consummate joy. I grinned.

I'd been a lone wolf for much of my life. An introvert. The kind of woman who never felt comfortable in her own skin. Aaron changed that for me.

The idea thrilled me to bits and, in turn, I instinctively stroked my own empty womb and thought how much I wanted my baby to have a friend.

JESSIE

TONIGHT MAKES FIVE DAYS since I've been asleep. It's my first night in my new place. I spend it not sleeping, but rather imagining myself dead. I think of what it must be like for Mom, being dead. Is there blackness all around her, a pit of nothingness, the blackest of the black holes? Or has time simply stopped for her, and there's no such thing anymore as the living and the dead? Sometimes I wonder if she's not dead at all but rather alive in the clay urn of hers, screaming to get out. I wonder if there's enough oxygen in the urn. Can Mom breathe? But then I remember it doesn't matter anyway.

Mom is dead.

I wonder if it hurts when you die. If it hurt when Mom died. And I think, in frightening detail, what it feels like when you can't breathe. I find myself holding my breath until my lungs begin to hurt, to burn. It's a prickling pain that stretches from my throat to my torso. It's reflexive, automatic when my mouth gapes open, and I suck in all the oxygen I can to soothe the burn.

It hurts, I decide. It hurts to die.

There's a clock on the wall, one that came with the house. *Tick, tock, tick, tock,* it goes all night long, keeping track of the minutes I don't sleep. Keeping count for me. It's loud, a conga drum pounding in my ear, and though I try and remove the batteries, the *tick, tock* doesn't go away. It stays.

I feel out of place in this strange place. The house smells different than what I'm used to, an earthy smell like pine. It's older than Mom's and my old home, where I lived my entire life. One of the windows doesn't close tight so that when the wind whips its way around the house as it does tonight, air sneaks in. I can't feel it but I hear it, the hiss of the wind forcing its way in through a gap.

I lie there in bed, trying hard to catch my breath, to not think about dying, to will myself to do the impossible and sleep. Beside me, on the floor, are four boxes, the only ones I brought from the old home. Some clothes, a few picture frames, and a box of random paperwork Mom kept, just an old white bankers box, kept closed with a string and button. It seemed important enough for Mom to keep, and so I kept it. A thought comes to me now: *Could my social security card be in that box, tucked away with Mom's financial paperwork?*

I climb out of bed and turn on a light, dropping to the floor beside the box. I loosen the string and lift the lid, meeting reams of paper head-on. If there's any sort of method to the madness, I don't see it.

I search through the paperwork for my social security card, to be sure the numbers I dashed off on the FAFSA form weren't incorrect. That I didn't write the wrong ones down by mistake. Because never in my life have I been asked to give my social security number, and so it's conceivable, I think, that I have the numbers mixed-up. I look for the card itself, grabbing stacks of paper by the handful and flipping through them one sheet at a time, hoping the card falls out. But instead I find the deed to our home, an old checkbook ledger. Gas and electric bills. Years' worth of tax returns that gives me pause, because if I know one thing, it's that Uncle Sam isn't about to pay out tax refunds without a social security number.

I set everything else aside except for the tax returns. My eyes go straight to the exemptions, the spot where someone would list their dependents and their dependents' social security numbers, meaning me and my social security number. Except that when I come to it, I find the line blank. Mom didn't list me as a dependent and, though I double-check the year of the form to be sure I was alive at the time, I see that I was. That I was eleven years old at the time the form was completed.

And though I don't know much about income taxes, I do know it would have saved Mom a buck or two if she had thought to use me as a tax deduction. A baby gift from Uncle Sam.

I wonder why Mom, who was frugal to a fault, didn't claim me as a dependent that year.

It was a mistake, I think. An oversight only. I dig through to find another 1040 in the tower of paperwork—this one older, when I was four years old—and search there for my name and social security number, finding it nowhere. Another year that Mom didn't claim me.

I sift through them all, six tax return forms that I can find—my movements becoming faster, more frantic as I dig—and discover that never once did Mom claim me as a dependent. Not one single time.

I turn off the light and get back into bed. I lie there, wondering why Mom didn't claim me as a dependent. What did she know about the IRS that I don't know? Probably a lot, I reason. I don't pay taxes. I've never once been sent a check from them. My only knowledge comes from hearsay, from eavesdropping on clients like Mr. and Mrs. Ricci, discussing whether they could claim Mrs. Ricci's shopping binges as exemptions, all those fancy clothes she toted home in the trunks of cabs.

Mom must've had a good reason for what she did.

I listen to the clock, *tick, tock*. I don't bother closing my eyes except to blink, because I know that I won't sleep. I pull the blanket up clear to my neck because it's cold in the room. Though the thermostat downstairs is set to sixty-eight degrees, I have yet to hear the heat kick on.

Fall is here and winter is coming soon.

I'm rubbing my hands together for friction, to try and create heat. To make myself warm. I rub them together and then press them to my cheeks. Rub and then press, rub and then press. And that's when I hear a noise.

It's sudden, the kind of noise that makes me sit up straighter in bed, that makes me hold my breath to listen.

The only way to describe it is a ping. A ping, and then nothing. Ping, and then nothing. It's a piercing noise when it comes, like some sort of mechanical bleep or chime, the second or two between each ping a welcome reprieve. I rub at my ears, certain at first that the noise originates there, in my own eardrums. That it's merely tinnitus, a ringing in the ears, something only I can hear.

But then I realize it's not coming from my ears.

It's coming from somewhere on the other side of the room.

I stare though the blackness but see nothing. It's too dark to see much of anything, aside from my own hand when it's pressed all the way up to my face. And so I push the blanket from me and rise, following the noise. I move blindly, feet guiding me, my steps small because I don't know what's in front of me. Where the bedroom ends and the stairs begin. I have to be careful so that I don't fall.

I skirt around the edge of the bed, where I find myself on the other side of the room, hunched at the shoulders because the squat ceiling doesn't allow me to stand upright. From there, the noise rises up from the floor to greet me.

I drop to my knees, running my hands over a metal grate by accident. There I discover a floor register, one of those metal contraptions that attaches to the end of an air duct and leads somewhere under the floor, to some other room in the home. That's where the ping is coming from, from some other room in the home. In my imagination, I see a mallet being tapped against the slats of another register in another room, because that's what it sounds like to me. Like metal on metal, rhythmic and fixed.

I lie on the floor, pressing an ear to the grate so I can hear it more clearly. The ping. Which makes me think only of sonar emitting pulses underwater and then waiting for them to return, to see if there's anything out there, anything like whales or submarines. Except the only thing here is me.

I'm overcome with the strangest thought then. An irrational thought but one that somehow makes sense.

Someone is trying to speak to me. To communicate with me.

I press my lips again to the cold metal grate and call out, "Hello?"

At first there's no reply. The ping disappears, and as I sit there, waiting foolishly for someone to respond to me through the floor register, I realize this is ridiculous. Of course there's no one at the other end of the floor register speaking to me.

Because if there was, that would mean they're in the carriage home with me.

A chill rises up my spine, one vertebra at a time.

Is there someone in the carriage home with me?

I rise to my feet and scurry across the room—quicker this time, forgetting altogether about falling down stairs. I reach out to flip on the bedroom light. A yellow glare spreads over the room, obliterating the darkness. I stand at the top of the steps, staring down over the rest of the carriage home, listening for sounds, watching for movement. But there are none.

"Is anyone there?" I call over the stairwell, my voice timid and afraid. My heart beats hard; my hands begin to sweat. For three or four minutes, no one appears and in time, logic begins to watch over me. I shake my head, feeling stupid.

Of course no one is here.

It's the newness of the home that's to blame. That's what has me on edge. Because for the first time in my entire life, I'm alone and somewhere new. I feel lost without Mom, not knowing who I am or where I belong. If I belong anywhere.

I turn off the bedroom light, and the room is once again plunged into darkness. It's darker now than it was before because my eyes have adjusted to the light. I creep across the room and back toward the bed, reminding myself that this house is old. Old homes come with all sorts of strange but innocuous noises. Rats living in the insulation, the settling of the home, water moving through the pipes. That's all that it is.

As I reach for the bed, I almost have myself convinced.

Until seconds later when the voices come. Female voices by the pitch of it, higher than that of a man. I suck in a gulp of air and hold it in, not believing my own ears.

Someone is there.

The voices are hard to hear, as if they're a million miles

away, the sound dampened by distance and the network of aluminum tubes that make up the ductwork. At first it's only sounds, the cadence of women speaking, but no words that I can make out.

Until I do.

"It won't be long now," I hear, and at first I'm scared. My knees buckle. My throat constricts. My hands go to my throat without meaning to, pressing hard against my vocal cords. My tongue turns to sandpaper and though I'm cold, sweat breeds on my skin.

I see women in some sort of insulated room, by the sound of it. Patients in a psych ward, the walls covered with plastic and foam; a door, padded on the inside, but reinforced with steel. No knob on the door. No way to leave. That's where I imagine the women are.

I stagger back to the floor register, setting myself down over it. I press my ear to the grate, willing the voices to return again, but at the same time hoping they won't. Because I pray that no one is here.

I call into the floor register, my voice mousy at first, scared, "What? What won't be long now?" Though my words are a whisper only, and if they were standing in the very same room as me, two feet away, they wouldn't hear.

I cup my hands around my lips, pressing them flush to the floor register this time, so close I taste the bitter metal in my mouth. I call out, voice louder and more emphatic than it was before, "Can you hear me? Is anyone there?"

The only words I hear are low and plaintive. "She's dead to the world." But to my question there is no reply. Whoever is there can't hear me.

The voices are hollow at first before they go silent. They disappear completely as I sit there, pressing my ear to the floor register in vain. But the only sound that I hear now is the *tick, tock* of the wall clock.

My pulse is going at a breakneck speed. It pounds hard through my temple, my wrist. Wind rattles the carriage home, hissing its way in through the window's gap.

A noise returns from the floor just then and I think that they are back. The women, the voices. The ping. I press my ear to the metal grate and listen.

But this time the only thing that comes is a rush of lukewarm air blasting into me.

The heat. The heat has finally kicked on.

I think of the maze of tubes that work their way through the home and into this room from the furnace. The pipes and fittings and ducts. The ductwork, which, for a home this old, whimpers at every bend like the high pitch of female voices speaking, a whimper that my tired mind only doctored into words. There were never any women there.

It was the furnace's burners igniting, starting to produce heat. The furnace spurting air into the home. It comes out with a whine this time, and I press my hands to the grate to thaw them out.

I'm aware suddenly of just how much my entire body aches.

The insomnia has taken my sleep from me, and now it's taking my mind. Turning the gray matter to sludge. How long can I go on, I wonder, without sleep?

I return to bed and lie down on the mattress, staring out the open window at the sky. It's turned black now, though before I can sleep, dawn will be here. Not in the blink of an eye because that's not the way it is with insomnia.

Time is as slow as the three-toed sloth when you can't sleep.

EDEN

August 2, 1996
Egg Harbor

THE DAYS HAVE GROWN longer now that the task of getting settled into the cottage is through. The walls are painted; the unpacking is done. The garden has become a waiting game, staring at the soil, waiting for something to appear. Always waiting.

Every day, once Aaron has gone off to work, the next ten hours last a lifetime to me. Ten hours with nothing to do but wait until Aaron comes home to keep me company. Afternoons alone are lonely; dinners alone are lonely. I can't fall asleep until Aaron, completely tuckered out from another work shift, drops into bed beside me, nor can I bring myself to admit to him that I am lonely and bored.

Before leaving Green Bay I worked reception for a local pediatrician. It wasn't anything glamorous or ambitious, answering phones, greeting customers, coding medical records, tallying up bills, but it was *something.* But now Aaron has suggested that I not work, that I stay home, that soon enough we'll have a baby to raise and then I'll have something to do.

On occasion Miranda and her boys stop by for a visit, their afternoons long and lonely as well. We sit in the backyard, watching Jack and Paul wreak havoc on the tree swing, and as we do, I listen to Miranda depreciate parenthood, complain about her husband and her kids, knock the tedium of her everyday routine: the frozen waffles, the syrup in the hair, the messy bath times and all the books that she and her children are meant to read but never do because it's far too easy to just let them watch TV. Her husband—Joe—wants her to limit TV time to an hour a day, and Miranda laughed at this, saying Joe didn't have the first clue what it was like to be pregnant, what it was like to raise rough-and-tumble boys like Jack and Paul. She'd take any quiet time she could get, even if it meant they sat perched in front of the TV for five hours at a time, so close they were liable to go deaf and blind. She didn't care. Anything so long as they were quiet.

These were the words Miranda used and I stared at her openmouthed; I could hardly believe my ears. I agreed with Joe, treading carefully, delicately, saying how I'd read that too much TV can lead to obesity in children, to aggressiveness among other things, and she made light of this, saying I didn't know the first thing about being a mother.

"Just wait until you're a mother," she said. "Then you'll see," while hoisting her bare feet onto my patio chair and drinking her lemonade.

And then when adorable little Paul ran over and made every attempt to scamper onto her lap, hot and sweating, Miranda shirked away, saying, "Come on, buddy, it's too hot for laps today," while pushing him off as if he was some sort of bug who'd landed on her legs.

In that moment, what I wanted to do—what I ought to have done—was pull him up onto my own lap. Let him rest his tiny head on my shoulder for a while. He was tired too, in addition to hot and sweating, his eyes begging for a cool bath and his afternoon nap, though Miranda was too busy whining about the drudgery of motherhood and wasn't yet ready to leave.

Suddenly I wanted to feel the weight of him on my own two legs; I craved the heat of his skin on mine. I wanted to press those blond curls away from his eyes.

I've started noticing kids with more frequency lately. Little kids, big kids. Babies. Kids at the park. Kids at the market. Kids walking down the streets of town, holding hands with their fathers and mothers. It seems everyone in the world suddenly had kids, everyone but Aaron and me.

Had they been there all along and I failed to notice?

Or did they arrive just then and there the moment Aaron and I decided to conceive?

I didn't welcome Paul onto my lap as I wanted to do, but watched instead as he pouted and walked away, forced off Miranda's lap with her own two hands. His eyes were downcast, his bottom lip thrust out. He cried, not big crocodile tears but rather quiet and ashamed tears, the tears of someone who'd been told one too many times not to cry.

And, as he disappeared to a corner of the yard to be sad, Miranda released a massive sigh of relief, grateful Paul was gone and she could once again breathe.

August 14, 1996
Egg Harbor

It's starting to become apparent that sex alone doesn't lead to a baby.

When I woke this morning with blood dotting the inside of my underwear, my belly seized by a cramp, I knew another month had come and gone without a child. After the second month of trying, that blood in my underwear came as a startling blow, and there in the bathroom, hunched over the toilet seat, staring at the candy-apple red flecks on the lining of my favorite lace underwear, I began to sob. I kept it quiet and stifled, so that Aaron, in the kitchen brewing our morning coffee, couldn't hear. I didn't want him to know that I was upset. For whatever reason, I'd convinced myself over the last few days that every single twitch and prick I felt were the earliest signs of pregnancy. The tenderness in my chest, the desire to lay waste to almost everything I could find in the pantry, especially that which was high calorie, high fat.

These weren't signs of pregnancy after all, but rather signs of my period. The same ones I'd felt every single month for the last fifteen years of my life, since the middle of seventh grade when I started my period in science class, red blood seeping through a pair of white jean shorts. And now my biological clock had only convinced me I was pregnant. I'd been sure I was nauseated, morning sickness *already*, when what it was was a change in hormones, my uterus clearing the decks, paving the way, getting ready to welcome a life that wouldn't be.

I feel empty now, robbed of something that was mine, but why?

How can I grieve for something I never had?

After Aaron left for work, I scrubbed my underwear clean with detergent and bleach and headed into town. I couldn't bring myself to tell him about the blood. Of course we don't much talk about babies and pregnancy or use words like *ovulation* or *conceive*. Ostensibly, we just have sex, though inwardly what I'm thinking about, what we're *both* thinking about, as we lie together in the moments afterward, my head draped across his chest, his warm hands massaging me, moving yo-

yo-like up and down my back, is the end product, our handiwork, our creation, Aaron and me coming together, the best of him and the best of me fusing to create a baby.

I know he wants this as much as I do.

Only one time did Aaron whisper to me as we lay there in the darkness of the bedroom, still trying hard to catch our breaths after we were through, that he wondered what she would look like and when I asked, "Who?" he said, "Our baby girl. Our baby girl." I beamed there from ear to ear and when I told him I didn't know, he said, "I bet she'll look like you."

And then he kissed me slowly and deeply, the kind of kiss I felt all the way to my every extremity, and though he didn't say it, I knew that in Aaron's eyes if our baby girl looked like me, that she'd be the most beautiful girl in the world.

In all my life no one has ever made me feel as special as Aaron makes me feel.

I've watched him garden, watched the way he carefully carries the peat pots from greenhouse to garden, his every move screaming of paternal instinct; the way he digs the perfect holes, assessing their dimensions twice for accuracy; the way he lays the tiny biodegradable contraptions inside as if setting an infant in a crib, scattering soil over the top as gently as drawing a blanket to a sleeping child's chin. He waters and watches and waits, and as he does, I watch him, this solid figure who, by his stature alone should be anything but gentle and soft-spoken, and yet he is. He wears his chestnut hair short these days, easier to hide behind the chef's cap so there can be no false claims of hair in food, at least not from him, his hands and forearms marked with a selection of scratches and burns. For as long as I remember, he's had them, those scratches and burns: badges of honor, war wounds dating back to his culinary school years.

There are times I find that I can't take my eyes off those scars.

Each time he steps carefully through the garden, tending the seeds, careful not to step on our seedlings, it strikes me what a good father Aaron will one day be, so patient, so protective, so loving, the way he is with me.

And so, to say the words aloud now, to tell him I've started my period, would be to confess to Aaron that though we *tried* again this month, *tried* to conceive a baby, we failed.

After I wiped my eyes, I joined him on the dock for coffee and together we watched the boats pass by and shortly before two o'clock, as always, he left for work and again I was alone.

JESSIE

EVERYTHING CHANGES WITH THE break of day.

As the sun rises, gliding over the horizon, the world turns bright. The oppressive burden of night disappears. For the first time in eight long hours, I can breathe.

In daylight, I find myself standing above the floor register on the bedroom floor, feet straddling it. I stare down at the black rectangle between my legs. There's nothing ominous about it; it's just an ordinary metal grate, cold now, the furnace no longer producing heat. I rub at my arms in an effort to warm them up.

I shower and dress and head out into the day. Outside it's a cold start, no more than forty degrees that will rise up to sixty-five by midday. The sky is blue for now, though there's rain in the forecast. The grass is wet with dew. My fingers are cold as I lock the door.

From where I stand, I catch a glimpse of my landlord through the window of her own kitchen. It's the back of her, just a pouf of hair and the ribs of a blue sweater before they meet with the wooden slats of a chair. It is a distorted image at best, muddled by the reflection of the outside world on glass. She doesn't see me.

I could knock on the door, make an introduction, but that really isn't my thing.

I round the side of the carriage home, gathering Old Faithful from the alleyway where I left her, leaned up against the side of the home. Ivy grows up the brick of the garage, the leaves starting to turn red. The alley is abandoned. There is nothing more than garage doors and Dumpsters here. City of Chicago garbage bins. No people. No rats. No feral cats. No signs of life anywhere. I settle Mom and her urn into the basket on back, nothing more than a metal milk crate that I keep secure with bungee cords. We set off down the street.

It's no secret that Chicago is the alley capital of the country, with over a thousand miles of shadowy backstreets. The kind of darkened corridors where people like to hide their trash and vermin, and nobodies like me.

Morning traffic, as always, is a mess. Millions of people move this way and that like cattle in a cattle drive. My first stop is the same as always: coffee. I take it to go with a sugar twist from the bakery, where the donuts are fresh and the coffee is hot and cheap. I don't have six bucks a day to spend on coffee, and the owner knows me, sort of. She always says hello and calls me Jenny, and I don't have the heart to tell her that, after all these years, she's got it wrong. I set my coffee in the cup holder, pedaling away, making my way toward the Loop. I take my time, moving in wide circles around cars and trucks illegally parked in the bike lines, careful to avoid the city's sewage grates. I stay away from potholes.

Having no luck finding my social security card in the box of Mom's paperwork, I started the day with an idea in mind:

getting a new one. That and figuring out how to get my name removed from this inauspicious death index it's on. I head toward the Social Security Office and there, wait in line for a mind-numbing hour, only to learn that in order to get a new social security card, I need to prove who I am. Something more legitimate than just my word. I need to provide some sort of official identifying documentation like a driver's license or a birth certificate that says I'm Jessica Sloane, neither of which I have.

On the advice of an employee at the Social Security Office, I head next to the Cook County Clerk's Office in the Richard J. Daley Center—the Bureau of Vital Records—in the hopes of tracking my birth certificate down.

When I arrive at the Daley Center, the plaza is teeming with people. I tie Old Faithful up to the bike rack outside, watching as men and women in business suits take wide strides across the plaza. I rush past the Picasso and into the imposing lobby, where I wait in line to pass through security, looking on as others empty their pockets with the speed of a snail. I make it through the X-ray machine and the contents of my bag are searched. When I'm deemed harmless, the guard sends me on my way to the clerk's office, which is in the lower level of the building.

A surge of people wait before the elevator doors and so I take the stairs alone, heading down where I take my place in a long line, sighing in solidarity with those who also wait, avoiding eye contact, losing patience.

When it's my turn, an employee beckons, "Next," with a hand held up in the air so that I see her there, hunched over a computer screen, shoulders sagging. I go to her, telling her what I need.

Suddenly it dawns on me all the information I'm liable to

find when the woman locates my birth certificate. Not only the documentation I need to prove I'm Jessica Sloane, but the place where I was born. The exact time I slipped from Mom's womb. The name of the obstetrician who stood below, waiting to catch me as I fell.

My father's name.

In just a few short minutes, I'll know once and for all who he is. Not only will I have proof of my own identity, but of my father's as well.

I would never have done something as flagrant as seek out my birth certificate from vital records if Mom were still alive. That would have broken her heart, my having access to all these things she never wanted me to have. Searching our home seemed innocent enough, but tracking down my birth certificate feels like a really egregious act were she still here.

But Mom told me to *find myself*, and that's what I'm trying to do. To get into college, to make something of myself. To do something that would make Mom proud, all of which I can't do without a social security card.

"I need to get a copy of my birth certificate," I say to the employee. My heart quickens as she slides a request form across the counter. She tells me to fill it out. I reach for a pen, completing as much of the form as I can. It isn't much. I can't answer the question that pertains to place of birth or anything having to do with my dad—what his name is, where he was born.

It's only as I pause in my writing that the worker takes pity on me. Her eyes soften ever so slightly and she says, "You don't have to fill it all in," while staring uncomfortably at the urn in the crook of my arm, seeing the way the pen in my hand hovers above the words *father's name*. "Just as much as you know," she adds, telling me she can try and look it up with what little

I know. I slide the form back to her, half-complete, and she says she'll just need the payment and to see a photo ID.

A photo ID.

It's easy to explain why I don't have a photo ID. Because by this point in most people's lives, they have a driver's license, which is something I also don't have. Because the cancer came the year I turned fifteen, the year I was meant to enroll in my high school's after-school drivers' education program. Because after we learned that Mom had an invasive tumor in her left breast, knowing how to drive a car—in a city where we didn't need or own a car—didn't take top priority. Because my afternoons were tied up with Mom from then on, riding the bus with her to bajillions of doctor appointments or working to help pay for our home and her care. Because once I knew there was a good chance Mom would die, I wanted to spend every minute I could with her.

And yet I'm loath to tell the worker the bind I'm in because I know how it will sound. And so instead of coming clean, I root around in the pockets of my jeans, extracting the lining. I dive a hand deep into the depths of my bag searching for something I know isn't there. I pluck thirty dollars out of my wallet—the cost of the birth certificate is only fifteen—and try handing it to the woman. "Keep the change, please," I say, bemoaning in a low voice how my license was in my bag just this morning. How it must have fallen from my wallet on the way in. How it was there, but now it's gone.

I press the urn to my chest, hoping the woman's mercy will prevail and she'll pocket the extra fifteen bucks and get me what I need. She stares at the money for a minute and then asks whether I have any other form of ID. An insurance card or voter registration, but I shake my head and tell her no. I don't have either of these things. Mom had health insurance.

A rock-bottom plan that helped pay for cancer treatment, though I'm still in the hole more than I care to think about. But Mom never added me to her insurance plan because she said it wasn't something I needed. I was young and healthy and the rare trip to the clinic could be paid for with cash. Those required school vaccines I got at the Department of Public Health because they were cheap.

"Got any mail with your name on it?" the woman wants to know, but I shrug my shoulders and tell her no. She gives me a look. Disbelief, I think. I'm as much of a skeptic as the next guy; I know how this sounds.

"Please, ma'am," I beg. I'm tired and I don't know what else to do. My eyes feel heavy, threatening to close. There's the greatest desire to lie down on the floor and sleep. Except that it's only a tease, my body playing tricks on me. Even if I lie outstretched on the linoleum tiles, I still wouldn't sleep.

"I really need that birth certificate, ma'am," I say, shuffling in place, and it must be something about the way my voice cracks or the tears that well in my eyes that makes her lean forward and snatch the money from the countertop. She gathers the bills into her hand, counting them one at a time. Her eyes take a quick poll of the room to see if anyone else is watching, listening, before she whispers, "How about this. How about I see if I can find anything first. Then we'll figure out what to do about the ID."

I say okay.

She takes the form and begins typing information onto the rows of keys.

My heart pounds inside my chest. My hands sweat. In just a few short minutes, I'll know who my father is. I start thinking about his name. Whether he's still alive. And if he is, if he thinks about me the way I think about him.

By now, there are at least twenty people in line behind me. The room isn't large by any means. It's stodgy and drab, and everyone is looking at everyone else like they're a common criminal. Ladies clutch their purses to their sides. A kid in line screams that he has to pee. As he yells, I glance over my shoulder to see this poor kid, maybe four years old, hand pressed to his groin, eyes wide and ready to burst, his mother reading him the riot act for nature's call.

"There were no records found," the woman says to me then. Not at all the words I expected to hear. My face falls flat; my mouth parts. For a second I'm confused, unable to produce coherent thoughts or words.

I fight to find my voice, asking, "Are you sure you spelled it correctly?" imagining her hunting and pecking for the letters, clipping the corner edge of some surplus letter by mistake, misspelling my name.

But her face remains motionless. She doesn't attempt another search, as I'd hoped she'd do. She doesn't glance down at the computer or check her work.

"I'm sure," she says, raising a hand into the air to beckon for the next customer.

"But wait," I say, stopping her. Not willing to give up just yet.

"There were no records found, miss," she tells me again, and I ask, feeling incredulous, "What does that mean then, *no records found*?" because what I'm suddenly realizing is that, instead of being *dead*, the crux of the matter is that there is no birth record on file for me.

I can't be dead because I haven't yet been born.

The Bureau of Vital Records doesn't even know I exist.

"Of course you must have found something," I argue, not

waiting for a reply. My voice elevates. "How can there be no birth certificate for me when clearly I'm alive?"

And then I pinch a fold of skin on my arm, watching as it swells and turns red before shriveling back down to size. I do it so that she and I can both see I'm alive.

"Ma'am," she says, and there's a shift in posture, her empathy quickly giving way to aggravation. I've become a pest. "You left half this form blank," she says.

I argue that she told me I could. That she was the one who said I didn't have to fill it all out. She ignores me, continues to speak. "Who's to say you were even born in Illinois? Were you born in Illinois?" she asks, challenging me, calling my bluff, and I realize that I don't know. I don't know where I was born. All my life, I only assumed. Because Mom never told me otherwise and I never thought to ask.

"No records found means that I couldn't locate a birth certificate based on the information you gave me. You want to find your birth certificate, you need to fill in the rest of these blanks," she tells me, slipping the request form back to me as I stare down helplessly at all the missing information, *name of father, place of birth*, wondering if what I filled in was even correct to begin with.

Was Mom always a Sloane like me? That I'd also assumed. But if she was married when I was born, then maybe she had a different last name, one she ditched at some point over the last twenty years for some reason I don't know?

"And next time," the employee tacks on as I back dismally away, losing hope, running blindly into another woman in line, "be sure and bring your ID."

I make my way out the door, climbing back up to the first floor two steps at a time. The building's stairwell is industrial and dark, a flash of gray that comes at me quickly. It spirals upward in circles for thirty floors or more. When I arrive on the first floor, slipping through the stairwell door, crowds flood the lobby of the Daley Center. I'm grateful for this, for the anonymity of it all. I camouflage myself among the wayward teens who've been summoned here for court, those with purple-dyed hair and heads hidden beneath sweatshirt hoods. I make my way back outside, nowhere closer to finding my father or proving my identity.

As far as the world is concerned, I'm still dead.

EDEN

September 14, 1996
Egg Harbor

THE TOWN WAS MOBBED with people today as it always is on Saturdays, vacationers trying hard to take advantage of the last few warm days before fall arrives. It's September now, days shy of the equinox, and as September eventually bleeds into October, the seas of people will finally leave. They come for the hundreds of miles of shorelines, the extensive gift shops, the food. But by December, this far north into Wisconsin, the temperatures will hurtle to twenty or thirty degrees, mounds of snow will obstruct the streets, and the skies will be endlessly gray. And then no one will want to be here, least of all me. Aaron and I will spend the Midwest winter as we always do, imagining the warm places in the world we hope to one day go, places where cold and snow don't exist. St. Lucia, Fiji, Belize.

Places we will never go.

I spent the day while Aaron was at work wandering the town's streets, simulating a tourist. I visited gift shops; I bought a T-shirt and ice cream, a book on sailing. I rode the Washington Island Ferry through Death's Door, spending the late-afternoon hours exploring the crystal clear waters and the polished white stones of Schoolhouse Beach, trying to skip rocks out over the lake, and like getting pregnant, failing at that too.

Back in town I watched families wander from store to store, mothers with buggies, fathers with toddlers perched on their backs. I stared at them as afternoon blended into evening, seated on a bench at Beach View Park, watching as families laid out blankets, staking their claim to a patch of land for the night's sunset display.

The children were everywhere, and I started to wonder why something in so much abundance could ever be hard to achieve.

October 8, 1996
Egg Harbor

Each time Miranda and her boys stop by, she has a new suggestion for me, some tip on how to hasten conception. No subject is too personal or too taboo to discuss, from the style of Aaron's underwear to various positions that supposedly aid in fertilization as she lounges on my back patio or living room sofa, weather depending, and cites for me the reasons she believes Aaron and I are not yet pregnant—though never once did I ask.

As she talks, Jack and Paul loiter before us, performing for me a song they learned, a magic trick, how they can make their eyes go crossed. They stand before me as Miranda spells out the effects of tight underpants on the male genitalia, saying over and over again, "Look at me, Miss Eden. Look what I can do," while folding their tongues in half, or trying to make them stretch clear to the ends of their noses, and, as Miranda talks louder to counter their escalating tones, it hits me how attention-starved they are, how they would give anything for her to watch them for a minute, to praise their talents. Every day, there is dirt wedged beneath their nails and some sort of food on their cheeks and chins. Their outfits are cobbled together with clothing that doesn't match and hardly fits.

I clap my hands for Jack and Paul, but Miranda tells them to go away. To go play.

Every day.

As her baby bump swells more and more, I'm pestered by Miranda to *hurry up*, to get knocked up, so that her baby and my baby can still go to school together as I've promised her they would.

If I wait much longer they'll be in different grades.

That's what Miranda has told me.

"September is the cutoff, don't you know?"

According to Miranda's timeline, I have until September of next year to have a baby. Twelve months, which leaves only three to get pregnant.

"It's not that we're not trying," I've tried to explain, and she counters with a flip of the hand and a slapdash "I know, I know," and then it's back to the underwear we go. To help with Aaron's and my fertility issues, she suggested a pillow beneath my hips to help steer sperm in the right direction. "It's all about gravity," she says.

At every visit I watch the size of her own baby bump swell, her maternity shirts no longer able to cover its overwhelming girth. I tell myself that her suggestions are only old wives' tales, not rooted in truth, but how am I to know if that's true?

But today when she lounged on my sofa, peering at me with that same expression on her face—mouth parted, eyebrows raised—and asked if I was keeping track of my ovulation, I realized how stupid it was of me, how naive.

This was Aaron's and my first foray into babymaking. I was sure it was something that just *happened*, that there was no need to time or plan. In the moment, I told her yes, of course I was keeping track of my dates, because I couldn't bring myself to say otherwise, to admit to her that it never occurred to me to figure out when I was and when I wasn't ovulating. Aaron and I both come from large families, and the number of grandchildren our parents have been blessed with is in no way in short supply. It seemed a given that after ample time, after many months of waking up in the morning to Aaron's soft fingers tracing my bare skin, thumbs hooking through the lacy edges of my underpants, gliding them proficiently over my thighs, sooner or later we'd succeed. We'd make a baby as we intended to do.

But for the first time I've come to realize that this is going to take more than time.

After Miranda left I drove to the library and sought out a guidebook on pregnancy and there, in the stacks of books, plotted out my approximate menstrual cycle. I figured out the first date of my last period. I counted backward; I did the math. It wouldn't be perfect, that I knew—my periods had never been perfect—but it would be close. And close to perfect was better than nothing for me.

And now, knowing that in just two days' time I will be ovulating fills me with an abundant amount of hope. Aaron and I were doing it wrong all along, missing out on the best times to get pregnant, likely omitting my most fertile days, those negligible hours when conception can occur. On the way home I stopped at the market and picked up a pocket-size calendar and, at home, with a red pen, circled my most fertile days for the next three months, through the end of the year.

This time we'll get it right.

JESSIE

I PUSH MY WAY through the turnstile doors and step outside, making my way across the plaza. Beside the Eternal Flame, I pause, overcome with the sudden urge to scale the fence and lie down beside the puny little fire in the fetal position. To fall to my side on the cold concrete, beside the memorial for fallen soldiers. To pull my knees up to my chest in the middle of all those pigeons who huddle around it, trying to keep warm. The land around the flame is thick with birds, the concrete white from their waste. That's where I want to lie. Because I'm so tired I can no longer stand upright.

People breeze past me. No one bothers to look. A passing shoulder slams into mine. The man never apologizes and I wonder, *Can he see me? Am I here?*

I head to the bike rack, finding Old Faithful ensnared beneath the pedals and handlebars of a dozen or more poorly placed bikes. I have to tug with all my might to get her out and still I can't do it. The frustration over my identity boils inside me until I feel myself begin to lose it. All this red tape preventing me from getting what I need, from proving who I am. I'm starting to question it myself. *Am I still me?*

The debilitating effects of insomnia return to me then, suddenly and without warning. General aches and pains plague every muscle in my body because I can't sleep. Because I haven't been sleeping. My feet hurt. My legs threaten to give. I shift my weight from one leg to the next, needing to sit. It's all I can think about for the next few seconds.

Sitting down.

Pins and needles stab my legs. I wrench on the bike, yanking as hard as I can, but still she doesn't budge. "Need a hand?" I hear, and though clearly I need a hand, there's a part of me feeling so suddenly indignant that I turn with every intent of telling the person that *I've got it.* Words clipped. Expression flat.

But when I turn, I see a pair of blue eyes staring back at me. Royal blue eyes like the big round gum balls that drop down the chute of a gum-ball machine. And my words get lost inside my throat somewhere as I rub at my bleary eyes to be sure I'm seeing what I think I'm seeing. Because I know these eyes. Because I've seen these eyes before.

"It's you," I say, the surprise in my voice clear-cut.

"It's me," he says. And then he reaches over and hoists Old Faithful inches above the other bikes, those that have held her prisoner all this time. It's effortless to him, like nothing.

He looks different than the last time I saw him. Because the last time I saw him he was folded over the cafeteria table, drinking coffee in a sweatshirt and jeans. Now he's dressed to the nines in black slacks, a dress shirt and tie, and I know what it means. It means that his brother has died. His brother, who was hurt in a motorcycle accident after a car cut him off and he went flying off the bike, soaring headfirst through the air and into a utility pole without a helmet to protect his head.

He held vigil beside his brother's hospital bed while I held vigil beside Mom's. And now, six days later, his eyes still look tired and sad. When he smiles, it's strained and unconvincing. He's gotten a haircut. The dark, messy hair has been given a trim and though it's not prim or tidy—not by a long shot—it looks clean. Combed back. Much different than the hair I saw those days and nights in the hospital cafeteria, his head stuffed under the hood of a red sweatshirt. We only spoke the one night, him fussing about the coffee, telling me how he'd rather be anywhere but there. But still, there's the innate sense that I know him. That we shared something intimate. Something much more personal than coffee. That we're bound by a similar sense of loss, united by grief. Both collateral damage in his brother's and my mother's demise.

He sets Old Faithful down on the ground and passes the handlebar to me. I take her in my hand, seeing the way his nails are bitten to the quick, the skin torn along the edges. A row of rubber bands rests on his wrist, the last one tucked halfway beneath the cuff of the dress shirt. A single word is written on the back of the hand with blue ink. I can't read what it is.

He runs his hands through his hair and only then do I think what I must look like.

It can't be good.

"What are you doing here?" I ask, as if I have any more right being here than him.

He speaks in incomplete sentences, and still I get the gist. "The wake," he says. "St. Peter's. I needed some air."

He points in the direction of some church just a couple of blocks from here, one that's too far to see from where we stand. Though still I look, seeing that the sun has slipped from the sky and is hidden now behind a cloud. While I was inside the building, the clouds rolled into the city, one by one. They changed the morning's blue sky to one that is plush and white, filling the sky like cotton balls, making the day ambiguous and gray.

I don't ask when or how his brother died and he doesn't ask about Mom. He doesn't need to because he knows. He can see it in my eyes that she has died. Neither of us offer our condolences.

He rams his hands into the pockets of his slacks. "You never told me your name," he says. If I was the kind of girl that felt comfortable in situations like these, I'd say something snarky like *Well, you never asked.*

But I don't because it's not that type of conversation, and I'm not that girl.

"Jessie," I say, sticking my hand out by means of introduction. His handshake is firm, his hand warm as he presses it to mine.

"Liam," he says, eyes straying, and I take it as my cue to leave. Because there isn't anything more to say. The one and only conversation we had in the hospital, words were sparse, but unlike in the hospital we're no longer killing time, just waiting for people to die. That night, before the conversation drifted to quiet and we sat in silence for over an hour, sipping our coffees, we talked about private things, nonpublic things, things we weren't apt to tell the rest of the world. He told me about his brother beating him up when they were kids. About how he would lock him out of the house in the rain and shove his head in the toilet, giving him a swirly when their folks weren't home. *Such a bastard*, he said, though I got the sense that that was then and this was now. That over the years, things changed. But he didn't say when or how.

I told him about Mom's hair and fingernails, both of which she lost thanks to chemotherapy. Her eyelashes too. I told him about the clumps of hair that fell out, and how I watched on in horror as Mom held fistfuls of it in her hands. How there were whole clods of it on her pillowcase when she awoke in the morning, masses of it filling the shower drain. I said that Mom never cried, that only I cried. It grew back, after the cancer was in remission for the first time, soft fuzz that grew a little thicker than it was before chemotherapy. A little more brown. It never reached her shoulders before the cancer returned.

"You should get back to the wake," I tell him now as we stand there in the middle of Daley Plaza. But he only shrugs his shoulders and tells me that the wake is through. That everyone split.

"The funeral's tomorrow," he says as I wrap my fingers around Old Faithful's handlebars. I don't know what to say to that. There isn't anything to say to that.

Turns out, I don't need to say anything. "You never said what you're doing here," he says then, but as I'm about to explain I realize that there's no easy answer for it, because the reason I'm standing outside Daley Center is far more convoluted than his. And so instead of answering, I sigh and say, "Long story," thinking that he'll just say okay and walk away because chances are good he didn't want to know in the first place. He was probably only being polite because I asked what he was doing here, and so he thought he should too, that he should reciprocate out of courtesy.

But as he shifts in place and tells me, "I have time," I realize that he wants me to stay.

There's a sadness in his eyes, the likeness to mine uncanny.

We walk. Out of the plaza, down Washington and toward

Clark Street, me towing Old Faithful by the handlebar. We walk in the street because it's illegal to ride a bike on the sidewalk in the city. I don't know what time it is, but what I can say is that the haste of rush hour is past, the clog of morning traffic like hair in a shower drain. Impossible to get through. It's gone, as if some plumber stopped by and dropped a gallon of Drano on the street, ameliorating the clog. People move slowly now. They take their time. Without the blockage we easily slip through, weaving in and out of pedestrians and cars.

"I stopped by vital records," I say. "I needed to get my birth certificate. Except that didn't go as planned," I explain as we turn a right on Clark, which is a one-way street around here. All the cars come directly at us. They miss us by a hair's breadth at times because there are no bike lanes. Not that it matters because half of the time when there are, cars and trucks illegally park and I have to veer around them and into traffic. The number of bike-related deaths in the city is staggering; I just hope that one day one of them isn't me.

Liam asks why getting my birth certificate didn't go as planned. He's a good ten inches taller than me, broad in the shoulders but narrow around the hips. At just over five feet, I've always been on the short side. My whole life, for as long as I can remember, I've been short. Kids in school used to make fun of me. They'd call me names like shrimp, peanut. Squirt.

He towers over me, his body slim but in the tailored clothes, he doesn't look too thin. I remember him in the hospital—oversize sweatshirt and jeans, getting swallowed up by fabric. Then he looked thin.

I start at the beginning and tell Liam the whole story. Otherwise it won't make sense. And even then it doesn't make much sense because I'm having a hard time wrapping my head around it myself. I tell him about applying to college, the phone call from the financial aid office. The woman's cheery voice on the other end of the line, laughing, telling me I'm dead. I tell him about the wasted time spent trying to find my social security card, the worthless trip to the Social Security Office. The one that led me here, to the Daley Center in search of my birth certificate, though that too was a waste.

"I don't have a birth certificate," I close with. "At least not one in the state of Illinois. And without a birth certificate or a social security number, there's no way to prove who I am or that I even exist. But what freaks me out even more," I admit, "is this implication that—"

But before I can get the words out, birds swarm around me, moving in from all directions. Pigeons with beady eyes and little bobbing heads, pecking at something on the street. They fight over it, their squawks loud and angry. I try to sidestep them, but their movements are arbitrary, aimless; there's no predicting where they'll go. I step on the tail feathers of one by chance and it scurries, wings slapping together to get away from me.

As I go to take another step, I see what the skirmish is all about. It's another pigeon, dead, lying on the street where my foot should go. The other birds move in on it, pecking at it, trying to eat it, and just like that, there's nowhere for me to put my foot. It throws off my stride, makes me lose balance. The dead pigeon lies on its back, spread-eagle-like. Its wings are fanned on either side of its body, white belly exposed, its neck turned too far in one direction, broken I think. I see only one beady eye, the other somehow missing. Its beak is tucked into the crook of a neck, and on the street beside it are flecks of blood.

I nearly step on the carcass as my body lurches forward, stumbling, and I'm sure I'll fall. My heartbeat kicks up a notch or two, hands sweaty, and like that I'm at the mercy of the bird and the street.

I let go of Old Faithful's handlebars by accident. I watch as she topples onto the street, certain I'm about to go with her. People turn to see what the racket is, the clang of the bike on the street, the sound of my scream. My hands reach for something to latch on to, coming up empty until Liam grabs me by the wrist, steadying me.

"Jessie?" he asks, and I have to fight for a minute to catch my breath. I'm breathing hard, seeing only pigeons nipping the bloody flesh of a dead bird. And I'm thinking about that bird, wondering what happened to kill the bird. How did it die? If it was killed by a car or a bike, or a run-in with a building window maybe. Maybe it flew headfirst into the Thompson Center before sliding down, down, down to the ground.

"Jessie?" Liam asks again because I still haven't replied. His eyes watch me, uneasy, as he makes sure I'm steady on my feet before leaning down to reclaim Old Faithful from the street.

"Are you okay?" he asks, and, "What happened?" and I shake my head and say, "The damn bird. Those pigeons."

"What bird?" he asks. "What pigeons?"

I turn to point them out to him. But when I look back on to the street behind me, there's no bird. No pigeons. The only thing there is a squandered hot dog that lies on the asphalt. Half-eaten, gravel stuck to what remains of it. Chunky green relish spilling from the bun, red ketchup splattered here and there like blood.

There's no dead bird.

There was never a dead bird.

The world loses balance all of a sudden, the street beneath my feet unpredictable and insecure. I think of sinkholes, when the earth suddenly decides to give, roadways collapsing like Play-Doh, sucking people in and swallowing them whole.

I shake my head. "Just tripped over my own feet," I say, but I can see in Liam's eyes: he doesn't believe me.

We move on.

Liam waits for me to finish whatever it is I was saying before I saw the bird, but now my train of thought is gone. I can think only of the bird, the pigeons, the flecks of blood. And so he reminds me. And then I remember.

What freaks me out the most, I tell him, is the implication that I'm already dead.

He asks about the death database. What it is and what it's called, and so I tell him what the woman from the financial aid office told me.

"The Death Master File," I say, which in and of itself sounds like something the grim reaper must carry along with him, a listing of all the souls he's sent to collect. Liam looks it up on his smartphone, and soon finds out that access to the file is restricted. That not just anybody can look at it. He tells me what I already know. That it's a listing of millions of people who have died, them and their social security numbers. It's used as a means to prevent fraud and identity theft. To stop living people from opening credit cards and getting mortgages in the name of someone who's already dead.

"So somehow I got placed on this list, and now my social security number is good for nothing until I clean up this mess. Because on paper, I'm dead. And I can't find my social security card or figure out how to get a new card because I don't have the other documentation I need to do it."

"Listen to this," Liam says as a disclaimer pops up on his phone and he reads, quoting verbatim, "'In rare instances it is possible for the records of a person who is not deceased to be included erroneously in the DMF.'"

I ask him how that can happen. "A clerical error," he says, meaning with the stroke of one wrong computer key someone who's alive and well is suddenly dead. Or not dead but undocumented, which is almost as good as being dead, I'm quickly learning.

The only reason my own death went unnoticed for all this time, I think, is because I haven't once been asked to give my social security number. But sooner or later it was bound to happen. When I sought out a driver's license, made an attempt to open a credit card. An attempt that would have been denied.

As we scoot onto the pedestrian side of the Clark Street Bridge and cross over the Chicago River, I think of people in the same situation as me, unable to access their own bank accounts and going broke. Those who don't have the money for food or shelter, though they *do* have the money; it's just that it's tied up in some bank account they can't access because the bank is certain they're dead.

"People get locked out of their own lives, interrogated by police for suspected identity theft when the person whose identity they've supposedly stolen is themselves," Liam says as he drops his phone into the back pocket of his pants, and I utter under my breath, "What a mess."

I stare down below, beneath the metal grates of the bridge, where a tour is underway, tourists exploring the polluted grayish-green waters of the Chicago River. The tour guide steers passengers' attention to the bridge—built in 1929, a bascule bridge, she says—and all eyes move to Liam and me, taking photos, pointing upward some twenty feet or more to the bridge on which we stand.

"You really are Jessie, aren't you?" His words are dry, meant to be funny, though they're not. His tone is deadpan, his face expressionless.

And though I know it's in jest, it's a question that nags at me.

I am Jessie, aren't I? Am I Jessica Sloane?

We continue to walk. Down Clark and left on Superior, my feet following Liam's lead. We're quiet. We don't speak much. He asks if I've been sleeping. He says that I look tired and I pause, looking at my own reflection in the glass facade of a building. I see what he sees. The sunken eyes surrounded by puffy red skin, the tip of my nose red.

I make light of the insomnia. I say that sleep is a waste of time. That there are so many more productive things I could be doing instead of sleeping.

"It's not good for you, Jessie," he tells me. "You need to sleep. The melatonin," he says, same as he did in the hospital when he slipped those pills into the palm of my hand. "Give it a try." *I did give it a try*, I think. I tried the melatonin—that and the clonazepam—and slept right on through Mom's death. Never again.

I tell him that I will but I won't.

And then he stops beside a mid-rise, saying, "This is me. This is where I live."

This building beside us is five or six stories tall, flanked with floor-to-ceiling windows. A sign out front offers spacious open-plan lofts for sale. A doorman patrols the revolving front door and there's something very moneyed about it that makes me feel out of place and ill at ease. The Liam before me is suddenly at odds with the Liam I remember from the hospital, the one who was bedraggled, a bit dog-eared like me.

A look of confusion must pass on my face. "My brother and I lived here together," he explains. His voice is deep and there's no rise or fall to his intonation as he speaks, telling me, "He was a software engineer."

I fill in the missing pieces. His brother made the money. He paid for the condo. And now he's gone.

"You'll be okay?" I ask, and his reply is detached.

"What's that they say?" he asks, plucking at the row of rubber bands on his wrist so that I see now what it says on his hand in the blue ink. *Adam.* His brother's name, I think. "About death and taxes?"

That nothing is certain but death and taxes. That's what they say. But he's not looking for an answer. What he's saying is that he may or may not be okay, but there's no way to know right now. Same as me.

We say our goodbyes. I watch as he slips through the doors of the apartment building, disappearing behind a wall of glass.

EDEN

November 14, 1996
Egg Harbor

IT'S NOVEMBER NOW.

The gray skies have descended, everything perpetually overcast and sad. The boats have been pulled from the bay, leaving it barren and empty, like my womb. The seasonal shops are closed. The tourists took their cue to leave.

Two weeks ago, on the first of November, Miranda had that baby of hers, a seven pound, three ounce beautiful baby boy who she and Joe named Carter. I visited in the hospital the day after he was born, her only visitor aside from Joe. I saw it in her eyes as soon as I entered the postpartum room, Miranda swaddling baby Carter with a look of arrant dissatisfaction on her face. Her lips were pursed, her eyebrows creased, crow's-feet forming around the eyes.

As I walked in—swapping places with Joe, who went to the cafeteria for coffee—her disillusioned eyes rose to mine and she confessed aloud so that baby Carter could hear, not bothering to lower her voice or to press her hands to his ears to muffle the rotten words, "All I wanted was a baby girl. Is it too much to ask for one little girl? But instead it's another goddamn boy."

Her words knocked the wind out of my lungs. They made it hard to breathe. They were so ugly and vile, and I saw a look in Miranda's eyes as she spoke of him, eyes dropping to his. A look that made my heart hurt. Only a day old and already she abhorred her baby boy.

I asked if I could hold him and she said yes, handing him off with too much inclination, too much ease, as if grateful to be rid of him. I took baby Carter to a chair in the corner of the room and peered at his inappreciable wisps of blond hair and his heavy, tired eyes, thinking to myself, *What difference does it make if he's a boy or girl, only that he's happy and healthy?*

And I felt angry for the first time at Miranda. Not just annoyed but truly angry. Angry that she had three beautiful baby boys and I had none. Angry that she didn't love her babies or value her babies, that she couldn't understand another woman—one like me—would give life and limb for a child.

Oh, what I wouldn't give for a child.

I had a thought then.

Would Miranda care if I rose to my feet and carried baby Carter from the room?

Would she even notice?

The hospital experience, for Miranda, was a welcomed furlough from motherhood. From what I'd been told, Carter spent his time in the nursery, being cared for by nurses round the clock except when he needed to eat, and only then did nurses carry him, crying and discontent, to his mother, and she welcomed him grudgingly, embittered to her chest. And then as soon as he was full, his eyes drifting lazily to sleep, she asked the nurses to take him away so that she could sleep.

Spread out on her hospital bed in an indiscreet polka-dot

gown, I watched Miranda sleep. Or pretend to sleep at least, so that she didn't have to tend to her child. She was exhausted, yes, from many hours of labor and delivery, from the every-other-hour feedings, and yet I wondered if her eyes were merely closed so that she could remain insensible to her baby boy, who lay limply in my arms, head misshapen, skin wrinkly and pink as a newborn's should be. Miranda's hair was brushed away from her face, pulled taut into a ponytail that lay flat against the bed. Her arms and hands were stretched out by her sides. She breathed with her mouth open, nostrils flaring with each inhalation and exhalation of air.

I whispered her name. There was no reply.

It was almost as if she was asking me, begging me, daring me to take her child.

And so I did.

I stood from the inflexible armchair, slowly, gradually, piecemeal-like so that the chair wouldn't make a sound. So that the floor wouldn't cheep. So that my own two feet wouldn't betray me. I flexed one muscle and then the next until I was standing upright, holding my breath.

I crossed the room, creeping by degrees so my shoes wouldn't squeak on the floors. Miranda's eyes were closed, enjoying the peace and serenity of having someone else care for her child.

It didn't occur to her for one instant that someone might try and take her baby.

I slipped into the hallway without a peep. Two left turns and there Carter and I were, standing before the nursery, staring through glass at a half dozen sleeping babies. They lay bundled like burritos in their pink and blue blankets, with knitted hats atop their near-bald heads. They were sleeping, every last one of them, completely tuckered out. The newborns slept in rolling bassinets all arranged on display so that grandmas and grandpas could see. If it wasn't for the slip of paper in each bassinet with the baby's name and date of birth in blue ink, there was no telling them apart aside from the obvious distinction of pink and blue.

How easy it would be for two to be swapped, or for one to up and disappear.

One nurse stood guard of them all, a shepherd in the pasture keeping watch over her sheep. What I wouldn't give to be that nurse, to be tasked with caring for the infinite number of newborn babies that rotated in and out of the nursery each day.

I wondered if she ever had a weakness for any one of these babies. A fondness. Was there ever one colicky child who caught her eye, the runt of a litter of multiples she wanted to bring home as her own?

From down the hallway a door opened and I saw the main hospital on the other side, areas other than the labor and delivery ward. A common hallway. The hospital's information booth. The doorway was twenty steps away at best, and there was nothing but two unlocked doors to prevent Carter and me from leaving. There was no alarm, at least none that I could see. There was no system to buzz people in and out. It was an open door, an invitation.

How easily Carter and I could just leave.

I looked around; the nursery nurse had her back in my direction, attention now focused on one little baby who was trying to wake up. Behind me, there was only a single woman at the nurses' station, a middle-aged lady on the phone. Other than that, the ward was quiet and still, all patient doors pulled closed, mothers on the other side in the throes of labor or fast asleep.

I peered to the doorway again, those swinging double doors

just twenty steps away from where I stood. I didn't think about the rest, about what I would tell Aaron or what Miranda might do when she awoke and realized Carter was gone. My heart beat quickly as desire and instinct told me to do it and to do it quickly, to move with purpose, to not draw attention to myself. In my arms, I held the very thing Aaron and I had been trying for for months. A baby.

Miranda didn't want him anyway. I was doing her a favor, I reasoned.

How easily this baby could be mine.

I thought of only one thing in that moment as I stood frozen, staring through glass at the plentiful sleeping babies.

How easy it would be to just go.

I didn't do it, of course, but it would be remiss to say the idea never crossed my mind.

JESSIE

I PEDAL TOWARD ROSCOE Village. As I do, I stare over my shoulder, back into the Loop at the peaks of skyscrapers that rise into the sky like distant mountain summits. I watch as the urban streets become residential.

Once in Roscoe Village, I duck into a burger joint on Addison. My stomach is empty by now, the morning's sugar high having given way to a glucose crash, one which makes me irritable and edgy. I've had nothing to eat but a donut all day—a donut and coffee—though since Mom's death, my hip bones protrude from my waistline and the bones of my rib cage are startlingly transparent.

I'm not *not* eating on purpose. I've just had no desire to eat.

I order a hamburger and take it to the counter to eat. There, I stare out the window at the world as it passes by without me. A bus goes by, the 152 heading east. A plastic bag floats through the air, surfing the airstream. Middle school kids amble by in private school uniforms—starchy plaid split-neck jumpers; burgundy sweater-vests; pressed pants—with backpacks so heavy they nearly tip over from the weight of them. An older woman stands beside the bus stop. The 152 gathers her up and goes, disappearing in a puff of smoke.

I eat part of my burger, wrapping the rest up for the trash. As I'm about to go, a voice stops me. I turn to see a woman standing beside me in jeans and a cardigan, a pair of white gym shoes on her feet. Her graying hair is wound back into a bun.

"Jessie? Jessie Sloane? Is that you?"

But before I can say one way or another if it's me, she decides for me. "It *is* you," she declares as she tells me that she remembers me when I was yea high, her hand pegged at about thirty-seven inches in the air. And then she embraces me, this strange woman wrapping her thickset arms around my neck and declaring again, "It is you."

Except that I don't know who she is. Not until she tells me.

And even then, I still don't know.

"It's me," she says. "Mrs. Zulpo. Eleanor Zulpo. Your mother used to clean my home when you were a girl. In Lincoln Park," she tells me, tacking on details as if it might help me remember. "Tree-lined street, beautiful box beam ceilings, rooms flooded with natural light," she says, though she and her husband don't live there anymore, not since the housing market crash when she had to give up her home. When they had to downsize. That's what she tells me.

I draw a blank. I don't remember.

Like me, Mom used to clean homes. Mostly upscale places that we could never afford. She taught me everything I know. My first foray into the family business came when I was about twelve years old and would get down on my hands and knees beside her and scrub floors.

But before that, when I was too young to clean, Mom would lug me along on assignments and there I'd spend my days playing pretend in strangers' homes. Cooking imaginary meals in their palatial kitchens, tucking my imaginary children into their mammoth beds before Mom scooched me out of the way so she could wash the sheets.

"You don't remember me," Eleanor Zulpo decides, realizing that it must have been sixteen or seventeen years ago or so, when I was three or four. "Of course you don't remember," she says, loosening her hold on my neck, telling me that I look just the same as I did back then. "It's those dimples," she says, pointing at them. "Those adorable dimples. I'd know these dimples anywhere.

"I read about your mother in the paper," she says then, sitting beside me on her own stool, unwrapping a hot dog. The sight of it alone, that hot dog, lying out on a foil wrapper, slathered in ketchup and relish—that and the smell—reminds me of the dead bird. The pigeon. And instead of a hot dog, I suddenly see blood, guts, gore, and I gag, vomit inching its way up my esophagus. I reach for my drink and force it back down, gargling, trying to get the taste of vomit from my mouth.

Mrs. Zulpo—*Eleanor,* she says to call her—doesn't notice. She keeps going. "I saw her obituary," she's saying. "It was a great write-up, a lovely tribute for a lovely woman," she says. I tell her that it was.

I submitted the death notice to the newspaper. I covered the cost of the obituary. I found an old photo of Mom to use, one that was a good six years old at least, taken back before she got sick.

We'd lived our entire lives in private, but for whatever reason I felt the whole world should know that she was dead.

"There have been other cleaning women since your mother. But never anyone as good as she was, as conscientious, as thorough. She was one of a kind, Jessie," she says, and I tell her I know. Eleanor tells me stories. Things I didn't know, or maybe I did. Memories that have been lost to time, erased clear from my brain's hard drive. About the time I helped myself to her Wedgwood china when Mom was cleaning. How I snatched it right from her hutch and set the dining room table to have a tea party with. "Wedgwood china," she tells me, grinning. "A single cup and saucer go for about a hundred dollars each. They had been my own mother's, given to me when she died. Heirlooms. Your poor mother," she laughs. "She nearly had a heart attack when she found you. I told her it was fine, that it wasn't like anything had gotten hurt. And besides, it was nice to see the dishes being put to use for a change."

And then she tells me that, at her suggestion, the three of us sat down at the dining room table and drank lemonade from the Wedgwood china.

It fills me with a sudden sense of nostalgia. A yearning for the past.

"What else do you remember?" I ask, needing more. Needing someone to fill in the gaps for me, all those details I can no longer remember.

Eleanor tells me how her children were grown by the time I arrived, and so it was nice to have a child in the house again. She didn't work outside of the home. When Mom and I came, she was grateful for the company. She used to look forward to the days we'd come. Usually she'd play with me while Mom cleaned, hide-and-go-seek in her home, or build forts from the newly washed sheets.

"You were a funny girl, Jessie," she tells me. "Silly and strong willed, a great sense of humor to boot," she says. "A bit ornery too. But those dimples," she adds as she takes a bite of the hot dog, speaking through a full mouth, "with those dimples you could get away with murder, Jessie." She laughs.

She says that anything Mom wanted done, she had to ask me twice. That the lunch Mom brought along for me, I refused to eat. That I was a far cry from shy, and would spend half of my days in her home creating a show to perform for her and Mom before we'd leave.

"You used to march around, insisting like the dickens that your name wasn't Jessie. Because you didn't like it back then, I think," she says then, saying I was adamant about it, insistent that my name wasn't Jessie. That my name was something else, but she doesn't remember what. "You would pout your face and stomp your foot and insist that people stop calling you Jessie. *Stop calling me that*, you'd cry, face turning red. Your mother would go along with it for a while, trying to ignore your antics. Because she knew you were doing it for attention and, if she didn't give in to you, sooner or later you'd quit. Though rarely did you quit," she smiles, telling me I was a headstrong little girl.

"You knew what you wanted," she says.

Eventually Mom would have enough of it, Eleanor tells me, and she'd get down to eye level and say, *That's enough, Jessie. We talked about this, remember?*

But I have no memory of this at all.

Why would I go around masquerading as something other than Jessie? I don't have time to come up with an answer because soon Eleanor is telling me how I used to carry an animal everywhere I went—a stuffed dog or a bear or a rabbit—but I couldn't care less about that because what I'm wondering is why in the world I would be so unrelenting about that name. About the name Jessie. Why I would insist it wasn't mine.

"And then there was your mother's name," Eleanor says

before I have a chance to think it through, and I ask, "What about it?"

Her eyebrows crease. She removes a pair of glasses and sets them on the countertop, rubbing at her eyes. "It's just that most little girls call their mother *Mom* or *Mommy*."

She leaves it at that and so I ask, "And I didn't?" thinking suddenly that Eleanor is mistaken. That she's wrong. Time has altered these memories of hers, or she's mistaken Mom and me for some other cleaning lady and child. Another child with dimples like mine. Because in all my life, she's only ever been one thing to me—Mom—or so I think.

Eleanor shakes her head and at the same time I see my hands before me, gripping the edges of the countertop, also shaking.

"You didn't," she says. "You called her by her given name."

Eleanor tells me that Mom would put up with it to a certain extent but then every now and again she'd get down and whisper in my ear, *We've talked about this, Jessie. Remember?* Same as she said about my own name. *You're to call me Mom.*

"For a short while, you'd remember. You'd remember to call your mother *Mom.* But before too long, you'd forget and go back to calling her by her Christian name. Eden."

I don't remember doing that.

EDEN

January 16, 1998
Chicago

I drove the speed limit the entire way, not wanting to draw attention to myself. It snowed much of the time and the roads were slick, though being a Midwesterner, I'm quite accustomed to driving on slick roads. This wasn't my first time with snow. And yet it was my first getaway, my first flight. My first vanishing act of what I hoped wouldn't be many, because I prayed that the world would let me disappear, that he would let me go.

I found myself staring in the rearview mirror nearly the entire time, all along Highway 42 and to the interstate, knuckles turning white from their grip on the steering wheel, though I knew there was no logical way he knew where I was, or that he watched me leave. But still.

He might just be there.

When I arrived, the first thing I did was find an apartment that I could afford, which wasn't easy considering I have so little in the way of money, nearly nothing at all, quite literally ten dollars more than was the rent payment, which means that for the immediate future, we'll be eating bread and cheese. I purchased a paper at a newsstand and, on a snow-covered park bench, scanned the for-rent ads, settling on a studio apartment in Hyde Park. The building is all wrapped up in a creamy yellow brick facade that's gone to rack and ruin; it looks abandoned, uncared for and unloved, like me. The ad trumpeted a French Renaissance charm but if it's there, I can't see it.

On the way into the building, I watched a drug deal transpire on the street. It happened right there, right before my eyes, two shadowy figures lurking beside the building, where the tall structure obstructs the sun's rays, making the men harder to see. They were men, of course, because I find it hard to believe that two women would stand on the street corner trading money for drugs, a wad of folded-up cash for the clear plastic bag of pills that passed from one hand to the next. I never saw their faces or their eyes, for their heads were cloaked in the hoods of sweatshirts like headscarves. And yet the men were tall, lanky, flat. Undeniably men.

We passed by quickly, my eyes tethered to the broken concrete of the street, feet kicking up pebbles as I went, certain I could feel their eyes on me. I inserted my key and ducked into the foyer of the apartment complex, grateful to be separated by a wall of glass.

We can't stay here forever. It isn't safe, I don't think.

And now, inside the apartment, I bolt the door behind me and stare out the peephole for a minute or two, to be certain no one followed me in. Not the drug dealer or his buyer, and not anyone else. I move to the window next, parting the dusty, broken mini-blinds with my fingertips, peering out, my fingers turning gray with dust. I survey the street below to be sure we haven't been followed, that no one knows we are here.

The last tenant had been recently evicted, her belongings never reclaimed. Because of this, I've been endowed with a foul-smelling sofa, a banged-up table, a mattress with worrisome stains. That and a carton of eggs that expired last week. I don't think we'll eat them.

I open the newspaper and again turn to the classified ads. But this time, instead of searching the apartment listing, I go to the wanted ads, searching for a job as a house cleaner because really, that's the extent of my qualifications, and after the stunt I pulled at the hospital, references are out of the question. *Must be courteous, conscientious, previous experience preferred,* I read. *Must speak English. Have good communication skills, a great work ethic.* The wages are noted; I tally the number of hours I will need to work to pay another month's worth of rent in this shoddy complex. Sixty hours—that's what I'd need to work. Though we also need to eat.

This is no longer just about me.

I try to relax but she's kicking and upset now, thrashing about, and I find that I can't relax. I tell her it's okay, that she doesn't need to worry, that she's safe here with me, though even I don't know if that's true because I have yet to decipher if we're safe here, if I'm safe. I stroke her, running my hand along the flushed skin, and for a moment—only a moment—she stops fighting. She gives in.

I try on a name for size.

"Jessie," I say, taking her stillness as consent.

I'll call her Jessie.

I'm not a bad person, I remind myself, though in that moment as I sit—watching a roach as it scurries across the worn carpeting, reaching a wall, shimmying along the baseboards to where the rest of its family no doubt lies waiting—reflecting on the last twenty-four hours of my life, the last twenty-four days and weeks, I'm not entirely certain that's true. All sorts of emotions get churned up inside me, everything from sadness to regret and shame, and I think of him standing unsuspectingly at the cottage, knocking on the door in vain.

"You're not a bad person," I incant, believing that if I think on it long enough, if I say it enough times, a thousand times over, it might somehow turn true.

I didn't set out to do the things I did. There was never any willful intent, any malice, only a pining for something I didn't have, something I so desperately needed. You wouldn't condemn a famished child for stealing a loaf of bread, now would you? A homeowner for shooting an armed intruder to protect his family?

I'm not a bad person, I decide, far more resolute this time.

I only did what I had to do.

JESSIE

WHEN I FINALLY MAKE my way back to Cornelia Avenue, it's evening. The colors of the sky have begun to change. Shadows fall across the street. The sun is thinking about going down.

I walk along Cornelia beside Old Faithful, staring at the million-dollar homes that fringe the street. They're mostly newly gutted homes with small tracts of grass. For each home lies a single tree on the road verge, fully grown. Its leaves form a canopy over the street where it joins with the tree on the other side. Conjoined twins.

The temperatures have fallen. It's no more than fifty-some degrees outside, a cold that creeps under my clothing, chilling me to the bone. The heat in the carriage home is stingy at best, when it runs. Though I toyed with the thermostat this morning, setting the temperature to seventy-two degrees, the furnace never kicked on before I left. When I arrive, it will be cold inside.

As I make my way along the street, the dread of nighttime

creeps in. The fear of eight long hours of darkness with nothing to do and only morbid thoughts to keep me company.

The front door of the greystone is open as I approach, though Ms. Geissler is nowhere to be seen. I stop on the sidewalk, wondering if I should let her know or if I should keep going. What I want to do is keep going, but my conscience says otherwise.

There's a garden on the front lawn of the greystone, one I didn't notice before, but now I do. It's not huge because city living doesn't allow for things to be huge. But it's magical. A blanket of yellows and oranges and reds that warms the earth. Tiny white butterflies hover above the blooms, levitating midair.

I blink once and they're gone because most likely they were never really there.

I make my way down the walkway, climbing the steps toward the front door. The home is large; three stories tall with a garden apartment to boot, one that peeks at me from beneath street level, hidden behind a black metal fence.

As I knock on the door, it pushes open more than it was before. My eyes take in the foyer, a carpeted runner, an unlit chandelier that dangles from the ceiling. "Hello?" I call out into the empty space, but if my landlord is here, she doesn't hear me.

My fingers press the doorbell and I hear the chime of it from inside, but still, there's no reply. "Hello?" I call again, laying a hand flat against the door and pressing it the rest of the way open. My feet cross the threshold as I step into the home.

I reach for a light switch and toggle it up and down, but nothing happens. The chandelier above me remains dark. It's not black in the home because the sun has yet to go all the way down. There's still some light outside, but it's fading fast. Soon it will be gone.

"Ms. Geissler?" I call out, explaining who I am and why I'm here. "It's Jessie," I say. "Jessie Sloane. Your new tenant. I just moved in to the carriage home," I call out, and at first I think the worst, that she's here somewhere, but that she's hurt. That she's had a nasty fall. That she can't answer me because she's lying on the ground just waiting to be found. That she's dead.

I don't think the obvious. That Ms. Geissler's in the shower and can't hear me. That she forgot to close the door on the way out rather than the way in. That she's not here.

"Ms. Geissler?" I call again, with an urgency to my voice this time. "Hello? Are you here?"

And it's only then that I hear the sound of a piano playing from upstairs. Classical music, I think. The kind you've heard before because it's famous. Mozart. Beethoven. I don't know which. The piano is quieted down from the distance, diluted, but still I hear it, the music staccato-like, sharp and disconnected.

And I breathe a sigh of relief because she's here. Because she's fine.

I could go home now.

I *should* go home now.

I should pull the door fully closed behind me and leave.

But instead I find myself hesitating at the base of the stairs. My hand grips the baluster as I stare up the flight of stairs, into the dark, cavernous second floor of the home. Because now the classical music has turned into some sort of ballad, and I find that it's haunting and beautiful.

That it's calling me, summoning me up the stairs.

Begging me to come and listen, to come and see.

And instead of leaving, my feet carry me up the stairs before I can think this through. I hold my breath as I go, listening only to the sound of the piano. Climbing upward, one step at a time.

The house is large, each room sprawling and grand, though they're hard to see for the scarcity of light, which becomes even more dim with each minute that passes by. Upstairs, my legs carry me to the bedroom from which the music comes. The only room that, as far as I can see, boasts light. The door is pulled to and so there's only a sliver of it. Only a sliver of light peeking from beneath the door slab.

I go to it.

Standing before the closed door, I listen to the sound of the piano play. My hand drops to the door's handle and it's unintentional when I turn the knob. I can't help myself; it just happens. I press a hand flat against the door and push it open, so slowly so that it doesn't squeak. I see her there on the piano's bench, her back to me. Her fingers move nimbly over the piano keys, foot pressing against the pedal with obvious expertise. I find myself entranced by her song, by the rhythmic motion of her hands and feet.

And then she stops playing.

And it strikes me suddenly, an awareness.

She knows that I am here.

I shouldn't be here.

All at once I feel like a trespasser. Like I've gone too far. This is not my home and I have no business being here.

She doesn't turn. "Something I can help you with?" she asks and I gasp first before I laugh. A nervous laugh. An exhausted laugh. One I can't make stop though I try. And only then does she turn and look at me as I press my hands to my mouth to smother the laugh.

Ms. Geissler looks to me to be about sixty years old. Her

hair is short, a dyed blond that's feathered around the edges. She wears glasses, dark, plastic frames that sit on the bridge of her nose. There's a frailty about her, her body gaunt, cloaked in a cotton dress. She rises to her feet and only then do I see that she's petite. There are lines on her face, laugh lines, frown lines, crow's-feet. And yet they look more regal than old. She's a beautiful woman.

"Jessie, isn't it?" she asks, and though it takes a minute to find my voice, I say that it is. She says that it's nice to meet me. She steps toward me, slipping her hand into mine. My hand shakes as it did this afternoon, a quiver that won't quit.

"I'm sorry," I stammer. "I didn't mean to interrupt," I say. Though I've done far worse than interrupt. "I rang the doorbell. I knocked. The front door was open," I explain, voice as doddery as my hands, just barely managing to scrape the memories together and remember why I'm here. "You left your front door open," I say again, for lack of anything better to say.

"Oh," she says, chastising the door latch. How it's old. How it doesn't work properly. How she needs to get it fixed, as she needs to get many things in this old home fixed.

"How is everything with the carriage home?" she asks instead, and I tell her fine. I say how much I like it. I compliment the hardwood floors because I can think of nothing else to say. I say that they are pretty. I thank her for letting me stay there. She says it's no bother.

It's awkward and uncomfortable, all the conversation forced. I think then that I should leave. I've overstayed my welcome because I was never welcome in the first place.

But just as I'm about to say my goodbyes and go, a noise comes from somewhere upstairs. From the third floor of the home. What it sounds like to me is the thud of a textbook falling. Something heavy and dense. I glance upward, finding a hatch there, a pulldown ladder that when folded up and stowed away becomes one with the ceiling, as it is now.

"What's that?" I ask, but Ms. Geissler's face goes suddenly blank, and she shakes her head, asking, "What's what?"

"The noise," I say. "Is someone there?" as I point up toward the ceiling.

"I didn't hear anything," she replies.

I hold my breath and listen in vain for more noises coming from up above. But they don't come. The house is silent, and I know then: I made it up.

My eyes burn. I rub at them, making them more red than they were before, still aware of my shaking hands.

"I must be mistaken," I say, holding my hands out before me so that I can see the way they tremble. They're cold. But that's not the reason for the trembling. It's something far worse than that, I think. Something neurological. I have my brain to thank for this. Because after all these nights without sleep, my brain functions are out of whack.

I try and convince myself that the shaky hands aren't degenerative. That they aren't getting worse. And yet there's no denying the fact.

My hands are shaking far more than they were this afternoon.

It's as if she can read my mind.

"You've been having trouble sleeping," she says, more of a statement than a question. She's not asking me because she knows. Behind the glasses, her eyes are a soft gray, staring at me in pity. I wonder how it is she knows I haven't been sleeping. Does it have something to do with the dark circles under my eyes, the bags, the red pools of blood that flood my sclera?

"I saw your light on late last night," she says by means of

explanation, and I think of myself last night. Hearing the strange pinging sound through the floor register, the voices, and turning the light on to investigate. It was nothing, of course, though still I spent the rest of the night lying in bed unable to sleep, forever indebted to the sun when it finally decided to rise and I headed off in search of caffeine, my magical potion, which becomes far less potent with each passing day that I don't sleep.

What makes not sleeping even worse than the crippling fatigue is the boredom that infiltrates those nighttime hours. The misery. The morbid thoughts that keep me company all night long. Last night I found myself thinking about ashes and bone fragments. That's what remains after a body has been incinerated. When Mom came back to me from the crematorium, I expected something soft, like the ashes left behind in Mom's and my fireplace. On cold nights, she and I used to toss in a few logs, sit on the floor beneath the same blanket, trying to stay warm. When the fire burned out, the ashes that remained were soft. Delicate. I didn't know that Mom's ashes would be coarse like sand, like cat litter, and not soft like ashes. Or that there would be bone fragments.

After Mom's 130 pounds were reduced to just 4, I didn't have the wherewithal to bring the urn to the crematorium with me so that they could place her inside. And so instead she came to me in a little baggie in a sturdy box. I was tasked with making the transfer to the rhubarb urn, this straight, canister-like contraption that's anything but the round body, narrow neck of your classic urn. You wouldn't even know it was an urn except for Mom's name impressed in the clay along with the years of her birth and death. Her stint on earth. Forty-nine years.

I made the transfer at the kitchen table, the day after I

brought her remains home from the crematorium. The same table where we used to eat. I used a funnel. Same funnel we used to use when transferring sugar cookie icing to the piping bags. When I was done, a fine mist of Mom covered the tabletop. I wiped her away with the palm of a hand. Then Mom was stuck to me, and it wasn't like I could just wash her off with soap and water. Because it was Mom. I couldn't just wash Mom down the kitchen sink.

These are the things you don't think about when someone has died. You don't want to think about them.

And yet these are the thoughts that keep me up all night. A fine mist of Mom on the palm of my hand.

"I couldn't sleep," I say, leaving it at that, pretending it was a one-time thing, not letting on to the fact that I haven't slept in all these nights.

"Try a glass of warm milk," she offers. "It always helps me sleep like a baby," she says, and I tell her I will. But I won't. I've tried that already and besides, I hate the taste of warm milk.

But then it comes again. The noise, one I'm certain I didn't imagine this time. Another dull thud.

And it's unintentional when my shaky hand lifts up to tug down the ladder and see for myself what's inside.

"You don't want to do that," Ms. Geissler snaps, her words brusque.

I freeze in place, insisting, "There's something there," and only then does she reconsider.

"I didn't want to scare you," she explains, and I breathe a sigh of relief. I didn't imagine the noise. It was there.

"It's squirrels," she tells me. "They've taken over the place," she laments. "I haven't stepped foot up there for a while." She says that she's been working with a pest control service to have them removed, but she's quite sure the service is more adept at bringing squirrels into her home then getting them out. The space is uninhabitable for now, until the problem gets sorted out. She can't bring herself to go up there, not until the squirrels are gone and her contractor repairs the damage.

"The squirrels," she complains, "have chewed holes in the walls. They've gnawed their way through electrical wires. They've ruined a perfectly good lamp. I've switched services, mind you. But getting rid of squirrels is no easy task. I need a roofer to come and replace the tiles and block the squirrels' way in, but the roofer won't come until all the squirrels are out. The darn things have it in for me," she says, sighing exasperatedly, and it doesn't once occur to me not to believe her.

I say to her, "Sounds like a mess."

Out the window, I see that the sun has finished setting. Darkness has arrived, anchoring itself to the earth for the night. Ending another day.

"It's getting late," I say, excusing myself, saying my goodbyes, and leaving.

I make my way around the periphery of the house, cutting across the patio and onto the lawn. There I pause midstride, hands on hips, and look skyward to see that the stars are lost somewhere behind the clouds. That there isn't a star in sight. The moon is there, but only a sliver of it. A crescent moon that doesn't do anything to light up the night. The fall air is cool; goose bumps appear on my arms. I rub at them, hoping the friction will make them go away. For now it does, though I'm dreading another night in the freezing cold carriage home.

The home is enveloped in blackness as I arrive. I have to fight to get the key into its hole. Twice I drop it, scrabbling around on the stoop to hunt it down.

The sound of a siren in the distance startles me. As I glance backward, over my shoulder to see the red and blue emergency lights whirling through the sky, I find Ms. Geissler standing in the back doorway of her home. She's illuminated by kitchen lights, easier to see than me, who stands in total darkness.

And yet her eyes are unmistakably on mine as if she's been watching me the entire time.

I find the keyhole and open the door. I hurry inside.

As I climb the lopsided steps, I feel the weight of fatigue bearing down on me. Fatigue from physical exertion and fatigue from lack of sleep. I lie down on the mattress, staring at my shaky hands before my eyes. There's an anemic quality to them. Blanched and mealy, the skin at their edges disappearing somehow, evanescing, like a loose thread being tugged from the hem of a shirt, the whole thing unraveling, coming apart at the seams. That's me. Coming apart at the seams. Little by little, I'm disappearing.

I look again at my hands, and this time they are fine. Intact. But still shaking.

I close my eyes and even though sleep is there within reach and I stretch my hand out to grab it, it's unattainable. Elusive and shifty. It moves away, mocking me. Laughing in my face.

For as tired as I am, I still cannot sleep.

EDEN

December 21, 1996
Egg Harbor

FOR MONTHS NOW, AARON and I have become slaves to the red circles on my pocket-size calendar, our intimacies slated out in advance. During my most fertile days we make love two, sometimes three times a day, though there's something inorganic about it now, something mechanical and forced. Our entire world, it seems, has become about making a baby, and I struggle to remember what our lives were like before we made the decision to start a family.

Two nights ago I stayed up until he was home from work, in bed, reading my book. Twice I rose from bed to look outside, searching through the bare trees for signs of headlights in the distance—a shock of blinding yellow against the blackness of night—rambling down the long, winding drive. But there were none. The night was pitch-black, no moon anywhere, not a star to be seen. It seemed to take forever for him to be home.

The bedroom lamp was dimmed, a candle burning on the dresser for ambience, though when he finally did arrive,

Aaron took one look at that candle and blew it out, thinking I'd gotten tired and plumb forgot about the burning candle. The small room filled with the noxious smell of smoke as he pulled his chef getup from his body, dropping it to the floor. He climbed into bed beside me, saying how he was so tired, how his feet hurt. His words were slurred with simple lethargy and fatigue. He didn't bother to turn off the light. I smelled the chophouse on him, the garlic, the Worcestershire sauce, the flesh of chops and steaks.

And yet there it was, another red-circled date on the calendar.

Beneath the blankets I wore a satin robe and beneath the robe nothing, though in it I didn't feel nearly as sexy as I'd thought I would, as I'd *hoped* I would, a feeling that was only exacerbated when I untied the ribbon from around my waist, revealing myself to him, and in Aaron's eyes spied a moment of hesitation, an excuse ready to form on his lips.

"Remember?" I asked, childlike hope in my eyes. "I'm ovulating," I reminded him, and before he could speak, before he could tell me why it wasn't a good night, I lowered myself beneath the sheets and easily changed his mind.

I don't think he minded that I did. In fact, I think he was quite pleased.

When we were through, Aaron pulled away and moved to his side of the bed, leaving me and my elevated hips alone in the hopes that this time, gravity might work its magic.

For three days in a row now it's gone like this, though tonight Aaron did object and it was much harder to make him acquiesce, and even when he did there was little satisfaction in it, little pleasure, but rather the knowledge that he was doing this for me. Because I wanted him to. Because I was making him do it. There was resentment in it, disgruntlement in his every move. When we were done I offered a pitiful *thank you*, which felt entirely wrong, as we each drifted to our own side of the bed, an ocean of space spread between us.

It's become apparent that these days we do it because we have to, not because either of us wants to have sex. We skip any sort of foreplay and get straight to the grunt work, finding sex as pleasurable as brushing teeth or washing dishes. Our movements have become as repetitive and predictable as cleaning laundry.

Just like any other of our daily chores, we've begun to grudgingly make love for three days out of the month, finding the other twenty-seven to be a blissful reprieve.

January 9, 1997
Egg Harbor

It took nearly thirty minutes to get to the obstetrician appointment, and all along the way, all I could hear was the grinding of snow beneath the tires' tread. Outside it was cold, a frosty thirty-two degrees, and the plump clouds looked like they might burst apart at the seams at any moment, burying us with three more inches of snow. Aaron was torn, worried we wouldn't be home in time for his shift, but feeling the need to go too. To be at the appointment. He vacillated about it for a good five or ten minutes, standing in the open doorway, letting the cold air into our home.

In the end, he decided to go so that as we drove south on Highway 42, both of us quiet, I felt a great guilt about it, knowing that if he was late to work, it would be my fault.

The obstetrician was in Sturgeon Bay, a seventeen-mile drive. He was the closest I could find and also came with a recommendation, one from Miranda, the only woman in town I knew well enough to ask. Miranda, who drove her three boys to my home last week in her Dodge Caravan—windshield caked with ice crystals still, so that it was near impossible to see through the rimy glass—because it was far too cold to walk.

Miranda, who sat sprawled on my sofa, feet raised to the coffee table, while I rocked her crying two-month-old baby, Carter, to sleep.

Miranda, who was so overwhelmed with motherhood that she couldn't stand to be alone with her own three kids.

Miranda, who revealed to me that she was pregnant again, that it was a mistake this time, that they hadn't been trying. "Because who in their right mind tries for more when they already have three kids?" she asked, staring at me sadly as if I should take pity on her for this obvious misfortune, but what I felt instead was infuriated and sick, anger and bile rising quickly inside me.

Miranda confessed to me that though she and Joe had waited the recommended six weeks after Carter was born to fool around, sure enough, Joe managed to knock her up on the first try, and already the morning sickness had set in so that her boys were forced to watch even more TV than ever before because Miranda didn't have the stamina to entertain them all day, let alone feed them. "The nerve of that bastard," she said of Joe and his evident virility, and then she asked what in the world was taking Aaron and me so long to conceive.

"You don't think," she asked, eyes wide, "that you're infertile, do you? That that handsome husband of yours is shooting blanks?"

As I sat beside him in the car, driving to the obstetrician appointment, listening to the pulverization of snow beneath the wheels, staring at the clouds, I couldn't help but wonder if that was the case. Was Aaron shooting blanks? Was Aaron *infertile*?

Aaron, who could do anything, who could fix anything, could not create a child?

Aaron, to whom everything came so easily, had difficulty making a baby?

The thought alone made me angry and annoyed. Angry at Aaron because why, for all the things he was so capable of doing, was he incapable of doing *this*?

Why couldn't he fix this? Why couldn't he make this right?

Assigning fault seemed to be the name of the game these days, pointing fingers, attaching blame. Whose fault was it that we didn't yet have a baby?

March 11, 1997
Egg Harbor

What I've come to learn after being referred to a fertility specialist is that even though I get my period each month with moderate regularity, my body isn't ovulating correctly, isn't always ovulating. *Anovulation*, it's called, a word I've never heard of before but now think about at every waking hour and when I should be asleep. If I'm being honest, this comes as little surprise to me. My body is simply going through the motions, the preparations of the endometrium—the lining of my uterus readying itself to welcome a fertilized egg—and then sloughing off when no egg moves in. It's not that the egg wasn't fertilized by Aaron's sperm. It's that it simply wasn't there to begin with.

Today I began my third cycle of Clomid. After months of this, I have no sense of humility left, no modesty. I've paraded my private parts for every doctor, nurse and technician in the fertility clinic to see, while all Aaron ever had to do was drop off a sperm sample and endure a simple blood draw. It hardly seems fair. The first month I didn't ovulate. Last month we upped the dosage and, though Dr. Landry spied two follicles when he performed his ultrasound—forcing the transvaginal ultrasound probe between my legs so that I should rightfully have felt violated and ashamed, but no longer did, sending Aaron and me home with strict orders to have sex—we didn't get pregnant.

The pills make me weepy all the time, for no apparent reason at all, though having seen the inventory of potential side effects, I consider it a blessing that the only one I'm doomed to endure is the predisposition for crying. I cry at the market; I cry in the car. I cry at home while mopping floors and folding laundry and standing in the doorway to one of the spare bedrooms, wondering if it will ever hold a child, steeling myself for another cycle of Clomid that will likely end again with my monthly flow.

To counter Aaron's low sperm motility, as it's called, he's switched to wearing loose-fitting underpants (I don't tell Miranda this), and is tasked with finding ways to reduce stress in his life, stress which neither of us knew he had. He now sleeps until after ten o'clock every morning so that we no longer share our day's coffee on the dock, which is fine anyway seeing as the eternal winter has trapped us indoors and there are no sailboats to be seen on the bay, none until spring. He takes herbal supplements and when the temperatures aren't too abysmal will go for a walk or a run, so that our days together are mere hours at best. This too is fine, seeing as we don't have much to talk about anymore, nothing that doesn't involve the many things the world is reluctant to let us have: strong, capable sperm; regular ovulation; a positive pregnancy test; a baby.

It isn't that Aaron doesn't have enough sperm—he does—it's that what he has doesn't swim properly and isn't able to travel the four inches or so to where my egg may or may not be waiting.

In short, we're both to blame, though there isn't a moment that I don't wonder which of us is to blame more and even though I think it's me, I *know* it's me, there is a part of me aggrieved that I'm the only one forced to record my body temperature, to take ovulation tests, to cry in public for no sound reason at all, to travel to the fertility clinic again and again, to be probed so that some doctor or technician can gaze inside me and at my ovaries, while all Aaron has to do is take an herbal supplement from time to time and exercise on occasion.

It doesn't seem fair. It doesn't seem right.

I've come to resent Aaron for this, as I've come to resent him for many things.

March 13, 1997
Egg Harbor

I field questions nearly every day about when Aaron and I are going to have a baby, often from my stepmother or Aaron's mother, calling on the phone when he's at work, asking not-so-subtly for grandchildren.

When can they expect them? When will there be good news to share?

It's not that grandchildren are in short supply because they aren't. Instead it's that Aaron and I have been married for over two years, and society doesn't take well to that: two nearly thirty-years-olds, married for over two years without kids, as if there's something unthinkable about it, something taboo.

Is there something wrong with that?

It feels as if there is.

A married woman of my age without a child is quite the anomaly these days.

I can't bring myself to say aloud that we're trying, *trying and failing* to make a baby because I don't want pity and I don't want advice. And so instead I tell Aaron's mother and my stepmother *soon*, wishing that my own mother were still alive because hers is the only advice I want and need.

I spend my days waiting. Waiting for Aaron to wake up, waiting for Aaron to leave, waiting for Aaron to get home so I can again close my eyes and sleep. Waiting for a new cycle of Clomid to begin, to ovulate, to make love to Aaron like robots would do, hasty and unfeeling, and then waiting for the negative pregnancy test results, the loyal, trusty blood.

It's the only thing I can depend on anymore. That sooner or later, my period will come.

March 14, 1997
Egg Harbor

Spring looms on the horizon.

It's weeks away still, but every now and then a day blooms before me, fifty or sixty degrees and full of sun, so that it's easier to get through than the endlessly gray winter days.

These rare springlike days I leave the cottage when Aaron is away and head into town. I've discovered a dance studio there, completely by chance—I didn't seek it out—a small single-story cottage on Church Street that tiny ballerinas move in and out of all day.

The first day I spotted the studio, I saw an empty park bench nearby, which was warm and welcoming, set directly in a shaft of sunlight so that even though it was no more than fifty-two degrees outside, I felt snug, my skin warm from the sun's generous beams.

For nearly an hour I watched the ballerinas, toddlers mainly in leotards with their hair pinned neatly back in buns. Their little voices were happy and high-pitched, like birds, as they clung to their mothers' hands, coming and going like clockwork, nearly every hour on the hour.

There was one group in particular that caught my eye. A group of sixteen—eight mothers and their daughters—who arrived en masse around noon, a whole bundle of giggly girls with women trailing behind, women who sipped lattes and gossiped while I sat alone on a park bench, feeling sorry for myself, isolated from society because I didn't fit in. Because I didn't have a child.

The women were beautiful, every last one of them, which for whatever reason made me feel dirty, self-conscious and ashamed. I smiled as they walked by, but not one looked at me and no one smiled in reply. They wore peasant tops and floaty skirts; cowboy boots; big, baggy sweaters; hobo bags; while me, on the other hand, I sat wrapped up in a sweatshirt of Aaron's that had faded and shrunk in the wash, feeling alone, bloated, desperate, wanting for a child.

How different I am from those mothers.

I could never be one of them, one of those women who travel in a pack, whispering secrets about their husbands, their children's nighttime habits, which little ones still wet the bed. All because I didn't have a child. Because without a child, I had nothing to offer them.

Because I'm nothing, I easily reasoned then, if not a mother.

There's no other justification for my life.

I watched them as they walked by, as they closed in on the dance studio. And then, after the women had passed and I assumed the parade was through, I noticed one little girl straggling behind, nearly stagnant on the sidewalk. Struggling to keep up. Too busy examining the buds on the trees. Smaller than the rest, which made me think of the piglet in Charlotte's Web. Wilbur, saved from slaughter by little Fern. I was captivated by her, holding my breath as she passed by, joining the others in the studio. Only when she was gone did I allow myself to breathe.

And now twice, sometimes three times a week I find myself sitting there on that bench, watching the dancers come and go, wishing one of them, any single one of them—but especially the littlest one, a head shorter than the rest, straw-colored hair and a collection of freckles, whose tiny feet always lag behind so that one day I worry she'll be forgotten—was mine.

I've become an addict really, and the only thing that eases the symptoms of withdrawal is seeing children, is being in the company of children. They are my fix, an antidote for the restlessness, the irritability, the tremor of my hands that is only exacerbated with each passing month that I don't get pregnant.

The little girl can't be more than three years old, pudgy arms, legs and cheeks still padded with baby fat that will one day wear away, no doubt, so that she'll look like any one of the ladies she tags along after, with their long limbs and their long hair and their coffee.

I don't like the way I feel sitting there on that park bench, eyeing children who are not mine. But I have nothing better to do with my time, and I don't think I could stop if I tried.

I suggested to Aaron that I look for a job, for some diversion from the long, lonely afternoons while he is away. Aaron isn't game. He'd rather I *not* work, which makes no sense to me. The financial burden of fertility treatments is steep; we could use the additional income. We've begun to argue about things like the cost of ground beef, the cost of electricity.

Aaron and I are monitoring the Clomid cycles, which means for each failed attempt we are quite literally throwing away hundreds of dollars for the medication, blood work and ultrasounds to see whether my body is releasing eggs, and when. Insurance won't cover these costs because, of course, some high-and-mighty insurance company doesn't give a darn whether Aaron and I ever have a baby, and so the procedure is considered *elective.* We are electing to waste thousands of dollars to try and conceive a baby, while other parents, far less capable or worthy parents, are given one for free.

"You're under so much stress already," Aaron said when I suggested applying for a job, and "Why not just focus on this?" meaning making a baby, as if somehow I'd been unfocused, and as if that lack of focus was the reason we were still without a child. I'd been too cavalier about it, too casual, too devil-may-care. He didn't use those words, not a single one of them, and yet that's exactly what I heard when he came home from work after midnight that night and, though I lamented about being bored all day, about being alone, he suggested I not apply for a job, but rather focus on *this*, with a sweeping gesture toward my vacuous womb.

I screamed at him then. I slammed a door. I locked him out of the bedroom so he slept on the sofa for the night.

Never before have I screamed at him. Never before have I raised my voice.

He didn't object to sleeping on the sofa. It was one in the morning. He was tired, he told me. "Eden, that's enough," he said with a sigh while gathering his pillow from the head of our bed. "I need to sleep."

I sat there in the bedroom that night, in the dark, propped up against pillows and not lying down. My hands still shook even hours after my fit was through. A headache slunk up the base of my neck and consumed my skull so that every part of my head hurt. My eyes burned from crying and though I tried to blame the medication for this—after all, mood swings and a propensity for crying were both common side effects of the Clomid—I didn't know whether or not they were to blame this time.

Maybe it was just me.

I felt sorry come morning.

But I didn't apologize and neither did Aaron. Instead he left for work earlier than ever before and I returned to the dance studio, an addict in need of a fix.

March 19, 1997
Egg Harbor

When Clomid alone failed to work, Dr. Landry suggested IUI. Intrauterine insemination. Placing Aaron's sluggish sperm directly into my uterus so that they don't have to paddle through those four inches of mucousy space all on their own, so that they will have an easier time finding and fertilizing my egg without getting lost, swimming in circles in my vaginal canal as they are apt to do. Each month, Aaron and I have quite literally thrown away money, frittered away follicles and eggs, doled out hundreds of dollars on medication and ultrasounds for nothing. My trips to see Dr. Landry have been a waste. It's time to try something new. Intrauterine insemination will add a couple hundred dollars to our monthly expenditure, but will also increase the likelihood of conception, especially in cases like ours where low sperm motility is to blame.

There it was again, that word: *blame.*

There is also the added benefit that with IUI Aaron and I won't have to have sex, which is a blessing in and of itself. Aaron is capable of collecting his sample all on his own in the comfort of a private room at the clinic, complete with pornographic videos and magazines, where sexy, buxom women far more appealing to the eye than me will help us create a child. It mortified him to have to do this, and yet after months of invasive ultrasounds and repeated blood draws, after digesting medication that made me moody, that made me cry, after poking myself in the gut with shots of hormones for months on end, this seemed only fair. This seemed right. The nurse tendered my assistance, saying I could keep Aaron company if I'd like, but with a sideways glance, he went in without me and closed the door, and there was a spasm of jealousy, a shooting pain searing through my head as though someone had momentarily lodged an ice pick into my skull.

I envisioned Aaron on the other side of that door, aroused by some strumpet on the television screen and not me.

And then hours later, after the sperm had been collected and cleaned, it was my turn to be put to work, to lie on the exam table, completely undressed from the waist down with only a drape sheet to provide that false sense of privacy, while Dr. Landry placed first a catheter and then Aaron's sperm inside me.

And then sent us home to wait.

Aaron, as always, went to work, leaving me alone and bored, and so I drove into town and sought out that small dance studio on Church Street and sat on the park bench, watching the little ballerinas come and go, searching for the smallest one with the straw-like hair and freckles, a head shorter than the rest, who always struggled to keep up with her mother and friends.

I had to wait awhile, but eventually she came and my heart skipped a beat. My hands went numb. I held my breath.

I saw her ambling first through the double blue doors of the studio, already lagging behind before she'd ever stepped foot outside, grappling with the weight of the door because there was no one around to hold it for her. Her tiny head barely surpassed the door's crash bar. The others were already a good five or ten paces ahead, moving down the concrete sidewalk in the direction of town, little girls gabbing merrily about an afternoon playdate while their mothers followed behind, paper cups of coffee in hand. Only once did a mother turn around to see where she was, calling out, "Snap to it, Olivia, or you'll get left behind," and then she turned again, facing forward, never again checking on Olivia, who brought up the rear, the caboose on some sort of high-speed train that had somehow gotten off track.

She had a name now. *Olivia.*

But Olivia's mother was fully immersed in a conversation with the ladies, listening to one of the other mothers complain about her husband's long hours and relentless travel schedule. He was in Tampa Bay this week on business, and that new admin assistant from the office had gone along too, the one her husband talked about at the dinner table, so that she couldn't help but be concerned.

"You don't think?" asked one of the other ladies, and Olivia's mother piped in with "Oh, you poor thing."

And it was decided then. This woman's husband was having an affair.

Through all this, no one paid attention to Olivia, who had fallen even farther behind.

I had no intent of rising from the park bench as she passed by. None at all. The thought didn't cross my mind until a single bobby pin fell from her hair, a silver sprung hairpin that dropped to the ground at such a frequency only I could hear. Little Olivia kept walking, leaving the hairpin behind. Her mother kept walking, now nearly twenty or thirty paces ahead. Only I paused to retrieve the hairpin, falling in line behind Olivia and the rest of her troupe, six steps behind and struck dumb.

I couldn't speak.

I could have called her by name; I could have tapped her on the shoulder and handed her the bobby pin. But I didn't. Instead I shadowed her by a mere three feet, eyes gaping at the lavender leotard and tutu, the sheer white tights, the hair done up in a bun, starting to lose its hold as strands of brown and yellow drifted through the springlike air. Beside our feet, the snow had melted, leaving puddles that returning birds paused to drink from. On the trees there were buds, tiny shamrock-green buds about to burst forth with leaves.

I never once thought about taking her, about grabbing a hold of her with my hand pressed to her mouth so that she wouldn't scream. I didn't think of luring her away, bewitching her with the promise of a puppy or ice cream. I only wanted to watch for a while, to walk a breath behind and pretend for just this one moment in time that she was mine.

As I followed Olivia down the sidewalk, a conversation played out in my mind.

Slow down, baby girl, I thought to myself, whispering the words in my head. *Come hold Mama's hand*, I urged, and in my imaginings I held out my hand as little Olivia slackened a bit, slowing down, turning to me so I could see the color of her eyes, the wealth of freckles she'd no doubt one day either outgrow or grow to hate. She slipped her hand inside mine and I squeezed tight, careful not to let go as we passed through an intersection while the traffic on either side paused to let us through. Olivia's hand was easy to hold. Her steps fell into sync with mine.

It was the raucous laughter of the other girls that broke my trance, bringing me back to the earth, back to my physical existence. To reality. They had all turned at once, calling Olivia a snail, a slowpoke, waiting for her to catch up so they could go get ice-cream cones, and even though I knew it was all in jest—Olivia's piping laughter was proof of this, no?—my heart ached for her for being called names, for being the poky little puppy, always lagging behind.

And then my heart ached for me when she skipped off with her friends, leaving me behind, standing alone on the sidewalk with her bobby pin in my hand.

I hoped that just once she would turn and see me and know that I was there.

I kept Olivia's bobby pin as a token of luck.

Ten days later, my period arrived.

And now another month has come and gone without a baby.

JESSIE

MY NIGHTTIME THOUGHTS CAN be grouped into four categories. They follow the same pattern, the same predictable rotation each night. Wash, rinse, dry, repeat.

It all begins with the morbid thoughts where I obsess over death and dying, of being dead, trapped inside an urn, unable to breathe. They settle in around twilight, when the sun sinks beneath the horizon, slipping away to play with kids on the other side of the world. It's then that I start to wonder how much time I have left on earth. I think about how and when I will die. Will it hurt when I die? Did it hurt when Mom died?

These morbid thoughts soon mutate into grieving, sinking ones where I miss Mom so much it hurts. By this point in the night, the world has turned black and I lie on my mattress in a black room, confined by blackness. A prisoner of the night. In all my life, it was always Mom and me, like Batman and Robin, Lucy and Ethel. Shaggy and Scooby-Doo. We were a team. Without her I don't know what to do. I spend half the night pleading for her back. Because I don't know who I am without her. Because, without her, I am nothing.

I don't cry about it because my eyes are done crying. They've dried up. And so instead I think things like, if Mom isn't here, then I don't want to be here either. It's grim, and yet it's true.

My thoughts go on like this for what feels like hours because it probably is. Eventually they turn into a guilt trip, where I loathe myself for sleeping through Mom's death. For getting testy with her when she puked for the sixth time in a row, missing the toilet by a mile. For not speaking to her for weeks when she wouldn't come clean to me about my dad. For not holding her hand the time she chaperoned my fifth grade field trip to the planetarium, or bothering to thank her for the embroidery thread she got me in middle school—a half dozen colors to make friendship bracelets with. I'd only huffed and stomped off to another room, thinking how stupid could she be. Didn't she know I didn't have any friends? These memories haunt me now.

In truth, Mom and I hardly fought. The only arguments she and I ever had were mostly over my father. Mom never wanted to talk about him—she refused to talk about him—and so I snuck around her back to try and learn more.

I was six years old when I first realized I didn't have a father. Until then I was too oblivious to see that other kids did and I didn't. Mom and I lived alone. We kept to ourselves much of the time. I didn't go to preschool and I didn't have friends. I didn't know much of anything outside of my world with Mom, not until school began, and then my world grew exponentially larger, though still, in comparison to everyone else's, it was small.

It was my first day of kindergarten when I realized that all of the kids in the class, aside from me, had both a mom and a dad. I remember that day, organizing our belongings inside the bulky metal cubbyholes, while our moms hovered in the classroom, talking to the teacher, talking to other moms. Everyone except for my mom, because she stood there alone, talking to no one. This confused me. Why didn't Mom talk to the other women?

But what confused me even more was the huddle of men in the classroom. A whole busload of them. Not just moms, but moms *and* men. Who were these men, and what were they doing here?

I asked one little girl. I pointed at the giant of a man standing by her side. *Who is that?* I asked, eyes wide, looking skyward. She said it was her dad, and though I'd heard that word before, it wasn't one that was readily in my vocabulary.

I tallied up the men in the room, realizing that every single child had one but me.

The mention of my father didn't come up again until later in the school year, when some kid asked where he was. We'd had a music performance and, while everyone else had a mom and dad in tow—grandma and grandpa too—I only had Mom. And things like that, when you're six, are big news. How Jessie Sloane doesn't have a dad.

Where's your dad? the kid asked, all dressed up in a sweater-vest and pants.

I don't have one, I said, thinking that was the end of it. But he came back with some comment about how *everyone has a dad*, and others started to laugh.

I asked Mom about it that night at home. I had to know. *Where's my dad?* I asked, standing in her bedroom doorway while she lay on the bed, bare feet crossed at the ankles, reading a book. Even at six years old, I could see that she was tired from a day spent cleaning someone else's home.

I didn't wait for her reply. *Joey Malone said everyone has a dad*, I told Mom as she uncrossed her ankles and set her bookmark between the pages of her book. *So where's mine?* I asked, feeling aggrieved all of a sudden. As aggrieved as a little kid can be.

Mom was keeping something from me.

Mom had a secret that she wouldn't share with me.

Mom's face turned as red as hot coal. *Joey had no right to say that*, she told me. *Not everyone has a dad. Not you.*

But her answer came with no explanation.

Maybe he was dead. Maybe they were divorced. Maybe they were never married in the first place. Or maybe I never really had a dad.

Still, I started snooping around the house to be sure, in case there was something hiding there that I might find. Evidence. A clue.

A few years later I became more tenacious about it, more annoying. I asked Mom again where my father was. What had happened to him. *Is he dead?* I wanted to know. I said that word with the testiness of a preteen. The exasperation. *Dead.*

But she wouldn't say. Time and again, she changed the subject; she pretended not to hear me ask. She had a brilliant way of mincing words, of making me forget what I had asked. Of clamming up and saying nothing.

And yet, again and again, I asked. A hundred times after that. But never did she tell me.

I became ruthless about it.

When I was twelve I set a place at the dinner table for him. Whoever he might be. Just in case he decided to show. Mom swiped his silverware from the table post-haste. Flung it back in the drawer.

Let's not do this, Jessie, she said.

I searched city streets for his face. Never sure what I was looking for, but always looking. I wondered if he had blondish hair and dimples like me. Or if he was a brunette, a redhead, maybe even some other ethnicity.

Maybe we looked nothing alike.

Or maybe we were the kind that could pass for twins.

I learned that dimples are inherited. A dominant trait. Meaning only one parent would have to have them for me to have them. And seeing as Mom had none, I easily reasoned that they came from *him*. From *Dad*. That, barring some sort of genetic mutation, I'd inherited them from my father.

What a dimple really is is a birth defect. A short facial muscle that pulls on your skin when you smile, causing indentations in the cheek. My father and I are, therefore, both defected.

I made up names for him. Occupations. I sized up men with dimples at random, wondering if any of them were him.

I imagined him with a different wife and kids. Me with half brothers and sisters, a family. In my delusion, every last one of them had dimples.

Before bed, I'd leave the porch light on, so that he could find our home if ever he came to visit. So that he'd know which one was ours. Which bungalow in a sea of bungalows belonged to me.

When I was fourteen, I attempted a crop top for school. It wasn't my thing, bearing my belly button for all to see. But it was a camouflage T, soft and green, and I was fourteen. Feeling rebellious. Trying to fit in with the crowd but failing. Instead I stood out like a sore thumb, always light-years behind the latest fad.

Mom's mouth dropped. She shook her head. She said no to

the crop top, told me to march upstairs and change. To *march*. I put up a fight, standing with my hands on my hips, pouting. Sputtering the nonsense of a fourteen-year-old girl.

But Mom would have none of it. It wasn't up for discussion, she told me, saying for a third time to *march*. Pointing at the stairs.

My words were brisk. *I bet that if my dad were here, he'd let me*, I said. She looked hurt, visibly wounded. I'd hurt her and I was glad I did.

Are you ever going to tell me about him? I asked. It was a fair question. I deserved to know, or so my fourteen-year-old self believed I did. I didn't once consider the reasons she kept him from me, or the ramifications of knowing who he was. But Mom did.

Qui vivra verra, Mom replied, holding her hands up in the air. Her favorite saying, one that rolled eloquently off her tongue. *Only time will tell* is in essence what it means, but this time what it was was a way to be evasive. To avoid my question yet again.

I stormed out of the room. Marched up the stairs and slammed a bedroom door. I put on a sweatshirt that covered every square inch of me.

Not a year later, the cancer came.

And then I started wishing I'd never asked about my dad.

I dwell on those memories now, hating myself for what I put Mom through.

But every night around 3:00 a.m., when I've exhausted all the thoughts of death and grief and guilt for a single night, my imagination begins to take flight. My imagination or my memories, though some nights I have a hard time determining which is which. Tonight it's a memory, I think, one so far-flung that my brain has to cobble pieces of it together, adding to the gaps so that it makes sense. Filling in the blanks. I see that kindergarten classroom, a poster of the golden rule taped to the cinder block walls. A big bookcase, a rectangular rug with the alphabet depicted on it—the alphabet plus simple pictures, an apple for *A*, a bird for *B*—the American flag. A chalkboard with the teacher's name written on it in perfect penmanship. I see Mom standing there before the teacher, making an introduction, saying to the teacher that she is Eden and I am Jessie, and then the teacher squats just so and reaches out a hand to me and I shake it. Her smile is warm and sincere as she rises back up to Mom.

Mrs. Roberts stands with the clipboard in hand, making sure each child's paperwork is complete and that they've brought their supplies. Mom hovers self-consciously before her, hands behind her back, fingers laced. Mom and Mrs. Roberts talk and as they do, words reach my ears—*birth certificate*, I think I hear—and Mom stiffens at Mrs. Roberts's request.

"Pardon me?" Mom asks, and Mrs. Roberts explains how there's a note from the school office that she's yet to provide a copy of my birth certificate with the other registration materials. A certified copy, with the raised seal.

Mom doesn't miss a beat. She says something about a house fire. "We lost everything," she says, and Mrs. Roberts's face turns sad.

"How awful," Mrs. Roberts says consolingly as I, six-year-old me, asks unsuspectingly, "What fire?" Because there was never a fire. Not in our home. We didn't lose a thing.

Mom shushes me. Mrs. Roberts lays a hand on Mom's arm and says just as soon as she can get a replacement, that would be fine.

But then, like that, the memory disappears, and I have to wonder if it was a memory at all or only my imagination.

Tonight as I lie on the mattress in a misplaced belief that if I lie here long enough, eventually I will sleep, I think of a dead three-year-old Jessica Sloane, having to remind myself that it's a typographical error only, that she doesn't exist.

The room is quiet as I lie in bed wondering what she looked like. For three years old, I picture chubby wrists and knees, innocent eyes, an endless smile. I wonder if that's what she looked like. But then again I remember. There is no other Jessica Sloane. She *is* me.

A heavy silence flattens me in bed, filling every crevice in the room like a poisonous gas. I think that maybe it could kill me, that silence. Displacing all the oxygen in the room with a smothering quiet. The only thing I hear is the *tick, tock, tick, tock* of the wall clock, keeping time.

I rise to my knees and gaze out the window into the yard, seeing only the back of Ms. Geissler's home from here. It's tall and imposing, three floors of limestone and brick. Such a big home for one woman alone.

There's a balcony in the back of the home, a basic, rudimentary sort of thing. Wooden scaffolding that soars up three floors, a wooden slab to stand upon. It looks unsafe to me. Unsound. Not up to code.

As I kneel before the window, I rest my elbows on the sill. Foolishly believing that I blend into the blackness of the room, that no one can see me from here. The house is dark, except for a single light that's turned on. A yellow hue fills the margins of a window. The rest of it is blocked by a drawn window shade. I can't see into the room, just that frame of light around the window shade.

Ms. Geissler must have forgotten to turn the light off before she went to bed, I rationalize, because it's the middle of the night, and no one should be awake but me.

But as I stare, I see that the frame of light behind the window shade is moving, because the window shade inside it is also moving. It's a gentle back and forth motion, as if a person had been standing just seconds ago behind it, lifting the edges of the shade to peer out.

I imagine her at the window, gazing out, seeing me lying on the mattress, pretending to sleep. I think of her own admission—*I saw your light on late last night*—and imagine that last night, like this, she stood at the window, staring at me. Me, who naively obliged, leaving the shades open wide, basic white roller shades that I didn't once think necessary to pull down.

But now suddenly I do.

I watch the motion of the window shade as it slows and then stops.

And then, like that, the light flicks off.

The yellow edges of the window disappear. The greystone is engulfed in total darkness. I'd think nothing of it, but then it occurs to me that the light was coming from the third floor of the home. The place with the squirrels. The place where Ms. Geissler doesn't go.

She was lying to me.

Why would she lie to me?

I crawl back into bed. I throw the covers over my head.

I make poor attempts to placate myself, to convince myself that the light is on a timer. That it's automated. That it goes on and off of its own free will. That a heat vent was spewing warm air directly at the window shade, making it move.

But it's not so easy to believe.

EDEN

May 14, 2001
Chicago

I watch as, beside me, Jessie sleeps. She's out for the count now—finally, after a long, feverish night—spread out on a blanket on the floor, arms splayed in opposite directions like the wings of a jetliner. Her pale face is placid and calm, unlike last night when it was a fiery red, the fever and the fury creeping up her neckline, inflaming her forehead and cheeks. She'd cried out all night in discomfort, wailing, unable to get a hold of her own breath. Her fever capped at 103 degrees and I was grateful for this, for the fact that it wasn't high enough to necessitate a visit to the emergency room. I don't know if I'd have had it in me to go to the hospital had we needed to. I find that the very notion of hospitals—the antiseptic smells, the insipid hallways, the vigilant eyes—still gets under my skin sometimes, like some form of PTSD, I think, because just thinking about being in one rattles my nerves, makes me dizzy, makes my chest hurt. I don't know that I could ever go back to one, not after what I've done. I'm certain they'd see clear through me, that—even with all these miles spread between us—they, the doctors, the nurses, the ladies at the reception desk, would know just exactly who I am, as if I have my own scarlet *A* forever etched into my shirt as a reminder of my guilt.

I stare at Jessie, sound asleep on the quilted blanket beside me. Her hair fans out around her face. Her arms, both of them, are thrust upward and over her head now like goalposts. There isn't a single line on her skin anywhere, and though I don't want to wake her, I stroke the back of a finger across her tranquil ivory cheek, grateful she still sleeps.

It takes my breath away sometimes, the way that she looks absolutely nothing like me, but is instead all blond hair and blue-eyed. And then there are those dimples—those dimples!—the most telling of all, so that I've tried sucking my cheeks in from time to time in the hopes of replicating them on my own skin. It doesn't work, of course, and instead of dimples I'm left with a fish face that makes Jessie laugh. There are times I find that I have to remind myself that I am a mother, that I am her mother, and I wonder if others see the hesitation in me, the doubt, or if it's only in my mind.

Yesterday as we were walking from the French bakery, the one with the luscious petits fours for which I had a sudden craving, the woman behind the counter wished me a happy Mother's Day, and there was something querying about it that I didn't like. It rubbed me the wrong way. What started as a polite greeting turned into a question instead, as if she doubted at that last moment—words already out of her mouth, too late to pluck them back—whether she should be wishing me a happy Mother's Day.

Was I the child's mother? Was I a mother? After all, we looked nothing alike, and of course the lack of a wedding ring raised a red flag. Perhaps I was only the child's babysitter, her nanny, the au pair.

As I thanked the woman I saw her turn red with shame, believing she'd misspoken. But I grabbed for Jessie and said,

"Come along, my darling girl," as if that might validate it for both her and me. As if it might make my maternity more real.

All afternoon I found myself overthinking, wondering what exactly that woman saw that made her question whether I was Jessie's mother. Was it the manner in which I carried myself, the way I spoke, the lack of a physical resemblance? I thought about it all day and night, wanting to know, needing to know, so that whatever it was, I could next time disguise it better.

JESSIE

THE DAY BEGINS WITH a cleaning assignment, the first in two weeks. It's a good thing for more reasons than one. These days, cash is in short supply, and I need something to do with my time. Something better than to obsess over my social security number or lack thereof, Ms. Geissler staring out her window, watching me—which, even by the light of day, still rattles me. So much so that before I leave, I eye the window shades in the carriage home, fully intent on pulling each and every one down so that no one can see inside while I'm gone.

I slip out of the carriage home quietly, setting the door closed.

I make my way down the alleyway in back, avoiding Ms. Geissler.

At 7:30 a.m., I arrive at the home on Paulina, a typical workers cottage. I have to ring the doorbell twice before Mrs. Pugh comes to the door and even then, when she draws it open, there's a deliberateness about it. It's not the breezy way she typically throws open the door and welcomes me in. Her voice is out of joint, uncharacteristic of her typical chirpiness. "Jessie," she says at seeing me standing there. The word falls flat, her eyes dropping to the mop and bucket in my hands, the cleaning caddy stuffed up under my arm. It's far more than my two arms can carry, so that I feel clumsy though I haven't dropped anything. Not yet.

As the sun rises, it lands on the nape of my neck, making it warm, which is a relief from the near-hypothermic way I spent the night in the carriage home. Cold enough to freeze. My teeth chattered all night, body wrapped up in the one blanket I could find. Three pairs of socks on my feet.

It isn't so much a welcome. "Jessie?" is what Mrs. Pugh really means, a question more than anything, as if she's surprised to see me, as if she's asking why I'm here. She stands before me in a robe and slippers, shielded by the door. There's no workout attire as expected. No yoga mat and no gym shoes. She must not be feeling well, I guess, because at eight in the morning Mrs. Pugh has yoga, so that by seven thirty, she's always dressed, hair done up in a ponytail with strands that hang loose and frame her face. But not today.

"Am I early?" I ask, looking at my watch, which tells me it's seven thirty. I'm not early because I'm right on time. I hear Mr. Pugh call from the distance, "Who's there?" he asks.

"It's Jessie," she says.

"Jessie?" he asks, the tone of his voice equally confused. As if he doesn't know who I am, which of course he does. I've been cleaning their home for years. Every Tuesday.

"It's Wednesday," Mrs. Pugh tells me. "You're not early, Jessie," she says. And I can't make out that expression on her face, but I can see that she's not happy. "You're a day *late*. You were supposed to be here yesterday," she tells me, and it startles me, this sudden revelation that today is Wednesday. That it's not Tuesday after all, in which case my whole week's been mixed-up. I wonder what else I missed. I feel groundless all of a sudden, standing high on a ledge with nothing to hang on to.

My apology is effusive. "I'm sorry," I sputter. "I'm so, so sorry," as I try and make my way past Mrs. Pugh and into their home to clean it now, but she stands in my way and says not to bother. "We had friends over last night, Jessie. Parents from the preschool. We needed the home cleaned," she says as she tugs tighter on the cord of the robe to keep whatever's inside concealed.

"I had to find someone else to clean it," she says as she stares at me, not into my eyes, but somewhere beneath. She raises a finger, points at my chest so that I look down but see nothing. She says, "Jessie, your..." but then her voice drifts off. She reconsiders. Puts her hand down and says instead, "I tried calling you. You didn't answer."

"I'm so sorry," I say again. "I could rake the leaves," I suggest, though the number of leaves on their lawn is negligible. It's too early in the season for many leaves to be falling. But I say it so that I'll have something, anything to do. "Mow the lawn?" I ask, hearing how desperate I sound, but she shakes her head and tells me, "We have a service. They take care of the yard work."

"Of course," I say, feeling stupid. I back away, not bothering to turn and look where I'm going, missing the one concrete step that separates the front stoop from the walkway. One step, a ten-inch rise. I drop straight down, landing gracelessly somehow or other on the balls of my feet, whacking my teeth together in the process. I don't fall, but the mop slips from my hands, its clang echoing up and down the street.

I turn to leave, tripping over the mop as I do, and only then does Mrs. Pugh take pity on me. "Our company," she begins, "last night. Six kids and twelve adults can make quite the mess."

She opens the door wider and invites me inside. My thanks is as over-the-top as my apology. It has nothing to do with money, but everything to do with time. Everything to do with keeping myself occupied.

I wipe down the kitchen countertops and cabinets; I wash the floors. In the bathroom, I scrub like the devil, taking out all my anxiety on the subway tiles. It doesn't help.

As I move from the bathroom to Mr. and Mrs. Pugh's bedroom, I catch sight of a computer sitting on a writing desk and it gives me an idea. The desk is minimalist, as is the computer. A sleek silver laptop that prompts me for a password as I lift it open and press the return key, holding my breath to listen for the sound of footsteps sweeping down the hall. It doesn't take a genius to figure this one out. Taped there to the desk is the password, as well as the password for every one of Mr. and Mrs. Pugh's financial accounts. Their credit cards, their bank accounts. Their Vanguard funds. I type the code and easily get in. I could probably appropriate a few hundred thousand from them if I wanted to. But that's not what I'm here to do.

Mr. Pugh has gone off to work and so for now it's only Mrs. Pugh and me. Mrs. Pugh, who sat in the sunroom drinking her coffee and reading a book when I excused myself to clean. I pray she stays put, that she doesn't come wandering into her bedroom and catch me meddling with her things.

I pull up a search engine and type my own name into it. Jessica Sloane. I'm not sure what I expect to find. Or rather what I expect to find is nothing. But instead I find an interior designer with my name, one that takes up the first two pages of results. Around page three I find a doctor named

Jessica Sloane. Even farther down the page, a Pilates instructor. A Tumblr account for a fourth woman of the same name.

But me specifically, I'm nowhere there. Though it's not like I'd have a reason to be on the internet. I've done nothing noteworthy with my life; I don't have social media; I've never been on the news. For the last twenty years, Mom and I have lived as sequestered a life as we could. Like nuns, except that we didn't pray. We just kept to ourselves.

I click on the tab for images. Hundreds of photographs load before my eyes. Hundreds of photographs of rooms the interior designer Jessica Sloane has designed. They're dramatic and fussy and not at all my style. There are photographs of her too. Her and Jessica Sloane, MD, all decked out in a white lab coat with a stethoscope slung around her neck, smiling. Trying hard to look empathetic and intelligent all at the same time. I click the news tab at the top of the page, finding articles about them too.

I pause then, hands frozen above the keyboard, hearing a noise from down the hall. The house is long and narrow, each of the rooms small. I listen, hearing water streaming from the kitchen faucet, the coffee maker warming up to brew another pot. Mrs. Pugh is making herself more coffee.

Only when Mrs. Pugh's gentle footfalls drift away do I return to the screen.

On a whim, I insert my middle name, certain the search will come back empty. But instead it narrows the results down to a manageable thirty-two, which is not at all what I was expecting, and at first I think the computer is wrong.

It's the top hit on the page that catches my eye, a newspaper clipping dated seventeen years ago. The headline reads Hit-and-Run Driver Kills Girl, Age Three.

It takes my breath away. My eyes can't believe what they

see. The words. The picture. The caption beneath the image that reads, in italics, Jessica Jane Sloane.

That's me.

My hands clutch the edge of the desktop, squeezing hard, white-knuckled from the grip.

I go on to read an article that describes a child walking into traffic and being struck by a car. The car sped on, it says, leaving the girl for dead in the street. According to witness accounts, the car was going too fast, driving erratically. Assumptions were made that the driver was drunk, though no one got a good look at him or her, nor did anyone catch a glimpse of the license plate number. There were discrepancies as to the color of the car, which went to prove the unreliability of eyewitness accounts. They couldn't be trusted. The girl, Jessica Jane Sloane, was carted to the local hospital via ambulance, and there she died.

I click back on the images tab and spy a photograph of little Jessica Sloane in a purple bathing suit. In it, she's happy. She's three years old.

My head spins. My fingers go numb. They lose feeling completely as I stare at the little girl's face and think, *Who is this girl and what's she got to do with me?*

EDEN

March 29, 1997
Egg Harbor

THEY SAY THAT VODKA has no smell to it, and yet it was clear as day to me, the smell of it on Aaron's breath as he dropped into bed beside me tonight, the clock trumpeting 1:13 in the morning. Over the last few weeks, I'd noticed a gradual shift in his work schedule, each night him coming home later than ever before.

At first he said nothing, just stared blankly at me when I asked if he'd had something to drink. He didn't say yes, but he didn't say no either, and it seemed reasonable enough to assume he *had* been drinking, though he need not say one way or the other because I could smell it on his breath.

It just so happened that Aaron and a couple of coworkers had stuck around for a nightcap after their shift was through. It had been a bad night, *shitty* was the word Aaron used, Aaron who didn't ever used to complain. Damien was a no-show and Aaron was in the weeds all night, struggling to keep up on the line.

"It was just one for the road," he said. "It's not like I'm

drunk, Eden. It was one drink. One stupid drink," he said as he set the pillow over his head.

I didn't need to remind him of the effects of alcohol on male fertility. He knew. He knew because Dr. Landry had told us all those many months before when we discussed ways to better improve Aaron's low sperm motility.

I didn't need to tell him how I had been alone all day, for eleven hours this time. Nearly twelve. He knew this too. He knew that I didn't like to go to sleep until he was here, in bed beside me. He knew that most days the boredom and loneliness consumed me, and what else was there to do for those eleven or twelve hours besides think about how much I craved a baby?

I rolled over onto my side of the bed, taking the blanket with me.

"So now you're mad?" Aaron asked as he sat there, exposed. I didn't say yes or no but I didn't need to say one way or the other because Aaron could see my posture, could sense me tense up in fury and rage. He tried to reach out for me, but I pulled away. He sighed. "I needed to unwind for a bit. To have a little fun," he said by means of explanation, but it only made things worse, imagining him with coworkers, drinking vodka and having fun.

"What's so wrong with that?" he asked. "Do you have any idea how stressful it is for me at work?" but I had a different thought then, one that went back to money. Not only was Aaron coming home later each night, drinking after work with friends—*female friends?* I wanted to ask, but couldn't do it quite yet, too afraid to know the truth, that Aaron was throwing back shots of vodka with the pretty cooks and waitresses while I sat, a prisoner in my own home—he was blowing our money on booze. Money that could otherwise be saved for fertility treatments. For a baby.

"You don't need to be wasting our money like that," I said. "We hardly have enough as it is."

And then I did ask him who he was drinking with and he rattled off names. Casey. Riley. Pat. Names that were all conveniently unisex. Names that kept me up half the night wondering if they were male or female.

"Who's Casey?" I asked, censoriously, and when he didn't reply I created her in my mind's eye: tall and svelte with long butterscotch hair and pecan eyes. Flirtatious and tactile, predisposed to standing too close and touching so that I envisioned her, this make-believe woman, with her nimble hand on Aaron's arm.

Perfect teeth.

A flawless complexion.

An effortless laugh.

I've gained ten pounds now due to the many months of fertility treatments. I'm bloated all the time, in addition to moody and upset. The water retention has made my fingers grow fat. Most days my wedding ring barely fits with the water weight and stays hidden at home in a dresser drawer.

And then Aaron asked, "What happened to you, Eden? You used to be so much fun," while pulling the blanket from me. His final hurrah.

I lay there in the dark, completely exposed.

There was a part of me that remembered that Eden, the fun Eden, but in the moment she seemed so far gone, she was hard to remember anymore.

April 14, 1997
Egg Harbor

Today I watched a mourning dove in the gutter of our home get pelted with hail. She was female, a mother-to-be, beautiful with delicate beige plumage, perched on three oval eggs in the aluminum gutter. She'd spent days with her man friend, methodically assembling the nest of twigs and grass blades—while I watched on from the second-story window as they scurried back and forth from tree to trough, collecting materials and sticking them flimsily together—not thinking once of the rainwater that would soon stream past her shanty or the pellets of frozen ice that would one day take her life.

It was golf ball–size hail, a fusillade of machine-gun fire streaming down from the pale green sky. I've never felt so helpless, watching as she sat there, hunkered down over her eggs, protecting them until the bitter end. It went on for six and a half calamitous minutes, and when it was through she lay there, unmoving, folded lifeless over the eggs like a hooded cloak and I didn't know what to do. There was no blood. I would have expected there to be blood, and yet the internal damage was no doubt worse than that which I could see from the outside, evidence of the great lengths some mothers will go to protect their children. She could have flown away, sought shelter beneath the elm or cottonwood trees that crowded the yard, diminishing our view of the lake.

But she didn't. She stayed.

The storm passed. The clouds drifted away and the sun began to shine. A rainbow appeared in the sky. The hail melted. Rainwater evaporated. The only sign of the storm was the dead bird.

Aaron watched on as I schlepped the old wooden ladder to the back of the cottage and began to climb. He asked what I was doing as I shimmied up those steps in bare feet, the shaky ladder teetering on the lawn. At the top rung I saw her, splayed sideways, head lolling over the edge of the gutter. I pressed a single finger to her chest, feeling for a heartbeat and, at finding none, removed her body from the trench. Beneath her corpse, the eggs were still intact.

She died a martyr.

I buried her beneath the trellis, which the snowdrift clematis had overtaken at this time of year, white flowers powdering the wood.

They say that mourning doves mate for life. As far as I could tell, her man friend never returned to grieve his loss or to check on the eggs.

Sometimes this is the way it is with men.

April 24, 1997
Egg Harbor

I can't trust myself to stay at home all day anymore.

All too often, I drive into town and park outside the dance studio, watching the little ballerinas come and go. It rains many days now, this time of year, and so they come toting umbrellas, skipping over puddles, walking faster than ever before, though always, *always*, does little Olivia lag behind, and on the most inclement of days, when no one else wants to be outside, I am sure that she will be forgotten. It makes me sick to my stomach to do so, to watch the ballerinas in their leotards and tutus and tights, a Peeping Tom by my own right; it isn't perverse, there's nothing depraved about the thoughts that run through my mind, and yet I know in my heart of hearts that it's unhealthy, pining this way for someone else's child.

And so, against Aaron's will, I found a job. Some useful way to spend my days other than keeping vigil of the ballet studio, watching the ballerinas come and go.

We rarely talk these days anymore, other than that time spent in limbo each month, while they wash Aaron's sperm before injecting it inside me. Then we talk. About what, I don't know. About nothing. When I ask him questions, I'm astounded by the brevity of his replies, one-or two-word responses that leave no room for dialogue. He doesn't make eye contact. He asks me nothing. We kill time in the lobby of the fertility clinic before my name is called and only then am I granted amnesty, a pardon, a reason not to have to sit in the lobby and speak to my husband.

The job is at the hospital. The position is in billing as a medical coder, one I have ample experience in after all those years working for a pediatrician in Green Bay. And so now, I spend eight hours a day reading through patient files to figure out what they're to be billed for; I enter data; I submit to insurance companies; I mail invoices to patients. It feels good to be doing something with my days, to be earning an income.

And yet the position comes with its fair share of downsides too.

Yesterday as I sifted through patient files, I came across a little girl, a toddler killed in an auto-ped accident. In other words, she wandered into the street when her mother wasn't looking and was hit by a passing car on the roadway, a four-lane highway that cut right through town. The little girl (and though I, myself, never laid eyes on her, I conjured her up in my mind anyway, her tiny, broken frame still clad in a pair of denim overalls with blood-stained pigtails in her light brown hair) was transported to our hospital by ambulance, and there, received a multitude of treatments, from a CT scan to assess brain damage, to an operation to control internal bleeding and swelling in the brain. A decompressive craniectomy, as was noted in the extensive patient chart. There were blood transfusions. She was on narcotics for pain. An anesthesiologist was called to deliver a local anesthetic to put her to sleep for the surgery. The surgery itself lasted six hours, and each of these items came with an exorbitant price tag, one the family's shoddy insurance company was loath to pay. For six tortuous hours while the little girl's mother, I can only imagine, sat on a chair in the waiting room, biting her nails to the quick, a neurosurgeon, along with a team of doctors and nurses and scrub techs, removed part of the girl's brain to allow room for the swelling inside.

Still, she died.

By the time the paperwork made it to me in coding and billing, it had been days since the angels carried her away. Her mother no longer stood within the hospitals' walls, sobbing for her child. Her body had been removed from the morgue, transported to the funeral home, buried in the ground.

And yet for me, it's a fresh wound. One that will stay with me for a long time to come. As I typed the billing codes into the system, I cried for a little girl I've never met, tears snaking down my eyes and onto the computer keys, knowing that she will never truly be anything more than a name and a social security number to me, but still it makes me cry, grieving for someone I don't know, consumed with the unwanted knowledge that healthy little girls—like the sick and the elderly—die too.

But there are perquisites to the job too.

I wear a name badge that gains me access to every nook and cranny in the whole entire hospital, including the birthing center, where I can watch newborn babies being tended to in the nursery, lying immobile in their rolling bassinets, bundled like burritos with knitted hats on their perfectly pink and misshapen heads. I didn't seek them out—in fact, I swore to myself that I would abstain from visiting the newborn babies—but I saw them anyway when a pair of grandparents-to-be stopped me in the hall and asked the way to labor and delivery. I had no choice but to lead them there, to steer them through the mazelike hospital halls, through the double doors and into the unit where the newborn babies caught my eye.

And now I stand there for what feels like hours, staring through glass, coming to terms with my fait accompli. No workday passes without at least one visit to the nursery room and as I sit at my desk coding patient files, it's all I can think about, seeing those babies. Getting my fix. I've come to know the nurses now—thanks to the frequency of my visits. They address me by name, sometimes holding up the newest infants so I can see their puffy, half-closed eyes, their still-bowed legs from being cramped inside a warm, cozy uterus, their cone-shaped heads from being suctioned through their mother's vaginal canal and into the world.

When they ask, I tell them I'm training to be a nursery room nurse myself, that I'm in the process of earning my associates' degree in nursing and, that as soon as I do, I'm going to apply for a job here, in our hospital's nursery room. I tell them I come to watch and learn, to see how the experts do it. I flatter the nurses so they don't think it odd that I spend every free second away from billing and coding staring at babies who are not mine. They smile and say how fantastic that is and sometimes, if I'm really lucky, they sneak me inside so I can stroke the soft skin of a tiny babe.

Though that, of course, isn't the real reason I come.

JESSIE

IT'S NOT YET TEN in the morning when I leave the Pughs' home. The day stretches out before me like the Sahara, massive and deserted and dry. And now I'm even more agitated than I was before, all nervous energy with nothing to do. Nowhere to go. No one to talk to.

I carry with me in my bag a printout of the newspaper article I found on the Pughs' laptop, grateful when Mrs. Pugh called down the hall that she was stepping out for a bit, and I was able to send it to the printer without her hearing me. Because if I knew one thing, it was that I needed to take the article with me.

I hop on Old Faithful and ride. I turn aimlessly, unplanned at each intersection, my head lost in the clouds. I move in circles so that three times I pass by the very same delicatessen without meaning to. I speak to Mom. I ask her questions about my lack of a birth certificate, my missing social security card, the girl in the article. Who is she, and what does she have to do with me? Does she have anything to do with me? *Tell me, Mom*, I scream in my head. *Tell me!*

It isn't until a woman standing on a street corner stares at me like I'm crazy that I realize I've been speaking out loud.

In time I find my way into the Loop. It isn't intentional. I don't go there on purpose. It's something far more subliminal than that, that makes my legs pedal hard, steering me to the Art Institute on Michigan Avenue, where I park Old Faithful just steps from the bronze lions and walk.

I don't go to the museum.

Rather I head to the south end of the building where, just off Michigan Avenue, I slip into this secret world of raised flower beds and a grove of hawthorn trees. I'd never have known what kind of tree they were, but Mom knew, Mom who found this spot by accident one day when I was young and we were exploring. It was fall and the trees were angular and uneven, a brassy shade of copper that peeked through the green of nearby trees as they do now.

Let's see what this place is, Mom had said that day, grabbing a hold of my hand and drawing me in. That first day, I didn't want to go. Rather I wanted to climb on the lions' backs and ride. But Mom had said no. The lions were to look at. They weren't for riding, though she let me pet them as we passed by.

The entrance to the garden is guarded by honey locust trees, which keep the rest of it hidden from the urban world on the other side. I slip in. I walk down a handful of steps that dip inches below street level. I move between the trees, lost in an enclave beneath an awning of leaves. Transported somewhere hundreds of miles from a city street.

There are people here. It's not as if I'm the only one who knows about this place. And yet those that are here are placid. Quiet. Drinking coffee and smoothies, reading books, staring into space. A woman picks at the edges of a muffin wrapper, offering scraps to a nearby bird.

This was one of Mom's favorite spots in the city. We'd come here and she'd spend hours sitting on the edge of the raised beds. She'd watch as I scaled them with my arms extended, imagining myself as a tightrope walker. They're large—a good twenty feet by twenty feet or more—so it was always quite the feat when I could get around without falling.

Mom let me do it for hours. She never got bored.

There was one place in the garden Mom liked more than the rest because it was secluded, set back from the street entrance, the water fountain and the pool. Even in the most secluded of places, she found the most covert place to hide.

I make my way there now because I think that somehow I might feel closer to Mom if I sit there. That somehow we'll be able to commune.

But when I get there, that spot is already occupied. A man sits there, reading the newspaper. Truth be told, it makes me crabby, thinking what nerve he has to sit in Mom's favorite spot. And so I sit opposite him on another bed, twenty feet away or more, watching him, waiting for him to leave. I stare at him, thinking it'll make him uncomfortable and he'll go.

But he's not uncomfortable because he doesn't even see me staring. He's too preoccupied by the newspaper in his hands.

I can't say one way or the other if he's tall or short because he's sitting. He's got his legs crossed, ankle to knee, and his clothes are all sorts of nondescript. Pants, shirt, shoes. Nothing noteworthy about them. They're clothes. The sleeves of his shirt are thrust to the elbows. There, on his left arm beneath the cuff of the shirt, is a scar. It peeks out from beneath the sleeve, a six-inch gash that's healed poorly. The skin around it is puckered and pink.

His face looks sad. That's the first thought I have. That the expression on his face—that and his body language—is one of sadness. The way his mouth pulls down at the corners, a slight tug there at the edges of his lips. The way his shoulders slouch. I should know because each time I look in the mirror, I see the very same thing. On his face is a patch of hair, a tight beard, trimmed and tidy. It gives off an aura of mystery and regality. His skin is tanned like the hide of a moose, stretched and dried in the sun before being smoked over a fire. Like he's spent too much time outside in the sun.

He isn't thumbing through the newspaper, but instead he's got his eyes peeled to some story on the top page, the paper folded so that he can hone in on it. Something bad has happened in the world, I think. Something bad always happens. I wonder what it is this time. Terrorist attack. Women and children being slaughtered by their own leaders. A shooting in an elementary school. Children murdered by their own moms and dads.

I watch his eyes, the movement of them as he scans the story. Moving left to right. Dropping down to read the next line. But his eyes are lowered, gazing down on the newspaper and so I can't see much, none other than the lashes and the lids. He bites a lip. He bites hard so that the pain of the lip overrides whatever it is he's feeling on the inside. I do that too.

He reaches for a cup of coffee set on the marble edge of the raised bed. I read the corrugated sleeve on the cup. A coffee bar on Dearborn. I've never been there before, but I know the place. I've seen it before.

And then he gets up to go, and I ready myself to make a move for his seat. He slips an orange baseball cap over the brown hair, though as he goes, he leaves his newspaper behind. Because he's sad. Because he's distracted.

He walks away and I notice a shoe is untied, the cuff of a pant leg stuck in the shoe's tongue. He leaves it there. For a second or two I watch him go.

But then, standing and making my way to the raised bed, I call to him, "Sir," while grabbing the newspaper so that the wind doesn't have a chance to scatter it around the garden. "Sir," I call again, "your newspaper."

But he's walking away and before I can run to him, something leaps off the page at me. It grabs me by the throat so that I can't speak and I can't move. I'm frozen in place, a bronze statue like the lions who stand before the Art Institute, guarding its entrance.

There on the top of the newspaper is Mom's beautiful face. Her beautiful brown eyes and brown hair, both watered down by the black-and-white newsprint.

Her obituary. The one I put in the paper because I needed the world to know she was dead. To solidify it. To make it real. Because only then, when it was written in print for all of the world to see, would I believe it.

This man. The sad man sitting in Mom's and my spot in the garden. He was reading her obituary.

He had the newspaper folded so that Mom's face was on top, and it was these words his eyes spanned as he bit his lip so that he wouldn't cry.

Mom's obituary is what made this man sad.

I read over the words. Mom's death notice, which was brief because there wasn't a whole lot of information to provide. No memorial service. No one to send flowers to.

The final line reads "Eden Sloane is survived by her daughter, Jessica."

My legs lose feeling. I go slack jawed. Because there's one word on the newsprint that the man has circled and it's my name. Jessica.

EDEN

July 12, 2003
Chicago

The park is named after some poet, I've come to learn. Though no one pays attention to things like that because, to most people, it's just a park where kids romp around on the playground and, on the other side of a chain-link fence, boys play basketball, the repeated *thump, thump, thump* of the ball on concrete a steady refrain. They're older boys mostly, teenagers, and they spout from their mouths a flurry of curse words at regular intervals, and I feel grateful Jessie is still too young to know what any of it means, though she pauses from time to time to watch them. To just stand on the playground and stare.

There are baseball fields off in the distance, and on the other side of a bridge, a path that snakes along the river where she and I sometimes walk, but not today. Today she played on the playground, and for the first time ever, found a friend. Not the kind of friend we'd keep in touch with after today or invite over for a playdate. No, Jessie and I don't have those types of friends.

Rather she's the kind of friend who, for fifteen or twenty minutes at best, is a bosom body. A soul mate.

I watched as Jessie and the little girl chased each other in dizzying circles, up the stairs and down the slide. Again and again and again. As far as I knew, they never exchanged names. Because that's the way it is with kids. Uncomplicated. Straightforward. Easy.

There was no one else on the playground but the two of them, and the only ones sitting on the periphery of it were the little girl's mother, pushing a newborn in an old-fashioned buggy, and me. It took some time, a few awkward glances my way, before she rose from her own park bench and came to mine, standing before me, offering a hello. I too said hello, staring down into the buggy at the infant sound asleep beneath a yellow blanket.

"How sweet," I said.

The baby, Piper, she told me, was twelve days old, born on the first of July. The woman moved guardedly, as if in pain, and I didn't ask before she told me, "Piper was breech," telling me how her baby was fully intent on entering the world feetfirst. "The doctors did everything they could to change that. But no such luck," she explained, sitting softly beside me on the park bench and describing in too much detail what a C-section is like. The incision. The surgical staples. The scar she'd no doubt have. She lifted the hem of her shirt then so that I could see it myself, and I blushed at the sight of her still-pregnant belly, at the bloated butterfly tattoo that sat just inches from the healing incision, at the canvas of fair skin. She was oversharing and I blamed the newness of childbirth for it, the fact that to her it was still fresh. The only thing these days that occupied her mind.

"With Amelia it was different," she admitted, and I made the easy assumption that Amelia was the older of the two, the little girl, maybe five years old, who Jessie made a train with at the top of the slide—wrapping her skinny legs around the midsection of a girl she hardly knew—and together they catapulted down to the wood chips below, landing on their rear ends, laughing. "Twenty-some hours of labor, three hours of pushing," she said, going on far too long about the gush of water when her membranes ruptured, like the pop of a water balloon. Her, worried only that she might poop on the bed, as one of her girlfriends had done. The broken blood vessels left behind on her face from hours of pushing, thin, red veins that snaked this way and that across her skin. Some doctor she didn't know delivering her baby. Her breasts engorged, her unable to produce milk following childbirth. Having to relent to formula, which her mommy's groups abhorred.

I felt uncomfortable, if I was being honest, about this sudden revelation of information from a woman I didn't know. But it dawned on me then that this is the type of thing women do, this is the type of thing *mothers* do: share their experiences, swap stories, foster camaraderie.

She looked at me expectantly, as if it was my turn to share. She was quiet, watching me, and when I didn't respond, she prompted, "And your girl?" and I knew then that I must tell her something, that I must offer up some version of the truth. I pictured those wide hospital halls, the glaring lights. "She was a vaginal birth?" she asked, that word alone—*vaginal*—making me turn redder than I was before. Because these were the kinds of conversations I didn't have. Intimate. Friendly.

Most of my conversations ended at hello.

I felt my head nod without my permission, and I knew I must say more, that a nod of the head alone wouldn't suffice.

And so I told her about the hospital room. I told her about the huddle of people who gathered around me, the nurses clinging to either of my legs, encouraging me to push. Incanting it in my ear—push, push—as I gathered handfuls of bedding in my hands and bore down with all of my might. The epidural had worn off by then, or maybe it was never there to begin with. All I felt was pain, a pain so intense it was as if my insides were on fire, about to rupture. I was certain I would soon explode. A hand stroked the sweaty hair from my face, whispering words of encouragement into an ear as I screamed, this crude, ugly scream, but I didn't care how crude or ugly it was. The nurses wrenched on either of my legs, stretching me apart, making me wide. *Push*, they said again and again, and I did, I pushed for dear life, watching as that flash of black spilled from inside of me and into the doctor's gentle hands.

But then I remembered.

That wasn't me.

JESSIE

BEFORE I CAN TEAR my eyes from Mom's face on the newspaper's obituaries page, from my own circled name, the man has slipped from the garden and disappeared from sight. I attempt to run after him, barreling through the rows of hawthorn trees as quickly as my legs can carry me. But still, when I come rushing out onto Michigan Avenue, chest heaving, breathing hard, he's gone. The sidewalk is inundated with people, with kids, a middle school field trip to the Art Institute, and they're all lined up in two parallel rows before the museum's concrete steps. Clogging the sidewalk. I push past bubbly preteens who are incognizant of my desperation, who don't care. By the time I reach the other side, there's no sign of the man anywhere. The man with the sad eyes and the untied shoe.

I stare up and down the street, completely aghast. A muscle in my eyelid twitches, a spasm. Something involuntary, something I can't make go away though I try. It's extremely annoying. The street is a wide six-lane divided street jam-packed with people and cars, a median strip in the center that's plugged with flowers and trees, making it even harder to see the other side. But still I walk, searching the streets for the man.

I hurry down Michigan with a heavy, desperate tread. The wind is a wall by now, and I lean into it to walk. It's exhausting. All the while, my eyelid twitches. I turn left at Randolph, a temporary reprieve from the militant headwind, which now comes at me from the side so that I slope laterally, a perfect seventy-five-degree angle. At Clark, I turn right, not quite knowing where I'm going, but trying desperately to find the man. I climb northward, gazing into storefronts to see if he's there. I stare down alleyways, out of breath by the time I come to a six-story building on Superior Street, one that's flanked with floor-to-ceiling windows and looks oddly familiar to me.

I spin in a circle, taking it in, the doorman in uniform, the sign outside that reads Spacious, Open-plan Lofts for Sale. Inquire Inside. I know where I am. I've been here before.

Just like that, I'm standing at Liam's front door.

I didn't know I was coming here. I didn't come here on purpose. But here I am, and now that I'm here, I make an attempt to scoot past the doorman and into the building. Because maybe Liam can help me think this through. The little girl in the car accident, the man in the garden. He'll make me see that there's nothing sordid going on. That it's only a coincidence.

The doorman stands on the curb, hailing a cab for a resident. "Can I help you, miss?" he asks, catching sight of me out of the corner of his eye, as he steers the resident into the back seat of the cab and closes the door for her.

He steps closer to me. "I'm here to see Liam," I say.

His smile is mocking. Wary. "Liam who?" he asks, playing dumb, and I freeze, realizing only then that I don't have a last name. That to me he's just Liam. That until yesterday he wasn't even that, because before yesterday he didn't have a name. He was only the guy from the hospital, the one with the blue eyes.

But I also realize that the doorman knows fully well what Liam's last name is. He isn't curious. He's testing me, checking to see how well I know Liam before he lets me in.

"I don't know his last name," I admit, feeling uncomfortable as my feet shift in place. At first he's hesitant, not sure he wants to phone Liam or not. For all he knows, I'm someone Liam is avoiding, someone he doesn't want to see. And that's his job, to keep unwanted visitors at bay, unwanted visitors like me.

He sizes me up and down. He asks twice what my name is. Both times I say Jessie, though for the first time I start to doubt that it is. I feel disheveled, disoriented, and though I have no idea what I look like, I can see it in the doorman's eyes. It's not good. I run my hands through my hair; I rub at my twitching eyes.

"Is Liam expecting you?" he asks, and I'm not quick enough on my feet to lie. I tell him no.

"Can you call him for me, please?" I plead, the desperation in my voice palpable to both him and me.

The doorman reluctantly phones Liam for me, but Liam doesn't answer his call. "He's not home," he tells me, setting the phone down. I feel the skeptic in me start to take hold. He's lying. He didn't call him. He only pretended he did, but he didn't. I think that maybe the number he dialed wasn't Liam at all, or maybe he didn't push enough digits for the call to go through. Or he hung up before Liam had a chance to answer.

I'm about to get angry, but then I remember. The funeral. Liam's brother's funeral is today. He's at the funeral. He's not home.

I excuse myself, walking from the building, feeling muddled. There's a convenient mart next door to the apartment building. I slip inside and buy a Coke, hoping the caffeine will make me feel less mixed-up. Or, at minimum, curtail the throbbing in my head from the day's lack of caffeine.

Back outside, I drop down onto the curb to catch my breath. I need to think things through, but my mind can focus on only one thing. What if Jessica Sloane with my social security number did die when she was three? She wasn't erroneously classified as dead because she was really dead. Then I've been living with a mistaken social security number all this time, with a mistaken identity.

Is it possible that the other Jessica Sloane and I have social security numbers so close they're off by only a single digit, or have two numbers that are interchanged? Maybe she died and someone unwittingly typed my social security number into the death database. The names matched, so they didn't think twice. An oversight only.

Doubtful.

And then my mind gravitates to the man in the garden. Who is he, and what was he doing there? What does he want with me?

"Jessie?" I hear, and when I look up from the street, I see Liam making his way toward me. All dressed up in a black suit and tie. Looking undeniably sleek but also tired like me.

I rise from the curb and bridge the gap, and, as we close in on one another, his face darkens. "Your shirt," he says as he points to it, to my shirt, and tells me that I've got it on inside out. Which wouldn't be so obvious were it not for the label sitting smack-dab beneath my chin, a blaring thing. I pluck it from my skin for a better look.

Not only do I have my shirt on inside out, but it's backward. And now that Liam has pointed it out for me, I feel the high neckline, the cotton taut in places it isn't meant to be taut. In that moment I have no memory of ever grabbing the shirt from the closet, slipping it from its hanger, of ever putting it on.

It's a blessing that I'm even dressed.

"Come inside," he says, his eyes hanging on a little longer than they ordinarily would. "You can fix it there."

But I say, "No," shooing him off, feeling suddenly asinine. "It's just a stupid shirt anyway; it's not like anyone noticed." And then I sigh, feeling completely exasperated. Exasperated and exhausted. He hears it in my voice.

"Jessie," he says, his voice far more resolute this time. "Come inside. Keep me company."

We step inside the building and wait for the elevator to come. "Did you sleep last night?" he asks. I don't say yes or no, but my silence gives it away. In my head, I tally the days up. I lose track at number four and have to start again, counting on my fingers this time, reaching seven.

It's been seven days since I've slept.

"I looked it up," Liam tells me as the elevator comes for us. Though it doesn't align with the lobby floor—a fact that I realize all too late—and so I trip on the way in, stumbling over that one-inch rise. Liam latches on to my arm, steadying me. He doesn't let go. Not until I draw my arm away, stepping closer to the wall so that I can use it for leverage if need be.

"Looked what up?" I ask as the elevator sweeps us up to the sixth floor. I feel suddenly rocky on my feet. Nauseous.

"The longest a person has ever gone without sleep," Liam says.

He tells me how people die from lack of sleep. About lab rats who died from lack of sleep. "How long?" I ask.

"Eleven days," he says. "Eleven, Jessie," he repeats to drive the point home, I think. "You need to sleep."

"I will," I say, but chances are good that I won't.

I ask how the funeral went because I don't want to talk about my lack of sleep or the fact that in four more days I'm liable to die because of it. The funeral, he says, went as well as to be expected for a funeral. His shoulders shrug and his expression is flat. He doesn't say more.

The elevator arrives at the sixth floor. He leads us to his apartment, walking a half step ahead of me. At the door, I stop a few feet back, waiting as he opens it. Inside, the space is big and roomy with ceilings that are extraordinarily high, track lighting, exposed brick. Sunlight pours in through floor-to-ceiling windows. "You coming?" he asks.

I walk past him and into the apartment as behind me he closes the door.

He offers me something to drink. I say no because I have my Coke, which I uncap and take a swig of. But as I raise the bottle up to my lips, there's that tremor to my hand again, the one I can't make stop.

Liam tugs the tie from his neck and slips the suit jacket off. Throws it over the arm of a chair. Unbuttons his shirt. Rolls the cuffs of it to his elbows. Finds himself a water in the refrigerator and sinks into a low-slung chair. He never asks what I'm doing here.

I give the article to Liam, my hand still shaking as I do. I sit on a chair opposite him. I don't bother fixing my shirt.

"What's this?" he asks, but it's one of those questions that isn't really a question because already he's reading the story of Jessica Sloane, who was killed by a hit-and-run driver at the age of three. When he comes to the end of it he tells me what I already know. He says that this is strange.

I assert, "I mean, it's just a coincidence, right? A mistake?"

His face is impassive. He doesn't say an emphatic *yes* as I'd hoped he would; he doesn't put my mind at ease. This time, there are too many holes that don't line up.

"I don't know," he admits, saying, "It's just that it's strange, Jessie. I mean, yesterday it was a coincidence. Yesterday it was a mistake. Yesterday someone screwed up. But now it's like it isn't so much an accident as it is someone intentionally trying to keep you off the radar. You have no birth certificate, you can't find your social security card and the social security number you think is yours matches up with that of a dead girl. One who might just have the same name as you."

The expression on his face says it all. Something sordid is going on here. Something bad.

"It's just hard to believe that she's not you," he says while motioning to the photograph in the article, but when I look at the child's face, I see nothing but a stranger looking back at me. I've never seen this girl before.

"But it's not me," I argue, voice trembling. "She doesn't look a thing like me. Look at the shape of her eyes, her nose. It's all different," I allege, rising to my feet. "It's all wrong."

"I didn't mean that," he says, his voice gentle. "That's not what I meant, Jessie. I just mean," he says. "I just mean that I think it's possible there's something going on here, some sort of identity theft."

"What do you mean, identity theft?" I ask, except I know what he means. What he's suggesting is not that my identity has been stolen, but that I've stolen the identity of someone else—unpremeditated on my part, but still identity theft.

"Jessie," he starts, but I shake my head and he stops.

At first there's nothing but silence. I drop back down into my chair. I think it through. "You think my mother changed my name, gave me a phony identity and passed me off as a dead girl?" I ask, the words themselves unthinkable. Not something that could possibly be real. For a second I feel like I might vomit. The Coke gathers in my stomach, burning the lining of it. There's hardly any food inside me, which, when coupled with everything else, doesn't sit well. The pain starts somewhere around my navel and creeps up my chest. An agonizing lump that plunks itself behind the breastbone.

"But no," I say decisively, rising to my feet again and beginning to pace. Why would Mom do that? Why in the world would Mom steal the identity of a girl who had died and give it to me? "Why?" I ask out loud, though the answer slowly dawns on me, that if Mom went around passing me off as a dead girl, then no one would know she had stolen another child's identity. Because that child was dead.

I watch as Liam grabs for a laptop on the coffee table and types quick, harried words into it. He moves from his chair and comes to me and together we stare at the words on the screen. There's a whole word for it, he tells me. "Ghosting. Thieves open bank accounts and credit cards using a dead person's social security number," he says. "They pore over obituaries to see who's died, and then rack up thousands of dollars of debt in some stiff's name."

"But why?" I ask dumbly, though I'm not that dumb. I just can't wrap my head around it. People do this kind of thing for financial gain, but Mom and I were never rich. We weren't living a life of riches. We lived paycheck to paycheck.

Besides, Mom would never do anything to harm someone; she would never steal.

There has to be more to it than that.

If—and that's a big *if*—she took the identity of a dead child and gave it to me, then it was for some other reason than financial gain. But what? I can't even begin to guess.

I swallow the last of my Coke. It's like rubbing salt in an open wound. The pain in my chest gets worse so that I cough and, as I do, all I can think of is corroded pipes, the lining of my esophagus plugged up and rusty.

I let an idea dwell for a short time, and then quickly expunge it from my mind.

Find yourself, Mom told me. One of two wishes she had for me before she died.

Maybe she didn't mean for me to apply to college. Maybe it was far less esoteric than that. Maybe it was quite literal.

Find yourself, she said, because Jessie Sloane isn't you.

EDEN

May 28, 1997
Egg Harbor

AS SPRING RIPENS INTO summer, tourists reappear. The town comes to life with a certain vivacity that was missing during the dismal days of winter. Trees burgeon, flowers bloom.

Miranda and her three boys appear like magic at my front door each day that I'm not working—and often, I'd venture to guess, when I am—toting blueberry loaves and apple pies.

As the boys play in the tree swing (that by now was meant to hold my own child, the two of us nestled snugly together, he or she on the seat of my lap, weightless and grinning as we lift off from the ground and take flight), Miranda and I sip lemonade. As always she sells short the joys of marriage and motherhood, while little Carter crawls on the lawn before us on all fours, eating dirt. She complains about everything from what a jerk her husband, Joe, can be—coming home late from work, missing dinner, not helping with the boys' bedtime routine—to the monotony of her days, to the amount of food three growing boys consume. She can never keep the cabinets fully stocked, she tells me, because the minute she buys it they eat it all, which leads into an onslaught on the difficulties of grocery shopping with three boys, and she describes it for me: the poking and the prodding of each other, the name-calling—birdbrain, imbecile, idiot—the running off headlong down the market's aisles, bumping into strangers, begging and crying for things that Miranda has already said no to, trying to sneak it past her and into the basket, screaming and calling her names when she snatches it out of their dirty hands and returns it to the store shelf.

"That must be so difficult," I say, trying my hardest to sound empathetic, but when Miranda replies with "You have no idea, Eden. Can you even grasp how lucky you are, getting to grocery shop alone?" it's all I can do not to scream.

I would give life and limb to grocery shop with a child.

Miranda doesn't bother asking how the fertility treatments are going, though just last night Aaron and I made the decision to give in vitro fertilization a try. Or rather, I should say, *I* made the decision to give in vitro a try. The cost of it is extortionate, thousands of dollars for a single cycle, for Dr. Landry to go inside one time and pluck an egg or two from my ovaries to combine with Aaron's sperm, making an embryo, a *baby*, in a culture dish. As one grows bacteria. It seems scientific, synthetic, and yet there isn't anything I wouldn't do for a child.

I know this now.

But Aaron isn't so sure. As we stood in the kitchen last night, both of us speaking in acerbic tones, he calculated the costs we've paid over the year, all the pelvic ultrasounds and semen analyses, the Clomid cycles, the trigger shots, intrauterine insemination. The grand total tallied up to some ten thousand dollars already spent trying to create a child, an expenditure that will nearly double with one single cycle of IVF. Aaron and I don't have this kind of money. He reminds me of this relentlessly, as he reminds me how happy we used to be before we ever made the decision to start a family, and I have this vague recollection of a couple, a man and a woman—as if in another life—sitting on a dock, holding hands, watching sailboats float by on a bay.

"I think we should stop, Eden," he said, trying hard to reach out to me but I pulled away. "I think we should be happy with what we have."

"And what's that?" I asked, up in arms. What did we possibly have without a baby?

"Us," he said, looking sad. "You and me. That's what we have."

I wouldn't be deterred.

"We will do this," I told him of the in vitro fertilization. Hands on hips, my expression flat. An imperial fiat.

I left the room so it couldn't be further discussed.

I've taken out three credit cards in my own name, and charge each appointment with Dr. Landry to them in sequence. Never are we able to pay more than the minimum payment for each. The interest fees soar monthly as the cottage degenerates bit by bit. The furnace went out; we need to replace the plumbing throughout the entire home before the decades-old steel pipes wear out for good. The windows are drafty; they too need to be replaced before another winter comes or we'll spend an arm and a leg to heat the home, watching our money quite literally go out the window.

But each of these plays second fiddle to making a baby.

Aaron and I argue daily about money. The cost of groceries, the cost of clothes.

What concessions can we make so that we can save more for a baby?

Do we really need two cars, cable TV, a new pair of shoes?

"This is ridiculous," Aaron says as he holds up a shoe, the outsole flapping loose like a hangnail. "I can't go to work like this." And yet I argue with him, claiming he's being extravagant by not making do with the shoe. "Surely you can get another month out of those shoes," I say, suggesting he use some glue, though it isn't about the shoe, but rather what the hundred dollars for another pair of shoes will buy. An appointment with Dr. Landry, a hormone shot, a month's worth of Clomid.

But Aaron swears he needs the shoe, which inside makes me fume.

How selfish can he be? Where are his priorities?

At each unwelcome visit, when Miranda and her boys appear at my door without invitation, her belly continues to swell, another baby on the way, "Hopefully a girl this time," she says, fingers laced together in the air.

If Aaron and I hurry up, she reminds me for the umpteenth time, joining me in the backyard for another glass of lemonade, her baby and my baby can one day go to school together. They can be friends.

I smile.

And though I don't say it aloud, I think to myself that I'd rather die than have my baby and Miranda's baby be friends.

June 13, 1997
Egg Harbor

The hollyhocks are in bloom. Just the sight of them lined up defiantly against the weathered picket fence stabs me in the chest. They stand high above the rest of the flowers in the garden, six feet tall or more. Their bold bell-shaped flowers burn red against the greenery.

It's been a year then since Aaron and I planted the seedlings in the lawn against the fence where they'd be sheltered from the rain and the wind. And now here they are, exhibitionists in my flower bed, outshining the roses and lilies.

Reminding me of all the wasted time Aaron and I have spent trying to have a baby.

When Aaron was at work, I took a pair of scissors to them, cutting hard through the thick stem. I seethed as I did it, crying, taking out a year's worth of rage on the flowers. I screamed like a maniac, grateful that, thanks to the deep rim of trees surrounding our yard, no one was around to see or hear my outburst. I grabbed handfuls of stems and tugged with all my might, wresting the roots from the ground where I stomped on them like a child. I tore the flowers from their stems, shredding them into a million pieces until my hands were yellow with pollen and I was out of breath from the outburst.

When I was finished, I threw them away, beneath the garbage where all the negative pregnancy tests go.

The deer, I'll blame, when Aaron asks what happened to the flowers. I'll say that the deer have had their way with the hollyhocks, eating them to the quick.

And he'll be more upset about this than he is our lack of a baby.

After all our hard work.

"Such a shame," he'll say, before waging a war against the innocent deer.

JESSIE

I TAKE THE BROWN Line back to the carriage home, walking the last couple of blocks from the station at Paulina. I feel lost without my bike. I don't have my bike, Old Faithful, because I left it outside the Art Institute, tethered to some sort of loopy bike rack, when I walked to Liam's, chasing after the mystery man.

It's dark inside by the time I arrive, night falling quickly. I close the door behind me and jiggle the handle a couple of times to be sure it's closed tight. I'm in a trance, thinking about little else but the dead Jessica Sloane. The one who is three years old. The one who is me but not me all at the same time. Lines from the newspaper article run through my mind, committed to memory already.

A four-lane highway with a speed limit of just twenty-five.

The road twisted through the small seaside town.

The driver rounded a bend at nearly twice that speed.

Every time I close my eyes I see her face.

I have only a vague recollection of riding the elevator

downstairs; of pushing my way through the turnstile doors of Liam's apartment building; of walking to the Merchandise Mart to catch the train with him at my side. He'd offered to cover the cost of a cab for me but I said no.

Still, he walked me there, to the Merchandise Mart, and paid to stand on the platform beside me, waiting until the Brown Line came. And now that I look, I see his jacket draped over me, keeping me warm. He must've put it there, but that I don't remember.

I turn and walk up the carriage house's stairway, a rickety old thing with steps that are a bit concave, the edges worn away. The steps sink at their center. They squeak. The tread pitches downward from a century's worth of weight, and I cling to the railing so I don't fall.

When I get to the top I have to fight for breath. The steepness of the steps isn't to blame, nor for once my overwhelming fatigue.

What knocks the wind from my lungs is something else entirely.

Because as my feet hit the wooden floorboards and my eyes size up the open rooms, I see that the white window curtains I'd pulled shut before I left, so that no one could see inside while I was gone—every single one of them is open wide.

It's instinctive, the way the blood coagulates inside me. It becomes thick and gooey so that I can't move.

Someone was here.

My gut feeling is to hide. There's a closet nearby, a catch-all for coats and shoes. My eyes go to it. I could hide. I could bury myself in a dark nothingness and cower on the floor in fear. Because whoever opened the blinds might still be here. Inside the old home.

I listen for strange noises. For calculated footfalls coming for me. For the sound of restrained breaths, slow, repressed and controlled unlike mine. I listen for the groan of floorboards, but the only sound I hear is that of my own heartbeat.

I don't hide.

I've never been a particularly courageous person. Mom always said to face my fears, to take matters into my own hands, to fight for what was mine. And so I make my way slowly through the home, searching for signs of life.

Much of the carriage house is easy to see from where I stand. But then there are those places I can't see. An upstairs closet, the bathroom, under the eaves of the pitched roof where shadows make it hard to see. All of that is up another set of stairs, on the third floor of the home.

I ascend those steps on tiptoes, the arches of my feet beginning to burn. Convinced that if I walk on tiptoes, the intruder won't hear me, that he or she won't know that I am here.

Upstairs, I see a figure hunkered down beneath the sloped ceiling and my breath leaves me. It's hidden to the side of the mattress, trying to hold still and yet moving in a gentle rhythm.

What I see is a man on bent knee, crouched down, waiting to lunge at me as I reach the top of the staircase.

I gasp aloud, attempting to brace for impact. But instead I lose balance, slipping backward on the top step and sliding downward the eight-or nine-inch rise to the step below. I catch myself there, gripping tightly to the stairwell banister before I plunge down an entire flight of stairs, head over heels over head. Breaking my neck.

My heart pounds hard.

I cling to the banister and realize that no one has lunged at me.

And this time, when I look again, there's no one there.

It's just the shadow of a tree streaming in through an open window. The leaves are hair, the branches arms and legs. The gentle rhythm, the movement of wind. No one is there.

I turn to make my way to the bathroom. It's a small room, but as I come to it, I take note: the door isn't pressed flush against the wall as it should be. Behind the open door, there is enough space for a body to hide.

I have to muster every ounce of courage I have to go on. It isn't easy. My feet don't want to move, but they do. It's slow, deliberate.

When I reach the bathroom door, I don't step inside. I don't look behind the door.

Rather my movements are sudden and abrupt, an impulse. I kick the door as hard as I can, where it ricochets off the wall, the rubber stopper running headfirst into the baseboard, not bumping into a person first. Because there's nobody there to slow it down. There's nobody there at all.

As I make my way inside the bathroom, I find the shower curtain pulled tight, stretched from wall to wall. It billows slightly. Heat spews from a nearby vent, though that's not the reason for the movement. Instead what I envision is a figure standing on the other side of the curtain, the breath from his or her lungs making the curtain move.

Someone is there, hiding behind the shower curtain.

I tread delicately. On tiptoes. Two steps, and then three.

I reach out a hand, aware that the blood throughout my entire body has stopped flowing. That I'm holding my breath. That my heart has ceased beating.

I feel the cotton of the shower curtain in my shaking hand, the plastic of its liner. I grab a fistful of it and pull hard, finding myself face-to-face with the white tiles of the shower wall.

There's no one there. It's only me.

The carriage home is empty. Whoever was here has gone for now.

I do only one thing then, and that's check the fire safe box where I keep my money, to be sure someone hasn't swiped every last penny from me. Because why else would someone break into the carriage home except to steal from me? I keep the box in the closet these days, hidden in the corner beneath the hem of a long winter coat where, God willing, no one will ever find it. I open the closet door, drop to my knees and gather the box in my hands. The box is locked. When I slip the key inside, I find every dollar accounted for. Whoever was here didn't steal money from me.

I try not to let my imagination get the best of me, but to force logic to prevail. I tell myself that I never closed the shades in the first place. That I only thought about doing it, but never did. I think long and hard, trying to remember the smooth, woven feel of the white roller shade in my hand as I drew it southward and let go, watching it hold.

Did that happen, or did I only imagine it did?

Or maybe whatever springlike mechanism that makes the shades open failed to keep them closed. The ratchet and pin that hold them in place didn't work. Simple human error or mechanical failure.

Or maybe someone *was* there, lifting the roller shades one by one so that when I returned, they could see me. I tell myself no. That the front door was locked. And that, as far as I know, only one person but me has a key. My landlord.

I step from the closet and make my way to a nearby window where I stare out and toward Ms. Geissler's home. The room turns warm all of a sudden. Beneath my arms, I sweat.

There's no one there, no one that I can see.

And yet, as it was last night, there's a light on in the third-story window of the greystone home. The window shades are lowered, but not pulled all the way down. They don't lie flush against the window sill. There's a gap. Albeit a small one, only a couple of inches at best.

But still, a gap.

And as I stare at that gap for half the night, sometime around midnight I see a shadow pass by. Just a shadow, but nothing more.

EDEN

July 2, 1997
Egg Harbor

BE STILL MY BEATING heart, it worked! We're going to have a baby!

One single cycle of IVF and, as I sat on the toilet today after Aaron had gone off to work, the all-familiar pregnancy test cradled between my fingers, I spied not one single line this time, but two. Two! Two pink lines running parallel on the display screen.

My heart hammered quickly inside my chest. It was all I could do not to scream.

And still I had my doubts—after months of seeing only one line, it was easy to convince myself that I was imagining the second one there, that I had quite simply fashioned it in my mind. The one line was bright pink like bubble gum, the same dependable line that greeted me each month, bringing stinging tears to my eyes.

But the other, this new line, was a light pink, the lightest of light, the mere suggestion of pink, a whisper that something might be there.

I pray that it's not a deception of my mind.

I went to the market wearing mismatching shoes. I drove above the speed limit with the window open, though outside it poured down rain. I ran into the store without an umbrella, saturating my hair. If anyone noticed my shoes, they didn't point it out.

I purchased three additional pregnancy tests of assorted brands in case one had a tendency toward being inaccurate. I took them home and urinated on them all, every last one of them, and in the end, there were six lines.

Three additional pregnancy tests.

Six pink lines.

Aaron and I are going to have a baby.

July 5, 1997
Egg Harbor

For days we've been living in a constant state of euphoria.

I walk around the home, floating on air. I dream up baby names for boys and girls. I go to the hardware store and get samples of paint for the nursery room walls.

At home alone, I find myself dancing. Spinning in graceful circles around the living room floors. In all my life, I've never danced before. But I can't help myself. I can't stop my feet from swaying, my arms wrapped around myself, holding on to the life within. Dancing with my unborn child. I find an old record and set it on the turntable. I carefully place the needle on it, and move in tune to the music as Gladys Knight sings a song for me.

The day I discovered the positive pregnancy tests, I phoned Aaron at work to deliver the news. He was euphoric in a way I'd rarely seen him before. He left work at once and came home earlier than ever before, pulling his car in to the drive minutes before eight o'clock.

He brought me ice cream in bed; he fed it to me with a bent-out-of-shape spoon. He lay in bed beside me and rubbed my back. He massaged my feet. He stroked my hair. He told me how amazing I was, how gorgeous, and how already I had that beautiful pregnancy glow.

He stared at me then, just stared, and inside my heart began to cantor, a kaleidoscope of butterflies flitting inside me. I knew what would come next and it was then that my body began to want him, to need him like it hadn't for so long before. I soughed at his touch, my skin breaking out in gooseflesh as he ran a hand across my arm, lacing his fingers through mine. As he stared, he said again that if our baby girl looked anything like me, that she would be the prettiest thing around. And then he tucked a strand of hair behind my ear and I knew that in that moment, I was the most beautiful girl in the world to him.

Our baby girl.

He held me tightly and kissed me like he hadn't in months, slowly and deeply at first, growing ravenous, a starved man who hadn't been fed in years, and it was then that I realized I too was empty and famished.

My breath quickened as he slid a steady hand up the skirt of my nightgown.

"You think it's okay?" I gasped as Aaron withdrew my underpants and set them aside, though there was nothing more that I wanted in that moment than a fresh start for Aaron and me and our baby, to be able to erase all the animosity in a single moment, with a single deed.

"You think it's safe?" I begged, and Aaron assured me that everything was okay, and, as we moved together there on the bed, I believed him. For the first time in a long time, I believed him.

July 14, 1997
Egg Harbor

An ultrasound with Dr. Landry confirmed the pregnancy, though there was no need for Dr. Landry's attestation because I, for one, already knew that it was true, that the manifold of pregnancy tests didn't lie. The battle with morning sickness had begun already, a misnomer if I'd ever heard one for it was morning, noon and night sickness. Not once did I complain, but rather welcomed the nausea and the fatigue as a gift.

Dr. Landry told Aaron and me that our tiny embryo is currently measuring one-half of a centimeter from crown to rump. As I lay on the examination table, feet in stirrups, for once not put off by the wand inside me, the complete invasion of privacy that I've come to accept as par for the course, Dr. Landry pointed out the gestational sac and the yolk sac, but I couldn't take my eyes off that pint-size nub that would one day be a baby.

Aaron held my hand the entire time. He stroked my hair. He kissed my lips when the image appeared, dark and grainy and impossible to see were it not for Dr. Landry's informative voice and thin finger telling us what was the gestational sac and what was the yolk sac, and where our baby was growing, and then, once I found it, the embryo—a half centimeter long with paddle-like arms and legs and webbing between its toes and fingers, none of which I could see for myself though Dr. Landry told us were there—the one thing in the world I loved more than anything else, I couldn't divert my eyes.

There was a heartbeat. We couldn't hear it yet, but we could *see* it. It was there, the movements of it on the ultrasound screen. Our baby had a heart and a heartbeat, and blood that coursed through his or her tiny body. Its heart had chambers—four of them Dr. Landry said!—and beat like a racehorse, a heartbeat that easily trumped mine, though it too was going at a steady gallop.

I'm six weeks along. And we have a due date now.

By May, Aaron and I will finally have a baby. We'll be parents!

How will I possibly be able to wait that long to hold my baby in my arms?

July 16, 1997
Egg Harbor

I told my stepmother about the baby today. I didn't mean to; it just happened. We were on the phone when she asked—as she had so many times in the past—"How much longer are we going to have to wait for you and Aaron to have a baby?" and it wasn't so much that I told her, because I didn't, but it was the lack of a response that gave it away, the silence, because I was too busy beaming behind the handset, trying to no avail to manufacture a lie.

If Nora could have seen me, she would have noticed the way my skin turned pink; she, like Aaron, would have seen the way I glowed. She would have seen me run a delicate hand across the cotton of my blouse—a link to the life inside—and triumphantly smile.

She said nothing at first, nothing in response to my nothing.

"When were you thinking you'd tell us?" she asked then with the slightest hint of malice—Nora, of course, needs to be the first to know everything—followed immediately by "Does Aaron's mother already know?" and there was jealousy and skepticism in her voice long before she offered her congratulations and said how happy she is for Aaron and me.

I called Aaron's mother next before Nora had a chance to call for herself, boasting that she knew a whole thirty seconds before Aaron's mother did.

It was like a wildfire then, that instant burst of pregnancy news that caught quickly, spreading through the family from phone call to phone call like a raging inferno. By the end of the day, nearly everyone would know our news.

Miranda arrived as Aaron's mother and I were saying goodbye, and catching a glimpse of my hand still situated on the cotton of my blouse, she said to me, "It's about goddamn time, Eden."

And then she hugged me, a quick, careless hug, sending her boys into the backyard to play alone so she could lie on my sofa and rest. Little Carter didn't want to go; he, himself, was still a baby, and so she picked him up and plopped him in Jack's arms and said again to *go* and we stood there, watching them walk away, listening as Carter cried. She was massive again, still months away from giving birth to baby number four, and the evidence of it was everywhere: in her tired eyes, her unwashed hair, her inflated legs.

Pregnancy did not suit Miranda well.

Her maternity shirts no longer fit correctly, leaving a fraction of her stomach exposed, ashy skin drawn tightly around her baby, a black, vertical line etched on her body from belly button down. Miranda herself didn't have a pregnancy glow, but rather was covered in blotchy brown spots all over her skin; the hormones were not working in her favor.

"Just wait until you're as fat as me," she said, seeing the way I watched her drop onto the sofa, a giraffe making an ungainly attempt to sit.

"Well I have news too," she said then, as if she couldn't stand me being happy, as if she couldn't take a back seat to my glad tidings for once. "We're going to have a girl!" she screeched, clapping her own hands, going on to say how—though Joe didn't know it yet—she'd had a peek at her medical file when the obstetrician was out of the room during her last appointment, and there, in the margins of the paperwork, saw the Venus symbol written with black ink.

"Finally," she said, frowning out the window at her three boys, fifty-pound Jack lugging twenty-pound Carter around, Carter who still cried. "After everything I've been through," she said, and I wanted to be happy for her, I really did.

But I couldn't bring myself to be.

She didn't deserve another baby any more than a murderer deserves clemency.

I was grateful when, an hour later, Paul wet himself and they had to leave.

Aaron had wanted to keep the news of our pregnancy a secret for a while longer, but I couldn't help myself. I wanted to shout it from the rooftops, to let everyone in the whole entire universe know that I was going to be a mother. "Why wait?" I asked later that afternoon as he prepared for work. I frowned at him, feeling punctured that he would want to keep our baby a secret. We'd spent a year trying to achieve this, watched our lives and our marriage flounder to make a baby, drained our savings and accrued mass amounts of debt on our credit cards.

And yet I couldn't be happier. I couldn't be more thrilled.

This was the one thing that I wanted more than anything. More than *anything.*

I wanted everyone to know about it.

"Just in case," Aaron replied when I asked why we should keep our baby a secret, why we should wait to share the news.

"In case what?" I asked, provoking him, but he wouldn't say the words out loud. He was being cautiously optimistic, I knew, but what I wanted was for him to be jubilant like me. He stood before me in the kitchen, slipping his feet into a pair of new shoes, waterproof, slip-proof black loafers that cost us an arm and a leg. But none of that mattered now, not trivial things like the cost of groceries, the cost of shoes.

We were going to have a baby.

He stood and came to me, wrapping his arms around the small of my back, and I breathed him in, the scent of his aftershave and soap because Aaron, of course, didn't wear cologne. His hands were rough from years of hard work, the scrubbing of dishes, the scalding sauces that bubbled over onto his hands, burning them. The many near misses with a utility knife. The gashes and lacerations, healed now but always there. Aaron's hands were rough and worn, but also the softest things in the world to me as they slipped under the hemline of my blouse and stroked my bare skin.

He wouldn't say the words out loud, but he didn't have to. I knew exactly what he was thinking.

"We saw our baby," I told him, whispering the words into his ear. "We saw the heartbeat. Everything is fine."

JESSIE

I'M OUT THE DOOR early, hurrying to the side of the carriage home to collect my bike, but when I arrive, I see that she's gone. That she's not there. That the spot where I left her last night is completely empty.

There's a moment of panic.

Someone has stolen Old Faithful from me.

My heart picks up speed, my face warming with frustration and anger and fear. I look up and down the alleyway as my heart sinks. For a minute, tears well in my eyes. I could cry.

But then I remember leaving Old Faithful tethered to the bike rack outside the Art Institute. No one has taken her from me. I left her there.

I take the Brown Line out to Albany Park, getting off at Kimball. From there it's a walk to Mom's and my old home, a classic Chicago-style bungalow that's boxy and brick with a low-pitched roof on a street where every single home is a replica of the next. The desperation has gotten under my skin now, a do-or-die need to find my birth certificate, to find my social security card, to figure out who the hell I am. I need to make a final sweep of the home to see if there's anything there, anything I may have missed. Because the estate sale will kick off soon, and then it will be too late. Everything that was once mine will be gone.

I've only been gone a couple of days. But as I make my way down the sidewalk, I feel homesick. I miss Mom more than ever. I miss my home. The sight of the for-sale sign plunged into the green grass makes my stomach churn, my Realtor's pretty face smeared across the corner of it. I'd picked her, this Realtor, because I saw her face and name on a similar sign somewhere down the street. There was a number to call and so I called it. And like that, the house is on the market and soon, any evidence of my time with Mom will be gone.

The house looks different than it did before. The only thing still here are the ghosts we've left behind. Aside from our house, the rest of the block looks annoyingly the same, as if no one noticed that I'd left or that Mom died, which most likely they didn't. The only person I see outside is our neighbor Mr. Henderson from next door. There he stands on his own front porch, thinning hair standing vertical, a cigar in hand. Smoke billowing around his head. Mr. Henderson wears corduroy pants, slippers, a fisherman cardigan. Though as far as I know, he doesn't fish. Instead he teaches English lit at a local college and is pretentious as all get-out. Mr. Henderson couldn't be bothered to help after Mom's cancer spread to the bones, leaving her far more susceptible to fracture. She fell one morning when I was at school, shattering a hip, lying there on her back, calling out an open window for help.

He heard her cries as he sat there in his own front room, sucking away on his cigar. No doubt he heard her cries, though later, as the ambulance carried her away and he stood watching from his porch steps—merely a snoop and not a Samaritan—he claimed he did not.

I pay extra attention to the sidewalk as I walk along, taking care not to step on the cracks. Not that it matters because Mom wouldn't feel it anyway if my footfalls broke her back. *Step on a crack, break your mother's back.*

I cross the street, refusing to say hello to Mr. Henderson, refusing to meet his curious eye. I dig into my bag for the keys, climbing up the stairs and to the front door.

This neighborhood has been around for near forever. Most of the homes are circa 1920-something, during some sort of housing boom when thousands of bungalows sprung up overnight, fulfilling dreams of homeownership for that exploding middle class. Because the homes were practical and affordable. And because there were a ton of them. Up and down the street, all I see is nothing but trees and brick, trees and brick. Trees and brick as far as the eye can see. I have no doubt Mom chose Albany Park to live because it's relatively affordable, a good place to raise kids. Money was a luxury Mom and I didn't have. Not that I can say I grew up poor, because I didn't. But Mom was frugal and we weren't rich.

We planned a big dinner out for when the cancer was finally in remission for the second time around. Gibsons Steakhouse. Mom was going to buy a new dress to wear because she never spent money on herself. Any time there was a little extra to spare, she spent it on me.

Needless to say, Gibsons Steakhouse never happened.

The day Mom found out the cancer was back, she was sitting outside on the front stoop when I got home from school. She'd been to the doctor for back pain, the kind that no amount of ibuprofen could fix. Pain she hadn't told me about until that afternoon. She thought it was a herniated disc, back strain, sciatica. Effects of the job.

As it turned out, it was the breast cancer, back for vengeance. Metastasized to the bones, the lungs.

She told me to sit. She held my hand, caressed each finger one at a time while I committed to memory the length and shape of her fingers, the asymmetry of the knucklebones, the blue rivers of veins that swept across the thinning skin.

She said to me that day on the stoop, *Jessie, I'm dying. I'm going to die.*

I cried. But she said it was all right. She wasn't afraid to die. She was stoic. *When?* I asked, like some stupid child. Like Mom had any way of knowing exactly when it would happen.

What she said was *Sooner or later we all die, Jessie. It's only a matter of time. And this is mine.*

I unlock the door and step inside. I'm inundated with the smell almost immediately. The smell of Mom. Her hand lotion, Crabtree & Evelyn's Summer Hill. It nearly knocks me from my feet. It's diffused through the rooms and if I didn't know any better, I'd think that Mom was still here with me. Heart still ticking, not yet dead. I hear that death rattle, the saliva pooling there in the back of her throat. The nurses' gentle footfalls, close enough to touch. As if they're still there, still walking in orbits around me. Lathering lotion on Mom's hands and feet, turning her every few hours to keep bedsores from forming on her skin.

The smell of the lotion is overpowering. It binds to the millions of tiny little hairs in my nose, bringing me to my knees every time I breathe. *Mom.*

And I find that I'm looking for her, half-certain that when I turn she'll be standing there in the arched doorway of the kitchen, sagging body leaning against the doorway because she doesn't have the energy to hold it upright anymore, a soft cotton hat covering her bald head. Asking how I got along at school today in that way that she does, teeth gritted through the pain that managed to breeze in and past the narcotics sometimes.

How'd you get along at school today, Jessie?

But it's not real, I remind myself.

The nurses are not here.

Mom is dead.

And only then am I aware of the silence. Of the earsplitting silence that now worms its way through the cracks of our home.

I don't know where to begin. I searched the entire home already, but I look anyway, starting in my bedroom, planning to work my way down in search of the social security card. I pluck desk and dresser drawers from their tracks. I dig beneath clothes I've intentionally left in the dresser drawers, those I no longer need. I lift rugs from the floor and check beneath. I canvass my closet. No luck.

I make my way to Mom's bedroom, where I see that the liquidator has begun to tag items for sale. Mom's clothes now hang from a rolling rack beside her bed. I run my hands over a knit cardigan, her favorite. If I'd had my wits about me at the time, I would have had Mom cremated in the cardigan so she could spend all of eternity in it. But instead she wore a hospital gown, white and wrinkled with snowflakes, a single tie on the otherwise open back. The funeral home gathered her body from the hospital within hours after she died. But there was a mandatory waiting period before the cremation could begin. Twenty-four hours, in case I changed my mind.

I spent those twenty-four hours parked outside the funeral home's doors, sitting on the curb because they didn't have a bench. And because I couldn't bring myself to go home without Mom.

The liquidator will take some 40 percent of all sales, which is fine by me. Anything so that I don't have to be involved in the process, so that I don't have to watch our possessions walk out the door in the arms of someone new.

I pull open the closet door to reveal a large walk-in. It's empty now, all of Mom's clothes moved to the rack beside the bed. Only hooks and a mirror remain—a silver-framed oval mirror that Mom and I used to make silly faces in front of when I was a girl. I'd stand on a chair so that I could see inside, and there we'd stare at our reflections side by side in the glass.

The mirror hangs on the closet wall, an oversight only, for it won't be long before the liquidator pulls that too from the wall and sticks a price tag on it, snatching memories right along with it, memories of my crossed eyeballs, Mom's fish face.

I run a hand along the glass, remembering how sometimes we didn't make silly faces at all. How sometimes I'd just sit on the floor beside her feet and watch as Mom stared at herself, her dark hair and eyes so unlike the dishwater-blond hair that sat on my head, the tufts of eyebrow hair that stuck straight up, same as they do now. Unlike me, Mom didn't have dimples. My dimples are much more than simple holes in the cheeks, but more like deep comma-shaped gorges. I didn't get those from Mom. There isn't one feature on my face that came from her.

Even as a kid, I saw the way Mom looked when she stared at her reflection in the mirror. She looked sad. I wondered what she saw. For some reason I don't think it was the same pretty face that I saw.

I'm about to leave when I spot something out of the corner of my eye, something I've never noticed in Mom's closet before. Something that would have otherwise been hidden behind the hems of clothes, except that now there are no clothes to taint the view.

I have to look twice to be sure that it's there, that I'm not only imagining it's there. What it is is black, metal, covered in louvers. A door. A boxy little door that hovers less than a foot above the hardwood floors.

I drop to my hands and knees and pull on the door's knob, finding a crawl space on the other side. A *crawl space.* I never knew we had a crawl space before.

The space is dark and dingy, the ceiling low. The floor is dirt, covered only by a thick sheet of plastic. I can't believe I never found this place before. How many times did I dig my way through Mom's closet for clues as to who my father could be? But as it so happened, I never dug far enough. Instead I gave up when I got to the clothes, taking for granted that there was nothing on the other side but a wall.

Only one time did Mom bring my father up all on her own, without my begging. I was twelve years old. Mom had had a glass of wine before bed. She said to me that night, seconds before she fell asleep, head draped over the rock-hard sofa arm, *A long time ago, I did something I'm not proud of, Jessie. Something that shames me. And that's how I got you.*

The next thing I heard was the sound of her half-drunk snore, but by morning I couldn't bring myself to ask what she'd meant by it.

I reach inside the crawl space and drag something out. What it is, I don't know. Not until I get it into the closet's light do I see that it's a plastic storage bin, and the adrenaline kicks in at the prospect of what I might find inside. My social security card, for one, but more likely, something having to do with my father, which suddenly, in this moment, takes precedence. Something Mom kept tucked away so that I wouldn't find it.

I tear the lid off, finding photo albums inside. I find myself feeling hopeful, wondering what I'll find in them. Photos of Mom, photos of my father, photos of Mom and her own mom and dad.

But of course not. Instead it's me. All me.

I set the album aside to take back to the carriage home with me.

I crawl toward the crawl space, feeling blindly inside for another box. I can't reach far enough in to grab it, and so I have to crawl in through the door. Inside, the space is only about thirty-six-inches tall. I'm not fully in before claustrophobia settles in. The dirty floors and wooden beams close in around me. The darkness is smothering. The only light comes from behind. I find another storage bin and drag it out backward, through the access panel and onto the closet floor, grateful for a little elbow room.

I open the lid and have a look, hoping that this is the mother lode I've been in search of. The answer to all the questions I have. But it's not. It's nothing, just a bunch of inconsequential items in a plastic storage bin, which makes me realize this isn't a secret crawl space at all, but just a *crawl space.* For storage. For stuff Mom had no other place to put.

She didn't intentionally keep this a secret from me. I just never knew it was here.

I sigh, feeling uncomfortable and glum. I rise to my feet, stretching my hands above my head, arching my back. But my movements are quick and careless. The blood flees my brain as I stand up, leaving me light-headed and dizzy. All of these nights without sleep are taking their toll on me. I reach for the wall to steady myself, crashing into the mirror as I do. I watch on helplessly as the mirror loses its hold on the wall and I can't catch it in time. I'm too slow to stop it from falling.

It slips from its nail and slams to the ground, scratching the wall as it does, leaving a four-foot scrape in the paint. The entire mirror shatters before my eyes. Broken glass spreads like spiderwebs, chunks falling to the hardwood floors. And all I can think about is bad luck. Seven entire years of bad luck that await me now.

I curse out loud, wondering if there's any hope of salvaging the mirror. I start to gather the biggest chunks in my hand, careful that I don't step on the tiny shards of glass.

My eyes are so caught up in what's happening on the floor that at first I don't see the small compartment dug into the wall. A little recess carved there into the drywall, hidden behind where the mirror should go. A hole that's been fitted with a sturdy box.

And I think for a moment that my eyes deceive me. That I'm only imagining the compartment is there. Because why in the world would there be a secret storage compartment on Mom's closet wall? I rub at my eyes, certain it will disappear as I do. But sure enough, it's still here.

For at least twenty seconds I stare at that box without moving.

Mom had a stash of personal stuff she kept hidden from me.

I think of all the times Mom and I looked together in the mirror when I was a girl. All I ever saw was a mirror—our own silly expressions looking back at us through the glass—but for Mom it was a portal to her private world, a gateway to the things she didn't want me to see.

It feels an enormous invasion of privacy for me to snoop but I can't help myself. I reach my hand inside Mom's secret box. There's only one item there. It's a scrap of glossy white paper pressed into the corner of the box. My chest clenches. I hold my breath.

This could be something.

Or, like the plastic storage bins hidden in the crawl space, this could be nothing.

I have to use a fingernail to emancipate the scrap. When I do, I turn it over in my hands to see. It's a photograph that some part of my memory reminds me I've seen before.

But with the memory of the photograph comes the memory of Mom's face. Openmouthed and afraid. She knew I'd seen it. But what happened next has been wiped clean from my brain's hard drive. Either that or entombed beneath a gazillion other memories, harder than others to dig up.

Mom hid this photograph from me.

It's the kind of photograph that looks a little dated, a little old. Not crazy old, like archaic. But older than me. The colors are faded, the blues a little less blue, and the greens a little less green than they used to be. It's a picture of a lake. A long seashore of blue. Tan sand, darker where the water hits it. White ripples of waves. Evergreen trees line the edges of the lake. There is a pier suspended over the water, one that looks unsound, unsafe. Like at any moment it could sink into the lake and get carried away with the waves. If I squint my eyes up tight, there's a boat out there on the water. A sailboat, just a simple sloop with a single white mast. That's what I see.

Mom knew a whole lot about sailboats, which she relayed to me when we used to walk past DuSable Harbor on occasion, hand in hand. *See that one over there, Jessie?* she'd ask, slipping her hand away long enough to point at it. I'd pretend to look. Pretend to look because I didn't really care, her words falling on deaf ears. *That's a cutter*, or, *that's a catamaran*, she'd tell me. She had a book on them, a heavy coffee-table book called *Sailing.* Though as far as I knew, Mom had never once stepped foot on a sailboat in her entire life. At least not since I've been alive. I forget sometimes that Mom had a life that preceded mine.

But the lake and the sailboat are only an afterthought to the image I see, because there's also a man in the photograph, one with brown hair and a large stature. He's tall and husky with thick wrists exposed by a flannel shirt that's rolled up to the elbows. There's a watch on a right wrist, a hat in his hand. He stands with his back to the camera, blurred at the edges because he wasn't standing still when the shutter button was pressed. He's not centered on the photo paper, as if he was moving away when the picture was snapped.

The photograph wasn't meant to be of him.

The central object is the sailboat. The picture is of the boat. And the man only got in the way. By today's terms, a photobomb.

The man stands with his hands on his hips, left knee bent a bit. His head is pitched to the right. He has blue jeans on—saggy ones, not formfitting. The ends are fraying, turning white. One of his gym shoes is untied. Strands of hair move in the wind.

I wish that he would turn and look at me, so that I could see his eyes, the shape of his nose. Whether we look anything alike.

Is this man my father?

Why did Mom hide this photo from me?

Why did she not want me to know anything about this lake or this boat or this man?

I think of all those times I sat cross-legged on the closet floor beside her feet, watching as she stared sullenly at her own reflection in the mirror. What I thought was that she didn't like what she saw. A modest, unpretentious face, a bit earthy with dark hair and dark eyes.

And then, years later when the cancer settled in, that same face became cadaverous. She lost more weight than she had to spare, face thinning, cheekbones hollowed out—an image she despised. That's what I thought she was looking at when she stared in the mirror.

But now I think that maybe she wasn't looking at herself as much as she was looking through the glass, reflecting on the life she left behind, the one she kept hidden from me behind that mirror.

EDEN

July 21, 1997
Egg Harbor

WHAT AARON TOLD THE emergency room physician was that there was blood, "Some blood," he said, "spotting," which to me equated to a teaspoon or two, enough to dirty a single pad, but the amount of blood I saw was measured in liters and gallons.

It came gushing out of me, a deluge of blood pouring down from the sky, rivers and streams overflowing their banks, dousing the earth, sweeping homes from their foundations. Everywhere I looked there was blood.

The day was hot and I wore shorts, and the blood, it saturated my underpants first before snaking down the inside of my bare leg, a thin, red zigzag emblazoned against my fair white skin.

"I have my period," I told Aaron as we were there in the backyard—he staring openmouthed at me, on his knees, installing chicken wire around the flower bed so the deer couldn't poach from us again, making off with our beautiful hollyhock blooms.

In retrospect there were warning signs, maybe: the suggestion of a cramp, some lower back pain, tokens of pregnancy as well as menstruation and miscarriage. The fact that the nausea had abated during the last twenty-four hours was, to me, a welcome blessing and not once a sign of catastrophe.

"You're pregnant," Aaron said lightly, rising to his feet and coming to me, but I couldn't process his words, couldn't make sense of what was happening. It was my period again, come to me like it does every month without fail. There was dirt on his forehead, and his hands were red, etched with the impression of chicken wire. "You don't have your period, Eden," he said, dropping the wire cutters to the ground and taking my hands into his.

He wiped the blood from my leg with his own sweaty T-shirt.

In the car I sat on a kitchen towel.

We didn't speak on the way to the emergency room.

He told the attending physician that there was *some blood*, that I was *spotting*.

An ultrasound was performed. This time, there was no heartbeat.

The baby's heartbeat had disappeared.

Both Aaron's and the doctor's eyes wandered to mine, though I wouldn't meet theirs, too busy staring at the black gestational sac on the monitor, at the stillness of the screen, the lack of movement. The absence of sound.

Aaron reached out a hand to mine but I couldn't feel it. I only saw that it was there.

I was insensible. I was stone-cold.

"What now?" Aaron asked the physician who'd been sent down from obstetrics to perform the ultrasound, a woman who would soon return to labor and delivery to deliver someone else's healthy newborn.

"We'll perform a dilation and curettage," she said, "to eliminate any remaining tissue from the womb."

Tissue. As if only a few hours ago that tissue hadn't been a child.

In that moment, I couldn't speak. I couldn't even bring myself to cry.

They put me to sleep for the procedure.

I prayed I'd never wake up again.

JESSIE

I LEAVE ALBANY PARK, taking the train into the Loop, where I make my way to the Art Institute to collect my bike. From there, I pedal to the coffee bar on Dearborn, the one where the man at the garden had purchased his coffee, the name I'd read on the paper sleeve of his coffee cup. People are religious about their coffee and their routines, and so it seems logical enough to think that if he was here yesterday, he'll come again today. I need to find him. I need to ask him why he was in the garden—*Mom's and my* special garden—sitting there, reading her obituary. I need to hear why Mom's obituary made him sad. How does he know Mom?

I bring the photograph of the man with me. I carry it in the front pocket of my bag.

The man who I think might be my father.

At random stoplights I slip my hand into the pocket of my bag and pull it out. I try to spot some nicety I haven't yet seen, some minor detail in the image I've managed to overlook, like the swollen clouds or the gangly-looking bird that perches on a rock at the water's edge.

The sleeves of the man's flannel shirt are shoved to his elbows in the picture. A raised red line bridges a lower arm. Scar tissue, I think, or maybe just an anomaly in the photograph, a streak of light or a reflection. I wonder what any of it means. If it means anything. If the clouds or the birds or the scar can provide details about the man or the land on which he stands.

Where was this picture taken?

And more importantly, who is he?

I search in vain for the smoking gun to tell me who he is. How I know him. What this man has to do with me. I wonder if the answer is there, staring me in the face, and I simply can't see it.

And then the light turns green and I carefully shove the picture back into my bag and pedal on toward the coffee shop.

When I arrive, I press in through the door, past people who are coming out. The coffee bar is eclectic, cluttered with mismatching tables and chairs. There are stacks of magazines and books.

Between the grinding and gurgling of the espresso machine, the roar of people talking, the coffee shop is loud. I order a coffee and carry it to the kiosk to douse it with sugar. A blue velvet sofa lines a wall, and I help myself to it, sinking into the wilted center, watching as caffeine-deprived customers come and go. The line grows long enough that the last person stands in the doorway because he doesn't clear the doorframe. Instead he props it open with his body, letting the fall air in. Napkins blow from a table and litter the floor.

As I sit there waiting for the man from the garden to magically appear, I pull the photograph from my pocket one more time, taking in the man's stature, the color of his hair. Imagining his eyes. In the image, they're looking out toward the sailboat, away from the camera lens, and so I can't see them. I can't see what they look like, but I can imagine.

They're blue like mine, and he has dimples too.

I sip from my coffee, place the photograph back in my bag.

My mind drifts and I find myself thinking about the other Jessica Sloane. The one who is not me. And I know with a sudden translucence that I am not Jessica Sloane, but that I'm somebody else. That Jessica Sloane died when she was three and for whatever reason, Mom stole her social security number and gave it to me. This is no longer a hypothetical. I know.

But there are ways of finding out who you are, aside from a birth certificate, social security number or name. Because if I'm not Jessica Sloane, then I need to know who I really am. I think of forensic identification, stuff like fingerprints, DNA, handwriting analysis, dentistry. Ways to prove one's identity aside from birth certificates and social security numbers. Everyone in the whole wide world is supposedly unique, like the stripes of a zebra or the spots of a giraffe. Snowflakes. It's near mathematically and scientifically impossible that any two could be the same. Even the creases of our feet are distinct, which is one of the reasons babies' footprints are taken after birth. For identification purposes. Because no two footprints are alike. So hospitals know which baby is which if ever they get separated from their moms or dads. In case the ID bands slip from their ankles or wrists. I stare at my fingerprints, thinking the answer to who I am is sitting there, in all those miniscule lines that make me unique, a single snowflake, one in twenty trillion falling in a snowstorm, drifting aimlessly and alone.

I don't know who I am, but I'm not Jessica Sloane.

It's hours later when I catch a smidge of orange pass by the storefront window, and I know right away: it's him. It's the orange baseball cap that he wore, slipping it over his hair before he left the garden. He's here, come and gone for coffee and somehow, in a daze, I all but missed him.

I rise too quickly from the blue velvet sofa, spilling a lukewarm coffee, my third of the day, down the front of me, staining my shirt a translucent brown. I don't bother blotting it with napkins before I go scurrying for the door, knocking into a stanchion post along the way. I knock it over with a clang, leaving it on the floor as people stare. "What's the hurry?" I hear breathed through the air. "What's her problem?" followed by a giggle, a snort.

I press my way out onto the city street, following the pinprick of orange in the distance, a beacon of light as it slaloms this way and that down the street. I run, pushing my way past people walking too slowly, trying desperately to bridge the gap from him to me.

As I narrow in on him, I reach out and tug on something, my hand bearing down hard. A little boy cries out, and, as they turn to me, I see. A little boy in a superhero costume. The Flash. He's perched on his father's shoulders, making him tall. The costume is red and yellow with a mask that covers his face. It's the type of mask that covers everything, leaving only slits for the mouth, nose and eyes. Like the costume, it's also red and yellow. Not orange, though my mind mutated them for me, mixing the red and yellow, turning them into orange.

Once again, my eyes have deceived me.

He isn't the man from the garden after all.

EDEN

June 17, 2005
Chicago

It's been a couple of hours since it happened, and still I can't get my heart rhythm to slow. I feel off, a dull headache in the back of my neck that simply won't quit, my handwriting like chicken scratch from the shaking hands. Jessie is quiet now, tucked into bed with her lights turned off. I'd read her a story before bed, hoping it might help her forget. Hoping it might replace the photograph she saw with the fun of leading imaginary beasts on a wild rumpus around her bedroom. She was laughing by the time she went to bed, and I can only pray that she dreams tonight of Emile and Bernard, and not of Aaron.

I, however, will dream only of Aaron.

I think I covered my tracks quite well, but I won't ever know. There's no telling what goes on inside a little girl's mind, which details of our lives are committed to memory and which we forget.

For the first time tonight, past and present collided, and it made me realize one thing: that I have to be more wary of where I hide my things. Jessie is older now and more inquisitive. She's liable to have questions for me that I can't answer because I don't want to answer them. I have to be more careful if I'm going to keep my past from her.

It's not that I don't love her. It's that I do.

We'd just finished up dinner when it happened. I was in the kitchen, wiping down the countertops, and she'd disappeared down the hall to, presumably, go play. She was in her room, or so I thought at the time, quiet as a church mouse. That should have been my warning, because for as fiery and high-spirited as she is, Jessie is rarely quiet.

I don't know how much time passed—ten minutes, an hour while I was stupidly relishing in the quiet and didn't once think to check on her—when she appeared there in the doorway to the kitchen with an item in her hand, asking of me, "Who's this?"

Her eyes, when I turned to her, were doe-eyed, her hair falling into her forehead like it hadn't seen a brush in weeks. There were dust bunnies clinging to the fabric of her pants and I knew right away that she'd been somewhere she shouldn't have been, on her hands and knees, digging through things.

"Where'd you find this?" I asked, taking it from her hand. I heard my voice crack as I said it, and though I couldn't see it, I was certain my face was masked in fear. My voice wasn't angry. It was scared.

Jessie had found it under my bed, of course, where she'd been snooping. The photograph had been stashed inside an envelope, inside a box, and under the bed, the kind of thing one didn't just happen to stumble upon. She went searching for it. Or rather she went searching for something and she found it, because up until a few minutes before, she didn't know this photograph existed, the photograph I'd snatched all those years ago in the yard of our cottage, a photograph of our glorious view—the lake with a sailboat out at sea—meant to be only of the lake and the sailboat, though Aaron stepped into the frame just as I took the picture. He'd apologized and later, after the pictures were developed, we'd laughed over it. Aaron thought he'd ruined my photograph, but what he'd done was the opposite of that. He'd made it perfect. He'd made it complete.

Up until a few minutes ago, Jessie didn't know Aaron existed because those *Who's my father?* questions have only just begun to surface, and so far I've been able to quell them all with the suggestion of milk and cookies or ice cream.

"Who is it, Mommy?" she asked again when I didn't respond.

"Just an old friend," I said, trying to settle my jittery voice as I opened a kitchen drawer—the closest thing to me—and slid it inside. I'd find a better hiding spot later after she'd gone to sleep. I could feel my cheeks inflame, my hands start to shake.

"Are you mad at me?" Jessie asked then, eyes swelling with tears, mistaking what I was feeling for anger when what it was was sadness and regret and shame.

"No, baby," I said, dropping down to my knees and drawing her into me. "Mommy could never be mad at you," I told her, and then I smiled as widely as I could and grabbed a hold of her hand. "How about some ice cream before we get ready for bed?" I proposed, and of course there was no hesitation, no wavering. Jessie screamed an easy *yes!* while jumping up and down, and so we carried bowls of chocolate ice cream onto the front porch to eat, watching as the sun made its final descent beneath the horizon. I helped her with a bath and we read about the wild rumpus. I tucked her into bed. She asked me to lie with her as she always does these days, and so I curled under the covers beside her, and she pressed her body into mine, a lean arm flung across my chest, pinning me down.

This was everything I ever wanted and more.

I lay there until her breaths became flat and slow, and then I returned to my own room. There I sat on the bed, clutching the photograph of Aaron in my hand, still trying to catch my breath. This photograph had been hidden beneath the bed for years. I've known it was there, of course, but couldn't bear the idea of looking at it, not until it was forced quite literally into my hand. It was the only keepsake I kept of him, just the one single photograph—not our wedding photographs, not my engagement ring—because in it, he's looking away. He's not looking at me, and so I can't see that love and adoration in his eye.

I can't see the anger.

I stare at the photograph, wondering what Aaron must look like now. Is he graying slowly like me, or is his hair still a chestnut brown? Is he fuller around the middle, or maybe he's more slim? And then I start to wonder if he's eating okay, if he's sleeping okay, if some other woman now spends her nights beside him in bed. My mind gets stuck there, a skipping record. I can't unsee this image, imaginary as it may be, of a woman lying beside Aaron, peacefully asleep—her head tucked into the crook of his arm, his hand on the small of her back—where I used to be.

I won't let myself dwell on the past.

I move quickly, having to get rid of the evidence before Jessie wakes up and goes snooping again. I put the photograph where she'll never find it, and then, when it's done, I tiptoe back into Jessie's room and stand there at the edge of the bed, forcing the past to some locked chamber in my mind, the same spot where that woman's voice is buried, the high-pitched squeal as she chased me down on the street.

Get your hands off my child.

I slip back under the covers beside Jessie so that when she awakes in the morning, she'll never know I was gone. A simple sleight of hand.

JESSIE

THAT NIGHT, I CLIMB into bed with my clothes still on. I don't bother changing them. I just want to get into bed, to be in bed. The bed used to be my safe place. But after all these nights not sleeping—eight of them, eight days and nights without sleeping now—the bed is my torture chamber too.

I read once about a man who died because he couldn't sleep. Fatal familial insomnia, it was called. Within twelve months from the time symptoms appeared, he was dead.

I think this is what's happening to me.

It started with a single bad night of sleep. For whatever reason, his mind wouldn't shut off. Wouldn't let him rest. One night turned into two, and before long he'd gone weeks without a decent night of sleep. *Relaxed wakefulness* is what it was called, though it was anything but relaxed. He never made it past stage 1 of non-REM sleep, the stage between wakefulness and sleep. He never dreamed. It was a light sleep at best when he was lucky, lasting less than ten minutes at a time, the kind of sleep interrupted by a hypnic jerk, by an overwhelming sense of falling.

I have it worse, I think. Because a light sleep, to me, would be a dream come true.

He walked the earth in a stupor, asleep but awake. Awake but asleep. He spent his days in a hallucination of sorts, not sure if he was alive or dead. He heard buzzing noises all the time. People calling out his name though no one was there. A voice whispering odd decrees on repeat. *Just do it already. Just jump.* A hand touching his arm and he'd whirl around, agitated and afraid, to find himself alone. The panic attacks were infinite. His brain was on overdrive all the time. There was no way to hit the switch and shut it down.

As a result, his brain's tasks were all out of whack. His muscles twitched. His heart raced. His blood pressure soared. Coordination was lost. He could no longer function properly. It went on like this until he died.

The most gruesome part? Though the body goes to pot, the mind does not. Thought processes remain relatively intact. They're clued in completely to their own demise.

The ill sweat profusely.

They stop eating, speaking.

They shrivel to nothing but a glassy-eyed stare, eyes shrunken to mere pinpricks, like mine. And then they die. Because, after those long, agonizing nights lying in bed, failing to truly sleep, fatal familial insomnia is nothing but a death sentence for them. The grim reaper coming to steal their life.

I'm waiting for my time.

I sit up in bed. I don't delude myself into lying down because I know I won't sleep. And so I sit, engulfed in blackness, legs pulled up to my chest. The blanket is kicked to the end of the bed because, though it's cold in the carriage home,

I've begun to sweat. The sweat, it gathers under my arms and in my hairline. My palms are damp with it. The soles of my feet. The skin between my fingers and toes.

My heart beats rapidly.

My head spins.

I stare into blackness, seeing things that I hope are not there. I go through the motions. The typical night, thinking the morbid thoughts, followed by the grieving ones where I miss Mom so much it hurts. It's a pain in my sternum this time, like heartburn or indigestion. Except that it's grief.

And then when I'm done grieving, the self-loathing comes, where I despise myself for all of that which I *would've, could've, should've* done differently. Said I love you while she could still hear me. Hugged her longer and with more frequency. Run a hand over the dark chocolate fuzz that had started to regrow on her scalp after her last round of chemo was through.

I bullet point them all in my mind. All the things I should've done.

The silence and the blackness of the room become suddenly suffocating and I feel like I can't breathe. I'm drowning in silence. Being asphyxiated by it.

I turn to my knees and peel the shade back, gazing outside. The world tonight is dark, a carbon gray. Not quite black, but close enough. Little by little, my eyes adapt to it, and though it's dark outside, I can see. Not perfectly, but I can see something. A halo of light from a streetlamp, a half a block away. Orion the hunter, brightening the sky. His shield is aimed at me as he hovers, light-years above the greystone, club hoisted above his head with a dog at his feet. For whatever reason, the light makes me feel less alone and less scared.

And then, as the moonlight slips out from behind a cloud, it settles on the greystone. As my eyes adjust to it, the house begins to slowly take shape. My eyes rise up from ground level, grazing over the kitchen's sliding glass door, an enclosed porch, up the home's rear facade, and there they make out an amorphous shape standing in the open window of the third floor. The very same window, which, for the last two nights, radiated light.

Except that tonight it's dark. There is no light, but rather a pair of eyes.

The bile in my stomach begins to rise. I feel like I could be sick. I press a hand to my mouth to silence my own scream.

The moonlight reflects off the eyes, making them glint in the darkness of night. They're undeniable. They're *there*. I'm not just making them up.

But beyond the eyes I see little else. Just a formless, shadowy shape to let me know that someone is standing in the window, watching me.

I let the shade go and it falls closed.

I grab Mom and her urn from a bedside table and slip to the floor, thinking that I don't want to be here in this carriage home, that I want to leave. That I'd rather be anywhere else in the world but here. But also realizing that I have nowhere to go. I press Mom to me and hold her tight because with her in my arms, I feel less alone. I scoot to a wall and press my back to it, heart beating hard. I try to defuse my fears, to make myself feel better, by telling myself that it's only Ms. Geissler. That it's only Ms. Geissler watching me.

And yet it doesn't make me feel better. Because Ms. Geissler is a stranger to me. We've hardly met. I don't know a single thing about her, other than she lied about the squirrels inside her home, but for what reason, I don't know.

My heart pounds. My hands are moist. They sweat and again I'm sure that I am dying. That the perspiration is a symptom of fatal familial insomnia, which has stolen my sleep from me and is now coming to take my life.

I want to get out of here. I want to leave. And yet I paid nearly everything I have to be here. I can't get out of here, I can't leave. I have nowhere to go.

I pull my knees into my chest. I drop my head to them and close my eyes. I pray to sleep, over and over I say it. *Please just let me sleep. Please just let me sleep. Please just let me sleep.* I beg for morning to come, for the sun to rise higher and higher in the sky, chasing the nighttime away.

For eight days now it's gone like this. Eight nights.

How many more days and nights can I go on without sleep?

And then I hear something. Just a murmur, faint at first like the sound of a piano playing from some other room. A gentle melody. But, of course, that can't be because there's no piano in the next room, and no one here to play it but me. And I'm not playing a piano.

My ears stand at attention. My head tips. I listen, and though I want to stay, firmly anchored to the wall where I can see through the darkness to know what's coming for me, I lift my body from the floor, carrying Mom's ashes with me. It's unintentional when I press a single palm down on the ground to hoist myself up. The other clutches tightly to Mom, pressing her to my chest like a newborn baby. I stand to an almost-upright position, bent at the shoulders so I don't hit my head on the low ceiling. And still I do hit my head, crashing into a low-lying wooden beam, so hard that when I press my fingers to it I feel the undeniably sticky texture of blood.

I tiptoe down the steps, one tread at a time, so slowly that it's almost as if I'm not moving at all. As I descend, voices surface. Not just one, but two or three or four. One lead and a host of background singers to accompany the piano. It makes me gasp for breath. My legs become weak, incapacitated; they start to give as I clutch the stair railing for support, squeezing so tightly the muscles of my hands cramp.

I can't go on. I don't want to go on. But I do because I have to. Because there's nothing there, because there's some reasonable explanation for the sound. A car stereo playing outside the carriage home, maybe, the tune getting carried in through an open window.

But I won't know what it is unless I go see.

I force myself to creep down the steps. I edge across the floorboards, willing myself forward, creeping, one step at a time. Following the sound, which comes from a wall and not the window at all because the window is closed tight.

The song isn't coming from the stereo of a car parked somewhere outside.

It's coming from inside the carriage home.

I go after the sound, and it leads me to an old vintage pie safe pressed flush against a wall, a petite bookshelf with a couple of shelves and a door. It's one of the few pieces of furniture that came with the carriage home.

I grab a hold of the knob and pull the door open swiftly, dropping to my knees. As I gaze inside, I find that it's empty, which makes no sense because the song is in there. It's coming from the pie safe. I feel blindly with my hands, moving them up and down the edges of the shelves, feeling for something, though what I don't know.

And then a thought comes to me.

What if the sound isn't coming from the pie safe? What if it's coming from somewhere behind?

I don't think twice. I shove the pie safe out of the way. It isn't heavy, but it isn't light either. I press a shoulder into it. It takes some jostling as it skids across the floor.

And there, on the wall behind where the pie safe was placed, I discover a cast-iron air return grille. One of those wall-mounted vents that leads into the duct system. It's an air return, one that sucks stale air from the room and cycles it back through the home's ductwork, leading, I have to assume, to the floor register upstairs where I heard the undeniable ping the other night. Ping, and then nothing. Ping, and then nothing.

Except that nothing is getting sucked up in here. Instead it's getting forced out.

And it's not air at all, but music. Gladys Knight & the Pips, "Midnight Train to Georgia."

How can this be?

I press my whole body against the grille to listen to the song. Mom's favorite. One she used to play over and over again until I got sick of it. Until I pouted and told her to turn it off because it was old people music. Those were the words I used. *Old people music.*

I'm stricken with the most impossible of thoughts, one that makes the hairs on my arms stand on end.

Mom is there. Inside the home's ductwork.

I set the urn down on the floor and, at first, try to jerk the whole thing off the wall with both of my hands. It won't budge. I grip the edges of the grille and pull, but I don't have a good grip on it and it slips easily from my grasp. I tumble backward, falling to the floor. The air return grille is wedged on too tight, held to the wall with four screws, one in each corner. I make an attempt to unscrew each with a bare hand, pinching and twisting the jagged screws until the skin splits, catching a sharp edge of it, one that's been whet over time. My finger starts to drip with blood.

But the screws don't move. Not even a little bit.

I grit my teeth and pinch and twist harder, but still nothing. They don't budge the slightest bit.

And so I wedge a fingernail into the slotted screw and turn. But all that happens is my nail breaks, getting ripped in two, leaving my nails in tatters. I curse out loud from the pain of it before hoisting myself from the floor and hurrying to the kitchen for a knife. I shuffle through a cutlery drawer—tossing forks and spoons out of the way, spilling them one by one to the floor—and find a butter knife.

I run back to the air return. I fall again to my knees.

I stick the knife into the screw head, turning counterclockwise as hard as I can. Bearing down on that knife with my whole body weight.

This time, it turns.

I spin and I spin that knife, desperate, gasping, as if I might just find Mom inside the air return. Because for this moment that's exactly what I'm thinking. That that's where she is. Inside the air return. I don't know how or why, but she is. She's *there.* I'm just sure of it.

I pluck one screw from the wall and move on to the next one. And the next one. And the next. All four screws tumble to the ground.

The grille loses its grip on the wall and falls. The sound is clamorous. I shove it out of the way and look inside. It's some sort of stainless steel box set there behind the air return grille, one that changes course about a foot of the way in. I can't see far enough inside to see where it goes and so I reach in a hand, grasping, sweating, but come up empty, thinking that behind that curve there are miles and miles of pipes and tubes which somehow or other lead to Mom. Mom is at the end of those tubes, listening to her music, speaking to me.

I try going in headfirst and then feetfirst. But I don't fit and in time give up, because I don't know what else to do.

I spend the rest of the night lying on the floor beside the air return in the fetal position, listening to Gladys Knight sing to me.

EDEN

September 26, 2010
Chicago

We bought our first computer today, at Jessie's insistence. I'd been saving for some time for it, hoping to surprise her because, as Jessie says, we're the last two people in the world without a computer, which may or may not be true.

We had to take a cab to the store for it, so that we could tote the boxes home in the trunk of the cab, while the driver waited impatiently for us to load and unload, meter running the whole time, never once offering to help. And then, at home, after Jessie and I lugged the boxes to the office, we sat on the floor, methodically reading instructions and trying our best to decipher which cords went where. The directions might as well have been written in Japanese, the illustrations done up for a four-year-old.

When all was said and done, I was shocked to find that, when we turned it on, the thing came to life, some sort of revolving image—*a screen saver,* Jessie told me—moving about on the screen.

Jessie went straight for the internet. "Look yourself up," she encouraged me, and I asked what she meant by that, thinking she'd just use this computer to type up papers for school. I hadn't thought much of her fiddling around on the internet, but I saw quickly that it was the one thing on her mind, the reason she wanted this computer. To look stuff up on the internet.

"Go ahead," she said again with an enthusiastic nod of the head, dishwater hair falling into her eyes. "Type in your name," she told me, "and see what you find."

But I laughed only, telling her we wouldn't find anything, because certainly I'm not on the internet. That's the kind of thing reserved for celebrities and politicians. Not everyday, ordinary people like me. But Jessie was certain.

"The internet knows everything," she told me, emphasizing that word *everything*, and I filled instantly with dread, trying to assure myself that it was only the ramblings of an eager preteen, that certainly the internet couldn't know *everything*, like some sort of omniscient god.

But Jessie's hands breezed past mine, and with nimble fingers, she typed *Eden Sloane* onto the keyboard and pressed the return key.

It didn't happen right away.

No, there was a moment of naive disbelief while the computer did its thing. In that moment, I assured myself that we'd find nothing. Nothing at all. Of course the internet didn't know anything about me because why would it? What reason did I have to be on the internet?

But then an image popped onto the screen before us. And there was my name, highlighted any number of times. My stomach dropped at the sight of them, all these results the computer had gathered for Eden Sloane. Some of them, I saw—as my eyes sailed past the results one at a time, trying to decipher which secrets of mine Jessie would soon find—were not me. There was a split second of relief.

It's another Eden Sloane. It's not *me*.

But then one listing caught my eye, rattling me to the core. Because there, on the internet, for anyone to see, was my name and, beside it, the address of Jessie's and my home, our little bungalow on the northwest side of Chicago, where I thought no one could find us, where I stupidly believed there was no way to know where we were.

I was wrong.

Because now I see that any and everyone is privy to that information, that anyone who's looking for me can find out just exactly where I am.

It was unconscious then, the way that I rose to my feet quickly and moved to the window, pulling the curtains closed post-haste. When Jessie gave me a look, I blamed the glare of sunlight on the computer screen—a glare that wasn't ever there—and she believed me.

I haven't disappeared after all.

All this time, I've been out in the open, living right under everyone's noses.

My throat constricted and went dry. I choked on my own saliva. I coughed, a desperate, panicked cough, unable for a moment to breathe past the saliva that was lodged in my throat.

"You okay?" Jessie asked, patting my back, and I nodded my head yes, though even I didn't know if that was true or not. Was I okay?

When I could speak, I asked her to run down the hall and fetch me a glass of water.

As she did, I snatched the electrical cord from the socket, watching as the screen turned blissfully black. I started packing the computer back in its box the moment Jessie left and, that very same afternoon, planned to hail another cab and return it to the store.

When Jessie returned with the glass of water and asked what I was doing—as I sat there on my haunches, wrapping foam paper around the computer parts—I told her that the computer was broken. That there was something wrong with it, which of course there was. There was something very wrong with it.

I told her that it would have to go back. I avoided Jessie's eyes as, there in the doorway, her face quickly fell. "Can we get a new one?" she asked, and though I said yes, I didn't for one second mean it.

Because there would be something wrong with that computer too.

As Jessie and I stood on the drive, waiting for a cab to appear, I couldn't help but wonder, *What other secrets of mine did the internet hold?*

JESSIE

THE MUSIC GETS CHASED away with morning's first light, and now the house is silent and still. It startles me, the way the music suddenly stops, and now that it's gone, I have to wonder if it was ever really there. I sit up with a start, sticking to the wooden floor. I've been sweating. I say my own name aloud to be sure I can still speak, that fatal familial insomnia hasn't stolen my voice from me already. "Jessica Sloane," I say, my words slurred.

I find myself on my hands and knees searching for Mom's urn, knowing I left her here beside me last night. I comb through the planks of the hardwood floors, as if somehow or other she's slipped through the millimeter gap between boards.

It's a sinking feeling. A spreading, sinking feeling that comes to me at once.

I've lost Mom.

I don't know who I am anymore. I can't go on, I won't go on without her here. I hold my breath and refuse to breathe. And just when I think I'm about to die, I see her. Just two feet away, on the other side of me, right where I left her. My panic comes to a halt.

Mom is still here. She's not yet gone. I release my breath and, at the same time, somehow hear the labored sound of Mom breathing through the air return. Short, shallow breaths followed by no breaths at all.

Only in daylight do I give up my perch. I rise to my feet, arching my back from the stiff muscles that come with three or four hours of lying on the hardwood floors. I creep across the room slowly, deliberately, one step at a time, my legs half-asleep. And I'm jealous of them because at least some small part of me still knows how to sleep.

In the shower, I shampoo my hair. I reach for the conditioner and end up dumping another handful of shampoo on my scalp. I wash my body and then, because I can't remember if I did, I wash it again. Though later, when my skin starts to secrete a sour smell, I wonder if I washed at all.

I head off for a cleaning assignment. As I scrub away on the homeowner's porcelain floors, I notice that my fingernails are still intact. Not a single nail is torn. There's no dried blood clinging to my fingertips because they haven't been bleeding. Even now I feel the sharp edges of the screw head burrowing into my fingertips, and I'm not sure if that happened or if I only imagined it did.

I lock up before I leave. I load my paraphernalia onto the back end of Old Faithful. Mop, bucket, rubber gloves. The September day is sunny and warm. I ride in the street, on tapered one-way streets, which narrow with parked cars like the thickening of arteries with deposits of fat.

I stop for coffee and a donut, taking them to go. "Have a good one, Jenny," the owner of the bakery says to me as I leave, and I think maybe she doesn't have it wrong after all.

Maybe she knows something I don't know. Maybe I really am a Jenny, since I'm no longer Jessica Sloane.

I pedal past a police station. On the sidewalk before the brick building, I pause. I think about stepping inside, asking them to fingerprint me. Maybe they can look my prints up in their system and tell me who I am. But I'm not sure that's how it works. I'm sure they'd need a reason to fingerprint me, and I'm not sure I have one to give. Not a good one anyway. Not one that wouldn't raise red flags.

But then my mind drifts to the notion of DNA, one of those in-home kits that you mail away. Those that claim, with a simple swab of the cheek, to help you figure out your family tree, find distant relatives, discover unknown ethnicities. It's just what I need. To figure out who I am.

I return to the coffee bar on Dearborn and sit there on the blue velvet sofa, waiting for the man from the garden. Hoping he'll come today. I see orange everywhere I look. On a shirt, a shoelace, a flyer taped to a store window, in a flower bed. But none are the man.

I go to the garden, slipping back in between the honey locust trees and finding my way to Mom's favorite spot. It's empty, except for a bird, a little brown thing, a sparrow, pecking away in the dirt for food. I scare it away as I make my way to the edge of the raised bed, sitting on the marbled edge, my eyes circumspect but also tired. The twitch in my eye has yet to go away. If anything, it's gotten worse. It twitches incessantly, only stopping when I dig the heels of my hands into it and press hard.

After an hour or two, I give up. I take the long way back to the carriage home because I'm in no hurry to return. I bike past the elementary school at the corner of Cornelia and Hoyne, a stately structure made almost entirely of red brick, four floors that are tall and thin and deep. Kids play outside, on a parking lot playground beside the school building. The flag is at half-staff; someone has died. The kids are rowdy, unruly, loud, like howler monkeys defending their territory. They scurry to the top of the jungle gym, laying claim to the swings and slides.

I round the corner at Cornelia. A bell rings, calling the kids inside from play. They'll go home soon; it's midafternoon. Once they're gone, the world is suddenly silent. The trees stand tall and proud, the sun's light getting scattered at random through their leaves, dusting the sidewalk.

As I near in on the greystone, I watch as, across the street from it, a little boy schlepps a bucket, waddling down to the sidewalk with his mother on his heels. He flips the bucket upside down and a stack of chalk falls to the concrete. It makes a racket. A single blue piece nearly rolls into the street but he stops it in time, running awkwardly after it. His mother asks him what he's going to draw, waving her hand at me, calling out hello. He's going to draw a hippopotamus.

Ms. Geissler is also outside. She's bent at the waist, picking weeds from her flower bed, plucking and gathering them in her hands. She wears gaudy gardening gloves and, on her head, a wide-brimmed straw hat that keeps the sun from her skin.

I see her and feel a rush of anger well inside me. A rush of anger and unease, among other things. I think of Ms. Geissler there in the third-story window watching me at night. The third story, which is overrun with squirrels. The third story, where she claims she hasn't been in months. I think of the eyes, of *her* eyes, pressed to the window like the eyes of an owl, big enough and bright enough to catch prey on even the darkest of nights.

But it's more than that too, because I'm certain that someone has been in the carriage home when I wasn't there. Only two people should have a key to that home, and it's Ms. Geissler and me.

The carriage home is technically hers, but as far as I'm concerned, she shouldn't be allowed to come and go without reasonable notice. Without letting me know in advance, twenty-four hours in my opinion. It's one thing if the pipes had burst or sewage was overflowing from the toilet, but so far, that's not the case.

I think of what Lily the apartment finder said about carriage homes not abiding by the same rules as prescribed in the city's landlord-tenant ordinance. Living here, I wouldn't be protected in the same way, she'd told me.

Did she mean I'd have a complete lack of privacy? That Ms. Geissler could enter my home without permission? Open and close my window shades? Stare in through the glass at me?

For some reason, I don't think so.

At first I think I should keep going, that I should pedal right on by. But then I have second thoughts. I want to speak to her, because there's something nefarious going on here—many nefarious things—and I want to know what it is.

I force down the kickstand of Old Faithful and stand, hands on my hips behind Ms. Geissler. As I do, words emerge. I don't think them through.

"Why have you been watching me?" I ask.

Her smile is warm. "Jessie," she says kindly, as if she didn't hear my question or the tone of my voice at all. Instead she says that it's nice to see me today. "How about this weather?" she asks, hands elevated, praising the sun and the sky for this glorious day.

And I'm thrown easily off track, thinking then only about the weather. Forgetting about the pair of eyes watching me at night. Forgetting the fear I felt at stepping inside the carriage home and finding the shades open wide.

I snap to. "Why have you been watching me?" I ask, and her face clouds over in confusion. Her eyebrows crease.

"I don't know what you mean," she declares.

"I saw you," I assert, pointing a finger at the windows up above. The windows that are dark now, not a light on inside. They're obscure, shadows only. The only thing that I can see is the outside world getting cast back at me. A reflection. "Standing up there," I say. "Three nights in a row now," I say, though the truth is that I've lost count. It could be three. It could be four or more. "You've been staring into the house, watching me. Spying on me. Why?" I demand. "Why are you watching me?"

The smile slips from her face. Or rather gets replaced with one that's more pitying. Ruts form between her eyes, deep trenches in the skin. She pulls the hat from her head and a great big cluster of hair falls from her head, getting trapped in the straw brim. Like Mom's used to do before she bit the bullet and shaved it all off. I see her and me standing together in the shower basin. Starting with an electric shaver first, and then a cheap, plastic disposable razor. Rubbing gobs of aloe vera on it when we were through.

"Well, aren't you going to say something?" I ask when Ms. Geissler doesn't say anything. I can't stand to see her looking at me piteously, saying nothing. "You have no right," I say, my eyes lost on the clump of hair that has fallen out of her scalp. She grabs a hold of it, plucks it from the hat and releases it to the wind. "No right," I tell her, "to be spying on me."

"Jessie," Ms. Geissler says. Her voice bleeds of sympathy, empathy. Or darn good theatrics. I don't know which, but whatever it is, I don't like it one bit. "Jessie, dear," she says again. "You're still not sleeping, no?" she asks. I feel my knees become liquid. They soften. I want to say no, that I haven't been sleeping. I want her to tell me to try warm milk. A spoonful of honey. To listen to music before I go to bed. Calming music. Lullabies. Not because I trust her; I don't. But because I want someone to tell me about the music and the voices that come to life in the ductwork at night. About Jessica Sloane.

In that moment I see her, Jessica Sloane, in her purple bathing suit, lying dead on the street. Pigeons circle around her, staring at her with their beady eyes.

Ms. Geissler stands before me, staring. "Jessie, are you all right?" she asks, and only then do I realize that she's been speaking to me. That she's been speaking to me and I didn't hear a word. "You don't look all right," she decides, empathy in her eyes, but I won't let her divert me from my track. I look around, remembering where I am. Remembering what I was going to say.

"Slept like a baby," I lie.

I look to the ground for the clump of hair that fell from Ms. Geissler's head, but it's not there. All there is is a cluster of leaves, a mixture of yellows and browns that shrivel on the lawn. As my eyes rise to Ms. Geissler, she replaces the hat on her head. And there I see it. A single wilted yellow leaf, folded like a moth in its cocoon, clinging to the straw of the hat.

There was never a clump of hair. I'd only imagined it was hair. It was just leaves. Leaves falling from a nearby tree, getting snagged on the hat as she hunched over the lawn, tending garden.

"I see you there in the window. Every single night. I know you see me. You were in my home," I snap, my tone turning vitriolic. "That's trespassing, you know?" I say. "An invasion of privacy. I could call the police. I should call the police."

She's quiet at first. "Jessie, honey," she says, the look on her face one of concern. Condolence. Shame. "Oh, Jessie. Poor, poor, Jessie," she says instead, pitying me, ignoring my threat to call the police. She takes a step toward me, makes an attempt to stroke my arm with her gaudy gardening gloves. But I pull back. "You must be mistaken, dear," she says. "The third floor, I told you already," she says, making a sweeping gesture of the greystone behind her. "I don't go up there anymore. I haven't been up there in months."

It's a lie. I know that's not true. I know because she was there.

"I saw the light on in the attic. I saw you standing there in the window looking out. Watching me."

"No," she says to me, shaking her head, looking concerned and confused. "There are no lights up there in the attic. I'd had a lamp once, just an old floor lamp, nothing special, but the squirrels chewed their way right through the cord. Can you imagine?" she says then, tsking her tongue and shaking her head. "Pesky little things. It's a wonder they didn't electrocute themselves." And for the briefest of moments it sounds so genuine, so real, that I almost see the squirrels' overgrown teeth gnawing their way through the cord, cutting power to the floor lamp.

But not quite.

"I know what I saw," I insist.

But somewhere deep inside me, I also wonder if I do.

"You must be mistaken, Jessie," she says. "Maybe it was a dream. You've lost your mother. Grief can be a terrible thing. The isolation, the desperation—" But I stop her before she can cite for me the stages of grief. Her eyes now are chock-full of condolence. Sorrow. They mock me. I know what she's doing. With her pitiful eyes and her compassion, she's trying to make me question my own sanity, to make me think I'm crazy. A by-product of the insomnia and the grief.

But I know what I saw. There was a light on in the third floor. There were eyes in the window, watching me.

"Then let me see," I insist. My words are assertive. I attempt to call her bluff. "Let me go to the attic. Let me see for myself that there is no light there."

Her lips curve upward. She grins. Not a happy smile, not a mocking smile, but an appeasing one. She's placating me. "Oh, I don't think so. It's quite the mess, Jessie. I don't even think it's safe to go up there," she says. Not until she can get her contractor out to clean it up, which she says she really needs to do. It's been too long and the attic, for now, is just a waste of space. And then she says that she must go. Rain is on its way, she says, staring skyward. Until now I didn't notice the storm clouds rolling in. It was all blue sky and sun, but now it's not. Now there are clouds. "The weeds are calling me," Ms. Geissler says, turning, stepping closer to the thistle and away from me.

And then, in that moment, from up above, the clouds burst apart at the seams. Rainwater comes pouring down. Just like that, the sun-dappled sidewalks are gone, getting replaced with puddles. I take my eyes off Ms. Geissler, looking down, to see my feet submerged in a puddle of water. Across the street, the little boy's chalk hippopotamus gets washed away, rallying his tears. He begins to cry. But not before first throwing his chalk so that it breaks in two, screaming, "It's ruined," and then stomping off and heading inside, hot on his mother's heels.

I look back toward Ms. Geissler, but already she's gone.

In the distance, a screen door slams and there I am.

Hair matted down, wet clothes binding to me. All alone.

★★★

The rain, only a cloudburst, is through. Over and done with. No sooner had I fled the lawn for the cover of indoors than it stopped. The sun forced its way through the clouds again like a baby chick breaking free from an eggshell. The world turned yellow, golden.

Drop by drop the rain disappeared, going back up the way it came down. And then the sun set, turning the world to pink and then purple and then black, welcoming another sleepless night.

I stare out the window and into the third story of Ms. Geissler's home. I stare until my eyes get tired from it, so tired that my retinas begin to burn, the lid continuing to twitch. And yet I can't bring myself to blink because in those milliseconds, I might miss something, a flicker of light, eyes in the window staring back at me. The house itself blurs, softening at the edges because I've been staring too long.

But still, I don't blink.

The shades on the third-story window are drawn. All three of them pulled taut. Like the world outside, the room is dark. For hours on end, there's no one there. Evidence that I'm mistaken. Evidence that I am wrong. That Ms. Geissler hasn't been standing in the window watching me at night, and that my imagination only made it up. It couldn't have been a dream because when you don't sleep you don't dream. And so instead it was my mind playing games with me.

All night long, the window remains empty and black. It's cold in the carriage home because I've turned the heat completely off in an effort to prevent noises from sneaking in through the ductwork. So far, it's working. There are no voices; there are no pings. No music. But as a result, the temperature in the carriage home hurtles to fifty degrees. My fingers and toes go numb.

As I lie there in bed listening to the *tick*, *tock* of the wall clock, it dawns on me. Mom is not my biological mom. It seems so transparent, so *glaring* there in the witching hour. As if it's been staring me in the face all this time and I just failed to see. I look nothing like her, for starters, which doesn't necessarily matter because for all I know I'm a dead ringer of my dad. But still, it's cause for doubt.

If Mom is not my biological mother, then how did I come to be with her? How did I come to think of her as my mom?

Maybe it was something innocuous, like she adopted me as a child. And in an effort to keep me from my birth mom—who, for all she knew, would try and track me down in an attempt to regain custody—she stole a dead child's identity and gave it to me so that I'd be impossible to find. Maybe my birth mother was abusive, neglectful. Or maybe she was thirteen years old, a victim of rape, not ready to be a mother. A teenager who'd gotten loaded at a party and went too far with some guy. Mom was saving me from a life of abuse and neglect at the hands of a reluctant mother.

Or maybe it's not so innocuous after all.

Maybe it's more toxic than that. Maybe I wasn't adopted, but rather taken. Kidnapped. It's a thought I go to only because it's the middle of the night, the time my imagination most often takes flight.

Did Mom *kidnap* me?

I feel an overwhelming sense of guilt for thinking these things about Mom. That she took me. That I'm not hers. That she did something illicit, that she did something wrong. I think of myself, twelve years old, Mom, woozy on a glass of wine, confessing, *A long time ago, I did something I'm not proud of, Jessie. Something that shames me.*

And that's how I got you.

I know now what she means.

Eleanor Zulpo, the woman Mom used to work for when I was a girl, told me that as a child, I insisted my name was something other than Jessie. She remembered that I'd pout my face and stomp my foot and demand that Mom stop calling me Jessie.

Jessie isn't my real name. That much I already know. It's a name Mom forced on me, one I accepted with resistance, because even a three-or four-year-old knows their name and isn't quick to change it.

But not only did I call myself by a different name, but I called Mom *Eden*. Did I call her Eden because she wasn't my mom? Because she'd *kidnapped* me? Because my mom was someone else, and if so, then who?

In the back of my mind I tell myself that if, *if*, Mom kidnapped me—that word itself lumbering through my brain, clumsy and awkward, finding it hard to travel from neuron to neuron because the very idea of it is so incompatible with *Mom*, who was always so loving, so kind—she had a good reason to do it. She wasn't just some run-of-the-mill child abductor.

But something doesn't add up, like a puzzle with interlocking pieces, the rounded tabs and the carved-out openings that are all supposed to connect. They don't.

Because there's the photograph of the man. The one I hold so tightly in my grip that the edges of it begin to disintegrate with sweat. I spend the night holding the photograph of the man with the lake and the trees, knowing he meant something to Mom, that she intentionally kept this photograph and this man from me.

Who is he? I have to find him. I have to find him so that I can know who he is, if he's my father. Then I'll know how and when and why I came to be with Mom. Mom who is not my mom.

I look hard for something, for some clue that I've failed to see. The cut of his hair, the color of the lake, the type of trees in the backdrop. The way he stands, the brand of his jeans—the tag far too small to read, but still I try—that sailboat in the distance. Is it really white like I believed it to be, or is it more of a pale yellow, or white with pale yellow stripes? None of which matter.

And then I see it. It's a small thing, but significant enough to me. Because suddenly every detail is significant to me.

This man is left-handed. I know this, or convince myself I know it, because he's wearing his watch on his right wrist. It isn't one of those hard-and-fast rules, and yet it's common enough to be true. People tend to wear their watches on their nondominant wrists.

I think that there are only a handful of lefties in the world, which narrows down my search exponentially, though still the field is huge. Instead of being one in seven billion, the odds that I'll find this man are now more like one in seven hundred million.

And I know it then; I'll never find this man.

He could be anywhere. He could be anyone. Even if I found myself staring right at him, I'd never know it because I've never seen his face before.

I set the photograph aside. I'm so cold that my skin turns mottled and gray. It's got a purplish tint to it and looks like it's covered in lace, a white overlay to the purple skin. I sit there on the floor, staring at my hands, my legs. All that exposed skin, which is as cold and as mottled as Mom's was before she died.

And I come to one conclusion: like Mom, I'm also dying.

At first, everything around me is black. I can't bring myself to move. I'm too cold, too tired, too scared to move. I can't bring myself to throw the covers over my arms and legs. Night goes by with the speed of a sloth. Painfully slow.

But then it begins. Sunrise. Daylight. Morning comes. Out the window, I watch it happen.

It starts as a single pixel of light. The sun still tucked safely below the horizon, scattering its light into the atmosphere. A semidarkness. A soft glow of yellow and blue. The clouds thicken around it, getting drawn in, like nuts and bolts to a magnet. They flush at their edges, turning shades of pink and red. As if the clouds themselves are embarrassed.

The sun rises higher and higher into the sky.

And just like that, day has arrived.

The air in the room starts to warm thanks to the sun's rays pouring in the open window. My mottled, purple skin disappears, getting replaced with a healthy pink. I'm not dying after all. I'm still very much alive, it seems. For now at least.

EDEN

August 4, 1997
Egg Harbor

IT'S BEEN TWO WEEKS since they took my baby from me.

Today, Aaron and I sat in Dr. Landry's office.

"The good news," Dr. Landry said, face firm, undeviating, with no hint of a smile, "is that we now know you can get pregnant. Your body is capable of that. But maintaining the pregnancy is proving to be another matter."

We had only been there a couple of minutes. Aaron and I sat beside each other on matching tufted armchairs, Dr. Landry on a swivel chair behind his desk. In my hand I clenched a tissue, dabbing at my cheeks as Dr. Landry stared at me.

I asked him, "How long until we can try again?" meaning all of us, another round of IVF at the cost of another ten thousand dollars, money that Aaron and I most certainly didn't have because we didn't have it the first time around. I now had three credit cards in my name and each were nearly maxed out. The minimum payment alone was more than I could pay. I'd never been in debt before; I'd never been behind on payments; I'd never been in the red. I'd never been bankrupt. It made me anxious, and yet I easily reasoned that it was money well spent.

I'd sell my own organs—a spare kidney or the lobe of a lung—before giving up on a baby.

He was dressed down today, no lab coat as usual, and, as Aaron attempted to cling to my hand, I pulled away, folding my hands in my lap. The numbness, the narcosis, it stuck around me like a cold that wouldn't quit. When I wasn't in bed crying, then I was numb. I felt nothing. I had only two modes these days: sad and numb.

Dr. Landry replied with "There's really no definitive answer to that; we can try again whenever you're ready," but his words were blighted by Aaron's incredulous sigh because Aaron, as he'd already told me, didn't want to try again. He wanted to be through.

The reason was simple.

The reason was me.

For the last two weeks, I couldn't bring myself to get out of bed. Morning, noon and night, I cried for my lost child, wondering how it was possible to grieve for something that was never truly mine.

Man plans, and God laughs. Isn't that what they say?

Aaron didn't want me to make another appointment with Dr. Landry. He had other suggestions for whom I should call instead: a therapist, a support group. Maybe all I needed was some time away, he foolishly believed. A trip by myself to one of those places I've forever longed to go. St. Lucia, Fiji, Belize. As if lying by the seashore and drinking a cocktail might help me forget the fact that I'd just lost a child, might annihilate that desire to ever have a child, so that when I returned I'd feel fresh, revived, happy.

"I don't want a goddamn vacation!" I screamed at him then, lying in bed, blankets over my head, coming up from under the covers only for air. "I want a baby. Why don't you get that, Aaron? What's so difficult to understand?"

And it was only then in broad daylight, when I dared to poke my head out of my own dark cavern, that I could see Aaron's eyes were red and swollen, his heart visibly broken like mine. His shirt was wrinkled, the buttons lined up incorrectly, his hair standing on end. His facial hair had grown threefold, proof to me that he, like me, wasn't leaving the house, that he too couldn't bring himself to go to work.

But I didn't acknowledge this.

"I know what you're feeling," he said quietly, compassionately, his voice losing control as he wiped at his eyes with the back of a shirtsleeve.

"Trust me," he said. "I get it."

A better person would have realized that Aaron had lost something too. A better person would have consoled him, would have let him console and be consoled. But not me.

This was my loss, not his.

"Go away," I barked then, and I heard it in my own voice, heard it and hated it but said it nonetheless. "You have no idea what I'm feeling. Don't stand there and pretend you know what it's like to lose a child."

I returned to my cave, throwing the blankets back over my head where I could scarcely breathe.

"This baby. This pregnancy. This need to get pregnant," Aaron lamented as he stood in the doorway, urging me to eat, to get out of bed, to go for a walk, to get some fresh air. "They've gotten the best of you, Eden. They've turned you into someone I don't recognize anymore. Someone I don't know."

And then he reminded me of who I was before that day we decided to start a family.

Fun loving. Benevolent and genuine. Carefree.

"I'd give anything to go back to being Aaron and Eden. Just us. Just you and me," he said, and for a bat of an eye I remembered us on our wedding day, riding in on horseback on Aaron's family farm in a regal ball gown, exchanging nuptials beneath the nighttime sky. A celebration worthy of a fairy tale. I had found my everything. I had married my prince.

But suddenly my everything wasn't good enough.

I needed more.

"I want to try right away. As soon as we can," I told Dr. Landry today as we sat in his office, and it was then that Aaron stood up from his tufted armchair and left the room.

September 8, 1997
Egg Harbor

Aaron didn't show up at the fertility clinic for today's appointment.

For weeks I've gone through the whole rigmarole, the process of developing follicles, of returning to Dr. Landry's office every few days to have my blood drawn and an ultrasound performed to see if there were any viable candidates for the procedure. I've been injected with a legion of hormones, each which leave blood blisters along my skin and a gamut of side effects, from headaches to hot flashes to moodiness and pain.

Already, Dr. Landry has forewarned me that, should implantation occur, Aaron and I will need to administer shots of progesterone into my backside to not only make a baby this time, but to help maintain the pregnancy. We'll do it daily, for ten weeks or more. "It's not for the faint of heart," he assured me, but I told him I'm ready. "I'll do anything, *anything*," I swore to Dr. Landry as he listed the side effects of the progesterone shots—the weight gain, the facial hair, the unbearable pain—to have a baby.

And then, when a mature follicle was ready, spotted on Dr. Landry's ultrasound monitor where not so long ago sat the image of a baby with a heartbeat and webbed hands and feet, we scheduled an appointment for the egg retrieval, where Dr. Landry planned to insert a needle deep inside me to remove the eggs from my womb.

Today was that day.

Except it wasn't.

I sat for hours waiting for Aaron to come and deliver his sperm.

Three hours and fourteen minutes to be precise, watching as other couples—six, eight, ten of them—came and went through the glass doors.

I read each of the magazines in the waiting room two times.

I made an attempt to phone Aaron, but he didn't answer my call.

I told the receptionist, who stared at me with shame and regret, that Aaron was only running late, that he would be here soon.

That he was caught up in traffic.

And then, after another hour of waiting, I asked to speak to a nurse and one was fetched for me, and, standing closer to her than appropriate so that she had to take a half step back to regain her personal space, I wondered whether they had any of Aaron's sperm remaining from the analysis or our first round of IVF. Certainly they had some remaining in storage, a few drops even, a single sperm, half-dead, clinging to the edges of a petri dish.

But she shook her head remorsefully, apologized and said no.

"I'm sorry," she said. "There is no sperm."

The nurse took a step away, but before she could go I laid a hand on her arm and asked whether my eggs could be removed now, if they could simply be stored somewhere, held on to until Aaron came to make his deposit. It seemed completely possible, like layaway, but I was reminded then of the little life span an egg has after ovulation. "There isn't time," she said, and it was then and only then that I inquired about donor sperm, an idea that settled in my mind slowly, one morsel at a time, while I spent hours in the fertility reception room, reading pregnancy magazine after pregnancy magazine, waiting for Aaron to come.

Donor sperm.

Two words I thought I'd never have to use in my entire life.

The desperation in my voice was tangible to every single person in the room, but none more than me. "Can we use donor sperm?" I begged, latching on to her arm now, fingernails leaving crescent-shape indentations in her skin.

"Where is your husband, Eden?" the nurse asked, stepping away, pretending altogether that I had never uttered those words, *donor sperm*. She was speaking down to me, that I knew. That I could clearly hear, as she riffled through a patient file in her hands, another patient's file, obviously distracted and needing to be somewhere other than in the reception area with me.

"Where's Aaron?"

It was then that I told her how he must have gotten caught up at work, except that was a lie because it was Monday, the one day in which Aaron never worked.

I inquired again about donor sperm—certainly they had vials and vials of male sperm stored somewhere in this facility that I could use—but the nurse assured me that they would need consent from me and Aaron—from the both of us—to use someone else's sperm.

In other words, Aaron would need to be present to give his consent, he would need to be here, and Aaron wasn't here.

Aaron wasn't running late and he wouldn't be there soon.

He had no intention of coming at all.

He just didn't tell me.

Not until I came home from the fertility clinic to find him at the kitchen table, drinking a beer. A beer! Suffice to say I lost it completely, feeling enraged. I screamed at him then like I'd never done before, uttering words I could never take back. Coming at him with fists raised, thinking for a minute that I could hit him. That I *would* hit him. I'd never done a thing like that before, and my fists stopped just shy of him as I turned on myself instead, pulling my own hair, screaming like a maniac. Aaron didn't flinch. I'd scarcely ever raised my voice to Aaron before, and it left me feeling rattled long after he left the room, walking out on me midsentence. It was the medication doing it, I convinced myself as I stood there in the empty kitchen in silence, strands of my own hair in my hands, watching as outside the sun went down—an arc of pinks and blues setting over our share of the bay, heaven on earth as we once so foolishly believed—the myriad fertility drugs affecting my judgment. They were the reason why I screamed and yelled, and yet I had every reason in the world to be angry.

Aaron never showed for the appointment.

He never came to deliver his sperm.

My eggs were ready and waiting, but where was he?

"Where were you?" I demanded as I lifted his empty beer bottle from the kitchen table and hurled it against the wall, longing and hoping for the release of a thousand minuscule shards of glass when all it was was two. Two large chunks of amber glass falling to the floor with a dull thud, leaving me far from satisfied. I reached for a collection of mail then, set there on the table's edge, and hurled that every which way too, bills and late notices drifting to the ground like fallen leaves.

"I told you," he said after I'd followed him into the living room—voice remarkably composed because he had likely sat there half the day rehearsing what he was going to say—"that I was through. We've been at this for a year," he said. "Over a year. We're broke, Eden. Everything we've worked for is gone. We have no more money to invest in this," he said, holding out a bill for me, one that arrived in today's mail, a credit card statement with a seventeen-thousand-dollar debt. "Look what this has done to us. To our marriage. To you.

"I can't keep doing this," he told me.

"I meant it, Eden. I'm through.

"It's time for you to choose."

And then he reached for a packed bag that sat on the hallway floor.

The front door opened and then closed again, and I wondered if that was it then.

If that was the last time I'd ever lay eyes on Aaron.

JESSIE

I SIT ON THE sofa beside Liam, in his apartment. His laptop is on my thighs. I find my way to the website for the National Center for Missing & Exploited Children, thinking that if Mom stole me, for whatever reason, if I had a family before her, then maybe someone once reported me as missing. Maybe my real family is missing me.

On the website, I discover countless babies stolen from their cribs. Kids who got on the bus, but never made it home from school. Pregnant women last seen on the gritty footage of parking lot surveillance cameras. Infant twins missing after a parent was found dead. Babies lifted from hospital nurseries.

One by one, I become absorbed in the sad stories. The stories of the missing. Thumbnail image by thumbnail image, I open them all. I read about a toddler who was last seen playing on his own front porch in some small town in Georgia, where he lived with his father and stepmother in Jeffersonville, Georgia. He was last seen at approximately ten fifteen on a Tuesday morning, way back in 1995. His hair is sandy and his eyes are green. An age-progressed photo shows what he might look like today, if he's even still alive. He was taken by his mother in a custody battle. There's a picture of her too. In it, she looks a little agrarian, a little unsophisticated, a little mean. Her hair is sparse and thin, her skin weathered and blotchy.

I think that it's possible that, like the little boy from Jeffersonville, Georgia, I am a child stolen from my front porch or from my crib, a child that climbed aboard the school bus one morning and never came home that afternoon.

"What did you find?" Liam asks as I scroll through the website, finding a search form.

"Nothing yet," I tell him. But I hope I will soon.

I fill in as much as I think I know and leave the rest blank. I am child. I am female. These are things I know. I make up the dates I may or may not have gone missing. I fill them in, this three-year gap that stretches clear from the day Jessica Sloane was born until the day she died. Three years. Three momentary years. Shorter than a presidential term, than the span between Olympic Games, between leap years.

I watch as over one hundred cases load. One hundred little girls missing in a three-plus-year time span. One hundred little girls missing in a three-year time span that now, seventeen years later, still haven't been found. It makes me sad. I think of their parents, of their real moms and dads.

One by one I click on the images and they tell me everything I need: when and where the child went missing; the color of their eyes, their hair, how old they would be. There are age-progressed photos, though how accurate they are, I don't know. Ivy Marsh went missing at the age of two. She was last seen in Lawton, Oklahoma, a little girl with blue eyes, blond hair, dimples like me. Kristin Tate went missing on her third birthday, last seen in Wimberly, Texas. She too has dimples.

I scroll down the page and click the arrow, move to the second page, and then the third. The fourth. "What are you looking for?" Liam asks, glancing over my shoulder to see what I see.

"I don't know," I say, but then I take it back, telling him that what I'm looking for is me. I take in the age-progressed photos of children who went missing nearly twenty years ago, wondering if any of them might look like me. Though I tell myself that an age-progressed image of an infant wouldn't have the same accuracy as that of an older kid because of how the face changes over the years. All babies have big, round eyes, chubby cheeks. Enormous foreheads. Toothless grins. There's nothing distinguishable about them. They all look the same to me. So who's to say what a baby's face would look like in twenty years?

And it doesn't matter anyway because scanning the missing children, not one bears a resemblance to me.

I push the laptop away. I reach into my bag and for the first time show the photograph to Liam. He asks who it is and I say, "Just some guy," though I feel in my gut that there's more to it than that. Because of some primal instinct to be close to this man, to know who he is. I tell Liam where I found the photograph, hidden in the cubbyhole behind the closet mirror.

"You think he's your father?" he asks, both a question and a statement. I shrug. He takes the photograph into his hands, holds it closely to his eyes, examining it before he slips the photograph back into my hands. My hands still shake, the tremor that for all these days won't go away. The room goes quiet, all except for the steady beat of rain against the window. It's a drizzle only, not a complete washout, though the day outside is ugly and gray. The morning's beautiful sunrise has been clouded over now; it's long gone. The melody of rain on glass is calming. I find myself soothed by it, tuning out everything else but that sound, wanting to sing along with it somehow, like a song's refrain.

And then it happens again. My eyelids close. They do it against my will. My head slumps forward, my neck no longer able to hold it up. It lasts a second. Only a second.

For one blissful second, I am asleep.

But then a jolt of electricity tears through me and my head snaps to. I'm awake.

"Jessie," I hear. I see Liam's hand fall to my knee. I turn to face him, his blue eyes so well-meaning. I'm overcome with a sense of belonging that I've rarely known before, only ever with Mom.

He touches my hair and for a single moment, something inside me feels warm.

He urges me to lie on his sofa. He offers up a pillow and a blanket, but I say no thanks. That I'm all right. "Jessie," he argues, but I say it again. I'm all right, though we both know that's not true.

I excuse myself, pushing my body from the sofa as if I weigh three hundred pounds. In the bathroom I splash cold water on my face. I stare at my reflection in the mirror. My skin has a grayish-green tint to it. I look sick, like I'm dying. My eyes sink into their sockets, deep bags formed beneath each. I press a finger to them, watching as they sink and then swell. Sink and then swell. My lips are dry, chapped around the edges, blistered, my cheeks concave.

I count the days on my fingertips. The days since I've been asleep.

The longest anyone has gone without a drop of sleep is eleven days.

I stare at my own sunken reflection, not able to make sense of what I see, but knowing that by this time tomorrow, I will be dead.

EDEN

September 23, 1997
Egg Harbor

I TRIED NOT TO let the desperation get the best of me, too afraid of what I might do if it did. I tried hard to keep busy, taking on extra shifts at the hospital, working overtime because being at home, alone, threw me easily off balance and I didn't like the feeling of being off balance, of being desperate, of feeling like I was losing control.

My home, Aaron's and my utopian cottage, quickly became a dystopia to me, a place where everything was undesirable and sad, and where I was in a constant state of dysphoria; I couldn't stand to be there and so I took to keeping myself out of the home all day, every day, doing everything imaginable to avoid the pine floors and whitewashed walls, the glorious tree swing that had once deceived me into believing this place was home.

I spent ten hours a day reading through patient files, trying to decipher what they were to be billed for and entering it into the hospital's system. It was meaningless and mundane, and yet a wonderful way to waste time. I took odd jobs on occasion, answering ads for a temporary cleaning lady or a dog walker or a driver to take a sweet elderly woman for dialysis treatments, keeping her company for the four hours it took to eliminate waste from her blood three times each week. It kept me busy and more than anything, I needed to be busy.

Time passed.

Last week I came home to find a separation agreement in a manila envelope, set beside the front door. In it, Aaron left me the house and all of our assets, taking from me only the debt, as much as he could anyway, the credit cards that were in both of our names.

Even in divorce he was protecting me.

I signed the paperwork post-haste, knowing that the sooner I did, the sooner the divorce was complete, I could ask for donor sperm without Aaron's consent.

In the meantime, I did everything I could to keep busy, knowing it would take months, nearly six of them, until the divorce was finalized.

Could I wait that long for a baby?

Oh, how I would try.

But as they say, the road to hell is paved with good intentions.

Because the minute the well ran dry and I found myself with nothing better to do, I drove by the quaint dance studio on Church Street and sat on the park bench, watching the little ballerinas come and go, and it was different now because I hadn't been there in months, since springtime, but everything was still the same. The bigger girls scurried out of the studio first, followed by their mothers, who carried coffee and talked.

And then, just when I'd begun to think that was it, the end of the procession, there came little Olivia with her short legs lagging behind, waylaid by things like heavy doors and sidewalk cracks, struggling to keep up. Her hair had been cut short, no longer in a bun but pinned to the sides of her head with barrettes. She was still easily distracted, that I'd come to learn, sidetracked by things like birds and bugs and today a leaf, bright red on the white concrete, the first indication of fall.

She paused to poke and prod at it as if it were alive, examining the redness of the leaf, the shape of its lobes, while the others gravitated away at their own pace so that the distance between them grew exponentially, and this time, Olivia's mother was too caught up in her conversation that she didn't see her daughter on her haunches, examining the leaf with the concentration and single-mindedness of a microbiologist. The woman's feet hit the street and she crossed the intersection, unaware of the fact that she and her child were now separated by a highway, the very same highway that once took a little girl's life when her mother was also not watching.

Some women were not meant to be mothers.

And some who were, some who would make the very best mothers, were refused the right.

It didn't seem fair.

Oh, what a good mother I would be, if only the universe would let me.

Suddenly Olivia's eyes peered up from the fallen leaf and, at seeing that she was alone, she began to cry. It was a process that went by degrees, a feeling of excitement first at finding the leaf, followed by frustration that there was no one around to show the leaf to, before sadness crept in, a great heartache that the others had left without her, leading to panic. Sheer panic. Olivia gasped first, choking unexpectedly on her own saliva, and then she began to cry, quiet tears, choked-up tears, while her little knees shook beneath their shiny white tights.

I'd be remiss to say that a series of thoughts didn't move swiftly through my mind.

How would I hide her?

Where would we go?

What would I call her? Because surely if she was a missing child, she couldn't parade around town as Olivia still. She'd have to be something else.

I leaned forward from the bench to lift the leaf from the concrete and asked if she ever collected leaves and pressed them between the pages of a heavy book. The sound of my voice, the sight of her leaf in my hand, gave her pause. Her eyes rose from the earth and landed on my smile, and for a moment there was a cessation of tears as I extended the leaf toward her and she took it from me with a shaky hand.

I rationalized in my mind that it would be Aaron's fault if I took the child—not mine, no, not ever mine—because that was the name of the game these days: blame.

If only he had shown up at the fertility clinic…

If only he hadn't walked out of my life…

He and I still would have a chance at our own child.

I wouldn't have had to take one that wasn't mine.

"Why are you crying?" I asked, though of course I knew the reason why. I remained seated, not wanting to scare her by standing tall and towering over her small frame. Outside, the temperatures were dropping again, fall drawing near. Soon the tourists would leave. On her arms there were goose bumps as loose strands of dishwater hair clung to the puddles of tears.

"Where's Mommy?" she asked, eyes searching the street. But only I heard it in the distance: the sound of girls' laughter over the sound of the wind. Olivia didn't hear.

Through the trees I could barely make out the red sleeve of a cardigan, the pink of a tutu, a length of brown hair.

"You lost your mommy?" I asked and, extending my own hand to hers, said, "Would you like for me to help you find her? Would you like for me to help you find your mother?

"It's okay," I said when she hesitated. "I won't hurt you."

It would be a lie to say she took my hand with ease, that she didn't stare at it for a minute, overthinking, some disquisition about not talking to strangers coursing through her mind.

But then she did take my hand, slipping it inside. It was a great shock to my system to feel this small, soft hand within mine, and it was all I could do not to squeeze tight with instinct, knowing that might make her scream. I didn't want Olivia to scream. I didn't want to scare her, but more so, I didn't want to draw attention to ourselves. For all intents and purposes, this was how it should be. I was hers and she was mine.

And then I began to lead her in the opposite direction of where her mother had disappeared. The direction of my car.

Olivia stopped, peering the other way over her shoulder—even a young girl could remember which way her mother had last been walking—but I said to her not to worry, that if we took the car we might find her mother more quickly than if we walked.

I pointed to my car in the distance. "It's right there," I said.

She thought about this a moment, standing frozen on the pavement, hemming and hawing, eyes moving back and forth from me to the car. A band of clouds had rolled in, blocking the earth from the sun, and as it did, the wind picked up its speed, chasing the warm day away. Outside, the temperature dropped by as many as five degrees and the day turned gray.

Fall was coming; fall was here.

"Well, that's okay," I said then, letting go of her hand. "If you don't want to find your mother, we don't need to," and it was reverse psychology, of course, making her believe that if she didn't get in the car with me, I might just leave her behind.

I didn't want to scare her, and yet there was no other way.

I was only doing what I needed to do.

I reasoned that we would only drive to the next town and then stop for ice cream. That I'd have her just long enough to teach her mother a lesson. Then I'd return her. Certainly I wasn't planning to *steal* the child, because that's not the type of person that I am. A kidnapper and a thief. I only wanted to borrow her for a while, like a library book on loan. To satisfy my craving for the time.

I had taken no more than two steps away when I heard Olivia's tiny feet scurrying quickly on the concrete, running after me. It worked.

Her hand reached up, and she grabbed a hold of mine, squeezing tightly, careful not to let go. I smiled at her and she smiled back, the tears evaporating quickly from her cheeks.

"Your mother must be here somewhere," I said then, and we walked that way, hand in hand, for a good ten feet or more. We moved slowly—at Olivia's pace, though I wanted to tug on her hand and run—and still, it took twenty seconds or less to traverse those ten feet. But in those twenty seconds I convinced myself that in some minute, negligible way, we looked alike, Olivia and me, though in reality we didn't. We looked nothing alike.

I wondered if, once she and I were sitting across from one another at a local diner, eating strawberry sundaes with whipped cream on top, I'd ever be able to return her to her mother.

And then a new thought crossed my mind. I could drive farther south, south of Sturgeon Bay, south of Sheboygan, south of Milwaukee. We could live somewhere else, far away from here, where people might believe that we were mother and child.

They would have no reason not to believe.

I'd rename her. I'd call her something other than Olivia.

And in time, she'd come to think of it as her given name.

"I don't have a booster seat," I said as we approached the car, "but that's okay for now. The seat belt will do just fine." And as we closed in on the car I extended a hand toward the handle, reaching out to open the back door for Olivia to climb through. "It will only be a short drive after all," I promised her. "I'm sure your mother is here somewhere."

In a single moment, I thought this through. I made a plan and it went like this. Once Olivia was in the car I would speed off the opposite way, far from town, away from her mother, not stopping until we'd passed Sturgeon Bay. There I would stop only to buy Olivia ice cream, something to soothe her, to make her not be scared, to quiet her certain tears. Ice cream and a stuffed bear or a toy from a gas station store, something she could clutch to her chest to make her feel safe. We'd drive all night, as far as we could go. Far away from here.

And that's when I heard it.

Olivia's name screamed urgently, emphatically through the cold air.

It was a high-pitched screech, whiny like a whistle. A distressed sound. What followed were the footsteps of a stampede, thousands of wildebeests running down the street. That's what it sounded like anyway, and as I peered up, hand still six inches away from the door, I saw Olivia's mother and her herd hurrying toward me, eight ladies with seven little ballerinas in tow, shouting commands.

"Olivia, come here right now.

"What do you think you're doing?

"Get your hands off my child!"

My hands grew slick. My heart beat quickly, more quickly than it was already beating. Under my arms there was wetness. Sweat. My head suddenly hurt. My brain thought quickly to manufacture a lie, as one of the ladies pointed at me and said, "I've seen you around here before," and I ransacked my mind for words, any words, but the words wouldn't come. My mind was holding them captive, detaining my words from me, though what it did do was measure the distance—computing the distance from the ladies to me, the distance from me to the car—doing the math, figuring it out, whether I could get Olivia inside the car before her mother and the other ladies reached us.

I *could*, I decided. But there needed to be no hesitation.

I needed to go.

Go!

I needed to go *now.*

But my feet wouldn't work properly, and my hand, slick with sweat, let go of Olivia's hand and suddenly she was running in the wrong direction, running toward her mother and away from me and away from the car.

"Who in the hell do you think you are?" Olivia's mother asked pointedly as she gathered Olivia into her arms and hoisted her to her chest. "What did you think you were doing with my child?"

And though I was completely tongue-tied, it was Olivia who did the speaking for me, who struggled in her mother's arms to be set free and there, once her feet were firmly planted back on the concrete while twirling her red leaf in her hand, she said, "You forgot me, Mommy."

And with that she took six tiny steps away from her mother's reach and extended her leaf to me. A parting gift.

I took it in my hand. "She was helping me find Mommy," Olivia crooned, smiling a toothless grin, but still, I could muster no words.

And then Olivia's mother changed tack, and her tone softened. The lines of her face disappeared and instead of reprimanding me or calling the police, as one of the ladies in the backdrop suggested she do, she thanked me. *She thanked me.* She thanked me for helping Olivia. Her cheeks turned red and her eyes filled with tears, and in that moment she believed were it not for me, she may have lost her child.

"You should keep a better eye on your daughter," I threatened, my voice and hands shaking like the leaves in the trees, clinging to their branches for dear life.

EDEN

May 11, 2016
Chicago

I sit on the front stoop, hands pressed between my knees to curb their shaking. I stare expectantly down the street, searching for that first glimmer of yellow to come bobbing along, the school bus, with Jessie on it. I check the time on my watch, knowing down to the minute what time the school bus arrives, but not having the tenacity to wait another three, because if I have to wait much longer I might get cold feet.

I need to get this over and done with. I need for this to be through.

I've combed and curled my hair. I lathered blush onto my cheeks for color, not so that I'll look nice, but so that I look alive, my current pallid tone far more synonymous with death and dying than with vigor. If I look healthy and robust, then maybe Jessie won't be as concerned. I wear a nice shirt. I plaster a smile to my face, one that sours the longer I wait.

I practice the words I'll soon say, saying them aloud so that I can get control of my cadence and rhythm, so that my voice doesn't shake the way it often does when I'm scared. Truth be told, I am scared, yes. I'm absolutely terrified. Though I won't dare say that to Jessie; for Jessie's sake, I'll put on a brave face.

The braking of the school bus sounds to me like the screech of a barn owl. I watch as Jessie clambers down the massive steps on the heels of her classmates, eyes lost on the ground as they often are these days. Her backpack is heavy; she slumps forward to counter the weight of it and I force back tears, knowing that my days of watching Jessie emerge from the school bus are coming quickly to an end.

I smile and she knows, the moment she arrives, that something is wrong.

"What's happened?" she asks, staring at me with the deadpan expression of a teenage girl, one that hides a legion of feelings behind that single blank stare. Sadness, confusion, fear. Her eyes—oh, how blue they are! Even to this day, they shake me to the core—are poker-faced. But not for long.

As I take her in, I realize that though she's wise beyond her years, she's still a child. A child who will be an orphan soon. I pat at the step beside me and tell her to sit down, cursing myself for trying too hard to look nice. I forget in that moment everything that I'd planned to say—all the wise old adages on life and death that I prepared to quote—and say outright to her instead, "Jessie, I'm dying," my voice flat and even, just barely above a whisper, trying desperately to stay calm for her sake. "I'm going to die," I say as that inexpressive demeanor cracks before me and tears rush to Jessie's blue eyes, flooding them instantly, a flash flood of tears.

I stare at her stoically, trying not to cry as Jessie breaks down before me. But it's hard to do. Jessie rushes into me, throwing her arms around my shoulders and neck. She pulls me in tightly as I purr into her ear, "Now, now. Don't cry. Everything will be all right," enveloping her in my arms, patting her back, stroking her hair.

"I'm not scared," I tell her, lying through my teeth because these are the words she needs to hear. "Sooner or later we all die, Jessie. It's only a matter of time. And this is mine."

To say I'm not heartsick would be a lie. To say I don't feel ashamed would be too.

Because after everything I did to make Jessie a part of my world, I'm leaving her alone to fend for herself, and for this, I feel guilty as sin.

JESSIE

I'M LYING IN BED when I hear a noise from outside. It makes me jump suddenly, makes me spring inches from the mattress and into the air.

What I expect to see when I look outside is a garbage can lid getting hurled to the ground, one of those galvanized steel ones clanging to the concrete. Because that's the sound I hear, the din of metal on concrete, and I imagine a colony of hulking rats climbing on shoulders to scale the garbage can, working together to carry off whatever's inside.

But instead when I peel the shade back and gaze out, I see nothing.

The moon, the stars are nowhere to be seen tonight. It's pitch-black outside.

For hours on end I find myself staring into the black nothingness that is Ms. Geissler's home. My body shakes from the cold, though as always I sweat. And I think that I have a fever, because that's the way it feels to me. Icy cold on the inside, but sweating through layers of clothes, my skin damp with sweat.

My clothes stick to me as my teeth chatter. I'm not sure I have it in me to survive another night. I wonder what a panic attack feels like, a breakdown. I think that's what's happening to me.

My eyes adjust to the darkness, making out shapes. The blackened windows, the balcony suspended three stories in the air on stilts, the flat roofline, the porch, the sliding glass door.

As I stare, I watch a squirrel leap from the branches of an oak tree and onto the rooftop. It vanishes into the eaves of the rooftop, as voices speak to me through the floor register again. *Peripheral cooling*, they say this time, and *mottling of the skin*, their voices weak and watered down, far away from here. But I can't be bothered this time to run and throw myself down over the metal grate because I know they won't hear me if I do. Even if I scream at them through the vent, they won't reply because they never do. Because they're only in my mind.

I hear the sound of footsteps too, quiet, restrained footsteps that slink up through the floor register and into the room with me. A giggle.

Shh, someone says, voice suppressed. *Let her sleep.*

I can't turn away from the window. Like bugs drawn to a light at night, I can't bring myself to look away. The window is the color of ebony, of charcoal. It's jet-black, the window shade motionless, completely inert.

I take in the rectangular shape of the glass itself—narrow and tall—the stagnancy of the shade. There is no one there. Behind the window and the shade, the room is empty and dark.

Until it's not.

Because, at three in the morning, the light flicks on.

There's an immediacy to it, a sudden unexpectedness. So much so that I almost fall from the edge of the bed. It happens all at once. A lamp turns on and the shades go up at the same time. The room becomes flooded with light.

For the first time I have a clear view of the room inside. What I see is a bedroom of sorts. An attic room, one space divvied up by three windows. Like a triptych, a painting where three canvas panels come together to create one scene.

In the first, a bed's headboard is pressed up against a wall paneled with a dated oak that stretches from floor to ceiling. The bed is unmade, a marshmallow-white comforter pulled down a foot from the head of the bed, pillows lay flat. There is a lamp on beside the mattress that lobs the soft yellow light across the room.

In the second canvas is the foot of the bed and the bottom two vertical columns of a four-poster bed frame. There is a wooden door on the back wall that leads to a hall. Or a closet. It's closed, so I don't know where it goes. A random cord dangles from the ceiling, belonging to seemingly nothing. At some point in its life, it might have been a fan or a light.

In the third canvas is the man.

Which makes me clutch a hand to my mouth, to keep myself from screaming.

He's leaned up against the window, the very same window where someone has been standing behind the shade watching me. His back is turned to me, as he sits on a ledge, pressing his back to the glass. He's dressed in brown, all of it, everything I can see, blending into the walls. Camouflage, a disguise. His hair is brown, pruned close to his head. I can't see his face or his eyes.

I stare at him for minutes, unmoving, he and I both frozen in place.

And then he rises. And as he does, I see that he is tall. He stretches in place, hands above his head, back arched. His stride is long and decisive. He crosses the room in three easy steps—what might take me eight or ten—all with his back in my direction, as if he knows I'm watching him. As if he knows, and he's toying with me. Playing a game of peekaboo. Of blind man's bluff.

His hands hang limply by his sides. I set my own hands on the window glass, as if reaching for the man on the other side of it.

I can feel it beneath my skin, something I can't quite put my finger on. Something about this man strikes a chord with me. His stature, his posture, the color of his hair. I've seen him before. Like Michelangelo's statue of David. You'd know it by David's carriage even if you never saw his face. He stands with his hand on his hips, left knee bent just a bit. His head is pitched to the right, looking at something off in the distance, something only he can see. Not me.

As my eyes fall to his right arm, I notice a watch on his wrist. A watch on his right wrist, which means to me that he, like the man in the photograph, is left-handed. I think of the man standing there in Mom's photograph in the saggy blue jeans. An afterthought to the lake and the boat and the trees. An addendum tucked neatly away in parenthesis. Almost forgotten, but not quite. I race to my bag and withdraw the photograph, holding it to the window so that I can see.

The stature is the same. Not just similar, but the same.

He's the man from Mom's photograph.

And then he turns, wheeling toward the window, quickly, in an instant. My hand slips unintentionally from my mouth as a scream slips out. I hold my breath, taking in his trim beard and his sun-tanned skin, knowing I've seen him before. I don't blink and I don't breathe. Because I know this man. It isn't just a hunch. Because there on his forearm is the very same scar, harder to see from the distance, but undeniably there. A six-inch gash, one that stretches clear from his wrist to beneath the cuff of a shirt, the skin around it puckered and pink.

And only then do I remember that the man in the photograph also had a scar.

As did the man at the garden. The one who sat reading Mom's obituary and looking sad.

The scar is the smoking gun. The one I was looking for. The one I couldn't see.

They're not two men who I've been searching for, but rather one man. And though it feels unimaginable, impossible, outrageous and far-fetched, I know it's true.

This man is my father.

He knows that I am here. He knows that I am here and he's come for me.

Because why else would he be there?

Now that I see them, his eyes are like hazelnuts, small and dark. He stares at me. Like me, he doesn't blink.

And then he steps from the window and reaches for the lamp. It turns off and then on again. A distress signal. An SOS. Morse code. Three short, three long, three short flashes of light. Save me.

He's speaking to me. Communicating.

I rise from the bed, sitting on the edge of it. I force my feet into a pair of gym shoes. The shoes resist. My feet have been sweating. They're tacky and they don't slip easily on. The laces of my shoes remain untied, trailing me as I go down the treacherous steps. I race out the front door, leaving it open wide, and across the dew-covered lawn.

At first I don't think. I just go.

Blades of grass reach out to tickle my legs as I cross the yard. The grass is long, in need of a trim, and my legs are bare, wearing only a pair of shorts. The air is nippy and brisk, but still, somehow, I sweat. It comes streaming down my hairline, gathering like swimming pools beneath my arms.

And then, ten or twenty feet from the carriage home, I start to question myself. What am I doing?

Suddenly I'm scared.

Three times I stop to get my bearings, looking around, in front of me and behind. Listening. A tree reaches out for me, brushes my arm, its leaves like the gentle caress of a human hand. I jerk back, startled and afraid.

It's dark outside. So dark that I can't see what's three feet before my eyes. I don't know what's there, if anything's there. My heart pounds inside me. "Is anyone there?" I call out, but no one replies.

Above me, I'm keenly aware that the blaze of light from the third-floor bedroom has gone dark. The house is black, no light anywhere. I think about going back, about turning around and going home. Of crawling onto the bed, of hiding beneath the sheets where I'll be safely on base.

But then I come to a spot that's halfway to the greystone and halfway back. I'm stuck in the middle, and the thought of going back seems as ominous as moving forward, especially since I left the door open wide. By now, who knows who's let themselves inside.

I hear scavengers in the distance. Raccoons, crows, rats. A creature scampers away from me on the lawn. Ringed tail. Masked face. Footprints like human hands. And I imagine a contorted human crawling by on all fours, releasing a guttural growl at me. Running away.

I make my way along the brick paver patio and toward the front door. There I climb the steps to the front door. Nearly ten of them, each tread precariously thin. At the top I pause to catch my breath. I breathe in, holding the air in my lungs. Absorbing it. Letting it fill my cells and bob through my bloodstream like a buoy at sea.

Two sidelights flank the solid mahogany door. I see my bedraggled reflection in each as I stand with my hand on my heart, gasping for air. My hair stands every which way; my skin is a bloodless white, deathly pale. There are purple bags beneath my eyes.

I knock on the door. It's a knock that's uncertain at first, but one that becomes more certain with each second that passes by. Once, twice, three times I knock. There's no reply.

Before I know it, I've knocked twenty-three times, each knock progressively louder, so that by number twenty-three, the knock is a pound. I raise my arm again but before I can bang once more, the porch light switches on. It startles me, the abruptness of it. Though after all this time, it's anything but abrupt.

Suddenly I'm no longer trapped in a black hole but instead doused with a bright white light that makes me go momentarily blind. For a whole six seconds after the front door opens, I see nothing. Just blotches, spots, dots. "Who's there?" I ask, voice still breathless, knowing it can be one of two people standing in the doorframe: the man in the attic window or Ms. Geissler.

"It's three in the morning, Jessie," she says to me. Her words are tired and annoyed. It's Ms. Geissler, who, unlike me, had apparently been sleeping, spared from a night of insomnia, unlike me.

My eyes focus to see her wrapping a red cotton robe around herself, tying the belt into a bow and patting down her hair. "What's the problem, dear?" she asks, her eyebrows scrunched up. "Is everything all right?"

"He's here," I say quickly, taking two small steps toward Ms. Geissler, bridging the gap from her to me. She takes a step in retreat.

"Who's here?" she asks. And I say, "Him. A man. Upstairs."

And it's the blankness of her expression that gets me upset, that makes me snap. That and my overwhelming fatigue, my persistent irritability thanks to a lack of sleep. "You know who I mean. You know exactly who I mean," I say roughly because I know he's here, in her home. She has to know that he's here. She has to *know* him, because why else would he be here? "The man in the window upstairs. The one who's been watching me. He's here."

She presses a hand to her heart. Gasps, "There's a man here? In my home?"

Her face goes white. She makes an offhand effort to peer over her shoulder and into the vacuous foyer as I take another step forward, one that gets my toes just inside her home. But only my toes. She resists, grasping the door hard and putting a foot behind it. She nearly shuts the door in my face. I lose balance, stumbling back onto the concrete stoop.

"I saw him in the window," I tell her, pointing at the staircase behind her. "Upstairs. A man in the third-story window," I say, and at this she relaxes visibly and smiles. She shakes her head and tells me that there's no one in the third-story bedroom, her voice so sure that for a second I believe it. She says again that no one's been in that room for months. Not since the squirrel incident, and then I think she's going to rehash it for me, the whole story about the squirrels inhabiting the third floor. I know now that it isn't true because there were never squirrels in that room but rather a man, my father, who she's been hiding from me all these days.

"The attic ladder," she tells me this time instead, "it's a pulldown thing," at which, like a mime, she grabs for an imaginary string over her left shoulder and pulls. "Broken for a couple of months. Wouldn't you know it," she says, "the exterminator managed to break the darn thing. I just haven't gotten around to getting it fixed."

"But I saw him," I insist, and she says quite simply, "You must be mistaken. There's no one there. Because how would anyone get up there, Jessie, without a ladder?"

It seems so sensible, the way that she says it. And for a fraction of a second, I doubt myself as she hoped I would do. But then his image returns to me—him standing there in the window, looking out at me—and I know that she's lying. That she's keeping him from me. Hiding him from the world just as Mom has always done.

"Let me in," I insist, pushing the door against the weight of her, and she says to me, "Now, now, Jessie. You had a bad dream, that's all," but of course this can't be true.

"You were dreaming there was a man in the room," she says to me. She reaches out a hand to mine but I pull briskly away. "Just a bad dream, that's all. It will all be clearer come morning."

"I know what I saw," I tell her, voice cracking. But her face is suddenly so pacific, so kind, and she asks if I'd like for her to walk me back to the carriage home so I don't have to go alone. It's dark out, she says. Hard to navigate the way. "But not to worry," she tells me. "I know this yard like the back of my hand," and she reaches for my arm to lead the way home. She winks at me and says, "And besides, I have a flashlight." And there it is, in the pocket of her robe. She flicks it on as if this conversation is over, as if she's put my worries to rest and now I can go home, feeling assured that there's no man in this home. No man watching me.

But I yank my arm away. "Why are you hiding him from me?" I ask. My voice becomes elevated, high-pitched, defensive. "Why don't you want me to see him? Why don't you want me to know that he's there?"

And then I let slip the one thought that's put down roots in the back of my mind, that's replaced all logical thought.

"Why are you keeping my father from me?" I scream.

Her face falls flat and she goes white, even whiter than she was before. She shakes her head, presses a hand to her mouth but says nothing. Nothing at first, before she carefully breathes out, treading lightly, "You're quite sure you saw a man in there?"

My heart nearly sings in relief. She believes me. *She believes me.*

I nod vigorously.

"Perhaps you're right then. Perhaps someone is there," she says with concern as she draws back the door and lets me in. "Why don't you go see," she suggests.

I think of my father, so close within reach. I soar past Ms. Geissler on the staircase, taking the steps two at a time up to the second floor. There I stand beneath that little hatch that leads up to the third floor. I listen for footsteps at first, hearing nothing, but remembering that I've stood here before and heard something.

He was here that night. Standing above me. Was he trying to contact me, to get my attention? To let me know that he was here?

I reach for the cord and give it a tug. The ladder unfurls before me, unfolding into makeshift steps. Two of the steps are split. Another is missing, just as Ms. Geissler said.

She warns me, "The steps, Jessie. They're not safe," though I go anyway, clutching the hand railing, which is unstable at best. "Bring the flashlight with you," she says, attempting to hand it to me. But I don't take it.

"There's a light," I tell her. "I saw the light. I don't need a flashlight," but she tells me to take it anyway, as she gives it a shake. I take it only to appease her, tucking it under the crook of an arm.

I begin to climb. I move slowly, walking though I want to run. The fourth step gives on me, splintering, and I shriek.

"Jessie!" Ms. Geissler yells, asking if I'm okay.

"I'm fine, I'm fine," I say, gripping the railing harder and pulling myself up and over the broken step.

Ms. Geissler makes no attempt to follow, but stands instead at the bottom of the stairs. She crosses her arms against her chest, watching as I go. She tells me to be careful. She tells me to go slow.

I reach the top step and hoist myself into the attic. The room is murky. Out the open windows, the sun is lost somewhere beneath the horizon. It's still nighttime, and yet there's a flush to the sky. Morning will be here soon.

I barely make out a lamp, the same lamp that for the past few nights radiated light. One of those old Tiffany-style lamps, with the stained-glass shade. But when I go to turn it on, nothing happens. The lamp is dead, the lightbulb burned out. I turn the knob around and around but still nothing happens. All I hear is the idle click that mimics my heartbeat.

I orbit the room, looking for him. I trip over things that I can't see. I hold my breath and listen, but I hear nothing. "Hello?" I ask, more begging than inquisitive.

"Come out so I can see you," I whisper to the man. My father. I tell him I know that he's here. That I want to see him, to meet him. That I've been waiting my whole life. I take small steps around the room, using my hands as a guide. My heartbeat pounds in my ear as I hold my breath, listening for breath, for footsteps, for him. A game of Marco Polo.

"Marco," I chant aloud to myself, but there's no reply.

I reach for the flashlight Ms. Geissler gave me. I turn it on. It casts a meager glow around the room, not much but enough. The light bounces on the wall from the tremor of my hands.

What I find is a wall of cardboard bankers boxes—dozens of them—with holes chewed out. Rodent droppings and old building supplies. Gallons of paint, boards of hardwood, boxes of screws and nails.

A makeshift nest—clumps of twigs and leaves—is nestled into the corner of the attic, and on it, there's some hairless and fetal-looking thing that looks like it's just climbed out of its mother's womb. A mother squirrel stands over her baby, scowling at me.

What I don't find is a four-poster bed. A white comforter. A cord dangling from the ceiling. A man. None of those things are here. It's just a ratty and dilapidated attic inhabited by squirrels, just as Ms. Geissler has said.

I feel like I can't breathe. The pain in my chest is immense, in my arm, my jaw, my abdomen. The room is empty, though as sure as I live and breathe, I saw a man here.

I stand looking out the window and toward the carriage home. I don't know how long I stand there, staring, thinking that maybe he will appear. That somehow we'll have swapped places. But he never appears.

I make my way back down the steps, where Ms. Geissler stands waiting for me. On her face is a complacent look. An *I told you so* look.

"Find what you were looking for?" she asks, though I can't speak. A lump forms in my throat, but I will not cry. I cannot cry.

"I told you, Jessie," she gloats, and I know then that she did this only to humor me. "There is no man there. Squirrels. Only squirrels." And then she thrusts the ladder back up so that the squirrels can't take over the rest of her home.

She shows me the door, but before closing it on me, she first asks, "Did you ever think, Jessie, that you're only seeing what you want to see? You need help." She all but pushes me out of her house and slams the door behind me. I hear the sound of a lock clicking shut.

The porch light goes off, and once again I am submerged in darkness.

I set myself down on the top porch step, feeling exhausted. My body aches from the lack of sleep, from ten nights of my mind depriving me of sleep. It's an insidious way to die, I think, from lack of sleep because there is nothing gory about it, no blood, no guts, and yet the effects are just as gruesome. I know because I'm living it.

As the sun begins to rise on the eleventh day, it's only a matter of time until I die.

This is what it feels like knowing you're about to die.

This is what Mom must have felt like knowing she would die.

I sit on the stoop and talk to myself, blathering about what's happening to me, hoping to make sense of it, but striking out. I can't make sense of it. I count to ten to make sure I can still do it, losing track at number six. I cry, a proper cry, shoulders heaving, the first in a long time. My heart, my head, everything hurts. I fold over sideways on the porch step, rolling up into the fetal position, pulling my knees into my chest, wondering if this is where I'll die.

All at once I look up and have no clue where I am.

By now the sun is just barely beginning to rise. It turns the world from black to gray. One by one people appear on the street before me. Joggers, early-morning commuters.

As a hint of daylight fills the sky, I suddenly catch a glimpse of something on the other side of the street. It's a man in jeans and a jacket, bustling down the street with his hands in the pockets of his pants. His chin is tucked into the coat to keep warm, and there's a hat on his head, an orange baseball cap, and for this reason I know that it's him.

But how did he get here? How did he slip out of Ms. Geissler's home without me seeing him?

And that's when the answer comes to me. The balcony. The one that leads from street level up to the third floor.

He climbed down the balcony before I had a chance to go up the stairs, sneaking out as I cut across Ms. Geissler's lawn. That's when the light in the window went black. It went black because he'd already left. As I examined the attic with a flashlight, he was at ground level, looking in through the windows, watching me.

I rise quickly, calling for him, waving my hands to get his attention. I fall down the porch steps, all six or eight or ten of them. "Excuse me!" I scream, but if he sees, if he hears, he doesn't look and he doesn't wave back. He doesn't slow down. He never stops moving. He's in a hurry. He has somewhere to be.

I run as fast as my legs will carry me, which isn't fast.

The twitch in my eye has gone from one eye to two, so that they both spasm and I can't get them to stop. My hands shake. My arms ache, my legs ache, my back aches and, as I move across the street, not looking either way before I cross, a passing car nearly runs into me. The driver slams on their brakes to keep from hitting me.

I stand there in the street, three inches before the hood of the car, staring at the panicked driver, myself unfazed. Because I don't have it in me to be scared. The driver shoots me a dirty look. When I don't move, she douses the window with windshield wiper fluid, splashing me as she hoped to do. She screams out the window at me, and only then do I go.

By the time I turn away from the car, the man has advanced a quarter of a block or more. He's harder to see than he was before, farther away. Every now and then I see the orange cap bobbing and weaving down the street, but then it gets blocked by a low-hanging tree limb and I can't see him.

I panic; I've lost him.

But then again it returns, and I follow along.

I listen for the sound of footsteps, and though I'm a half a block away, I hear them. They're tenacious and quick, and for this reason, I know that they're his. I follow, having only the drum of footsteps to guide me, the drum of footsteps, steady like a beating heart.

But then, as I round the corner and pick up the pace, I hear something else too. They're words, breathed into my ear. *Earth to Jessie*, I hear, and I spin suddenly on my heels, glaring at a man who follows from behind. He's dressed in a suit and tie, an overcoat draped over him, smoking a cigarette. In the other hand, a coffee cup.

"What are you looking at?" he grills, tossing the cigarette to the ground. He grinds it into the concrete with the toe of a shoe and immediately reaches into his breast pocket for another. I turn away, saying nothing.

And then another noise comes. It's so soft, so subtle, hardly more than a whoosh of air against my ear, as I come to a red light and stop. *Psst*, says the noise, like the buzzing of a mosquito in my ear. I'm at a street corner, my eyes peeled to the walk signal, waiting for my turn to cross, hoping it was soon before I lose track of the orange cap. The street is congested, early-morning rush hour dissecting me from it.

Psst. Hey you, I hear, *hey, Jessie*, and I jump, my eyes turning away from the street to see who it is and who's calling me. The man with his cigarette is gone now, around the corner and out of sight, leaving a wake of smoke trailing behind. Behind me stands a corner coffee shop, the first floor of a three-story light-colored brick building. There are people milling around outside, just a small handful of them, though their bodies are turned away from me.

Jessie, I hear again, and I snap to attention. Who said that? Who's calling me?

There's a sudden chill in the air. I shiver. I pull my sweatshirt tighter around me, eyeing the people outside the coffee shop and taking them all in. But there's no one here that I know.

I turn away but still can't shake the feeling that someone is following. That someone is watching me. It's a gut feeling and there, at the fringes of my awareness, I feel it. Eyes on me though they're outside my field of view, burning a hole in my back.

On the other side of the intersection I pause, looking backward one last time, because I just can't shake that sense of being watched. And then I hear it again.

Psst. Hey. Hey, Jessie, and I turn suddenly, a spinning toy top on its tip. I almost lose balance; I almost fall to the ground. The world spins on its axis and I don't know what to blame for it, the lack of sleep or grief.

A man and woman walk behind me now, holding hands. Midthirties, pushing forty. They look slick and sophisticated, she taller than him in high heel boots, though they're both pinched and slim. "Did you call me?" I ask, but they exchange a look and tell me no. They part ways, slipping around me, one on either side. Once they pass, they rejoin hands, looking into each other's eyes before gazing over their shoulders at me. They laugh. I hear words giggled between them. *Lunatic* and *crazy.* They're talking about me.

And then there's a hand on my back. A warm hand that touches my bare skin from behind. It caresses me as every single hair on my arms and legs goes erect and I can't help myself. I scream. I jerk away, spinning around to find no one there. There's no one standing on the sidewalk behind me, though I hear it again. I feel it again. Lips pressed to my ear, whispering, *Earth to Jessie.*

I shake my head, willing it away, telling myself that it's nothing. That it's only the wind. I look up, coming to, realizing that I've lost track of the man I am sure now is my father. He's gone. I listen for the sound of his footsteps, searching the horizon for the orange baseball cap. I start to panic—eyes desperately lurching this way and that, hoping to see that pinprick of orange way off in the distance. I stagger down the street like a drunk. I can no longer hold my body upright because it's begun to collapse on me. I try running but I can't run, and so it's a shamble at best, feet dragging.

A hand latches onto my arm, a voice asks if I'm all right. I peer down at the hand on my arm, seeing a spindly hand, a bony hand. Rivers of blue veins roll across it. There's dirt wedged beneath the fingernails, lining the edges of the nail bed, and that's how I know. I know this hand; I'd know this hand anywhere. This is Mom's hand.

My eyes shoot up, taking in the woman draped all in white. She looks nothing like Mom. And yet, she says, "Jessie."

I'm so taken aback that I don't have it in me to respond. She stands before me, a halo of sunlight bearing down on her. She wears a wispy white blouse that billows in the early-morning breeze, the top button undone so I catch a hint of the pale skin beneath. On her bottom half is a skirt, a long one, stretching clear to her feet so that I can't be certain they're there. She looks fragile, delicate and, as she draws her hands through her hair, strands come with it. Clumps of hair fall from her scalp just like that, getting trapped between her thin fingers. Through the thin, floaty blouse I catch sight of her breasts. The breasts flat, nipples gone. Serrated suture marks criss-crossing her chest, the way Mom's used to be.

"Mom," I say. As impossible as it sounds, this woman standing before me is Mom.

"Mom," I beg this time, trembling as I reach for her, wanting nothing more than to draw her close, to wrap my arms around her shoulders and pull her in tight. I'm crying now, tears falling freely from my eyes. "Mom!" I plead, but before me she pulls suddenly back, sharply back, her eyebrows pleated. Her mouth drops open and she asks, "Do you need me to call someone for you? An ambulance, maybe?" as she stands a good three feet away and retreats a step for every step that I draw near. I grab for her again, but she tugs her arms out of reach from mine, setting them behind her back.

"I'm not your mom," she states. And it's so assertive, so firm, it gives me pause.

My eyes calibrate the image I see, the woman with the red hair and green eyes dressed in all white. Except that her hair is intact and what I saw as suture marks are instead lace.

It's not Mom.

I drop my hands to my sides, as she asks again if I need help, if there's someone she can call for me. I bark out *no*, though all at once I realize that I have no idea where I am, that the streets and the buildings are unrecognizable to me. That I've never seen them in my whole life.

Where am I?

How did I get here?

A siren wails off in the distance.

A car door squeaks open and then slams closed.

People push past me on the sidewalk, in a hurry to get here or there as the woman disappears into the crowds.

I cup my hands around my mouth, screaming up and down the street for my father.

And then, when I think all hope is lost, I see him. Out of the corner of my eye, somewhere in my peripheral vision, I catch a glimpse of orange as it slips behind the glass door of an apartment building on the other side of the street. I go to it, tugging on the door handle to follow him in, but find the door locked.

I press my face to the glass, staring inside. The lobby of the building is near empty. It's dated and retro with 1970s linoleum tile, the kind that seeps with asbestos. Where are we? Does he live here? Does he know someone who lives here? The tile is partly covered with some sort of commercial carpeting, bland and gray, to disguise the ugly tile. A postal worker separates mail into a million bins and though I knock on the glass for him to let me in, he ignores me. Either he can't hear or he doesn't care. He just goes about sorting the mail as if I'm not here, as if he can't see me, as if I'm invisible.

And I wonder then if I am invisible, if I am already dead.

I tug again on the tempered glass door. The hollow metal frame rattles in place. I smash the heel of my hand against the glass to no avail.

I begin to make my way around the building, in search of another way in. A freight entrance, maybe. But before I've gone twenty feet, a tenant comes tearing out of the building, eyes set on an incoming bus. I race back to the door, managing to slip in a hand in time to prevent it from latching. I sail inside. Behind me, the door closes tight.

My eyes look to the left just as a flash of orange disappears behind a door. A black-and-white sign beside it reads Stairs, the steps themselves explicated by a zigzag line. He's going upstairs. I follow along, racing toward the stairwell and after him.

I press hard on the steel door's push bar, making my way into the stairwell. I run, scaling the steps two at a time, clinging to the banister with a sweaty hand, pulling myself up the concrete stairs. The air is stuffy, suffocating, hard to breathe. There's a notable lack of oxygen in here. It's unventilated; there's no access to fresh air. I choke on nothing and it takes a moment to regain my composure, to stop myself from choking on the musty air.

There are sixteen floors in the building. Above me, I hear footsteps as they climb upward at a better clip than me. He's going too fast. I can't catch up. I call to him, but if he hears, he doesn't let up.

Somewhere between the eighth and ninth floors, my feet slip on the edge of the step, on some sort of tactile paving, yellow, rubbery lumps that are meant to have the opposite effect, to prevent people from falling. But not me. Rather my body keeps going, the momentum of the run thrusting me forward at a blistering pace. But, thanks to the tactile paving, my feet slow down, two things which are mutually exclusive because I can't stop and go at the same time. And so instead I trip, feet skidding beneath me. My body jerks, my hand latching on to the banister to keep me upright. Pain radiates down my arm, into my hands, seeping into the muscles of my rib cage, my neck, my back. But I keep going. He is right there, within reach. I can't lose him this time.

I scurry up yet another flight of stairs. I keep running, up the steps. Though before I know it, we've reached the top floor. The highest floor in the entire building, the sixteenth floor. The end of the line, I think at first, but not quite. Because he's still climbing. Because there's still one more flight of stairs, different from all the rest. More industrial, more heavy-duty. Not meant for everyday pedestrian use. It's more of an elaborate stepladder than stairs. But I scale it nonetheless, ten feet behind him. Beside it, a sign reads Roof Access.

There's a hatch at the top, a single slab of aluminum with a hinged lid. He pushes through it and I follow, mounting the last few steps of the stepladder and breaking free onto the rooftop of the apartment building.

At the top, the hatch door closes all on its own behind me. The wind forces it shut, the sound of it slamming closed, startling me.

I reach for the handle to tug it open again, finding it suddenly locked.

I'm trapped on the building's rooftop.

The city surrounds me. A panorama. With arms outstretched, I can't help but spin, taking it all in. Enjoying the view, knowing fully well this may be the last thing my eyes ever see.

The buildings and skyscrapers rise up like dominos around me and I stand on my own domino, waiting for my turn to fall. The lake is bluer than I've ever seen, a luminous blue that makes the blue of the sky inferior. An underling. Sunlight reflects off the glass of the buildings so that the whole world is suddenly aglow.

I circulate the building, looking for him, for my father.

Now that we're here, he's somehow disappeared. He's hiding from me. I call to him, but he doesn't reply. "Hello!" I scream. "I know you're up here!"

The roof itself is filled with all sorts of miscellany. An industrial cooling system. Exhaust vents. Access panels to this and that. It makes it hard to see. I search among various parts of the cooling system, looking for him. They're big, boxy things that make noise from time to time, like the whirring of a fan inside. I hold my breath. I refuse to breathe. Breathing makes noise and I don't want to make noise. I only want to listen.

A hand strokes me again, whispering into my ear, *Earth to Jessie.*

I pull back, drawing sharply away from the strange caress.

To the west end of the building, there's a fire escape, one that runs from ground level clear to the top, a thing so basic, so rudimentary, it terrifies me. It's little more than a metallic swimming pool ladder, four treads that lift you from the rooftop to the other side of the building.

That's where my father stands. On the fire escape. Now that the hatch is closed, the only way out of here, aside from a free fall, is the fire escape.

I go there, legs shaking. I call to him, voice more subdued now that I see him. Now that I've found him. Now that he's in reach. He's climbed over the roof wall, a three-foot thing, and onto the fire escape.

My hand reaches out for the ladder's handrail and I grab a hold of it and pull myself up. My hands are dripping and slippery. I go up one tread. It gives on me and I fall back down to the ground. I start again. One step and then two, watching on in horror as my father begins his descent without me, jogging down the steps at a steady clip, unfazed by the great height.

"Stop, please," I beg, hearing the anguish in my voice. "Please, don't go."

As I near the top, there's a moment of calm that comes and goes so quickly I almost don't notice it. For one split second the world is still. I'm at peace. The sun moves higher and higher into the sky, yellow-orange glaring at me through the buildings, making me peaceful and warm. My hands rise beside me as a bird goes soaring by. As if my hands are wings, I think in that moment what it would be like to fly.

And then it comes rushing back to me.

I'm hopelessly alone. Everything hurts. I can no longer think straight; I can no longer see straight; I can no longer speak. I don't know who I am anymore. If I am anyone.

And I know in that moment for certain: I am no one.

I think what it would feel like to fall. The weightlessness of the plunge, of gravity taking over, of relinquishing control. Giving up, surrendering to the universe.

There's a flicker of movement beneath me. A flash of brown, and I know that if I wait any longer, it will be too late. The decision will no longer be mine. I cry out one more time. And then I go, legs convulsing as I swing one leg over the edge of the building and onto the fire escape on the other side. I have to force myself to do it. It takes everything I have. All that's on the other side is a measly shelf, an overhang, that hovers seventeen floors above land.

I make my way toward him, but he's moving far too fast for me. And I'm scared, looking down where, beneath me, the earth tilts and sways. I'm overcome with vertigo. I feel nauseous; I feel like I could be sick. The steps of the fire escape are perforated to prevent snow and ice from forming, which does nothing for me now. I can see straight through them to the street beneath my feet. People like ants walk up and down the street, minding their own business, paying no attention to me. Cabs like matchbooks soar past.

The steps beneath me are corroded and weak. A handful are missing. In some spots, the fire escape pulls away from the building's masonry, bolts no longer holding tight. I take the steps two at a time, though they clatter each time my feet hit, the entire fire escape bucking beneath me. I have to take long strides over the missing steps.

I make it down only half a flight of steps before my knees give.

As they do, I lurch forward, staggering. I fall down the second half flight of stairs. The railing at the end is corroded, as much of the fire escape is. It's the red-orange of rust. As my body goes hurtling into it, the spindles give and I slip straight through, with nothing there to prevent my fall.

As I tumble off the side of the fire escape, my head swims.

I take one final look at the great distance to the ground, the distance I'll soon fall.

All at once, I'm falling. My legs follow the rest of me, feet making a last-ditch effort to cling to something, trying in vain to tether themselves to the steel of the fire escape. I try to grab it with a hand, but it slips straight through time and again, as I soar along beside it, unable to grab hold.

My arms and legs kick. They do the doggy paddle as I soar downward. I flail and kick, my body splayed as air rushes from beneath me, wrapping my hair around my face. I can see nearly nothing. Not that there's much to see anyway, other than the blue of the sky as I fall. There's no air resistance. The air does nothing to slow me down. My hands make a meek attempt to protect my head, some sort of Pavlovian response, as I thrust my feet downward, knowing my only chance of survival hinges on landing feetfirst. It doesn't work. I can't get them down. Another fire escape landing soars past but I can't get to it in time.

My insides scuttle to my center from the speed, from the velocity of the fall. A fall that feels like forever. Like I am forever falling. My face molded in fear.

I open my mouth to scream, but nothing comes out.

EDEN

October 3, 1997
Egg Harbor

IT'S BECOME AN ITCH that I can't reach. A hunger that no amount of food can satiate. A drought that a thousand rainfalls can't fix.

That unquenchable need to be a mother.

I think about it morning, noon and night.

At night I lie awake not sleeping, wondering how I will ever be a mother.

I don't know that I have it in me to wait until Aaron's and my divorce is complete.

There is adoption, of course, but as a single mother going through divorce proceedings and carrying an exorbitant amount of debt, I hardly think I'm a suitable candidate for adoption.

And so I must find another way.

I go to work early and I leave late, spending those extra few minutes staring at the babies through the nursery room glass. On my lunch break I eat quickly so that I have time to wander down to the labor and delivery unit and salivate over the newborns while the nursery room nurses tend to their every need, the bottles and clean diapers and the endless rocks in the rocking chairs.

I don't want to feel the way I do.

I'm not a bad person, not by any means, and yet it's an addiction to me. A disease. I'm unable to abstain from thinking about babies, from wanting a baby, from craving a baby as one does gambling or cocaine.

I've lost control of my own behavior. I don't know what I'm capable of, what I might do, and that in itself terrifies me. Once I was very rule abiding; I always did as I was told.

But now my neurotransmitters are in disrepair and quite simply, I'm not the person I used to be. That Eden is gone, replaced with someone I scarcely recognize anymore, someone I don't know.

October 7, 1997
Egg Harbor

Something happened today.

I had eaten my lunch—roast beef on rye from the hospital's cafeteria—sitting all alone at one of the smaller round tables, nibbling quickly, quietly and staring out the window at the visitors and outpatients who came and went through the revolving front doors, realizing how utterly alone I felt as the other tables spilled over with groups of four, five, six, all involved in conversations that didn't have a thing to do with me. Oh, how I felt so alone. When I was through eating, I set my tray beside the trash can and then went to visit the babies in the nursery.

A drug addict needing her fix.

As I stood there, peering through glass at the newborns sound asleep in their knitted blankets with their knitted hats, one little one in particular caught my eye, the name in the bassinet reading Jade Cutter. It was the name that caught my attention, not necessarily the baby herself, though she was perfect in every way, from the roundness of her head to the redness of her cheeks. But more so, it was the slip of pink paper in the bassinet that caught my eye, the one that listed her name, date and time of birth, pediatrician, and the names of her parents.

Joseph and Miranda Cutter.

Joe and Miranda.

They'd had their baby girl. They'd had their baby girl and they didn't tell me.

She was swaddled in a pink cotton blanket, eyes closed, mouth parted as she breathed in her sleep. A single hand had forced its way from the blanket, but Jade seemed unmindful of this, unlike other infants—I'd come to learn from my time spent observing them in the nursery—whose limbs needed to be controlled so that they could sleep. There was dark hair, a mound of it, that sneaked out from the edges of the pink hat and, though they were shut tight, I had to imagine her eyes too were dark like Joe's, though these, of course, were things that often changed over time.

And in that moment little Jade's eyes parted and she gazed at me, it seemed, and I was stricken with a sudden, purposeful, persistent need to hold her in my arms.

I stepped into the nursery, greeting the ladies there by name. There were two of them, one older and one younger, both of whom I knew fairly well. How many months had I been stopping by, telling the tale of how I was working hard to earn my degree so I could be one of them, nursery room nurses who tended to newborn babies? How many times had they let me into the nursery, allowing me to watch as they changed diapers and swaddled with the expertise of someone who'd done it a million times? How many times had they let me stroke an infant's cheek in his or her sleep, never once needing to remind me to wash my hands because I always remembered?

But not this time.

"You'll need to stay in the hall, Eden," the older of the two nurses said, a woman by the name of Kathy, and I felt a stabbing sensation in the chest as she pointed to the floor, to an imaginary line that dissected the nursery from the hallway tiles.

That's the line where I was to remain behind.

"But, Kathy," I attempted to argue, but she held up her hands and told me that there had been complaints that they'd been too lax of late, and hospital officials were cracking down on security protocols, and I wondered now if the babies were fitted with tiny security devices on their wee wrists or ankles to keep someone from walking out the front door with them. Someone like me.

"But it's just me," I reassured her, holding up my badge, reminding her that *I work here.*

Except that by that time, she'd turned her back to me and was attending to an infant who'd begun to fuss; she wouldn't let me in, and I could feel my hands begin to shake in withdrawal. There was a tightness in my chest and my head suddenly hurt. For a minute or two, I couldn't breathe. My heart was palpitating, strong, irregular beats that left me lightheaded, though neither of the nurses seemed to notice; no one noticed but me.

And then Joe was there coming to my rescue, as he appeared at the nursery to come lay claim to his baby girl.

"Joe!" I said too loudly, thrilled to see him, knowing that he was my key to that baby. Joe would get Jade out of the nursery; Joe would let me hold and coddle baby Jade as I needed to do.

He said hello to me, and what a nice surprise to see me, and at this, I felt a smile spread widely across my lips. My heartbeat slowed; the tension in my head and neck began to ease.

"Miranda called you to tell you the news?" he asked, but I said no, that I was working, that I had just come to visit the babies in the nursery when I saw baby Jade.

"Congratulations!" I said, offering an awkward embrace. Joe was not a man I knew well, and what I did know came from Miranda's own complaints about him. How he was a jerk, a lousy father. But I couldn't let this deter me now.

"How is Miranda?" I asked, and Joe replied as expected: Miranda was tired, Miranda wanted nothing but to sleep and already I imagined her, sore over her infant's need to eat.

Kathy glided the rolling bassinet out the nursery door to Joe's waiting hands, and when I made an attempt to follow, to accompany Joe to Miranda's room where I would sit on the corner armchair with Jade in my arms as I'd once done with Carter, he said to me, "Another time, Eden? My parents are here," meaning that they already had company, that Joe's mother and father were here to see baby Jade.

That I wasn't welcome in the hospital room with Joe's mother and father because as everyone knows, three's a crowd.

"Just for a minute?" I pleaded, staring at Joe, who looked worse for wear in that moment, tired and jaded. I could see it in his eyes: four children was too much.

I could help him.

I could take a single one off his hands.

Just one child.

"Just to offer my congratulations to Miranda and then I'll go?" I begged—and even I could hear the desperation in my voice—but Joe shook his head, and I felt like a child then, like a five-year-old child who'd just been told no.

Joe said that he'd pass my message along to Miranda and then he turned to go without me. He walked quickly on purpose, faster than my legs could go, and I felt the dismissal a thousandfold then. I was being brushed off, given the cold shoulder as if I carried a stigma on my sleeve.

The stigma of infertility, the stigma of miscarriage, the stigma of a woman whose husband was in the process of divorcing her.

I blinked and Joe was gone, disappeared down the hall and around the corner where I couldn't see him anymore, and immediately the headache returned, the palpitations, the sweat. The hospital walls began closing in on me as in a room nearby a lady, deep in the throes of labor, screamed, and instead of feeling sympathy for her, I felt a surge of jealousy and spite.

Oh, how I wanted to be the one screaming in the throes of labor pain! How I wanted to feel a baby inside me, wedging itself headfirst to get out. How I wanted to feel that baby press between my legs, to feel it crown as doctors and nurses gathered around telling me to push. *Push!*

My feet crept toward her room with instinct, setting my hand on the doorknob and turning it, opening it just a sliver so that I could see in. There was far too much happening inside the room for anyone to hear the door squeak. I stood in the doorway, inching a foot back so no one would see. A Peeping Tom. The door wasn't open and yet it was ajar, not quite closed tight, and through the crack I saw her laid out on her back, gasping from pain. I saw her gather handfuls of blanket in her hands and squeeze, pushing to get that baby out. I heard her scream, this throaty, guttural scream, crude and uninhibited as a nurse on either side told her to push.

"Push!" Her husband stroked her sweaty hair, brushing it out of her eyes. Between her legs was a shock of black and there I stared, wondering just where exactly she ended and the baby began as she pushed again, holding her breath—as I, in turn, held mine, parting my legs ever so and pushing too—bearing down, and this time, as she pushed, a baby came spilling out of her insides, covered in mucous, and the room was filled with a sudden rapturous bliss.

The door slammed shut in my face.

Someone had seen me.

I ran away, out of labor and delivery.

I was due back at my desk in just a moment. Soon the other women in billing would wonder where I had gone, and why I wasn't yet back from lunch. They would tell our manager. I would be given a scolding.

But I couldn't go back to billing at that moment.

I needed to get away.

I got behind the wheel of my car and I drove and drove.

I drove to the chophouse, needing to see Aaron, desperate suddenly to see him, for him to hold me in his arms, to stroke my hair and tell me everything would be all right. If I'm being honest, I was scared of the person I was, scared of the person I'd become. I was quite terrified, if Aaron didn't put a stop to it, of what I might do. My thoughts were scattered, sown like seeds in my mind, and there was no telling which ideas would bloom, the sensible ones like going home and putting myself to bed, or the misguided ones where I return to the hospital and force myself into Joe and Miranda's room, screaming like a lunatic, demanding that they give me their child.

I left the car parked haphazardly across parallel lines on the street outside, nearly a block from the chophouse. Parking in town was never easy to come by. I stepped from the car, my ankle giving on me as it sunk deep into a crater on the street. I shook it off, kept moving, feeling the ligaments beneath my shoes begin to ache and swell.

It had begun to rain outside, the sky darkening. The restaurants, the gift shops, the galleries that lined the street radiated light. They beamed from the inside out, while outside people scattered like roaches in daylight, hiding under canopies and slipping inside stores, seeking shelter, huddled in throngs beneath ample-size golf umbrellas, clutching one another, laughing.

But not me.

I made my way to the chophouse alone, fully intent on going inside. On speaking to Aaron. On begging him to help me, on pleading with him to take me back. I was desperate. What else could I do? The rain came pouring down, permeating my skin, so that I could feel it inside my bones. I hurried past people tucked warmly, drily beneath their umbrellas, no one offering to share. The rib of a passing umbrella poked me in the shoulder, but no apology came thereafter, as if it was my fault, as if it was my shoulder's fault for getting in the way of this man's umbrella.

I closed in on the chophouse, smelling that scent that always followed Aaron home and into bed with us, that coiled around us while we slept. Grease, Worcestershire sauce, the flesh of meat.

But before stepping inside, I caught a fleck of Aaron through the restaurant window, seeing his face through the small partition that separates the kitchen from the dining room. A flyspeck only, but in that flyspeck, there was a lightness about him, a nimbleness, a radiance to his skin. Rain streaked down the window, but I peered past it, watching as a smile danced on the edges of Aaron's face. In the very same fleck some other man made a wisecrack, I could only assume, because then Aaron was laughing, *laughing!*, the edges of his lips reaching upward to the sky like he hadn't done in years. Aaron was laughing and it was beautiful to see, an openmouthed laugh, nothing curbed or restrained about it, and I saw in Aaron's eyes a felicity that I hadn't seen in quite some time. Never did he press his hand to his mouth to hide the smile, but rather chuckled with all of his might.

Aaron was happy. Aaron had found his happy place.

Unlike me, his heart had healed and he was no longer broken. He was whole.

Oh, how I wanted to be there beside him, laughing too.

But I couldn't bring myself to do it, to shatter what had already been fixed. I'd ruin him, that I knew, if I stepped foot into the chophouse, as I imagined the laughter drawing to a sudden close if I walked in, that lovely smile vaporizing from his face at the sight of me.

And so instead, when a hostess poked her head outside and asked if I'd like to take a peek at the menu, I shook my head, scurrying the other way like all the other roaches, seeking shelter indoors from the rain.

It was an upscale restaurant where I went, fine dining with a bar attached, the kind where one might have a glass of wine while waiting for their table to be set. This hostess offered a table, but I strutted straight past her and to the bar—sopping wet, leaving a trail of rainwater behind me as I walked. I climbed onto one of the tall stools and ordered a chardonnay to drink. A chardonnay! The glass came to me full to the rim, a generous pour at the hand of a bartender with cavernous dimples and sparkling blue eyes, a man who must have been six years younger than me, barely old enough to be serving alcohol at an upscale establishment. And yet here he was, and in the moment I felt suddenly old, much older than my twenty-nine years, but that didn't matter. That was the least of my concerns.

With the wine he also brought a dish towel, which I used to towel dry the ends of my hair.

The first sip of wine tasted like battery acid to me.

It choked me on the way down, burning the lining of my esophagus so that the bartender raised an eyebrow at me and asked if I was all right. I pressed a hand to my mouth, nodding, but I wasn't sure that I was all right. The wine settled in the pit of my stomach, and the feeling was a mix of repulsion and nausea, along with a warmth and prickling that I quite liked.

And so I had another sip, wanting the warmth and prickling to have its way with me, to help me forget about Aaron and the miscarriage, all those wasted months trying unavailingly to create a baby.

How stupid I'd been in believing that with Dr. Landry's help we could outsmart nature. Aaron and I were infertile; that was the nature of the beast. That couldn't be changed.

The universe was laughing at me for my arrogance and my vanity.

I took another sip of wine and this time, I didn't choke.

I thought of my baby, of my unborn baby. Of my dead baby. I wondered what she would have looked like had she had a chance to grow full-term. Would she have looked like Aaron, with dark hair and light eyes, or would she have looked like me?

Would she have been a she, or would she have been a he?

I still think about her all the time.

Had she been a girl, I would have named her Sadie.

I raised my glass to my lips and swallowed a mouthful, wondering if she ever crossed Aaron's mind.

Wondering if I ever crossed Aaron's mind.

By the second glass, the wine was no longer battery acid to me. It quenched that *hunger*, that *thirst*, like nothing else in the world was able to do. It spilled through my veins, anesthetizing my arms and legs, dulling my senses. I hadn't had a drop to drink in quite some time and so it didn't take much for the room to start to blur at the edges, for the stool to feel insecure beneath my seat.

With every sip thereafter I became a more youthful version of myself, someone more energetic, someone more carefree.

With every sip I became blissfully forgetful, forgetting at once that I was a soon-to-be divorcée, a woman who would never have a baby.

It was a quiet night, a Tuesday night, and so the bartender happily filled his free time speaking to me—about what, I hardly remember anymore—and, after that second glass of chardonnay was poured, I plucked a credit card from my purse, one that wouldn't be denied, and the bartender started a tab for me, telling me his name was Josh.

"You have a beautiful smile," he said to me, and I blushed, grinning, and he pointed at it and said, "Yup, that's the one," while smiling his own beautiful smile. For whatever reason I dug a tube of lipstick from my purse, a light shade of pink, and applied it to my lips, leaving light pink prints around the rim of my wineglass that he filled each time with a bountiful pour.

I unbuttoned the top button of my blouse, leaning farther over the bar, fully aware of just how pathetic it was, me, a lonely, depressed woman hitting on a bartender in a near-abandoned bar.

I had become a cliché.

"What's your name?" he asked, setting a bowl of nuts before me, a single finger brushing against my skin as he did, and I told him that it was Eden. He equated it to the garden of Eden, in other words, *paradise*, and I smiled and said I'd never heard that before, though of course I had, from each and every one of the lowlifes who came before Aaron when they were trying to pick me up in bars far less classy than this.

"What are you doing here all by yourself, Eden?" he asked while swirling a dishrag in circles before me.

I shrugged my shoulders and said that I didn't know.

What was I doing here?

I reached for my glass and downed the last few drops. At once it was refilled, and I downed that too, scarcely able to recall what came next.

Only bits and pieces stayed with me until morning, a montage of what may have occurred. Sliding from the barstool with the third glass of wine. Laughing at myself as strange hands helped me to my feet, refreshing my glass. A face far too close to mine. The deep groove of dimples. Words whispered in my ear.

"Wait for me," he said.

Standing on the street corner in the dark autumn night, I leaned against a streetlamp that didn't give off an ounce of light. Getting absorbed by blackness until even I wasn't sure if I was still there. It was raining still, a fine mist in the air, one which seemed to levitate and not fall.

And then suddenly there were lips on my neck, hands kneading my skin, though who they belonged to, I couldn't see. It was far too dark to see, but it didn't matter to me. I knew only that my extremities were numb from the alcohol, and it was cathartic to me, strange hands wandering along the landscape of my skin, exploring the valleys and hills with a certain vehemence I'd never felt before. A body pressed against mine, pinning me to the streetlamp, whispering breathless words into the lobe of an ear.

"Where's your car? I'll drive."

I heard the sound of an engine gunning, the stars coming at me at a dizzying speed before the world turned black again, and then the scratch of facial hair on my cheek, a hand groping at my chest with the impatience of a sixteen-year-old boy. A hasty man pawed at me, tearing at my blouse. What buttons remained clung to the fabric by strings, as he pushed me into the back seat of the car, moving with the deftness and agility of someone who knew what they were doing, of someone who had a history of strange women in the back seats of cars.

I felt the force of my skirt getting thrust clear up to my rib cage. The scratch of a fingernail as he tore at my panties, pushing them aside. The sound of a moan, my own forced moan tolling through the airless space because, even with the continuous thrust of his hips into me, I felt nothing and I wanted more than anything to feel something, to feel *anything*, because feeling something was far better than feeling nothing, and in that moment all I felt was nothing. Nothing that mattered anyway.

Instead, hot breath on the lobe of my ear. Handfuls of hair being clenched between hands, tugged consciously or unconsciously, I didn't know. Reggae music on a car stereo.

He panted out a name in rhythm, "Anna, Anna." Did he think that that was my name, Anna, or was there another woman in his life, a woman named Anna, and he was only pretending that I was her? I replied with "Yes, yes!" deciding that I would be his Anna if that's who he wanted me to be. A seat belt buckle drilled a hole into the small of my back, plastic plunging itself into me with every thrust of his hips, leaving its mark, though still I felt nothing, nothing at all, not until finally a spasm tore through him like a lightning strike and he collapsed against me, and then there was the weight of him, no longer supported by his own hands.

The weight of him. That I felt.

And then weightlessness.

A car door opened and closed and then there was silence.

He was gone.

I woke up in the morning in the back seat of my car, parked at the far edge of a public playground parking lot, beneath the shadow of a tree, my skirt still thrust clear up to my rib cage, the rest of me exposed, hidden only by the dewdrops that had settled on the windows overnight.

JESSIE

MY HEART BEATS INSIDE me like a cheetah. I'm screaming.

"*Psst.* Hey you, hey, Jessie."

There's a hand at my shoulder, rattling me. It's gentle, but insistent. I jerk away from the hand, arms flailing. I'm no longer falling.

A mouth presses closely to my ear, speaks in a breathy voice. A stage whisper. "Earth to Jessie," she says, and it's a numbing voice. A hypnotic voice. The perfect opiate.

I imagine where I am. On the grass. Body in bits on the ground, bleeding and broken, hardly able to move. In the distance, the sound of an ambulance's wailing siren as my father walks away from the scene unscathed.

The voice says *it's okay, it's okay*, three times or more while stroking my hair. I can't open my eyes. And yet I see her, a woman hunched over me on the lawn, while others crowd around her. She's gawking, her eyes fixated on the most gruesome parts of my battered body. A leg that bends backward, organs that protrude from the skin.

I know the voice. I've heard it before. But I can't place it.

I'm swimming beneath water. Sounds are muffled above my head. The dropping of a needle onto an old vintage vinyl record. Voices talking. A measured, high-pitched ping. Ping, and then nothing. Ping, and then nothing. Ping, ping. Voices in the background. Talking. Saying things like *morphine* and *slipper socks* and *ice chips*.

When I go to open my eyes, they're sealed shut. Taped down. Impossible to open.

My hands rise and I'm surprised to find that I can still move them, my arms and hands. That they're not broken after all. Not shattered into a million pieces across the concrete.

I press the heels of my hands against my eyes and rub hard, wiping the crusty discharge. Inside, my heart pounds hard. A song begins to play. Quietly. Background music. It's a song I know well because it's Mom's favorite song.

When I finally get my eyelids to lift, all I see is yellow. A blinding yellow light.

And that's when I know that I'm dead. That's the first clue.

The yellow light charges my eyes. It stuns and overpowers them, making them close again because I can't stand to keep them open; it hurts too much. I blink repeatedly, trying to adapt to the light. To orient myself, to find a reference point, to figure out where I am.

The second clue that I have that I'm dead is Mom. Because Mom is also dead. And yet, as I open my eyes, she's here, sitting five or six feet from me. She sits upright, on some sort of reclining armchair with castors on its feet, her gaunt legs propped on the chair's footrest. She's dressed in a roomy gown that slips carelessly from a shoulder, the hair on her head merely fuzz, as it was the last time I laid eyes on her alive. Which is why I know this is some sort of afterlife we're stuck in. Mom and me.

The room around me is blue. Blue walls. Blue sheets. A comforting, pastel shade of blue. I'm not on the lawn after all. I'm not outside, lying in the shadow of the building from which I fell. Rather I'm in a room, on a bed.

A woman stands beside Mom, lathering lotion onto her arms and hands, massaging the purplish, blotchy skin. I know who she is because I've seen her before, at the hospital before Mom died. She was Mom's nurse, one of them anyway. A woman named Carrie who was more religious than any about applying lotion to Mom's hands and feet, about turning her so she didn't get bedsores. Even when I begged for them to leave her alone so Mom could sleep.

She looks over at me and says, "Well, it's about time," and that's when I know that we're all dead. Mom, the nurse and me. They've just been waiting for me to arrive.

I know how Mom and I died, but I wonder, how did she?

"That stuff knocked you out cold," says the woman who squats on her haunches beside me, a second nurse. Her hand rests on my shoulder, the very same hand that only moments ago rattled me, mouth purring into my ear, *Psst. Hey you, hey, Jessie. Earth to Jessie.*

"What stuff?" I ask, feeling dazed and confused. Behind me, from a record player, Gladys Knight sings to me. There's the greatest sense that I'm still falling, though I'm well aware that it didn't hurt when I hit the ground. That when I crash-landed into the concrete beside the apartment building, I felt nothing. I don't even remember it happening. I must've been dead by then, I decide. A heart attack, a broken neck.

The room whirls around me. I push myself up so I sit, perpendicular, no longer lying down on a bed. There's a puddle of blankets on the floor, a pillow beneath my head. The second woman rises from the ground beside me and pulls the strings of a window shade so that they rise. I've seen her before. She's the same woman who kept me company the night before Mom died, and now she too is dead like me. How can that be?

How can we all be dead?

More blinding yellow infiltrates the room, making it hard to see much of anything clearly. But Mom. I see Mom. My eyes go back to Mom. To Mom sitting there. Mom, in the flesh. No longer listless. No longer bed bound. She looks sleepy still, her eyes glazed over, and yet on her face, a smile. "How about some ice chips, Miss Eden?" Nurse Carrie asks, offering a single piece of ice from the end of a spoon.

"The clonazepam," I hear, and it takes a minute to realize the nurse is talking to me, that I asked a question and she's answering it for me. "The stuff doc gave you to sleep. He'll be happy to hear it worked. You needed a good night's sleep. You were dreaming," she says. "Calling out, kicking in your sleep. Must've been one hell of a dream."

And as I finally start to get my bearings, I realize where I am. I'm in Mom's hospital room. Mom. Who sits six feet from me, upright, sucking on a cube of ice. Not six feet under, but six feet from me. No longer ashes, but now whole.

The clonazepam. The melatonin. That I remember. My own bloody, inflamed eyes. The doctor, concerned, offering something to help me sleep. Watching a newsmagazine show on the TV, a story about identity theft, while waiting for the pills to kick in, the nurse tucking me into bed, telling me about her daughter, dead in a car accident at the age of three.

The purple swimsuit, her daughter collecting shells from the sea. That I remember.

By the time I woke up Mom was dead, except that she wasn't dead.

It was all a dream.

My eyes adapt. The light becomes less painful, less blinding.

And that's when I see a man in the room too, and I know straightaway that it's the man from the dream. And I wonder if I'm still dreaming. If this is like the purgatory of dreams and I'm trapped somewhere between sleep and awake, having to atone for my sins before I can fully wake up. His back is to me as it's almost always been because he's there on a chair before Mom. He sits, though I see it in the body posture, the carriage, and I know that it's him. I'm not chasing him anymore because now he's here.

Ping, I hear then. Ping. And I turn to watch the movement of lines across Mom's EKG, the spikes and dips of her heartbeat.

"Dad," I breathe, my voice gravelly and hoarse. My heart throbs. Because after chasing him for all those days and nights, after spending my entire life trying to find him, he's here.

He's been here all along, waiting for me to wake up.

Except that as the man turns to me, I see that he's different. His face is not the face from my dreams. There's no facial hair anywhere, and his eyes are a grayish-green like sage. They're not brown. His hair is streaked with gray and there are lines across his face, forehead lines mostly, deeply set. His arms are blotched with pale pink scars.

It dawns on me then, slowly. Of course he's different from the man in my dream. Because in real life I never saw his face. I only caught a glimpse of the back of him when I was a girl, before Mom snatched the photograph from my hand.

Before we read a book, before we ate ice cream. Now I remember. I never saw that photograph again until it returned to me in a dream.

There's a book on his lap.

He leans forward, gathering Mom's hands into his. Hers are limp. He strokes her cheek, and I see in his eyes the look that he has for her. A look of adoration, a look of love. It makes me feel embarrassed, watching them. This moment of intimacy. It's not for me to see.

In all my life, no one has ever looked at me that way. I doubt anyone ever will.

His smile is deferential, kind. "No, Jessie," he says as he lets go of Mom's hands and turns back to me. "I'm not your father," he tells me, and at first I'm speechless because if not my father, then who? My eyes well with tears—wanting, *needing* him to be my father—as I sputter, "There was a photograph Mom had of you. I remember seeing it a long time ago. She took it away, she hid it, but it stayed with me. It was a picture of my father. It was *you*. You have to be him," I say, and he leaves her side to come to me.

He sits down beside me on the bed, a gap spread between us. He pats my hand, tells me his name is Aaron. "I knew your mother a long time ago," he explains. "We were married. She was my wife," but then he pauses, his own eyes red, and gathers himself. He won't cry in front of me. "I don't have any children, Jessie," he says, as if that should make it clear, but it only makes me more confused. More angry and more confused. Because how could he be Mom's husband but not my father? Didn't he want me?

My tone is more scathing, more exasperated than I mean for it to be. "Then why are you here?" I ask, and I see the anguish in his eyes, the grief. I pull my hand from his, seeing then that he doesn't have a wedding band. He's not married and I wonder if, after he and Mom were married, he ever was. He divorced Mom, he left her, I think, and there's a groundless anger that swells up inside me.

This man hurt Mom.

"I loved your mother very much," he says, as if he can read my mind. But then he rethinks and alters it a bit. "I *love* your mother very much," he says, before holding up the book from his lap. "Eden," he tells me, "your mother, she sent this to me," and I look at it, a brown leather book with a stitched edge, and in his other hand a note, written in Mom's handwriting on a piece of stationery. Stationery with her own name engraved along the edge. "It's her journal," he explains, though in all my life, I never once knew Mom kept a journal.

He hands the note to me. I skim Mom's words. In them, she tells him she's dying. She says that she wants him to have this journal so that he can finally have closure, so he can finally understand.

The last line reads, *With love, Eden.*

"Understand what?" I ask. And there it is again, that exasperation.

But his tone is compassionate and warm, his eyes soft. He rubs at his forehead, confesses, "There were some loose ends, Jessie," he says. "Some unfinished business between your mother and me." He asks, "What did Eden tell you about your father?" and I shake my head and admit, "Nothing. She never told me a thing about him."

He passes the book to me, the journal. He says that he thinks I should read it, that it would help me understand.

"Everything she did," he tells me, voice cracking, "she did for you. You should know that."

And then he rises to his feet to leave, but not before first confessing, "I wanted to be a father, Jessie. I would have loved to be a father. I would have loved to be *your* father. But sometimes life doesn't go as planned."

I don't know what he means by that. But I grip the journal in my hand; I press it to my heart, knowing I'll soon understand.

He says that he'll give Mom and me a few minutes. And then he leaves the room.

My eyes turn to Mom's. They're unfocused and disoriented, the top lid puffed up. She sees me but doesn't see me all at the same time. I wave; she waves back. But not right away, as if there's a broadcast delay. Her lips are a length of string, pilled and thin. They're dry, chapped, some sort of gunk collecting around the edges, which no one bothers to wipe. Her skin is a washed-out shade of gray blotched with purple and blue. A lack of oxygen. Poor circulation flow.

And yet she's there. Sitting upright. Waving.

"You're alive," I breathe as I go to her one last time.

The nurse leads the way as we drift into the hall. I take one look over my shoulder as we go, saying to her quietly, in a whisper, "It's a miracle." Because I don't want Mom to know how close she came to dying. "She's better. She's all better. Just like that. Overnight, and she's better," I say, a smile as wide as the Grand Canyon on my face. And suddenly nothing else matters. All that matters is Mom. I clutch the nurse's hand, wanting to celebrate the moment, to savor it. Relief consumes me, seeing that Mom has her strength back, some of it anyway. That she can sit up, that she can swallow. I'm thinking of next steps already. We'll begin chemo again. Maybe there is some clinical trial that Mom can participate in, some new medicine we can give a try.

"Oh, Jessie," the nurse says as we watch a family pass by in the hallway, flowers and balloons tethered to their hands. Her face drops. It gets overpowered with empathy, and for a minute or two she's speechless. The only smile she has to offer is a comforting one. Not a happy one. Not a celebratory one like mine.

It's a sympathy smile.

"Jessie," she says as she ushers me to a nearby bench and we sit, just across the hall from Mom's room so we can still see inside. "Your mother," she says, hesitating. "She doesn't have much time left."

"But—" I argue, thinking of Mom, sitting there in the room in a chair. Mom, more energetic than I've seen for weeks. Mom, making what looks to me like a speedy recovery. There's a spark to her eye, just a dot of light that wasn't there the last time I looked, days ago when she last opened her eyes. She'd been comatose for days like that; she couldn't swallow, she couldn't eat. The doctor said it wouldn't be long. And now here she is. Clearly he was wrong. Through the doorway I see Mom reach a hand out to nurse Carrie, rub at her throat. She can't speak. But she's asking for more ice chips, for a drink. "Look at her. See for yourself. She looks *fine*."

"She looks better. But the cancer. The cancer is still there. This happens, Jessie. A death rally, we call it. She will relapse, honey, and likely soon. Maybe hours, maybe days. There's no way to know for sure, but her body is still deteriorating. The cancer isn't cured. It's metastasized to the lungs, the bones. It's getting worse."

Which I know. Of course I know. I've heard this all before, many times. But looking at Mom now, it can't be true. It's like she's had this surge of brain power and awareness. Like she's come back from the dead.

And then I understand.

Terminal lucidity. As imminent a sign of death as any. The final blessing I'd been hoping for. Five more lucid moments with Mom. That's all I asked for. And here they are.

The nurse graciously turns off the machine as it flatlines. I wonder if she always does that, if her hand shoots there automatically the moment a patient dies so their beloved family members don't have to hear the damn thing scream. The ping from my dream has finally gone silent.

Mom's doctor presses the end of his stethoscope to her chest and we all look to him for guidance, for him to tell us she's dead, though we already know that she is. Her body lies peacefully on the bed, skin going white, blood draining from it. Already she's colder and more synthetic feeling than she was before. Her hands and toes unclench; her body goes lax. The doctor speaks. "Time of death," he says, "Two forty-two."

And with it comes great relief.

Mom's battle with cancer is done.

Mom's death rally lasted a total of three hours and fourteen minutes. For some of it she sat up with me in the chair, while Aaron watched from the corner of the room. He thought he should leave, that Mom and I should have this time together, but I asked him to stay. I did most of the talking. Mom could talk once she warmed up to it, but talking didn't come with ease.

I spent the time trying not to cry. But then, when I couldn't hold it in any longer, I sobbed, gulping down air and choking on it. Because there were things that needed to be said and I didn't have much time left. If I didn't say them, I'd regret it forever, for the rest of my life. "I don't know who I am without you," I confessed. "I'm no one without you." And though

I didn't say it aloud, I thought to myself that I'm vapor without Mom around. I'm nothing. A nonentity. A rock, a clock, a can of baked beans.

Mom stroked my hand as she did the day she told me she was dying. Caressed my fingers one at a time, and forced a smile that was as sad as mine.

"You're *you*," she said. "The one and only Jessie Sloane," as she stroked my arm with an anemic hand, the white flesh darkened here and there with bruise-like marks.

I squeezed into the same chair beside her, as if I was still a little girl. I don't know how we fit, but somehow we did. We sat like that for a while. As we did, one of my earliest memories returned to me, one of the few that hadn't been lost to time. In it, I'm about five years old. It's the middle of the night when Mom comes to me in my room. I'm sound asleep when she kneels on the floor beside my bed, whispering into an ear, *Jessie, honey. Wake up.*

And I do.

She helps me get dressed. Not fully dressed, but instead we slip a sweater over my nightgown, a pair of leggings beneath its hem. Socks and shoes. I follow her out the front door and into the blackness of night, asking at least a gazillion times where we're going, though all she ever says is *You'll see.* We walk hand and hand down the street.

There's a rare giddiness about Mom in that moment. A frivolity. She isn't restrained as she often is, but instead is playful and bright. We only walk as far as the home next door, but for me it seems an incredible adventure, some sort of magical, midnight escapade. We have to walk to the far side of the Hendersons' home where the gate is, cutting through their lawn as we go. Mom stands on tiptoes—her feet, I realize only then, are bare—to unlatch the gate, pushing it slowly open so it doesn't squeak.

Where are we going? I ask, and she says, *You'll see.*

We creep through the grass to a tree at the center of the backyard. A tall tree, sky-high, as high as my five-year-old eyes can see. Though it's too dark to see, I'm pretty sure the crown of the tree stretches clear into the clouds. There's a swing hanging there from one of the tree's branches, just a slab of wood with a thick rope that's looped through holes on each side. Mom tells me to hop on and at first I resist, thinking we can't possibly ride on the Hendersons' tree swing without asking. But Mom's face is radiant, her smile wide.

She sits down on the wood herself, pats the thighs of her pants. She tells me again to hop on, only this time she means on her lap. And I do.

I scramble awkwardly on, Mom hitching an arm around my stomach to help hoist me up. I sit on her lap, leaning back and into her as she gets set to launch us from the ground. Mom holds onto the rope with a single hand, the other folded around my belly. She walks backward as far as her bare feet can reach and then all at once, she lifts her feet from the earth and, just like that, we fly.

"Do you remember," I asked, snuggled there beside her on the hospital chair, "the time we broke into the Hendersons' backyard and snuck a ride on their tree swing?"

For as long as I live, I'll never forget the smile that bloomed on her face right then. She closed her eyes, reveling in the moment. The memory of the two of us nestled together on that tree swing. "It was the best night of my life," I said.

Shortly after the memory left, Mom got tired. The nurses and I helped her back to bed. Minutes later, Mom fell asleep.

She drifted back into some sort of minimally conscious state and passed away two hours later with me there at her side.

It's only after the funeral director comes to collect Mom's body that I finally rise from the chair. The room is remarkably quiet. No music playing, no familiar sound of the EKG.

The only sounds I hear now come from down the hall where other people lie dying.

Before he leaves, Aaron asks if I'll be all right and I tell him that I will. "I may not be your father," he says, "but it would mean the world to me if I could be your friend," and I tell him that I'd like that very much. He goes, and after he does, I see the nurse has already begun to strip the sheets from Mom's bed. Soon another patient will be here, another family surrounding them, watching as they die.

"Where are you going to go?" she asks, and I shrug and say stupidly, "Coffee," because nothing else comes to mind.

Beyond that, I have no idea where to go, what to do with my life.

But there's a part of me that thinks I can figure this out in time.

I try to reconstruct the dream. As I move down the bright, buzzing hospital halls, I try to piece it back together. But dreams have a way of fading fast, the mind a habit of deleting nonessential things. It's as if there's a fifty-piece puzzle before me and I'm missing all but five pieces. I've lost forty-five and only some of them connect. I remember only squirrels. Hot dogs. A hippopotamus. But I don't know what any of it means.

It's only as I cut through the hospital lobby, passing by the cafeteria, that I'm struck with the sudden sense that something is missing. Something that makes it harder to breathe. I come to a sudden stop and as I do, a body plows into me from behind, making my bag drop to the ground, contents spilling across the hospital floor. Mom's stuff—her lotion, her ChapStick, her journal—as well as mine. My driver's license, my credit card, dollar bills.

"My fault, my fault," I hear as I turn to see a man scramble to the ground to pick up my stuff. "I didn't see you. I wasn't looking where I was going," he admits as he rises to his feet and holds out the bag for me, my things shoved indelicately back in.

As he does I catch a look at his face for the very first time, and only then do I remember. I gasp. It's him. "Liam," I breathe, taking in that shaggy brown hair and the blue gum-ball eyes, knowing with certainty that he was there in my dream with me. There's the vaguest recollection of sitting on a sofa beside him, of his hand stroking my hair. It's a thought that makes me blush as I take a step closer to him. And though I don't know him, there's the greatest sense that I do. That we're already friends. "Liam," I say again.

But his face only clouds over in confusion. He shakes his head, stares vacantly at me like I'm mistaken. He looks tired. Stubble has all but taken over his face, and his hair stands on end. His bloodshot eyes are even bloodier than they were before, rivers of red running through the white. He shakes his head. "Jackson," he says. "Jack." And I find that I'm thrown completely off, feeling out of sorts because he's not Liam. Of course he's not Liam. Because Liam was only a dream. This man is a different man completely, though our late-night confessions over coffee were real. That was real, I remind myself, finding it suddenly impossible to remember what's real and what's not.

"I'm sorry," I stammer. "I thought," and I feel silly all of a sudden. "I should go," I say, taking the bag abruptly from his hands, excusing myself, trying to sidestep him and leave. But he doesn't let me leave. Instead he steps in front of me, reaches out his hand and says, "You never told me your name," and for a second there's the sense that he doesn't want me to leave. That he wants me to stay.

His handshake is warm and firm. He holds on a second longer than he needs to.

I reply, "Jessie," knowing for the first time in a long while that I am. I am Jessie Sloane.

"You're leaving, Jessie?" he asks, and I say, "No reason to stick around here any longer."

I don't have to tell him that Mom is dead, because he already knows. He can see it in my eyes. "Your brother?" I ask, thinking of the motorcycle accident. His brother flying headfirst into a utility pole. "Is he going to be all right?" For a moment Jack—Jackson—is silent, but then he says, "Bit the dust last night," and my heart breaks for the both of us.

But there's also a sense of relief because, though we lost the war, the battle is finally through.

"Where are you going?" he asks, and I tell him I'm not sure. Anywhere. That I just have to get out of here, and he says he knows what I mean. His family waits upstairs in his brother's hospital room for the funeral home to arrive, to carry the body away. That's the last thing he needs to see. That's what he tells me. He shuffles from foot to foot, looking antsy and strung out, desperately in need of a good night's sleep.

I ask him if he wants to go for coffee, and together we leave.

That night, at home alone, I find the courage to open the journal. I caress its cover for a good fifteen minutes first, scared to death of what I might find inside. Maybe my father. Maybe not.

I sit on the sofa in Mom's and my home in Albany Park. Because for now it's not yet on the market, though I know that soon it will be. I carefully pull the cover back. A flattened leaf slips from its inside and onto my lap—red, with edges that fold up slightly at their edges—as does a photograph, which falls facedown on my thighs. There's a name etched on the back. *Aaron.* I know what the picture is before I ever look. The photograph I found as a child. The one Mom hid away in this journal so that I couldn't find it again.

My heart breaks at the familiar sight of Mom's handwriting.

My eyes wade through the pages, tears blurring my vision. Making it hard to take in the words. But I do anyway, curled into a ball on the sofa, beneath a blanket Mom and I once shared, listening to her favorite records over and over again on repeat.

Aaron showed me the house today, it reads. *I'm in love with it already—a cornflower blue cottage perched on a forty-five-foot cliff that overlooks the bay. Pine floors and whitewashed walls. A screened-in porch. A long wooden staircase that leads down to the dock at the water's edge where the Realtor promised majestic sunsets and fleets of sailboats floating by…*

EDEN

November 10, 1997
Egg Harbor

WHEN I AWOKE THIS morning there was the most unpleasant sense in my stomach, as if I'd swallowed some sort of gastric acid in the middle of the night and there it sat, lost somewhere between my throat and my intestines, not sure which way to go. Up or down. There was an awful taste in my mouth, as if I'd drunk a vat of vinegar before bed, and when I hurried for a glass of water to wash it down, I wound up hurling the water and everything else inside my stomach into the kitchen sink and then stood, clutching the countertop, tasting vomit, trying hard to catch my breath. There was saliva on my chin and tears in my eyes.

What did I eat last night?

Whatever it was, it wasn't much. I haven't eaten much for weeks, having subjected myself to a life of seclusion since my brush with that bartender in the back seat of my car. I haven't left the house other than for the bare necessities, for fear of running into him on the street. My home is my prison. I've been too ashamed to go outside.

Ashamed for a whole slew of reasons, my promiscuity only being one of them.

Overnight I had gone from being a respectable human being to a voyeur, a kidnapper, a misfit, a freak. The morning after my encounter with that bartender, I came home to find bruises on my neck from where he sucked my skin raw so that I couldn't leave the house until they healed, my skin returning to its usual shade of peach. Day and night I stared at those bruises, hating myself. What kind of person was I? What kind of person had I become?

I remembered the feeling of little Olivia's hand in mine.

Had that really happened, or was it only a dream?

Did I nearly steal another woman's child?

Two women's children?

The bartender had taken off with my purse too, snatched it right from the front seat while I lay in the back in a daze, leaving the car door unlatched, the interior lights on so that by morning the battery was completely drained. I walked the three miles home with a swollen ankle, clutching the plackets of my shirt together since the buttons had snapped clear off at his hasty hand. I spent the morning after on the telephone with various credit card companies, reporting the cards stolen, despising myself for getting into this situation in the first place, for letting myself be a floozy and a victim. I avowed to pay off my debt and cut the new cards the credit card company would no doubt send me to shreds.

I would never be a victim again.

I'd never trust anyone again.

I would never leave the house for fear I might try and pilfer someone else's child.

And so I've become a recluse, plunged into a state of depression where I go unshowered for days at a time, oftentimes not getting out of bed from morning until night. I eat only when I need to, when the hunger pangs are more than I can bear. I've lost my job, no doubt, though no one told me as much, but one can't expect to stay employed when they haven't gone to work for thirty-odd days. I'm drowning in debt, I assume, though I haven't found the energy to drag myself to the mailbox to retrieve the bills, but I'm certain I must be because just last night when I flipped a light switch on, nothing happened. I jiggled the toggle up and down and when that failed, tried another light switch.

It appeared the electricity had been shut off for nonpayment.

I went back to bed in the dark, planning to stay there for the rest of my life, which would be short as I swore off water and food too.

But then this morning the nausea wrenched me from bed, dragging me to the kitchen sink, where again and again I heaved, wondering what in the world was wrong with me.

And it was a slow dawning then, daylight arriving at its own sweet time, one shaft of light at a time.

For thirty-odd days I had lain in bed since my encounter in the back seat of the car, and in those thirty-odd days, my period—my ever-reliable period—hadn't come.

And now there was the nausea, the vomiting, and though every rational thought in my mind told me it wasn't true, it couldn't be true—after all, I was infertile; there was no way I could get pregnant of my own accord, without Dr. Landry's menagerie of drugs and devices—I knew instinctively that it was true.

I was pregnant.

To say I was happy would be a lie.

It wasn't that I didn't savor the thought for a second or two, that I didn't relish the idea of carrying a child, of birthing a child, of being a mother. There was no greater desire in the whole entire world for me. It's all I wanted; it's the only thing that mattered in my life.

But deep inside I knew this child would never come to fruition. A fetus it was, but a baby it would never be. It would be as it was the last time with the heartbeat that was there and then not there, the gallons of blood. I would lose this baby as I had the last, and it would be my purgatory, my punishment, being forced to endure weeks, maybe a month, of pregnancy, knowing as always that it would end with blood.

That trusty, reliable blood.

And so instead of being happy I stood there, back to the countertop, steeling myself for another miscarriage, to lose this baby like I had the last. Certainly the universe wouldn't let me keep this child. This, truly, was my penance, a gift that was given only to be taken away.

January 15, 1998
Egg Harbor

The joke is on me it seems, for I've made it through the first trimester without a single drop of blood.

The baby has survived thirteen weeks in my wasteland of a womb.

Only by necessity have I left the house, taking a job at a local inn where I clean rooms once the guests leave. There's nothing glamorous about it. Just stripping beds of sheets and washing endless mountains of laundry, scrubbing someone else's excrement off a toilet seat. The perk of the job, however, is that I essentially speak to no one, working alone in an uninhabited guest room or the laundry room, dealing only with dust spores and mildew, as opposed to the human race.

But the work itself is backbreaking. And those first thirteen weeks of the pregnancy were anything but fun and fancy-free. The morning sickness, the lethargy nearly got the best of me until the empty hotels beds were hard to resist—I envisioned myself sprawled out across them, wrapped up in one of the hotel's velour robes—but, for as much as I wanted to, I didn't give in to the whim.

Only second to a baby, I needed this job more than anything.

I haven't been to see Dr. Landry or another obstetrician, though there's a slight outgrowth to my midsection now, a bulge that makes my pants fit tightly so that I've taken to wearing sweatpants when I'm not stuffed into the uniform I wear for work, the polo shirt and the khaki pants, which I now leave unbuttoned so I don't flatten the baby.

The cottage is on the market again.

I can no longer afford to pay for it. I haven't been able to for months so that I'm in debt to the bank and the foreclosure threats have begun to arrive. The sign went in today, stuck there—forced into the nearly frozen ground—by the very same Realtor who sold us the home.

Oh, what she must think, looking at me now. How I've changed.

The Realtor didn't look the least bit different to me, but I was changed, hardly the same woman I was when we first met, less than two years ago.

After she left, I sat myself on the tree swing and swayed, moving back and forth through the nippy winter air. I did it until my fingers were numb and I could no longer feel the sturdy rope beneath my hands.

This was the closest my child would ever come to a ride on this swing.

The bay was empty now, not a boat anywhere, and snow

flurries fell on the dock, collecting like powdered sugar. There were birds in the trees, winter birds, cardinals and chickadees, but everyone else was gone, sunning themselves on one of those tropical islands where I only dreamed I might one day go.

The greenhouse door was frozen shut.

The flowers in the flower bed were dead.

I was still outside when I heard the doorbell ring, and thinking it was the Realtor—that she had an offer *already!*—I left my post to see.

But it was not the Realtor.

Aaron stood before me, his chestnut hair getting peppered with soft powdery snow. His eyes had a forlorn look about them, sad. He wore a coat, his hands set in the pockets of it, and as I pulled the door to, he offered a simple smile.

"Aaron," I said.

"Eden."

I couldn't bring myself to invite him inside, for the cottage was truly a mess, in a state of bedlam; I couldn't bring myself to show him what had become of our home. And so I stepped outside, onto the porch, my hair also getting peppered with snow. I pulled the door closed behind me. My feet were bare, covered only in socks, and against the concrete, they grew cold. Aaron, ever-obliging Aaron, ever-unselfish Aaron, ever-benevolent Aaron, shimmied at once out of his coat and wrapped it around my shoulders, saying to me, "You'll catch your death out here," and beneath the weight of his hands—which lingered there on my shoulders, gently liberating strands of hair that were trapped under the heavy coat, warm hands tucking them behind my ear, pausing there—I softened like a stick of butter left on the table too long.

We said nothing.

But I could see in his eyes that I had been wrong. That Aaron wasn't healed as I'd believed him to be the day I saw him through the chophouse windows. That he was only taped back together that day, a skimpy job at best, for the tape had come undone, it had lost its stick, and Aaron was once again broken, standing before me now, mere fragments of himself.

Oh, what have I done?

He hunched to my height, bending his knees ever so. He cupped his hands around my face—softly, delicately—as if those hands cradled an heirloom crystal vase, and I could see in Aaron's eyes that what he held was, to him, something fragile, something magical, something irreplaceable and beyond compare.

That, to him, I was irreplaceable and beyond compare as I'd always been.

That, in all these months apart, that hadn't changed for him.

His lips felt warm as he pressed them to mine, and there was nothing rushed about it, nothing presumptuous or brusque. "I want you back," he whispered into my ear.

"I need you back.

"I miss you, Eden.

"I am nothing," he said, "without you."

I am nothing.

Was it just my imagination, or did the baby inside me kick?

I stepped back from Aaron, tugging on the ends of my sweater to make sure that tiny bulge was concealed. Inside me the baby—not Aaron's baby, but the baby of some man I would never know—knew how to squint its eyes and to suck its thumb. Each day it grew bigger, arms and legs lengthening, organs and cells unfolding in my womb. It would come to be a person one day, a person perhaps with cavernous dimples and sparkling blue eyes, but never would I resent this child for the choices that I made.

Be careful what you wish for, the saying goes, but never would I harbor a grudge for all that I lost to have this baby. All that I will lose.

It might just come true.

I would have done anything for a baby. This I know without a shred of doubt.

The lump in my throat was nearly impossible to speak past. Something inside my larynx had swollen to two times its size and my eyes burned with tears. As they began to fall, Aaron wiped them from my cheeks with the pad of a thumb and again pressed his lips to mine, saying that everything was okay, that everything would be fine. He held me close, stroking my hair, pressing my hands between his to keep them warm.

"Can I come home?" he asked.

And I thought what it would do to him if I told him about the baby.

It would take those broken pieces of Aaron that remained and sliver them completely. It would pulverize them so that all that was left of Aaron would be ashes and dust.

"Yes," I said, feigning a smile, forcing the word past that knot. "Yes."

Aaron's knees nearly collapsed from the relief of it. He kissed me again, this time with passion and zest, then reached his hand toward the doorknob to let us both inside.

But I stopped him.

"Not yet," I said. "The house is a mess," I said. "Complete bedlam. Let me clean it first," I told him, and though Aaron tried to shoo it off, to tell me it didn't matter, that we'd clean it together, I said no.

That I wanted it to be just right.

That I wanted it to be perfect for him.

That *I* wanted to be perfect for him.

And at this he relented, and an agreement was made.

The following morning he would return with all of his belongings, and we'd start over with a clean slate. We'd be Aaron and Eden again. Just us. Just Aaron and Eden.

He kissed me goodbye—lips lingering on mine for what only I knew would be the last time—and then he was gone, his car pulling out backward down the long, winding drive, disappearing through dark tree bark. The leaves of the trees were gone, as soon I would be.

Life is full of regrets and this is only one of them.

It didn't take long to pack a bag.

By the time it was dark outside, I was heading south, south of Sturgeon Bay, south of Sheboygan, south of Milwaukee. Soon I would be living far away from here. My baby and me.

Dear Aaron,

I had a dream last night. In it, I was being chased. I ran in slapdash circles all night long, sweating and panicked as people tend to do in dreams, and for the longest time I couldn't see the angry face of the man who was chasing me. It wasn't until later, when I finally awoke, delirious and frightened, that I realized it was you, which puzzled me a great deal because after all of the grief and the heartbreak I've put you through, you have never been anything but selfless toward me. Compassionate and kind.

You, of all people, would never hurt me.

I remembered the way it is with dreams sometimes, how they have a habit of being less literal and more metaphoric, and I thought that sometimes with dreams like this, it's not about who's chasing you, but what you're running from.

I've spent the last twenty years running from the past, Aaron, from all the horrible things I put you through. And now I'm dying of cancer. I'm going to die. But I can't stand the idea of leaving this world without explaining things to you first so that you'll understand. It's only right that you have the closure you deserve. Every single day for the past twenty years I thought about calling you, asking you to meet. But I knew I'd never be able to verbalize all that I was feeling, that I could never put it into intelligible words, nor could I bear the thought of looking you in the eye and admitting what I'd done. And so for now, my journal will have to suffice.

I have a child, Aaron, a daughter, named Jessie, who means everything to me—and more. A mistake is what some might call it, but to me, she's perfection. Jessie has spent her entire life searching for her father. It should have been you.

With love,
Eden

★★★★★

acknowledgments

First and foremost, thank you to my smart, savvy and thoughtful editor, Erika Imranyi, for always having faith in me and my books, and for helping take my rough drafts and transform them into something that shines. I'm so proud of the work we do together and know with confidence that my novels are far better after you've left your mark on them.

Thank you to my wonderful and always encouraging friend and literary agent, Rachael Dillon Fried, for having my back, for knowing just what to say when I'm in need of reassurance and for always seeing the positive in everything I do.

Thank you to everyone at Sanford Greenburger Associates, Harper Collins and Park Row Books, including my publicity team of Emer Flounders and Shara Alexander; Reka Rubin for sharing my novels with the world; Erin Craig and Sean Kapitain for another gorgeous cover design; the copy editors, proofreaders, sales and marketing teams, and all those who play a role in getting my story into the hands of readers. I couldn't do what I do without any of you. I'm forever grateful for your diligence, enthusiasm and support.

To my wonderful friends who do not (I promise!) provide the inspiration for my less savory characters, but always supply an abundance of encouragement throughout the process, thank you! To the booksellers, librarians, book bloggers and the media who read and recommend my novels to your customers, patrons and fans, you are amazing! And to my readers worldwide, you're the reason I keep writing.

Lastly, thank you to my parents, Lee and Ellen; my sisters, Michelle and Sara; the entire Kubica, Kyrychenko, Shemanek and Kahlenberg families; to my husband, Pete, and our children, Addison and Aidan; and to Holly, who kept me company while I wrote—there will always be a spot for you by my side.

Read on for a special excerpt from Local Woman Missing, *Mary Kubica's newest riveting thriller that shows how some people will stop at nothing to keep the truth buried.*

PROLOGUE

11 YEARS BEFORE

THERE'S A SMUDGE OF lipstick on the collar of his shirt. She sees it. She says nothing about it. Instead, she stands there, bobbing the crying baby up and down like the needle of a sewing machine piercing fabric. She listens to his lame lies, his same, dispassionate *Sorry I'm late, but*s he reels off almost every night. He must have an arsenal of them amassed, and he uses them in rotation: a bottleneck on the expressway, a coworker with car trouble, getting stuck on the phone with some apoplectic policyholder whose house fire wasn't covered because of insufficient documentation of the damage. The more specific he is, the more sure she is of his betrayal. Still, she says nothing. If she presses him on it, he gets mad. He turns it around on her. *Are you calling me a liar?* For this reason, she lets it go. And also because it would be a double standard for her to make a big deal of the lipstick.

"It's fine," she says, taking her eyes off the lipstick.

They eat dinner together. They watch some TV.

Later that night, she puts the baby to bed, feeding her at the last minute so that she won't wake hungry while she's gone.

She tells him she's going for a run. "Now?" he asks. It's after ten o'clock when she steps from the bedroom in running clothes and shoes.

"Why not?" she asks.

He stares at her too long, his expression unclear. "When people do dumb shit like this, they always wind up dead."

She's not sure what to make of his words, whether he means running alone late at night or cheating on one's husband. She convinces herself it's the first one.

She swallows. Her saliva is thick. She's been anticipating this all day. Her mind is made up. "When else do you expect me to go?"

All day long, she's home alone with their baby. She has no time to herself.

He shrugs. "Suit yourself." He rises from the sofa and stretches. He's going to bed.

She goes out the front door, leaving it unlocked so she doesn't have to carry keys. She runs only the first block so that if he's watching out the bedroom window, he sees.

At the corner, she stops and sends a text: On my way.

The reply: See you there.

She deletes the conversation from her phone. Is she as transparent as her husband? Is what she's doing as obvious as the lipstick on his shirt? She doesn't think so. Her husband is hot-blooded. If he had any idea she was sneaking out to hook up with some guy in his parked car on 4th Avenue, where the street dead-ends a hundred feet from the last house, he'd have beaten her to within an inch of her life by now.

She walks along the street. The night is quiet. It's the only time of day she looks forward to, lost in the anticipation of some guy she hardly knows indulging her for a while, making her feel good.

He isn't the first man she's cheated on her husband with. He won't be the last.

After the baby was born, she tried to quit, to be faithful, but it wasn't worth the effort.

This guy says his name is Sam. She's not sure she believes it. She's been seeing him off and on for months, whenever he or she gets the urge. She met him when she was pregnant of all things. To some guys, it's a turn-on. He made her feel sexy, despite the extra weight, which is far more than she could say for her husband.

Like her, Sam is married. And he isn't the only guy she's been seeing on the side.

The few times they've been together, "Sam" takes his ring off and leaves it on the dashboard, as if that somehow mitigates what he's doing. She doesn't do the same. She isn't one for feeling guilty. She's made herself believe that it's her husband's fault she does what she does. Turnabout is fair play.

The sky is full of stars. She stares at them awhile, finding Venus. The night is cold and her arms are covered with goose bumps. She's thinking about his car, how warm it will be once she gets inside it.

She's looking up at the stars when she hears something coming at her from behind. She spins around, eyes searching the street but coming up empty in the darkness. She chalks it up to some wild animal rummaging through trash, but she doesn't know. She turns back, goes back to walking, picking up her pace. She's not one to get scared, but she starts thinking of what-ifs. What if her husband is on to her, what if he is following her, what if he *knows*?

She tells herself he doesn't know. He couldn't know. She's a very good liar; she's learned how to silence her tells.

But what if the wife knows?

She isn't sure what "Sam" tells his wife when he leaves. They don't talk about things like that. They don't talk much at all except for a few preliminary words to kick things off.

Don't you look pretty.

I've been waiting for this all day.

They're not in love. No one is leaving their spouse anytime soon. It's nothing like that. For her, it's a form of escapism, release, revenge.

Another noise comes. She turns and looks again—truly scared this time—but finds nothing. She's jittery. She can't shake the feeling of eyes on her.

She starts to jog, but soon trips over an untied shoe. She's uncoordinated and nervous, wanting to be in the car with him, and not alone on the street. The street is dark, far too dark for her liking.

She senses movement out of the corner of her eye. Is something there? Is *someone* there? She asks, "Who's there?"

The night is quiet. No one speaks.

She tries to distract herself with thoughts of him, of his warm, gentle hands on her.

She bends over to tie the shoe. Another noise comes from behind. This time when she looks, car lights surface on the horizon, going way too fast. There's no time to hide.

Don't miss the other riveting thrillers by *New York Times* bestselling author

MARY KUBICA

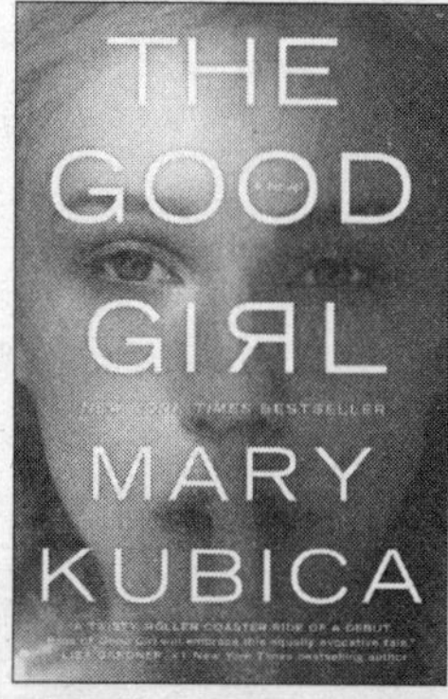

Available now.

Connect with us at:

BookClubbish.com/Newsletter

Instagram.com/BookClubbish

Twitter.com/BookClubbish

Facebook.com/BookClubbish

ParkRowBooks.com
BookClubbish.com

PRMK0775TR